Praise for DAVE DUNCAN and the TALES OF THE KING'S BLADES

"Just the sort of marvelous yarn that lured me into reading fantasy."
Anne McCaffrey

"A fantasist of most sophisticated subtlety."
Locus

"Duncan's people are marvelously believable, his landscapes deliciously exotic, his swordplay breathtaking."
Publishers Weekly (☆Starred Review☆)

"The author's unique vision reinfuses the genre with freshness and genuine wit."
Library Journal

"He explores heroism, betrayal, and sacrifice, all within the context of breakneck adventure . . . But in a Dave Duncan story, 'rollicking' should not be mistaken for 'insubstantial.' "
Calgary Herald

"The estimable Duncan manages, somehow, to be in tremendous form every time out."
Kirkus Reviews

Also by
Dave Duncan
from Avon Books/Eos

The King's Blades
The Gilded Chain

Coming Soon in Hardcover
Sky of Swords

The Great Game
Past Imperative
Present Tense
Future Indefinite

www.daveduncan.com

Lord of the Fire Lands

A Tale of The King's Blades

DAVE DUNCAN

An Imprint of HarperCollins*Publishers*

EOS
An Imprint of HarperCollins*Publishers*
10 East 53rd Street
New York, New York 10022-5299

ISBN: 0-380-79127-7
www.eosbooks.com

First Eos paperback printing: September 2000
First Avon Eos hardcover printing: October 1999

Printed in the U.S.A.

WCD 10 9 8 7 6 5 4 3 2 1

• Warning •

This book, like *The Gilded Chain,* is a stand-alone novel. They both cover much the same time interval and certain characters appear in both, but you can read either without reference to the other. The same is true of the upcoming third volume, *Sky of Swords.* However, the three taken together tell a larger story. If you read any of the two, you will note certain discrepancies that can be resolved only by reading the third.

These days I seem to be accumulating grandchildren faster than I write books, but I am very happy to be able to dedicate the longest of the latter to the latest of the former.

This one is for
Samuel Joseph Duncan

May he enjoy it years hence and carry the family name on into the far reaches of the next century, or even beyond.

I knew him, Horatio—a fellow of infinite jest,
of most excellent fancy. . . .

SHAKESPEARE, *Hamlet,* Act V, Scene I

· Contents ·

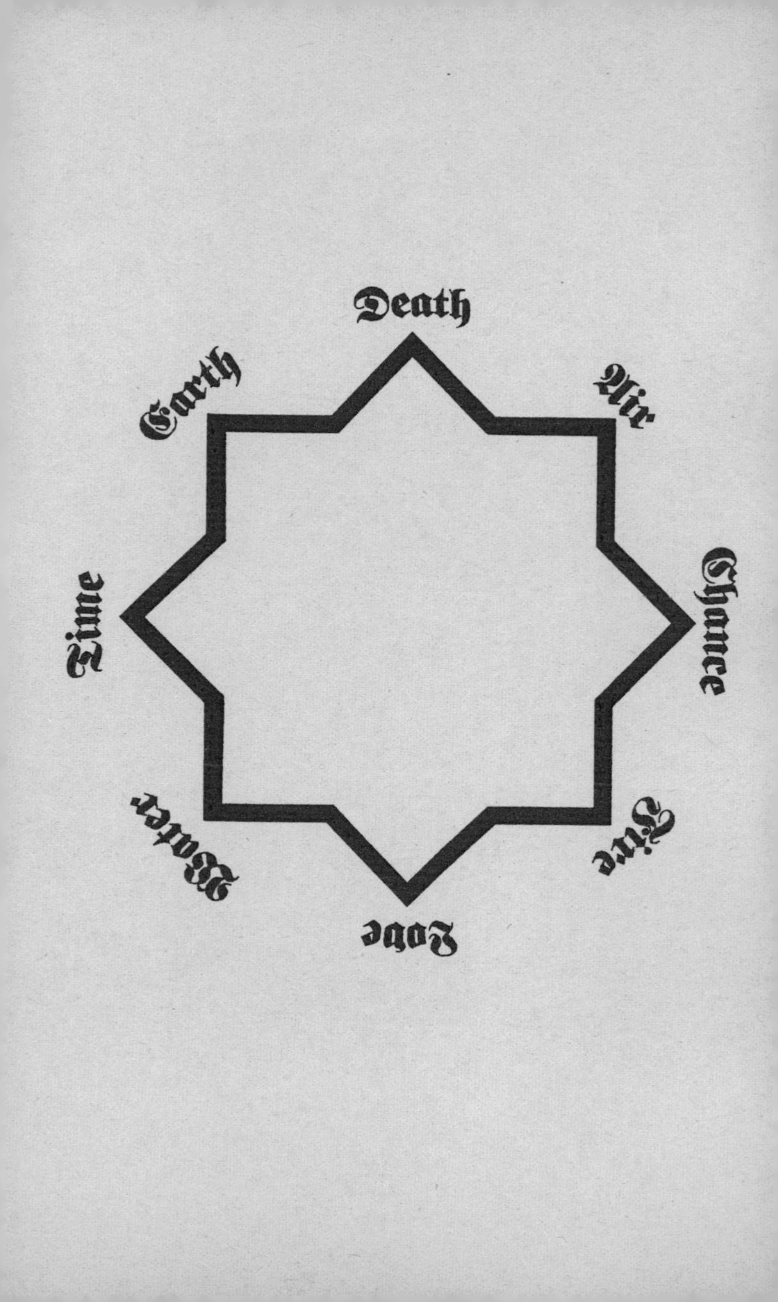
Death
Air
Chance
Fire
Love
Water
Time
Earth

• Notes on Baelish •

An archaic form of Chivian, Baelish is written much as English was written a thousand years ago. The alphabet contains twenty-four letters. Every letter is pronounced, even when this seems impossible, as in *cniht* or *hlytm.*

j, k, q, x, z were not then in use. Three letters have since been abandoned: *eth* (Ð, ð) and *thorn* (Þ, þ) are both pronounced like the English *th*, while the ligature *Æ* is a separate vowel sounded between *a* and *e* (roughly *a* as in "bade," *æ* as in "bad," *e* as in "bed").

c: before *e* or *i*, *c* is prounced like our *ch* (*cild* was "child," after *s* pronounced like our *sh* (*scip* was "ship"); otherwise, *c* was pronounced *k* (*Catter* was "Kater").

g: is tricky! It could be hard (*Græggos* would sound very close to "gray goose"), but it could sound like *j*, as in *hengest* ("stallion"); thus *hengestmann* was a stable hand and gave us "henchman." If a lord arrived with his stallion men, look out!

The suffix *-ing* (meaning "son of" or "descendant of") was probably sounded like the same letters in our word "finger," so Radgar Æleding would be "Rad-gar Al-ed-ing-g."

However *g* before *e* was usually sounded as "y" as in our "sign" or "thegn." *Gea!* survives as "Yea!"

(*ge* was a common and meaningless prefix attached to many words such as *refa* in *scir-gerefa.* As "shire-reeve," this metamorphosed into modern "sheriff.")

Some of the place names should now make a sort of sense if you puzzle at them. *Cwicnoll* means "quick-knoll," "live summit," which seems apt enough for a volcano. *Haligdom* would be pronounced "holy dome" and *Suðecg* not far from "South Edge."

Many Old English words have gone out of use: *wer* meaning "man" survives only in "werewolf." Others have survived unchanged—a *hwæl* is still a "whale." *Cniht*, which originally meant "boy," (*cnihtcild* was a "boy child") became "knight," and that *k* was still being pronounced when English spelling was standardized a couple of hundred years ago.

Lord of the Fire Lands

I

· 1 ·

"*The King is coming!*" The excited cry rang out over the sun-bright moorland and was picked up at once by a half-dozen other shrill trebles and a couple of wavering baritones. Alarmed horses tossed heads and kicked up heels. The cavalcade on the Blackwater Road was still very far off, but sharp young eyes could make out the blue livery of the Royal Guard, or so their owners claimed. In any case, a troop of twenty or thirty men riding across Starkmoor could be no one but the Guard escorting the King to Ironhall. At last! It had been more than half a year.

"*The King is coming! The King is coming!*"

"Silence!" shouted Master of Horse. The sopranos' riding classes always teetered close to chaos, and this one was now hopeless. "Go and tell the Hall. First man in is excused stable duties for a month. On my signal. Get ready—"

He was speaking to the wind. His charges were already streaming over the heather toward the lonely cluster of black buildings that housed the finest school of swordsmanship in the known world. He watched to see who fell off, who was merely hanging on, who was in control. It was unkind to treat horses so, especially the aging, down-at-heel nags assigned to beginners; but his job was to turn out first-class riders. In a very few years those boys must be skilled enough and fearless enough to keep up with anyone, even the King himself—and when Ambrose IV went hunting he usually left a trail of stunned and mangled courtiers in the hedges and ditches.

There went one . . . and another . . . *Ouch!*—a bad one.

No matter, young bones could be repaired by conjuration and the mounts seemed to be surviving. Unrepentant, Master of Horse rode forward to rescue the casualties. On this blustery spring afternoon in the year 357, the moor had masked its ancient menace behind a deceptive glow of friendship, soft and green and smelling of clover. The sky was unbelievably blue. Broom was bursting into yellow glory. There could be few things finer in all creation than having a reasonably good mount and an excuse to ride it flat out. As the race faded into the distance, he could see that the piebald mare was going to win, thanks more to her own abilities than the skills of her rider, Candidate Bandit.

Ten minutes after the sighting, the winner thundered in through the gate and yelled out the news to the first people he saw, who happened to be a group of fuzzies engaged in rapier drill. *''The King is coming!''*

In seconds the word was everywhere, or almost everywhere. The candidates—sopranos, beansprouts, beardless, fuzzies, and especially the exalted seniors who wore swords—all reacted with indrawn breath and sudden internal tenseness, but even the instructors narrowed their eyes and pursed their lips. The Masters of Sabers and Rapiers heard it on the fencing ground, Master Armorer in the Forge. Master of Rituals got the word in a turret room, where he was studying arcane spells, and Master of Archives in a cellar, where he was packing ancient records into fireproof chests. All of them paused to ponder what else they need do to prepare for a royal visit. The answer, in all cases, was absolutely nothing. They were more than ready, because it had been seven months since Ambrose had come to the school. In all that time, only one candidate had been promoted to Blade. The question now—of especial interest to the seniors—was: *How many would the King harvest this time?*

The lowest of the low was the Brat, who was thirteen years old and had been admitted to Ironhall only two days previously. On the theory that a man can get used to anything, he had concluded that this must be the third worst day of his life. Down on his knees, he was attempting to wash the main courtyard with a bucket of water and a small rag—an impossible task that had been assigned to him by a couple of beansprouts because trying to drive the Brat crazy was the juniors' traditional pastime. Having all survived Brat-hood themselves, they felt justified in giving what they had received. Few of them ever realized that they were being tested just as much as the Brat was and would be expelled if they displayed any real sadism.

An elderly knight passing by when the shout went up told the Brat to run and inform Grand Master. Grand Master was the highest of the high, but the Brat felt comfortable near him, safe from persecution. Grand Master did not dunk him in a water trough or make him stand on a table and sing lewd songs.

The old man was in his study, going over accounts with the Bursar. He displayed no emotion at the news. "Thank you," he said. "Wait, though. Bursar, can we continue this another time?" Then, as the other man was gathering up his ledgers, he turned back to the Brat and absolutely ruined his third worst day. "His Majesty will undoubtedly bind some of the seniors tomorrow night. You have heard of the ritual?"

"He sticks a sword through their hearts?" the Brat said uneasily. It was a sick-making thought, because one day it would happen to him.

"Yes, he does. It is a very potent conjuration to turn them into Blades. Don't worry, they always survive." Almost always. "But you will have a part in the ritual."

"Me?" the Brat squawked. Conjury? With the King present? That was worse than a *hundred* water troughs, a thousand. . . .

"Yes, you. You have three lines to say and you lay the candidate's sword on the anvil. Go and find Master of Rituals and he will instruct you. No, wait. First find Prime and make sure he knows about the King." Prime, after all, must have more interest in the royal visit than any other candidate, for his fate was certain now. Whoever else the King took, Prime would be first. "He'll be in the library."

Regrettably, Grand Master was wrong. The seniors were

not in the library that afternoon. The Brat had not yet learned his way around the school and was too unsure of himself to ask for help, so he never did deliver the message. By the time Raider heard of the King's approach, the royal procession was at the gates and escape had become impossible.

• 2 •

Even before the King's arrival, that day had been a memorable one in Ironhall. Two swords had been Returned and three names written in the Litany of Heroes. It was the Litany that was special. Returns were common enough, for the school had been turning out Blades for several centuries and they were mortal like other men. Unless a Blade was lost at sea or died in a far country, his sword came back at last to Ironhall to hang in the famous sky of swords.

Every newcomer began as the Brat. The ideal recruit was around fourteen with good eyes and fast reflexes, either orphaned or rejected by his family, and at least rebellious—preferably a holy terror. As old Sir Silver had said on numerous occasions: *"The wilder the better. You can't put an edge on soft metal."* Some of them were driven out by the hazing, a few gave up later, and very rarely a boy was expelled. Those who lasted the full five years emerged as the finest swordsmen in the world, companions in the Loyal and Ancient Order of the King's Blades, every one as sharp and polished and deadly as the cat's-eye sword he was then privileged to wear. The King accepted about half of them into the Royal Guard and assigned the rest to ministers, relatives, courtiers, or anyone else he chose. To serve was an honor, and Grand Master turned away many more boys than he accepted.

It was only four years since Lord Bannerville, the Chivian ambassador to Fitain, had bound Sir Spender as his third Blade. When Fitain had erupted in civil war, Spender and his two brother Blades, Sir Burl and Sir Dragon, had managed to smuggle their ward out of the chaos, but the latter two had died in the process. That morning Spender had Returned their swords.

Standing in the hall under that baleful canopy of five thousand swords, the survivor told the story to the assembled candidates, masters, and knights. He said very little about his own part; but his limp, his pallor, and the jumpiness in his voice backed up the eye-popping stories of his injuries that had been whispered around beforehand. Everyone knew that a Blade defending his ward was harder to kill than a field of dandelions. But death was not impossible, and many of the juniors were openly sobbing by the end of the tale.

The hero ate lunch in private with Grand Master and some other teachers. He wanted to leave right after the meal, but Master of Protocol persuaded him to stay and instruct the seniors on politics. Prime invited him to do so in the tower. Thus most of the seniors were in the tower that afternoon, which was why the Brat did not find them.

· 3 ·

Ironhall had never been a castle, but its wild moorland setting had inspired some long-forgotten builder to festoon parts of it with turrets, loopholes, and fake battlements. The most obvious of these follies was the tower whose attic served as the seniors' private lair. Generations of future Blades had idled in its squalor without ever having a single thought of cleaning or tidying. The furniture was in ruins and heaps of discarded clothes and miscellaneous clutter moldered in the corners. But by tradition—and everything in Ironhall ran on tradition—no one ever set foot up there except the seniors themselves—not Blades, not Grand Master, not even the King. No one had ever explained why any of those men should want to, but the invitation to Sir Spender was supposedly a great honor. It also kept Master of Protocol out.

Wasp was the first to arrive, trotting up the stairs carrying a respectable ladder-back chair for the guest, which he placed in front of the fireplace. He rearranged a few of the other chairs to face it and then nabbed his favorite for himself, leaning back in its moldering excretions of stuffing to watch the others arrive. Fox appeared and made a dive for the second-best chair; Herrick led in six or seven more; then there was a pause while Sir Spender came up one step at a time, escorted by Prime. More seniors clattered up behind them, chattering like starlings. They draped themselves on tables or rickety stools, propped themselves against the walls, or just sprawled on the boards.

"Flames and death!" the guest declaimed. "This place

is still the same disgusting midden it was when I left. Have those windows ever been cleaned?"

"Certainly not!" said Mallory, who was Second. "You can't break tradition that way in Ironhall!"

"Those look like the same ashes in the hearth."

"They're *traditional* ashes," said Victor, who fancied himself as a humorist. "And the cobwebs are priceless."

Spender limped over to the fireplace to hunt for his signature, for all the paneling and the steeply pitched roof and even parts of the floor were inscribed with the names of former candidates. *Wasp* was written near the door, very small within an overlarge initial; and he had found two other *Wasp* inscriptions, although Master of Archives had records of only one Blade by that name, an undistinguished member of the Royal Guard back in the days of Everard III. The other must have been even earlier and spectacularly mediocre. It would be the third Wasp who made the name memorable!

Herrick was very dark, Victor unusually blond, and Raider—who would not be coming—had hair as red as a Bael's; but with that trivial exception of coloring the seniors were as alike as brothers: all lean and agile, moving with the wary grace of jungle predators, neither too small to be dangerous nor too large to be nimble. Five years of constant effort, superb instruction, and in most cases a dash or two of conjuration had produced these fledgling Blades, awaiting only their master's call. Even their features seemed alike, with no extreme bat ears or crooked teeth. Wasp wondered if he was just noticing all this anew because Spender so obviously belonged there, an older brother come home to visit. Few Blades cared to remember any other home. Wasp was an exception there, but then he was exceptional in other ways too painful to think about.

Raider hurtled up the stairs three at a time and strode over to flop down on the floor under the south window, putting his back against the wall and stretching out his long legs. He caught Wasp's eye and grinned at his surprise. Wasp rose and went to sit beside him, putting friendship ahead of comfort and provoking a minor tussle as three men simultaneously tried to claim the chair he had abandoned.

"Thought you were drilling beansprouts in sabers?"

Raider's emerald-green eyes twinkled. "I wrapped Dominic's leg around his neck until he offered to help me out." He was lying, of course. Giving the juniors fencing practice was never the most popular of assignments; but only Raider would rather listen to a talk on politics, even with the Order's latest hero doing the talking. Dominic would have agreed to the exchange very readily.

The door slammed, then Fitzroy came clumping up the stair to announce that this was everyone. Wasp looked around and counted two dozen seniors present. Traditionally there should be less than that in the whole class, but the King had assigned only one Blade in seven months. Poor Wolfbiter had been twenty-one by the time he was bound last week. Bullwhip was twenty. The rest were all eighteen or nineteen, unless some of them were lying about their ages—as Wasp was.

As Prime, Bullwhip made a little speech. He was chunky by Blade standards, a slasher not a stabber—meaning saber not rapier—sandy-colored, the sort of man who would charitably be described as "stolid." He was certainly no orator. Spender thanked him, took the chair Wasp had brought, and began to talk politics, specifically politics that led to civil war.

Master of Protocol and his assistants had the unenviable task of preparing the candidates for life at court. That included teaching them dancing, deportment, elocution, etiquette, some history, and a lot of politics. By their senior year it was almost all politics—taxes, Parliament, foreign affairs, the machinations of the great houses. Frenetically active and athletic young men would much rather be fencing or out riding on the moors than listening to any of that stuff, with the possible exception of the racy court scandals. At least Spender was a novelty and hence more interesting than the usual fare. The King of Fitain had lost control of his barons and failed to rally the burghers. Even kings needed allies. And so on. Twenty-four young faces made earnest efforts to seem attentive.

Only Raider would not be faking, Wasp decided. Glancing sideways he saw that his friend was indeed very intent, nodding to himself as he listened. He had the strange perversion of finding politics interesting. He was probably the only man in the room who cared a snail's eyebrow about what had happened in Fitain. Everyone else just wanted to hear about the fighting and how it felt to keep on fighting when you knew you ought to be dead after having your thigh crushed and a sword run through you.

The sky was blue beyond the dirty panes.

Back in Wasp's beansprout days he had watched Lord Bannerville bind Spender. Dragon and Burl must have been there, attending their ward, but he could not remember what they had looked like.

No one had thought to open the windows and the room held too many people; it was stuffy. Attentions were wandering.

At the far side of the room, Herrick stifled a yawn.

Suddenly Wasp's jaw took on a fearful life of its own. He struggled desperately, but the yawn escaped. That one Sir Spender noticed.

Sir Spender exploded. "Smug young bastards!" he snapped. He heaved himself to his feet. "You don't give a spit about this, do you, any of you?" His already pale face had turned white as marble. "You don't think it matters! Doesn't concern you, any of you, does it?" He glared around the room, eyes flashing with fury, left hand steadying his scabbard as if he were about to draw. "You insufferably stuck-up unbearable latrine cleaners, all of you!"

Twenty-four seniors stared up at him in horror. Wasp wanted to die. How *could* he have done that? *Yawning!* What a crass, imbecilic, *childish* thing to do!

But Spender's rage was not just against him—it was directed at all of them. "I know what you're thinking!" He grew even louder. "You all think that the King takes the best for the Guard and it's only the failures he assigns as private Blades. Don't you? *Don't you?* Just nod!" he said, dropping his voice to a menacing growl. "If that's what you think, you young slobs, just nod once and I'll give you a fencing lesson with real swords. I'm a private

Blade and proud of it. Burl and Dragon were my brothers and they're *dead*! They didn't rank second to *anyone*!''

Wasp stared appealingly at Prime and so did everyone else. *Say something!* A week ago Wolfbiter had been Prime and Wolfbiter would have known exactly what to say. But Wolfbiter had gone, and in Bullwhip's case the sword was mightier than the tongue. He had straightened up off the wall, where he had been leaning. His mouth opened but no sound emerged.

Spender had not finished. ''You all think you're going into the Guard, don't you? Nothing but the best! Well, I tell you being a private Blade is a thousand times harder than lounging around the palace with a hundred others. It's a full-time job. It's a lifetime job! None of this ten-years-and-then-dubbed-knight-and-retire nonsense. We serve till we die! Or our ward does.''

Bullwhip's freckled, meaty face remained locked in an agony of embarrassment. Mallory, who was Second, seemed equally frozen, unwilling to upstage his leader—good manners but not good sense when a hero started having hysterics.

Wasp jabbed an elbow in Raider's ribs. ''Say something!'' he whispered.

''Hmm? All right.'' Raider flowed to his feet, unfolding like a flail. He was third in line, after Mallory. He also stood almost a hand taller than any other man in the school, long and lean; with that copper-red hair and green-green eyes he was never inconspicuous. Everyone looked, including Spender.

''With respect, sir, I certainly do not believe that. I doubt if anyone here does. Wolfbiter is the finest fencer Ironhall has produced since Sir Durendal and just a few days ago we all saw him being bound as a private Blade. He put all of us to shame with steel, yet the King assigned him to someone else, not the Guard.''

Twenty-three throats made earnest sounds of agreement.

''In fact,'' Raider added, perhaps hoping to change the subject, ''he assigned him to Sir Durendal and none of us can imagine why.''

Spender stared at him in silence for a moment. His color

flamed swiftly from its corpselike white to brilliant red. Wasp relaxed. Everyone did. They had been taught that pallor was the danger sign. Blushing meant apology or bluff. The hero sank down on his chair again.

"I'm sorry," he muttered. "Sorry, sorry, sorry!" He doubled over.

Bullwhip waved hands at the stair, meaning everyone should leave. Raider made contradictory signs—*stay where you are!*—and everyone stayed. No one ever argued with Raider, not because he was dangerous but because he was always right.

"Sir Spender," he said, "we are sorry to see you distressed, but you should know that we continue to admire you enormously and always will. We are proud to know you, and when we become Blades ourselves we shall be inspired by your example and what you and your two companions achieved. We think no less of you for being human."

Nobody breathed.

"The last entries in the Litany," Raider continued, "were made two years ago during the Nythian War. Sir Durendal saved the King's life outside Waterby. He defeated a team of four assassins single-handed and did not suffer a scratch. I mean no disrespect to him, Sir Spender, but he is so close to a legend that he hardly seems human. You inspire me. He makes me feel horribly inadequate. Your example means much more to me than his does, and that is because I know that you are flesh and blood, as I am." Nobody else could have taken over from Prime without giving offense, but Bullwhip was beaming gratefully.

The Blade looked up and stared at Raider. Then he straightened and wiped his cheeks with a knuckle. "Thank you. That was quite a speech. It means a lot to me. I'm afraid I've forgotten which one . . ."

"Raider, sir."

"Thank you, Raider." Suddenly Spender was in charge of the room again, sustained by the four or five years he had on all of them. "Sorry I lost my temper." He smiled ruefully, looking around. "Blame the King. He ordered me to come here and Return the swords. I shouldn't have let old weasel-tongue Protocol talk me into staying on. I haven't been away from my ward since the night I was bound. Commander Montpurse gave me his solemn oath that he would assign four men to keep watch over His Lordship day and night until I get back, but it isn't the same. And after what happened in Fitain, I'm extra sensitive. It's driving me crazy!'' He smiled at their horrified expressions. ''You didn't think being a Blade was easy, did you? You don't care about rebellion and civil war. Why should you? It isn't going to happen here in Chivial. And I need to be with my ward. So, if you'll excuse me now, I'll be on my way. The moon will see me back to Grandon.'' He was talking of an all-night ride and he looked exhausted already.

When Bullwhip tried to speak, Spender stopped him. ''You have other things to attend to. I promised not to warn you, but in return for the honor you have done me, I will. The King is on his way. He should be here very shortly.''

Raider spun around but not before Wasp was on his feet and looking out the window. Horsemen in blue livery were riding in the gate.

''He is!'' Wasp screamed. ''He's here! *The King is here!*''

His voice cracked on the high note. He turned around to face the glares of a dozen men who wanted to murder him on the spot.

· 4 ·

By tradition—and tradition was law in Ironhall—the King entered by the royal door and went directly up to Grand Master's study. There Grand Master waited, fussing around, vainly trying to flick away dust with a roll of papers and mentally reviewing his notes for the thousandth time. A small fire burned in the grate, a decanter of wine and crystal goblets waited on the table. He was a spare, leathery man with a permanently bothered expression and a cloud of white hair reminiscent of a seeding dandelion. Foolish though it seemed, he was presently as nervous as anyone in the school. This was the first time he had played host to the King. Usually the Blades' own rumor mill ground out warnings of the King's visits, but this time it had not.

The previous Grand Master, Sir Silver, had ruled the Order for a third of a century; but half a year ago the spirits of time and death had caught up with him at last. His memory still haunted this room—his ancient furniture, his choice of prints on the walls, even some of his keepsakes still cluttering the mantel of the fieldstone fireplace. His successor had added a tall bookcase and his own books, plus a large leather chair, which he had ordered made to his specifications in Blackwater as a celebration of his promotion. Nothing else.

Long ago he had been Tab Greenfield, unruly younger son of a minor family, which had disposed of him by enrolling him in Ironhall—the best thing that had ever happened to him. Five years later he had been bound by Taisson II in the first binding of his reign, becoming Sir

Vicious, enduring eight years of routine and futile guarding before being dubbed a knight in the Order and so freed. Having a longtime interest in spirituality, he had enlisted in the Royal College of Conjurers and had done some original work on invoking spirits of earth and time to increase the stability of buildings. He had even toyed with ambitions of becoming grand wizard, but eventually the opportunity to merge his two careers had brought him home to Ironhall as Master of Rituals. Last Ninthmoon he had been genuinely astonished when the Order chose him as Grand Master and even more surprised when the King approved the election. He was about to be tested in his new duties for the first time.

He had a problem, a candidate who did not fit the pattern.

The King was taking his time! Possibly he had ridden round to West House to inspect the fire damage. The noise of the carpenters working was faintly audible even here, although Grand Master had grown so used to it now that he never noticed it. He looked around the room yet again. What might a new Grand Master have forgotten?

Flames, his sword! Only a bound Blade could go armed into the King's presence, and Grand Master should be the last one to forget that. Appalled that he had so nearly made a major blunder, he drew *Spite* and stepped up on the muniment chest to lay her on top of the bookcase, out of sight. His baldric and scabbard he folded away in the chest itself.

He was just closing its lid when the latch rattled on the inconspicuous door in the corner and in walked Hoare—a typical Blade, all lean and spry. Until now his only distinguishing features had been a grotesque tuft of yellow beard and a vile juvenile humor, which his chosen name did not deny, but now he sported the baldric of Deputy Commander across the blue and silver livery of the Royal Guard. Smiling, he advanced with hand outstretched.

"Grand Master! Congratulations!"

"Deputy! Congratulations to you, also."

Hoare had a grip like a woodcutter. "My, we are coming up in the world, aren't we?'' His eyes raked the room. ''How does it feel to be chief keeper of the zoo?''

''Very gratifying. How does it feel to step into Durendal's shoes?''

Hoare shuddered dramatically. ''I expect it would make me very humble if I knew what the word meant.'' He shot a quizzical glance at the older man. ''Odd business, that! Did he by any chance drop any hints while he was here? Where he was going? Why the world's greatest swordsman needs a Blade to guard him?''

''Not a peep. I was sort of hoping you might tell me.''

They exchanged matching frowns of frustration.

Hoare shrugged. ''Hasn't been a word from anyone. Grand Inquisitor probably knows, but who's going to ask her? The Fat Man isn't talking. Never forget, Grand Master, that kings have more secrets than a dead horse has maggots, and most of them nastier. Even Leader swears he doesn't know.''

Grand Master would believe that when Montpurse himself told him so; he got on well with the Commander. ''Leader is not with you this time?''

''Yes, he's coming. Janvier? Something wrong?''

There was another Blade standing in the doorway, a younger one—Janvier, a rapier man who had been Prime very briefly and bound on the King's last visit, together with Arkell and Snake. He had always been quiet, acute, and self-contained, but why was he just standing there like that, head cocked, frowning as if listening for something?

Grand Master opened his mouth, and Hoare held up a warning hand. He looked amused, but Hoare always looked amused.

Sir Janvier marched unerringly across the room and stepped up on the muniment chest. ''There's a sword up there.'' He sounded more aggrieved than surprised.

Hoare grinned like a pike and waggled a reproving finger at Grand Master. ''Naughty!''

Incredible! ''How does he *do* that?'' Many Blades had instincts for danger to their wards, but Grand Master had never witnessed sensitivity on that scale.

"Wait till you hear about the wood sliver under the King's saddle! Tell Grand Master how you do it, brother."

Young Janvier had jumped down, holding *Spite,* and was admiring the unusual orange glint of the cat's-eye stone on her pommel. He looked up blankly. "I don't know, Grand Master. I heard it buzzing. It's you who should be able to tell me."

Buzzing? "There are some reports in the archives. . . . I resent the implication that my sword is in any way a danger to His—"

"Any sword can be a danger if it falls into the wrong hands," Hoare said. "You're supposed to set us kiddies a good example. Put that wood chopper somewhere safe."

Janvier headed for the corridor door, peering at the inscription on the blade as he did so. "Why *Spite*?"

"Why not!?" Grand Master snapped. Seeing another man handling his sword was a novel and extremely unpleasant experience. *Spite* was *his* and he had not been separated from her in almost thirty years.

At that moment the door at the bottom of the stairwell slammed. Hoare ran across to Janvier and shot him out of the room, *Spite* and all. He had the corridor door closed again and was standing with his back to it and his face completely blank when the heavy tread approaching reached the top step.

· 5 ·

The King ducked his wide, plumed hat under the lintel and paused to catch his breath. He stood much taller than any Blade and was visibly bigger than he had been on his last visit, much too large for a man not yet forty. The current fashions made him seem gargantuan—puffed, slashed sleeves on a padded jerkin of green and red hanging open to reveal a blue silk doublet, legs bulging in striped gold and green stockings, green boots. The tawny fringe of beard was flecked with silver, but Ambrose IV of the House of Ranulf showed no signs of relaxing the granite grip with which he had ruled Chivial for the last eight years. His amber-colored eyes peered out suspiciously between rolls of lard.

He acknowledged Grand Master's bow with a nod and a grunt. As he unfastened his mud-spattered cloak of ermine-trimmed scarlet velvet, Montpurse materialized at his back to lift it from the royal shoulders. Then the Commander turned as if to hang it on a peg, but Grand Master had been unable to think of any reason for that peg to be there and had removed it so he could hang a favorite watercolor in its place. Montpurse shot him a surprised smile and laid the garment over a chair. With flaxen hair and baby-fair skin, he looked not a day older than he had on the night he was bound. *Spirits!* That was just after Grand Master came back to Ironhall . . . was it really almost fifteen years ago . . . ?

The Commander closed the outer door and took up his post in front of it. Without removing his hat, the King headed for the new leather chair and settled into it like a galleon sinking with all hands. He was still short of breath.

"Good chance, Grand Master."

"Thank you, sire, and welcome back to Ironhall." Vicious reached for the decanter. "May I offer you some refreshment?"

"Ale," said the King.

Grand Master strode to the other door and peered out. Wallop and the Brat were waiting in the corridor as he had ordered—the Brat looking scared to death. But Janvier and Scrimpnel were standing there also with the patience of mountains, and Wallop held a tray bearing a large flagon, a drinking horn, two pies, several large wedges of cheese, and sundry other victuals. Wallop had been a servant at Ironhall since it was built, within a century or two, and he obviously knew the present king's preferences.

Granting him a sheepish smile of thanks, Grand Master took the tray and bore it back to the monarch. He laid it on the table as Hoare whipped away the wine to make room.

The King reached a fat hand for the flagon. "So how are you settling in, Grand Master?"

"With great satisfaction, sire. I welcome this opportunity to thank you in person for the extreme honor you—"

"Yes. When will the repairs be completed?" Ambrose put the flagon to his mouth and drank without taking his shrewd, piggy gaze off Grand Master.

"By the middle of Fifthmoon, sire, they assure me. We shall be . . . We are looking forward to it." The school was presently packed to the rafters, although a dozen elderly knights had been temporarily evicted to find other accommodation. To point that out to a touchy monarch might be dangerous, since the overcrowding was partly due to his delay in harvesting qualified seniors.

"Thunderbolts in the middle of winter?" The King wiped his beard with his sleeve and glowered suspiciously. "You are satisfied there was no spiritual interference? None of those batty old pensioners experimenting with conjuration? Kids holding midnight parties and upsetting candles?" His father had always seen conspiracies where others did not. Perhaps all kings did. Why else the Blades?

"Thunderstorms can strike Starkmoor at any season, sire. Some superstitious people tried to relate the accident to the death of my predecessor so soon before." Did the King's scowl mean that he was one of them? "I do not believe in ghosts, and if I did I could never believe Sir Silver would return from the dead to attack the Order he served so long and well. The storm brushed Torwell also. It roared half the night away here. We have some very deaf old knights among us and I don't think one of them was asleep when we were hit."

The King grunted and reached for the drinking horn. "So what have you for me this time? How many stalwart young swordsmen, hmm?"

"A great many, Your Majesty. A couple of them are outstanding. I fancy the King's Cup will be safe from outsiders for many years to come."

"I'll have you drawn and quartered if it isn't!" He laughed, and the famous royal charm dismissed any threat in the words. "We don't have Sir Durendal to rely on now."

Ah! "We don't?"

"No we don't." The King cut off that line of conversation. "Start with Prime."

Noting that he had not been invited to sit down, Grand Master stepped away from the fireplace in case he forgot himself so far as to lean an elbow on it. He folded his hands behind his back and prepared to perform like a soprano reciting the Ironhall creed.

"Prime is Candidate Bullwhip, my liege. A fine—"

"Bullguts!" The King glared as he filled the horn. Foam spilled over his hand, but he ignored that.

"Sire?"

"Bullballs! How shall I feel if I must address one of my guards at court when he has a name like that? In the presence of the Isilondian ambassador, perhaps? I *know* you said Bullwhip, Grand Master! I had occasion many times to reproach your predecessor for some of the absurd names he allowed boys to choose and that is an egregious example! I hope you will display better judgment!" Scowl.

Hoare, standing safely out of sight behind the King, stuck out his tongue.

Grand Master bowed, recalling that two days ago he had approved the registering of a Candidate Bloodfang who stood less than five feet high and had freckles. "I shall inform Master of Archives of Your Majesty's instructions." He wasn't going to change the tradition, no matter what the King said. The right to choose a new name mattered enormously to a recruit. It was a rite of passage, recognition that the old person was forgotten and from now on he was who he said he was, to be whatever he could make of himself. This was going to be a stormy audience if Ambrose objected to a name as innocuous as Bullwhip.

"Well, carry on!"

"Yes, sire. Bullwhip is an excellent saber man."

Silence. The King wanted more. He took great personal interest in his Blades, like a horse breeder in his stable.

"Not truly outstanding with a rapier, but of course that's speaking relatively. By any standards but the Blades' he is superb."

The King paused in raising the drinking horn to his mouth. "The man himself! If I'm going to have him under my feet for the next ten years, I want to know what to expect."

"Yes, of course—"

"I can still assign him to my Minister of Fisheries, you know!"

"Er, certainly, sire. Bullwhip is, hmm, solid. Popular. Not especially imaginative, but very, um . . . solid."

Hoare rolled his eyes. Grand Master resisted a temptation to throw something at him, preferably a sharp knife. Hearing no further comment from the King, he plunged ahead.

"Second is Candidate Mallory, sire." At least Ambrose could not object to that name. "A rapier man, a very fine rapier man. Personality . . . lighthearted, jovial, well liked. But not flippant at all, sire! Good all-rounder, I'd say. No problems." He was not doing well at this. In a year or two, when he'd had more practice and knew what to expect . . . He could feel sweat running down his temples, and the King could probably see it. The trouble was that all the candidates were good men. The weaklings had long since been driven out. He was expected to find fault where there wasn't any.

"Umph. And third?"

Wait for it . . . "Candidate Raider."

The royal glare chilled the room. "That is *another* example!"

Five nights ago, right here in this room, Grand Master had asked advice from the celebrated Sir Durendal, who was one of the King's favorites and reputed to handle him better than anyone except possibly Montpurse. "Never let him bully you," Durendal had said. "If you don't know, say so. If you do know, stand your ground. He respects that. Give him an inch and he'll trample you into the mud.''

''With respect, sire, perhaps not! I mean,'' Grand Master added hastily as the royal temper glinted, ''that 'Raider' is certainly a foolish name, but I cannot at the moment recall whether it was ever formally approved. I never chose to be called Vicious.''

''You didn't?'' The King did not like to be contradicted. He had probably been saving up some pointed observations on the subject of *Sir Vicious.*

''No, sire. I wanted to be *Lion.* I was entered in the rolls as Lion, but the sopranos had already named me Vicious and it stuck. When the time for my binding came, I had grown into it. Candidate Raider is unusually tall. Even when he was the Brat he was big, and he has very, hmm, very red hair.'' The ground was especially treacherous here, for Ambrose's hair and beard had a decidedly bronze hue.

''Oh, *that* one!'' Ambrose said with welcome signs of amusement. ''Year by year as I've come here, I've watched that flaming red head moving up, table by table. I'll be interested to meet its owner at last.''

''Hmm, yes, sire. At first sight they called him the Bael, of course, because of his hair. This was while the Baelish War was still raging, and stories of atrocities were drifting in almost every week—piracy, raiding, slaving. He wore it long when he arrived, so the first night the sopranos hacked it all off him. Naturally! I mean, how could they resist? But it took six of them to hold him down and when they thought the scramble was over, he did not agree. One can start a fight but it takes at least two to stop it. Raider wouldn't stop. He broke one boy's jaw and knocked teeth out of several others.''

''Broke his jaw?'' The King raised his tawny brows. This was exactly the sort of childish tale that impressed him. ''How old was he then?''

''Thirteen, sire.''

''Broke a jaw at thirteen?'' Ambrose chuckled, releasing a gleam of the royal charm. ''No milksop, obviously!''

''Far from it, sire. That was only the beginning. By the

time his term as the Brat was up, he'd cowed all the sopranos and most of the beansprouts, and I don't remember anyone else ever managing that. He sabotaged their clothes and fouled their bedding with horse dung. He woke them in the night. . . . They could gang up on him, of course, and they did, but they couldn't stay together in a pack all the time. Whenever Raider could get one of them alone, he would jump out and take his revenge. One-on-one he could pummel any of them. I have never seen so many black eyes and split lips. It was a reign of terror. *They* were scared of *him,* and it's supposed to be the other way. They named him Raider, sire!''

Ambrose roared out a thunderclap of laughter that seemed to shake the building. ''Feels good to tell me that, doesn't it? All right, we shall issue a royal pardon to Candidate Raider for being Candidate Raider. He obviously earned that name. If he ever goes near the coast with that hair they'll lynch him. They have long memories for those evil days. You suppose his mother was raped by a Baelish raider? Tell me more about this demon.'' He reached for a pie.

Grand Master breathed a silent prayer of thanks to the absent Durendal. ''But the point is that he isn't a demon, sire! He's affable, courteous, sociable. Self-contained, inclined to be meditative. Very popular and respected. We find this often. No matter what their background, once they've been through their testing as the Brat, as soon as people start to treat them like human beings, they begin to behave like human . . .'' He recalled another of Durendal's tips: *Never lecture him.* ''Yes, well, Raider's a future commander of your Guard, sire. I'll stake my job on it.''

This threat to the royal prerogative caused the porcine eyes to shrink even smaller. ''You will, will you? I'll remember that, Grand Master. By the eight! I don't recall your predecessor ever making so reckless a prediction.'' He emptied the drinking horn and bit a chunk out of the pie.

Hoare was grinning, so he had guessed what was coming.

''He made this one, sire. He made it several times. A

superb judge of men. And he was taken from us *before* the night of the fire. It was Raider who ran back into the building and made the rescues. Two knights and one candidate are alive today only because of him."

The King must know all this. Grand Master's reports on the seniors were officially addressed to Commander Montpurse, but he certainly passed them on. Ambrose could probably quote them word for word if he wanted to.

"So he's lucky and he's foolhardy. How is he with a sword, hmm?"

"Adequate."

The royal scowl darkened the room again. "Is that the best you can say about this paragon? *Adequate?*"

"I am confident his skills will not be found wanting." The truth was that the fencing masters refused to commit themselves on Raider's swordsmanship. Fencing was an obsession for most of the boys, but not for him. He was easygoing, even indolent, practicing no more than he had to and frequently letting his opponents score—he admitted he did that, although holding back was regarded as a major breach of the code. Winning mattered more to them, he said. He had been ranked as "disappointing." But one day, just once, he had taken offense at something Wolfbiter did or said, and then he had given the school wonder a thorough trouncing with foils, around and around the courtyard. It had been the talk of all Ironhall for days. He had been unable to repeat that performance since and nobody knew whether he could do so in a real sword fight.

The King had sensed the evasion but he let it go. "Well, they can't all be heroes. Bullwhip, Mallory, Raider . . . Who's fourth?" He reached for the second pie. There was gravy in his beard.

"Wasp, rapier man. Fine swordsman. Popular, sharp . . ." Grand Master hesitated one last moment, and then said it. "I have reservations about him, sire."

"What sort of reservations?"

"He's only a boy."

"Shaving yet?" the King asked with his mouth full.

"Probably not. Wasp is not ready, but there are a dozen

first-class men waiting behind him. It seems very unfair to hold them up because of him.''

That was the rule—candidates must leave in the order in which they arrived. Awkward though this ancient edict often was, it did encourage cooperation in the Order. The faster learners worked hard to help the slow ones. Any other arrangement would make them compete against one another, leading to bad blood and feuds within the brotherhood. Thus was it done and thus shall it always be done.

The King was scowling again. Monarchs liked to think they were busy people, and Ambrose grudged the time to come to Ironhall. It was a duty he could never delegate, for a Blade must be bound by the hand of his ward. ''His fencing is good?''

"He lacks the heft for the heavier weapons, but with a rapier he's brilliant. He'll be even better when he stops growing so fast—it skews his coordination.'' It was his very skill that was the problem, of course. He was too young to handle the deadly abilities Ironhall had given him. A band of drunken aristocratic fops poking fun at a boy Blade might provoke disaster. ''I'm sure there's nothing wrong with the man himself, sire. He's just immature—suffering from a bad attack of adolescence. He can neither swim with the tadpoles nor jump with the frogs. One minute he expects to conquer the world, next minute he's convinced he's human trash and a total failure; or his friends have left him behind and life isn't fair—that sort of thing. We all go through some of it in our time, but he has a severe case. His terrible experience in the fire set him back. And he is an Ironhall swordsman!''

Hoare was pulling faces again.

Ambrose had started on the cheese. ''How old?'' he mumbled.

''He says eighteen, but he may have lied when he came in. A lot of them do and it rarely matters. He was orphaned by a Baelish raid—must have been about the last one of the war. He turned up at the gate here alone. Normally we don't accept a boy unless a parent or guardian sponsors him, of course. Wasp claimed to have walked all the way from Norcaster. He was in a very weak state—close to starvation, feet bloodied, incipient pneumonia."

"Are you accusing your predecessor of being motivated by *pity,* Grand Master?"

The Durendal gambit again: "I am sure he was, sire, many times. But he very rarely made a mistake." The ensuing silence was encouragement to continue. "And in this case, he may even have been anxious to find a Brat to replace Raider before he devastated the entire soprano class!"

Ambrose munched for a moment, then took a gulp of ale. "How did the rat pack deal with him?" It was an unexpected question, a reminder that a king who looked like a butter churn might yet have a sharp mind.

"They hardly touched him. Partly, I think, they were sorry for him. Most of them are here because they made the world too hot to hold them, but Wasp was different. More important, Raider was still resentful and opposed to the hazing. He put the new Brat under his protection. They have been staunch friends ever since." Grand Master saw that Hoare had picked up the hint, so it was a fair bet that Ambrose would raise the matter if he tried to shirk it. "Inseparable friends."

"Like *that*?" It was known that His Majesty disapproved strongly of *that.*

"No, not like *that,* sire," Grand Master said firmly. "If it were like *that,* then there would be jokes and gossip, and there aren't. You cannot keep such secrets in Ironhall." Not easily, anyway. "I'm sure they are just what I have said, very close friends. It is common enough in the Order. Boys arrive here rejected or recently orphaned. The school is harsh—it is no wonder that they reach out for friendship."

The King grunted skeptically. Hoare rolled his eyes.

Grand Master said, "Wasp's misfortune is that he was young when he came and he has turned out to be a slow developer."

And now he was inconveniencing his sovereign lord, who was displeased. "You have conjurations to nudge them along!"

"They are not infallible, sire. Even the ritual to stop a boy growing taller than Blade limits did not work for Raider, although it is one of our standards. There is a maturation-enhancing ritual we could have tried on Wasp, but I never risked it when I was Master of Rituals and I will not allow it now. The danger is that it invokes only spirits of time, and such monoclinal adjurations risk perturbing the diametric complement, which in the case of time is chance, thus hazarding aberrant and unpredictable eventualities. The College has records of children dying of old age before the . . ." The menace in the King's face stopped him.

"You're lecturing!"

"Your pardon, sire!" Grand Master hesitated and then decided that in fairness to the boy they were discussing he must tell the rest of the story. "There is more, sire. His entire family had died in a fire, understand. When we had the fire here, last Eighthmoon, he became separated from the others. I suspect . . . Well, there is no doubt, really. He panicked. When everyone else went down the stairs, he must have run the wrong way or hidden somewhere. . . . We counted heads and discovered he was missing—this was after Raider had already helped the two knights out. We tried to stop him, but he went back a third time to look for Wasp and carried him out just moments before the roof collapsed. There is absolutely no doubt that he saved the lad's life. The boy has not quite recovered from that experience even yet. He needs more time. . . ."

"Tragic!" rumbled the King. "But we cannot let one boy's problems disrupt our Royal Guard. I do not want tearful tales, Grand Master, I want recommendations. This is a difficult situation, one that your predecessor faced more than once. I look to you for judgment."

Grand Master sighed. "Yes, Your Grace. It depends entirely on the urgency of Your Majesty's needs. If Commander Montpurse requires up to fifteen new Blades, Ironhall can supply them, and fourteen will be entirely satisfactory. Probably the fifteenth will also perform as required and I am just worrying overmuch, like a mother hen. On the other hand, if three will tide the Commander over for a couple of months, then I would recommend that this be Your Majesty's decision."

"Two months?" the King growled. "Sounds like the boy needs two years."

"With respect, sire, he will be Prime. That is a considerable test for any candidate and those with apple cheeks most of all. I suspect the Commander could confirm that statement for you." He glanced around, and the fair-faced Montpurse grinned and nodded agreement. "Wasp will not have his hero to rely on any more. The candidates behind him will guess that he held them back and seniors can make Prime's life utter misery if they want. So can Grand Master, if he must. I will guarantee, sire, that within two months, Candidate Wasp will either have snapped like a cheap sword and run away across the moors screaming, or he will have hair on his chin. It may not be visible to everyone, but it will be there. And in that case, both Your Majesty and the Order will have gained an excellent Blade."

For a long, uncomfortable moment the piggy eyes assessed Grand Master as if he were a juicy acorn. "And if you're wrong?"

"Minister of Fisheries, sire."

The King leaned back in the big chair and uttered a couple of deep whoofs that grew into a sort of deep-seated chortling, a peculiar eruption that made his bulk shake. "So you can be ruthless? I confess I wondered if you were man enough for the job, Grand Master. I am pleased to see my doubts were unjustified. I need men who know when compassion is no kindness. Commander, can you live with just the three paragons for now?"

"For two months, yes sire." Montpurse had obviously been amused by the exchange. He must have witnessed many similar sessions. "Longer than that might be troublesome."

"Then you have your two months, Grand Master. Bring on your swordsmen. We shall leave the Wasp in his nest for now."

· 6 ·

Ever since the fire in West House, the senior seniors' dormitory had been a room in New Wing big enough for two beds but containing six. Bullwhip's and Mallory's were next door. Herrick and Fitzroy had to climb over Wasp's or Raider's to reach theirs. The King's unexpected arrival had thrown all the seniors into panic until they realized that they were already wearing their best outfits, which they had put on for the Return that morning and had not had cause to change. All that was required was some washing, straightening, and combing. Herrick had shaved again, because his jowls were permanently blue, but now six men—five men and a boy—were stretched out on their cots awaiting the King's pleasure.

Herrick chewed his nails. Fitzroy cracked his knuckles. Mallory was polishing his boots for the fifteenth time. Bullwhip kept getting up, looking out the door, closing it, sitting down again. . . . And so on. The only calm one in the place was Raider, silently reading a book of poetry with his long legs stretched out. Wasp, who was always being accused of fidgeting, prattling, and making his bed squeak in the night, was absolutely determined that this time he would show no impatience *whatsoever*. None. He had his hands behind his head so they couldn't tremble and he was concentrating on not moving a single muscle. Not a blink! Like Raider. Trouble was that all the pressure seemed to be rolling into his stomach and he was fairly sure he was about to explode and sick up.

Not that his fake calm was going to deceive anyone after that farce he had staged when Spender announced the King was coming—leaping up to look out the window and then screaming like a *kid*! A *dumb* kid! What sort of swordsman made a fool of himself like that? And his voice cracking! Oh *flames*! It was two years since his voice changed. It didn't have to put him through that again. Not now, please not now, with the King in the school.

Bullwhip, Mallory, Raider, Wasp, Herrick, Fitzroy . . . Herrick and Fitzroy wanted to lynch him at once. So did all six men in the second seniors' dorm next door, and some others might be talked into it. All of them shaved or wore beards. Some of them had hair on their chests, too—Herrick without his shirt looked like one of the stable cats. But the King would not bind a mere *boy,* so Wasp stood between them and the Royal Guard.

Soon the summons would come. At the very least it would be a call for Prime and Second to report to Grand Master, but after seven months the King would certainly harvest more than one. However many he wanted, Grand Master would summon them and one more. That was the way it was done. Last week Wolfbiter as Prime and Bullwhip as Second. This week . . . What Wasp feared most was a summons for four: Bullwhip, Mallory, Raider, and Wasp. Three to be bound and Wasp to remain behind.

Then he would be *Prime*! Oh, flames! Mother confessor to a hundred candidates. "Prime, why can't I move up to the beansprouts' table?" "Prime, my neighbor snores. . . ." "Prime, why can't I keep my hands off myself in bed?" And this Prime was only a boy. The seniors would eat him raw. Death! The *sopranos* would eat him raw. He would be like that King of Fitain Sir Spender had described, with barons and burghers and peasants all after his blood at the same time.

He couldn't possibly need to go pee *again,* could he? At least he didn't wet the bed now, as he had for the first few nights after the fire, but he still woke up choking and sobbing, dreaming he was back in the burning dormitory, flailing around unable to see or breathe in the smoke, alone and deserted, or even all bundled up in a blanket, being carried out by a stumbling, cursing Raider. It had been a fiendishly close call, true, but what sort of swordsman wept in bed? And so often it got all mixed up with that other fire, the one he had almost managed to forget. . . .

Raider closed his book and laid it down. "The time has come, soldiers of fortune. I'd like to tell you all that I've enjoyed knowing you and I'm proud to have been your friend. May the spirits of chance grant you all the success you have earned."

After a moment's puzzled silence, Mallory said, "I'm sure we all feel the same about you, dread warrior, but surely we can storm the palace together?"

"No."

"We six!" Fitzroy protested. "The King will take at least all of us here, even if he doesn't—"

"No." Raider grinned but offered no explanation.

"What do you mean?" Wasp cried, and again heard that stupid squeak. Once a man's voice had changed it was not supposed to change *back*!

"Yes, what do you know?" Bullwhip was glaring as if his honor as Prime was being threatened, but the others were frowning too. If Wasp had spoken as Raider had, then everyone would have assumed he was just jackassing around, but Raider's pronouncements always carried conviction.

He smiled at each of them in turn, last and longest at Wasp. "I can't tell you how I know, but I do. For me this is good-bye. So good-bye. Good chance to you all."

Any further argument was blocked by a soft tap on the door. Bullwhip reached it in one bound from a sitting start, almost flattening Mallory, who was there before him. Between them they hauled it open to reveal the Brat dithering outside and about twenty juniors goggling in the background.

"Message for P-p-p-prime!" The kid had not stammered yesterday.

"Well? Let's hear it!"

The Brat dropped to his knees and bent his face to the floor—the sopranos had him well trained already.

"Never mind groveling," Bullwhip said, more gently. "We know why you're here. How many of us does Grand Master want to see?"

The Brat looked up and licked his lips. "F-f-f-four, honored sir."

Wasp's world shriveled up and died.

"You heard him," Bullwhip said harshly. "Let's go. Second. Raider. Wasp? Yes, Wasp." He sounded surprised, as if he couldn't believe Little Peach-face was so senior. "The rest of you kiddies can go back to fencing."

Wasp croaked, "Ready," and lurched to his feet. His stomach writhed and then steadied. It was probably waiting to do its atrocity until it could shame him in front of the King.

With the Brat trotting to keep up with those he was supposed to be leading, they marched across to First House and into the oldest part of that oldest building. The corridors were dingy and dark, still clammy with winter's chill. Halfway along the library corridor, they came on two Blades waiting at the bottom of a narrow staircase—Sir Hoare and Sir Janvier. Those stairs led up to the Flea Room, which was where Grand Master interviewed applicants. It was also where seniors met their future wards, so for most Blades it marked the beginning and the end of life in Ironhall. Yet Raider claimed that he had never seen it and Wasp remembered only dropping in a dead faint at Grand Master's feet.

"Brat, you can run and help the cooks," Hoare said cheerfully. "Tell them you're ready to start skinning the horse now. Prime! Congratulations!" He offered a hand. They all knew Hoare. His scathing humor was much admired and quoted for weeks after his visits. "The Guard's been waiting for you for too long and that is not your fault. The same applies to you, Second."

The candidates mumbled thanks for the compliments and moved on to be greeted by Janvier, who had been Prime before Wolfbiter.

"So you're Raider?" Hoare appraised Raider. "You're not quite as tall as the Big Man, but close. Congratulations on being called."

"Thank you. And congratulations on your own promotion, Deputy."

Only now Wasp noticed the narrow silver baldric. Everyone but Raider had missed it.

"Thanks. It's about time they got someone competent," Hoare said. "And you're Wasp. Tough luck, candidate. Next time we'll . . . Huh?"

Janvier was ignoring Raider's offered hand, staring up at his face with a puzzled expression.

"Trouble, brother?" Hoare asked. His hand slid to his sword hilt.

For a moment there was silence and the dingy corridor seemed to fill with menace.

"Something," Janvier muttered. "It's very faint."

Raider spread out his hands, showing that they were not near his sword. Very softly he said, "I can't see how I can be a danger to Good King Ambrose. I strongly suspect he is a danger to me, so perhaps that's what your talent is detecting, Sir Janvier."

"How do you know about his talent?" snapped Hoare.

"Snake told me about it when he was here last week." Raider's eyes never left Janvier's face.

"What *talent*?" Bullwhip demanded. He was ignored.

"Make up your mind, Janvier." Raider's gentle manners went only so far, as everyone knew. "If you want to try and kill me, I'll enjoy making a sieve of you. If you'd rather do it with fists, I'll be happy to reset your face the way I did last time. Otherwise stand aside, because I have business with the King."

Janvier did nothing. He seemed to be paralyzed.

"Brother, why don't we carry on now?" Hoare said. "We can mention your doubts to Leader and Grand Master before the binding tomorrow."

Reluctantly Janvier stepped back, still watching Raider.

"Fists for preference!" Raider looked to Hoare. "I think I know what's rankling him and it's no danger to His Majesty. Can we move on? I have to dye my hair tonight."

Hoare grinned. "I'm the joker here, candidate. Off with the swords, lads. Stand 'em up in the corner here and collect them when you leave. Remember, it's Grand Master who's summoned you. You go to him. When he presents you, you turn your back, drop your hose, and bend over. Anyone want to practice that now?''

"I'll do it and say you said to!" Bullwhip snarled.

"Me? I told you to kneel and kiss the royal fingers. Don't lick them, even if they do have gravy on them. Any questions?''

"Will he be hiding behind the door like Durendal was?''

"No," Hoare said patiently. "They only play that trick with commoners. Otherwise you'd have your backs to the King and that isn't proper. Spirits, cheer up! You all look scared shoeless. You're supposed to be swordsmen, not milkmaids. This is what you've all been working for all these years! Stick your chins out and swagger. He's a growly fat old bastard, but he's a fiery good king too, and we're all lucky to be able to serve him. Ready?''

"And I don't get asked, do I?" Wasp said.

"Not unless somebody drops dead. You get to stay home and be Prime, you lucky lad. Come along, kiddies."

The Flea Room was small and cold, with two unshuttered windows and an empty fireplace. Dusk had arrived there already, for outside the westward sky was turning pink over the moors and stars shone in the east. As the four candidates formed themselves into a line facing Grand Master, Hoare closed the door with himself on the inside of it. The King was watching from the corner—large and menacing, but smiling and presently officially invisible. The man lurking inconspicuously at the far end was Commander Montpurse.

"You summoned us, Grand Master?" Bullwhip said hoarsely.

Grand Master's swansdown hair rippled as he nodded. "Yes, Prime. His Majesty has need of a Blade. Are you ready to serve?''

This was the ritual. They had all heard tell of it a hundred times, but Wasp had been included so he would know exactly how it was done and could carry word back to the next crop and thus to generations yet unborn. Everything in Ironhall was ritual, tradition, ancient custom.

"I am ready, Grand Master."

The old man smiled approvingly and turned to bow, acknowledging the royal presence. "Your Majesty, I have the honor to present Prime Candidate Bullwhip."

Now everyone could take notice of the King. Wasp had never seen him close, only across half the length of the hall. He was very large. In his voluminous garments he made everyone else present seem small, even Raider. The plume on his hat almost touched the ceiling. Bullwhip made a full court bow, then walked forward and knelt to the sovereign.

"Glad to have you, Prime," he boomed. "Grand Master speaks very highly of your skill with the saber."

Bullwhip mumbled something appropriately modest and was permitted to kiss the royal fingers, rise, bow, step back into line.

"Candidate Mallory," Grand Master bleated, "His Majesty has need of a Blade. Are you ready to serve?"

"I am ready, Grand Master."

One more and then Wasp could go away and begin his ordeal as the Runt Who Wasn't Good Enough. He wouldn't have his friend Raider around to complain to. He would have no friends in Ironhall. Nothing was more certain than that. In a week or so some vapid aristocratic nobody would turn up with a warrant from the King to claim him and turn him into a lap dog. That was what they did with failures—palmed them off on worthless courtiers who needed a bodyguard like a third ear.

The King had been well cued. "A fine rapier man, I hear, to balance a saber one. Welcome to our service, candidate."

Mallory returned to Bullwhip's side.

"Candidate Raider, His Majesty has need of a Blade. Are you ready to serve?"

Raider said, "No, Grand Master. I regret to say that I cannot."

That was not part of the tradition.

• 7 •

The King put his fists on his hips and seemed to swell until he filled the room. Grand Master's face turned as white as his hair. Everyone stared at Raider as if doubting their ears. There was no ritual for this, obviously. There might not even be a precedent—had any candidate ever refused his sovereign? A private binding, maybe. That might be understandable, although Wasp had never heard even a whisper of any refusals, so they must be extremely rare in the three-century history of the Order. And to refuse the King!

Why? After all these years of hard work and effort? Any candidate was free to leave at any time. They were all told that on the day they were admitted, but they were also warned that they would walk out empty-handed, wearing nothing but a peasant's smock. Wasp had known many to disappear. But to give up after five years, at the last possible instant, in front of the King himself . . .

An astonishingly long silence.

"If I may have your leave to withdraw, Grand Master," Raider said quietly, "and an escort past the Blades on the gate, then I will leave Ironhall at once." He was easily the calmest man present. He had not been surprised, of course. This was what he had been hinting at back in the dorm.

Grand Master made a choking sound. "You certainly will!" He was not having much luck with his first harvesting.

"Wait!" The King stepped forward until he was right in front of Raider, almost nose to nose. He was not much taller, but taller he was, and bulky enough to make the boy look like a fishing pole. *"Radgar!"* he barked.

Raider flinched. It must be years since he had needed to look up to anyone, but that did not explain the flinch. Whatever the charge, he was obviously guilty. "Your Majesty?"

"Raider—Radgar! That's why you hung on to that stupid name, isn't it?" The King smiled, if every satisfied display of teeth must be classed as a smile. "I want to hear more about this. We shall talk with you later, young man. Stand over there. Carry on, Grand Master." King Ambrose spun around and stomped back to his place in the rapidly darkening corner.

"Carry on, sire?"

"That's why you have Second, isn't it? *Isn't it?*"

Grand Master made a visible effort to gather his wits. "Ah, yes, of course." He looked doubtfully at Wasp.

Eek! Wasp had become the center of attention. Of course technically Second must become Prime Candidate as soon as Prime accepted binding—or refused it. And so on down the line. That meant that he was now . . . *Eek! Eek! Eek!*

"Candidate Wasp." Grand Master pulled a face as if the name tasted bad. "His Majesty has need of a Blade. Are you ready to serve?"

Another silence . . .

Wasp wanted to look at Raider and see if he could offer any hints, even just a nod or a head shake, but Raider had been removed from view. Whatever was Raider planning? He had nothing: no money, no home, no relatives. All he had ever said about his family was that both his parents had died in a fire. That was something they shared, because so had Wasp's. A peasant's smock and nothing else. He did have his Ironhall training. Any nobleman needing a household guard or a fencing instructor would jump at a chance to hire an Ironhall man. So why let King Ambrose drive a nail through your heart and serve him body and soul for ten years or more? Looked at in that light, Raider had made a very logical decision. Ungrateful, larcenous, and rapacious, perhaps, but he could leave at any time. Those had been the terms offered.

Wasp's hesitation was becoming obvious. The King was glaring. Grand Master was glaring.

"Wasp!" Raider shouted from somewhere in the background. "Don't be a fool! Don't do it!"

Why not? They could go together.

"No, Grand Master. I am afraid I cannot."

• 8 •

Blades did not approve of upstart sword brats who insulted their liege lord. Hoare cracked no jokes now, and Montpurse's fair face was dark with anger. They removed ex-Candidate Wasp from the royal presence, jostled him along to the guardroom, and pushed him into a corner with his face to the stonework. He was told to stay there and say nothing. He was aware that Raider had been similarly placed in the opposite corner, because Raider tried to speak and then cried out when someone struck him. After that there was silence.

King Ambrose was not an absolute despot. Unlike monarchs of less enlightened lands, he must observe the law and truckle to Parliament to some extent. But if he chose to throw two friendless Ironhall orphans into the rankest dungeon in Grandon Bastion and leave them there to die of old age, who would call him to account?

As time dragged by, one thing became more and more certain—Raider had not acted on the spur of the moment. More than anyone else Wasp knew, he always kept his head and thought things through. Having decided to refuse binding, he would have counted on at least a few hours' grace to make his escape, because the King's visits were normally known in advance. He had not intended to provoke a confrontation. But he had, and then dumb-kid Wasp had jumped in and turned it into a conspiracy. They had insulted their king.

Enraged their king.

Guards came and went, for this was the Blades' own room at Ironhall. Words were spoken—not many, but enough to inform Wasp that a dozen astonished seniors had been summoned to the Flea Room and eleven had agreed enthusiastically that they were ready to serve. The King was now dining in the hall. Bullwhip and Mallory had been sworn to silence. If refusals were treated as state secrets, they might not be so rare after all.

Perhaps they buried the bodies on the moor.

Long after sunset the miscreants were fetched to Grand Master's study, which Wasp had not seen since his far-off days as the Brat. The King stood in front of the fireplace, showing no evidence that dinner had improved his mood. Behind him logs crackled cheerfully on the hearth and candle flames danced atop silver candlesticks on the mantel.

The prisoners were stood by the window, facing the King but on the far side of the book-littered table. Janvier was already guarding the outer door, and when everyone else had departed, Montpurse took up position before the inner one. That was all, just five of them, no Grand Master, no witnesses. Would the Guard commit murder on the King's orders?

Wasp had not had a chance to exchange as much as a wink with Raider since this catastrophe began. Raider must have reasons, or at least some plans, so when the King finished his glowering and started asking questions Wasp would have to take his cue from him.

The King cheated—he began with Wasp. "When is your birthweek?"

"First quarter of Fourthmoon, Your Majesty." His voice sounded very small, even to him.

"What year?"

There was going to be a problem here. "Um, 340, sire."

The King had very tiny eyes, and at that news they seemed to shrink even smaller. "You aren't even seventeen yet! How old were you when you were admitted?"

Gulp. "Eleven, Your Majesty."

"And how old did you say you were?"

Wasp whispered, "Thirteen . . . sire."

"So you gained admittance under false pretenses! For five years you have eaten my food, slept under my roof, worn my clothes, taken lessons from my instructors, and now you think you and your friend can just walk away without paying a copper mite?"

There was no answer to that. Wasp hung his head.

"Look at me, thief!" roared the King.

Wasp raised his chin. As he had come to Ironhall, so was he leaving. He was back to being the Brat again. Raider had not kept all the torment from him then, and Raider could do nothing at all for him now. No one could shield him from a bullying monarch with a phalanx of enthralled swordsmen eager to satisfy his whims.

"What's your real name?"

Something rattled its chain, wanting out. "I don't remember!"

Raider cleared his throat in quiet warning.

King Ambrose raised a fist. "Well, *boy,* you had better start remembering, because I'll get the truth out of you by whatever means it takes. I can have inquisitors here before dawn, and you can't lie to them. I can have you put to the Question. I can have you tortured. Or I can do it the easy way. Commander Montpurse, if I ask for three or four volunteers to interrogate this suspect, what sort of response will I get?"

"Enthusiastic, sire. Blades don't like ingrates and renegades."

"Some men never recover their health after that sort of experience—you understand, boy?"

"Yes, sire."

"Then what's your name and where did you come from?"

Even then the resentment straining at its chain made

him delay a moment before he answered, just to watch the King's anger mount. "Will. My father was Kemp of Haybridge by Norcaster."

"And what happened to him?"

Not fair! Everyone knew that admittance to Ironhall was a fresh start, that a man would never be asked for his old name or details of his old life. The slate was wiped clean. Even the law said that, the charter. But the King was the King.

"The Baels got him," Wasp muttered. His father, his mother, his brothers, and a few older relatives. It had been the last raid of the war—in fact the war had been officially ended and all Chivial celebrating with dancing and bonfires, but one Baelish ship had either not yet heard the news or had chosen not to listen. The King was waiting for details. "The squire rallied everyone into the big house, but the Baels burned it." Wasp had been out in the hills, gathering the cows for the evening milking. He had seen the glow of the fire in the dusk. . . . The raiders had come for the cattle and looked for the herd boy. He had hidden in a badger's sett, wriggling in feet first, terrified the badger might start chewing his toes but more terrified of the two-legged monsters hunting him above ground. In the morning they had gone, but there had been nothing of Haybridge left, nothing at all. . . . "I had nowhere to go, no one to turn to. I walked here. I lied to Grand Master because I didn't want to starve to death out on the moor."

The King's fat lips moved in and out as he considered this answer. "And tonight? Why did you refuse to be bound?"

Now Wasp could look up at Raider for help. But Raider was ignoring him, staring glumly at the King.

"My friend needs me."

"Why?"

"I . . . I'm a better swordsman than he is."

"And why does he need a swordsman?"

"Er . . . I don't know."

The questions flashed like rapiers. The answers grew more and more pathetic until Wasp was reduced to repeating, "He saved my life!" over and over and the King shook his head in exasperation. "Grand Master certainly nailed you in the gold. You're an idiot *child,* Will of Haybridge! A brainless, headstrong, immature *brat*!"

Wasp's anger had all gone. He just hoped he wasn't going to weep. *Anything* but that! "Yes, sire."

"You've thrown away everything and you don't even know what you chose instead. What's *your* name, Bael?"

The switch came without warning, but Raider smiled as if he had expected it. He glanced over the audience—Montpurse, Janvier, Wasp—and shrugged.

"You guessed who I am, Uncle."

Wasp jerked out of his misery and took a hard look at that familiar bony face with its invisible eyebrows and lashes, brilliant green eyes. Same man as always. *Uncle?* Had Raider simply gone insane? Had the King? Was that what all this was about—craziness? Raider had always denied being a Bael. How could he be the King's nephew if he was really one of those monsters? Aha! Wait a moment! Wasp recalled a dim memory of Master of Protocol mentioning some obscure and disgraceful connection. . . .

The King scowled. "Why did you refuse binding?"

"Because binding would kill me. I am already enchanted."

Montpurse's sword flashed into his hand.

Raider eyed him warily. "The conjuration cannot harm anyone else. If His Majesty wishes, I can demonstrate its effects."

"Sir Janvier?" growled the King.

Janvier seemed more puzzled than worried. "He does feel like a threat to you, sire, but only vaguely. . . ."

Ambrose dismissed this diagnosis with a snort. "Show us."

"Yes, sire," Raider said calmly. "Commander, I must remove my doublet."

Montpurse took a step closer, still clutching Talon, and Janvier drew his sword also. They watched like cats as the prisoner stripped off his jerkin and then his doublet. Moving deliberately, he rolled up his right shirt sleeve, exposing an arm like any ordinary arm—somewhat slender for a swordsman's perhaps, but a quite respectable pale-skinned and boyishly hairless forearm. "Now, Commander, if you would fetch me one of those candles?"

The King himself grabbed a candlestick from the mantel and stood it on the table. Raider drew a deep breath, set his teeth, and put his arm in the flame.

The King muttered an oath, but otherwise everyone just stared in disbelief. Obviously it hurt. Sweat streamed down Raider's face and his lips curled back in a rictus of pain. His arm trembled with the effort of will needed to hold it steady, but there was no visible change where the flesh should be blistering, turning black, smoking.

"That will do!" said the King sharply.

Raider snatched his hand away and wiped his forehead. He held out his arm to confirm that there was no mark on the skin. Now that the ordeal was over, he was trying not to smile at the King's obvious shock. Montpurse, testing a finger over the candle, winced and drew it back instantly. Raider rolled down his sleeve.

King Ambrose scoffed, but he had been shaken. "A clever parlor trick! What does it prove? Are all Baels immune to fire?"

Again Raider did not deny the insult. "No, sire. But a massive enchantment like mine will deflect any other conjuration, or at least distort the balance of the elements in it. I'm sure that's why Master of Rituals could not stop my growth. If you thrust the sword through my heart I will die. Besides, how would the sniffers at court react to me?" He smiled ruefully at Wasp. "I also showed you that my companion's loyalty is misplaced. Yes, I carried him out of West House, but I was in no danger. When my clothes burned, it hurt but did me no harm. I should not have claimed to be a hero when I wasn't, friend. I am sorry."

Ridiculous! "You didn't claim anything," Wasp protested. "What would have happened if you'd been half a minute later? What if we'd been still inside when the roof came down? I'd have died under tons of blazing timbers. What would you have done?"

"I'd probably have used a lot of bad language."

"Silence!" roared the King. "Any more insolence and I will have the Guard lay the rod on your backs, both of you. You can do tricks with a candle, boy, but you still have to convince me you're the lost atheling."

Raider raised his brows in impudent surprise. *"Gea! Ic wille mine æðelu gecyðan, pæt ic eom miceles cynnes. . . ."** The King's glare made even his cocksureness falter at that point. "I will tell you of my noble kin, Uncle, for it is true that you have granted me hospitality for the last five years and a guest's duties—"

"An uninvited guest! A freeloader, a thief!"

"Ah! Well, that depends."

Wasp wondered what the two Blades were making of this. He did not dare look. He did not dare look anywhere except at a king who seemed very close to explosion. Never had he felt admiration for anyone more than he felt for Raider now. In an impossibly unfair contest he had brushed aside the King's attack and drawn ahead on points. Not that it could ever be a fair match, for the King could break it off at any point and summon the inquisitors. His talk of a beating was no bluff, either.

"Depends on *what*?"

"On what orders Sir Geste had and who issued them."

The royal eyes narrowed. "Geste? Who's he?"

"A former Blade, Your Grace. He was the one who brought me to Ironhall."

"Don't recall any Geste in the Order. Do you, Commander?"

"No, sire," Montpurse said. "Shall I send for Master of Archives?"

"Perhaps later, when we have finally extracted the explanation we are still waiting for."

Raider bowed. "Gladly I will give it, sire. But my friend and I have been kept on our feet for about three hours now. I very much need to relieve myself. A drink and a bite of food would be a generous gesture."

The King scowled at Montpurse. "Send for some water and a piss pot." As the Commander was passing the word

*Yea! I wish my nobility made known, that I am from great kinfolk. . . .

to someone outside the door, the King sank into the big leather chair. He pointed at the oaken settle opposite. "Sit there and explain how you got here."

The command did not specifically include Wasp, but there was room for two on the bench and no one objected when he squeezed in beside Raider.

"How I Got Here?" Raider said thoughtfully. "I suppose the greatest blame should be laid on Gerard of Waygarth. A nice enough young man, I understand, yet sadly misguided. He was of no real importance in himself, but back in 337, during your father's—"

"Never mind him! You need not go that far back."

Wasp felt peeved. Why would the King not let Raider tell the whole story? What could have happened twenty years ago that he still wanted kept secret?

II

The story Raider wanted to tell would have gone something like this. . . .

1

Ambleport was a town of about a thousand souls on the southwest coast of Chivial. It thrived on trade, fishing, a little whaling in the spring, and more than a little smuggling. By day its inhabitants bustled about in its crowded little harbor and by night they slept unworried within its walls of honey-colored stone.

One foggy dawn in the spring of 337, four dragon ships floated into the mouth of the Amble River. They advanced with muffled oars, silent as trout in a pool, gray as ashes in the murk. The cold watchmen in their shack at the end of the breakwater rang no warning bell, because their throats had been cut a few minutes earlier by three wet, naked men who had climbed up the stonework with knives in their teeth. The hunters passed unchallenged into the harbor and tied up alongside the fishing boats. Two hundred well-trained raiders swarmed ashore without a word.

Brawny arms hurled grapnels, and these made some slight scraping noises as their teeth gripped the edges of the honey-colored walls but nothing loud enough to alert the town watch. The first men over opened the gates for the rest.

•

Everyone knew about Baels. Everyone had heard of the mindless havoc—women raped in the streets and screaming naked berserkers slaying every living thing. What happened in Ambleport was very different—well-trained troops following a plan with steely discipline. A band smashed in the door and rushed through the house, looking for opposition. If they found none, one or two remained, demanding loot, while the remainder continued to the next house. Many of the raiders spoke fluent Chivian and the rest could parrot, "Do not resist and you will not be hurt." If the residents quickly handed over some jewelry, a few gold coins, perhaps a silver candlestick, the raiders would grin politely and depart, taking anything else that caught their fancy—weapons, good textiles, metal pots. Only if they met resistance or found nothing of value did they resort to violence, and then they could be as nasty as the legends said.

Dealings were less civilized when youngsters were present. Adolescents and older children were ordered outside and herded down to the harbor for future consideration. In much less than an hour, Ambleport was stripped bare of valuables, and its young people stood in a terrified huddle on the quay. There had been almost no resistance.

Almost none. Gerard had been fast asleep in the Green Man, blissfully dreaming of Charlotte. He was wakened by someone kicking in the door of the room next to his and had just enough time to leap out of bed and snatch up his rapier. When his own door was smashed open by a red-bearded raider, he attacked.

He had never been in a fight in his life and had never expected to be. But he was a gentleman, and gentlemen sported either rapier or short sword. To gird on a weapon one could not use was folly, so he had taken lessons at a very respected school in Grandon—not many lessons, for his means were limited, but he was nimble and accurate. Alas, in this instance, also rash. The only crazy naked berserker in Ambleport that morning was Gerard of Waygarth. His victim looked more surprised than hurt when the steel point went through his beard and up into his brain, but he folded to his knees and collapsed on his shield and ax in an entirely appropriate manner.

Another Bael filled the doorway behind him—younger, shorter, and broader. With a blood-chilling scream he leaped over his fallen comrade. His shield brushed Gerard's rapier aside like a twig and slammed its owner back into the wall hard enough to stun. The fight was over even before the raider brought up his knee. This technique was not taught in the gentlemen's fencing schools.

By the time Gerard had stopped retching long enough to breathe again, the Bael had stripped his fallen comrade, piling ax, shield, dagger, helmet, and other equipment on the bed—even the man's boots. He had also searched the room and found the pouch containing Lord Candlefen's gold.

"This?" he demanded incredulously. "You killed a man for four crowns? A thegn's wergild is twelve hundred!"

Gerard could only moan and hope for a quick death. To his blurred vision the monster was a vague impression of broadsword, breeches, boots, steel helmet, close-cropped copper beard, and a truly murderous green stare. And a voice that said, "Put on warm clothes. You're coming with me."

As an added indignity, Gerard had to carry the blanket containing the dead man's gear plus his own rapier and document case, although he would have walked doubled over even without that load. The inn was put to the torch because a Bael had died in it. No other buildings were burning, but as he staggered down the muddy track to the harbor gate, he saw he had not been the only would-be hero. Four or five men had tried to defend their loved ones; their bodies had been thrown out of windows to discourage any further resistance.

The raid over, the raiders returned to the waterfront to load their booty. A large part of that booty consisted of the young people of Ambleport, huddled into a terrorized flock within a ring of glittering steel, but the first shock was starting to wear off. As the horror of their plight registered, they were growing restless and milling around, girls easing into the center and the older boys moving to the outside. The slavers selected one of the largest and ordered him to lead the way aboard a ship. He refused and was hacked down on the spot; then the rest did not argue. The astonishing discipline still prevailed—no raping, no wholesale arson, just clockwork perfection.

As the sun burned off the mist, the dragon ships spread their oars and departed on the ebb tide. They rounded the headland and were gone. They took Gerard with them, because he had slain one of their own and must suffer for it.

· 2 ·

Baels were savages inhabiting mountainous islands a few days' sailing northwest of Chivial. Perversely, they were also the world's finest traders, offering infinite diversity of riches: silk and jade, pearls and fantastic shells, sable and ermine, spice and perfume, ivory, precious metals, peerless weapons. Their ships were little bothered by the pirate scourge that made distant seas so treacherous for other nations. That was because most of the scourging was done by the Baels themselves, and the locals had learned not to meddle with them.

Whatever they got up to in distant waters, they marauded the coasts and sea lanes of Eurania at will. Baelmark's closest neighbor, Chivial, suffered more than most, seeing every year three or four ships vanish, a town or two raped. The Baelish King was very sorry, always; he did try to control the pirate gangs, so if the victims would just give him the culprits' names and say exactly where on his wild shores they had their lair, he would take appropriate action. No one believed him, but reprisals against Baelmark itself always ended in disaster. Once in a while Euranian authorities would catch a raider red-handed and hang the whole crew in a line, but not often. Some governments tried to buy safety by paying tribute, although even that did not always work. All monarchs benefitted from excise taxes on Baelish trade, and their courtiers had insatiable appetites for the exotic luxuries only Baels could provide. Commerce and slaughter ebbed and flowed in uneasy balance, rarely open war and yet never quite peace.

The distinction was moot to the Baels. When the ships that had sacked Ambleport rounded the headland and caught the wind, the crew shipped oars and unfurled a square sail on the single mast—not a red war sail, but an innocent brown one bearing an emblem of a goose in flight. The dragon's-head posts were removed from prow and stern. Unless inspected at close range, the ship was now a trader, and who could ever run down a Baelish ship to inspect it?

Gerard had been put in the lead ship. He thought it was also the largest but could not reliably judge size in a watery world bereft of landmarks. It was about three spans wide at its widest part and perhaps five or six times that in length, an open box with no covered decks. People and booty filled it like a herring barrel, except for a small area at the stern where the pirate chief stood holding the steering oar, exposed to the wind and spray as much as anyone. He ruled a crew of about fifty and now almost as many captives, who were all crammed together in the bow. The reason for putting the landlubbers at the downwind end became obvious as soon as the ship began to roll, although most of the Ambleport youngsters were far better sailors than Gerard proved to be. Within minutes he was so deathly seasick that he no longer cared what happened to him.

Far from displaying the wholesale brutality attributed to them by the legends, the raiders were considerate of their valuable and fragile livestock. They slung awnings across the width of the ship like very low tents as protection from the weather; they passed out furs and blankets. They themselves were well bundled up in garments of leather and oiled cloth. Near nudity was acceptable for warriors ashore—as an efficient garb for fighting or a means of intimidating enemies—but at sea they wrapped up warmly.

By evening the wind was a screaming gale, whipping spume from the waves and churning the sea into mountains. Sailors who could speak Chivian assured the captives that the wind was good because it meant a faster trip to Baelmark. The merits of that argument depended on one's point of view. Next day the weather was even worse and the crew even happier.

Needless to say, the prisoners were in despair. They all knew that Baels enchanted captives into mindless thralls and either set them to work in the fields or sold them in slave markets far away. Gerard suspected they would have worse tricks to try on people they seriously disliked. Unlike his companions, he was not being mourned. His parents might not notice his disappearance for weeks or months, and the senior heralds of the college would do no more than curse the unreliability of gentlemen employees. Nobody knew he had been in Ambleport that night. Enriched by his unexpectedly generous honorarium from Lord Candlefen, he had decided to return to Grandon by the coast road. The priory in Wearbridge was reputed to own some very old manuscripts, and if he could win permission to make copies, the college archivists would pay well for them. Alas, he had never reached Wearbridge and now never would.

On the third day the wind dropped, and the sea grew calmer. The awnings were removed so the crew could clean up and tidy the ship. The stronger, fitter prisoners were set to bailing. Even Gerard had accepted that life was possible in a world made up of green-glass hills and shadowed valleys. He had grown used to the reek of overcrowded bodies, constant creaking from the cables, the clink of the ever-shifting cargo, muffled sobbing among the captives. Around noon word was passed forward. A raider hauled him to his feet—and held him there, else he would have fallen. At the rear of the ship, the leader nodded.

"Sciphlaford þe gehateþ," the pirate said. *"Þu ga him."*

Gerard could not speak Baelish, but he could understand

some of it. Baelmark had been discovered by Chivian sailors and settled by Chivians, and many of the words the crew spoke among themselves resembled the archaic Chivian on the old charters and documents he worked with in the college. The sailor pronounced *sciphlaford* much like "ship lord," so his meaning was obvious enough, especially when he pointed at the helmsman with one hand and gave Gerard a shove with the other.

Gerard set off along the ship, a course that alternated between uphill and downhill, clambering the whole way on hands and knees over sacks of loot, trying not to jostle any men who were sleeping, lest they lash out with fists like mallets. Yet the journey was informative. He had already seen that the sailors' garments were beautifully made and frequently bore embroidery and strips of beadwork. Now he noted buckles and brooches elaborately decorated with gold and precious stones, like the hilts of the weapons that lay always ready to hand. The ship itself was put together with a clockmaker's craftsmanship, its oaken planks perfectly fitted, smoothed, and in many places embellished with low-relief carvings of whimsical sea monsters that served no practical purpose. Nothing could be more utilitarian than the chests on which the men sat while rowing and in which they stored their personal effects, yet even those were carved and inlaid with ivory or mother-of-pearl, as if to defy the harshness of the elements. That slavers might be rich was no surprise, but he had not expected savages to be lovers of art.

The ship lord was the blocky young man who had captured him. Although he had held the steering oar for at least two thirds of the time since leaving Ambleport, he showed no signs of weariness. In the worst of the storm he had needed the help of two other men; even now, when the gale had tapered off to a stiff breeze, steering was clearly hard work, for he had to move the oar up and down on its pivot as the ship rode the swell, straining constantly against the pressure, holding her close to the wind. That explained those shoulders.

He wore a long-sleeved, knee-length smock of green wool, gathered at the waist by a gold-studded belt. Below that showed cross-gartered leggings and soft boots; over it all he had a fur-trimmed cloak, pinned at his left shoulder with a gold brooch whose gems might well be emeralds and rubies. The hood of his smock was thrown back so his copper-bright tresses could blow out like a banner. Baels were said to regard any baby born without red hair and green eyes as seriously deformed, and would rush it to the nearest octogram so it could be enchanted to acceptable coloring. Certainly every man aboard flaunted hair somewhere between tawny and chestnut and they all wore it long, either loose or braided, although none of them could outdo their leader for sheer intensity of color.

Gerard gripped a stay to steady himself and waited to hear his fate. The raider studied him for a moment without expression. He had a broad, strong face to match his chest and shoulders, certainly not handsome, but plain rather than ugly. If he had one distinctive feature it was that his mouth seemed too large, giving him a deceptively jocular expression. He looked like a man who would be the life and soul of a party—any party, for love or mayhem.

"I am Atheling Æled Fyrlafing, tanist of the *ealdormann* of Catterstow and *sciphlaford* of *Græggos.*"

"Er . . . Yes, sir."

The stare softened slightly. "Æled son of Fyrlaf. *Atheling* means my father was king. Catterstow is the largest and richest shire in Baelmark, and the tanist is heir to the *ealdormann*—what you would call the earl." A corner of the big mouth twitched in amusement as he saw his prisoner's reaction. If he was telling the truth, he must be one of the most powerful men in the country. "None of which means much, but at the moment I am ship lord of *Gray Goose,* and that lets me do anything."

"I am Gerard of Waygarth, Your Grace."

Æled beamed, displaying many fine large teeth. "Gerard of Waygarth is a pretty name. Tell me more about Gerard of Waygarth, Gerard of Waygarth, because all I know of Gerard of Waygarth is that he slew my brother."

That last information helped not at all. "I am twenty-three, unmarried. I have no family, no estates. I earn my bread as a gentleman scholar, doing minor tasks for the College of Heralds.''

The tanist laughed. ''Gerard of Waygarth, you are in really *serious* trouble, you know? Killing one of my brothers was bad enough. That puts you in blood feud country, even if he was only a half brother and I have more of those than I need. What is *really* worrisome is that he was one of my thegns. I usually kill seven men for every one of mine who falls. You should not have done it, Gerard of Waygarth, you really shouldn't! Now tell me what you can do to make it up to me.''

Was this a serious negotiation, or was the Bael just taunting a man he intended to kill in some especially horrible way?

''Nothing,'' Gerard croaked. ''I mean, what could possibly console you for a brother's death?''

The coppery eyebrows soared high. ''Oh, lots of things. I told you twelve hundred gold pieces is a thegn's wergild. I might settle for tapestries. Bags of jewels. Or a dozen beautiful virgins. Be inventive! And quick about it.''

''Ransom, you mean?''

''Blood money. If you cannot pay the wergild, then you will be *witeðeow*.''

That was no term Gerard had ever met in the college archives. ''Meaning?''

Æled sighed. ''A guilty man sold into slavery so the money may go to the dead man's family.''

''You are trying to scare me.'' And succeeding marvelously.

''I am trying to save you, Gerard. We must find a way for you to pay off your debt.''

''I told you. I'm only a poor artist-clerk. I can paint portraits for you or inscribe your family tree in a fair hand.''

''Provided I don't burn out your brains by enthralling you, you mean?''

''I suppose so.''

Æled shook his head. ''Not enough, Gerard of Waygarth. Not *nearly* enough.''

Gerard tried to think.

That was a mistake, because the fact that he was trying to think implied that he had something to think about. Spray hissed across his face as *Græggos* lowered her stern and raised her prow to the next swell.

Æled turned to look over his crew and then bellowed, "*Steorere?* Toðbeorht!" A man the size of a bull rose on his hind legs and came to take the oar. The captain showed him where to keep the shadow of the mast, then laid a hand on Gerard's shoulder to urge him over to the other side of the deck. Gerard could no more have resisted that hand than he could have thrown the steersman overboard. He gripped the gunwale and waited to discover if the tanist was about to throw *him* overboard. He would not put anything past this soft-spoken, smiling killer.

"Do not think I do not mourn Wærferhð," Æled said. "It was not easy for him, because his mother was a thrall. The thrall-born are rarely smarter than jellyfish. But Wærferhð had the run of the palace, and I always liked him and spoke to him. I helped him. When his beard grew in I loaned him a heriot—war gear—and found him a place among my *werod.* He was trying hard and learning to be brave. He would have been a good thegn. You killed him."

Perhaps it was time Gerard learned to be brave. "What of all the men you killed in Ambleport?"

"What of them?" The pirate's green eyes widened. "Had they done as they were told they would still be breathing."

"Given up their children without a fight?"

Æled shook his head sadly. "It is ours or theirs. Baelmark is a small, poor land, Gerard. We cannot raise enough crops to feed our families, and weeks go by when the fishing fleet cannot put to sea. We must earn our bread by trade, and slaves are the most profitable cargo. Do you think there are no Chivian slavers in the world? I assure you that there are! It is true you do not market people openly in Chivial itself or enthrall them openly, but there are peasants tied to the land, yes? If you had enough money and wanted an ever-willing bed partner, some elementary in Grandon would sell you a pretty thrall, surely?

These captives will be well fed, highly valued, and they will never worry about anything ever again. There are worse fates.'' To emphasize that point, he laid a hand over Gerard's on the rail. A rower's hand was twice the size of an artist's. ''You know why I speak Chivian so well?''

''I suppose your mother was a slave?''

''Ah, you are a clever man, Gerard. Do you understand how we Baels choose our kings?''

''No.'' Why did that matter? Gerard did not dare try to pull his hand free—he was afraid the other's might tighten and crumple his to paste. The last three days had left him far too weak to match wits with this glib monster. He could not even meet those inhumanly bright green eyes. It was no help that his last encounter with the thug had left him unable to stand straight even yet, and nausea still throbbed in his gut. He felt horribly vulnerable.

''You Chivians are satisfied to take the first male in the royal litter. We Baels insist on a man who is not only *cyneboren* but also *cynewyrðe*. That means he must be of royal birth—we have several royal families, not just one. He must also be *cynewyrðe*, worthy to be king.''

''And how is that decided? By this month's civil war?''

''That is decided by the witan and sometimes by personal combat.''

''Your family is royal, I assume?''

The tanist's hand tightened over Gerard's. ''I am a Cattering! We Catterings are the *most* kingly, because we descend from Catter, discoverer and first king of Baelmark. We have given Baelmark more kings than any other family. Times are out of joint when a Cattering does not rule in Baelmark.''

''As now, I assume?''

Æled smiled. He removed his hand and patted Gerard on the shoulder as he might have comforted a horse. ''A clever man! You see the problem. My father fell in the Gevilian War when all his sons were very young. The witenagemot elected a Tholing; and the present king is a Nyrping, which is even worse. To be true to my manhood and my forefathers, I must win the throne back for the

Catterings. You will assist me. This is how you will pay wergild for poor Wærferhð."

"You are crazy! I am a penniless clerk. How can I possibly help?"

"You will think of a way. I will help you concentrate." With no visible effort, the ship lord picked Gerard up and dropped him overboard.

The world was green agony and icy cold. Gerard struggled violently and blew bubbles. Moments before he was about to drown, daylight brightened and he was slammed face first against the planks of the ship's side as the water dropped away, leaving him hanging head downward. He managed to gulp in air and was plunged again back into bottomless ocean, battered and rolled along the hull by the current. The iron band around his right ankle must be Æled's fingers.

Four waves later, he was hauled back aboard—half aboard, because he was left doubled over the rail, draining water and blood back into the ocean. His nose would never be the same again, and the rest of his face seemed to be full of splinters or barnacles. He had ripped his hands and arms on the timbers.

The tanist leaned a heavy arm on him to help expel the water. "I can keep this up all the way home, Gerard of Waygarth. Can you?"

"My father owns some land," Gerard mumbled, "but only two hides and a half share in a watermill."

"Gerard, Gerard! You stay in the best room in the inn. You wear gentlemen's clothes—or they were gentlemen's clothes, no one wants them now. You have been taught the rapier. Your hands are soft as butter and your skin pale as cream. Your leather box is full of scrolls in strange scripts and many colors that must be very potent spells. Most men in your position would be bragging how rich they are, not how poor. Think more, Gerard!"

His struggles had no effect whatsoever. Again he went overboard, dangling there for another dozen waves. The kid must have an arm like an anchor chain and probably could keep it up all day, as he said, for he did not sound at all winded the next time he let the water drain out of his victim's ears.

"Any ideas yet, Gerard?"

Gerard croaked, "Two hundred crowns?"

Æled chuckled appreciatively and ducked him again, but now he held him lower, so he did not always get his head out in the troughs, and when he hauled him up to question he did not even give him time to stop choking and spewing. "No progress? Well, keep trying. Concentrate!" Down again.

Gerard realized that the thug was quite prepared to continue this torture until he got what he wanted or his victim died, which was becoming more probable with every ghastly minute. One more death would be nothing on his conscience and he might be doing all this just to entertain his crew anyway. No man could be expected to endure both repeated drowning and the constant battering. When he was about to be sent down for the fifth or sixth dunking, Gerard flailed his hands wildly and managed to make croaking noises between spasms of vomiting seawater.

"You have thought of something already?" Æled inquired.

Gerard nodded vigorously. *"Arrrh arrrh arrrh!"* He was left hanging there upside down to drain, but it was several minutes before he had coughed enough ocean out of his lungs for him to croak anything intelligible. "I'm King Taisson's cousin."

The Bael flipped him inboard and hugged him like a long-lost brother, drenched though he was. "Dear Gerard! Why didn't you say so at the beginning?"

· 3 ·

Nothing was too good for the King of Chivial's cousin. A band of slavers stripped him, toweled him till he glowed, dressed him in dry wool garments. A villainous-looking thegn with a delicate touch packed his battered nose to stop the bleeding, rubbed salve on his scrapes, bandaged his hands. The ship lord himself wrapped the prisoner in soft blankets and emptied half a bottle of fine brandy into him. That brought the day to a peaceful close.

Next day Gerard was one raw bruise from knees to ears, but the pirates treated him like a valued senile invalid, a rich grandfather who had not yet made his will. They kept him aft, under a canopy far from the other prisoners, and pampered him as much as was possible in the middle of the ocean. A freckle-faced talkative youngster named Brimbearn tended him all day long, changing his dressings, swilling beer into him, feeding him by popping morsels of hard bread and pickled fish in his mouth.

"I goodly speak Chivian," Brimbearn explained, "because my mother was Chivian. Never she was thrall-made. Thrall-wrought? Enthralled! Thank you. Likewise not was Æled Tanist's mother. Thrall mothers raise stupid childs." He leered. "I like woman with fight in her."

That was probably just an innocent joke, but Gerard dared not ask for details. He wondered what Charlotte would think if she could see him now.

Young Brimbearn went on to claim that he, too, was a Cattering, although from a minor branch of the family that had produced no kings for so long that it could no longer be considered royal. He worshiped Æled as a paragon of thegnhood who gathered more loot with fewer losses than any other raider currently active. He also shared it fairly, worked as hard as anyone, avoided fights when he could but fought like a hurricane when he must. He was already being compared to legendary heroes like Wulfstan, Smeawine, or even Bearskinboots. He had won his place as tanist the previous fall and was sure to challenge for the earldom itself very shortly. "Not good is," Brimbearn admitted, "when earl and tanist from same family not sprung."

"I can see that," Gerard remarked. However perilous his own present state, it probably compared favorably to that of an earl with a designated successor like Æled waiting in the shadows. The constant scratch of knives being sharpened must grow hard on the nerves eventually.

His efforts to learn more about the election of kings foundered on Brimbearn's lack of interest. The kid was not stupid. Despite his youth, he had visited half the countries of Eurania and many far-off lands Gerard had never even heard of. He spoke with apparent truth of brown people and yellow people, of seeing palaces of ivory, whales longer than *Græggos,* single stone buildings bigger than all Ambleport, monstrous land animals with tusks and humps. He obviously had a very shrewd knowledge of trade goods and markets. When it came to politics, though, his only concern was to back Æled Fyrlafing to the hilt, whether figuratively or otherwise.

He spoke eagerly enough about the ship lord himself. Although Æled had mentioned having many half brothers, it seemed that they were all thrall-born, like the late Wærferhð, and such men were regarded with contempt. They could never be considered throne-worthy, so the political ambitions of the Cattering family depended on Æled and his one full brother, Cynewulf, surviving sons of the late King Fyrlaf by a Chivian captive who had not been enthralled. That made her a *læt,* a slave—well above thralls, but below ceorl commoners.

"Æled is king-worthy?" Gerard could not imagine anyone better qualified to rule a nation of gangsters and brigands.

"Æled is *especially* throne-worthy," Brimbearn agreed. "Fyrlaf King married was when he was born. A fine lady, Maud Queen, much honored still. You go her see in Waroðburh. Most throne-worthy! Men fight to join Æled's *werod* and win booty and honor."

"So Æled is legitimate, but he has an older brother who isn't. Must a man be born in wedlock to be throne-worthy?"

Brimbearn looked puzzled. "That is no matter," he muttered. "It is Cynewulf himself that . . ." He glanced around uneasily to see who might be listening, then changed the subject.

Several times the tanist came and sat beside his prisoner. Like his crew, he seemed to spend most of his off-duty time talking and combing out his hair. He offered his captive more of the excellent brandy but took no offense when it was refused. He chatted pleasantly, apologizing when his Chivian failed him, which was rarely. No topic seemed to be off limits.

"There are more than a thousand islands in Baelmark," he explained. "Most are only rocks awash at high tide or stacks the gulls and terns use. About two score are inhabited. Fyrsieg is the largest. Three shires share Fyrsieg—Catterstow, Eastrice, and Grætears. Catterstow is the richest of all shires in Baelmark and Waroðburh the biggest town."

"And who is earl of Catterstow these days?"

"Ceolmund Ceollafing." Æled smiled without explaining what was funny.

"Not a Cattering?"

"His family is not even royal!" The scorn would have melted bronze.

"Am I right in assuming, Your Highness, that—"

"Not 'highness,' Gerard! You Chivians have too many foolish titles. I am not high. I am shorter than you are, if somewhat wider and deeper. We address our king as 'lord' and nobles as *ealdras*. You call me *ealdor*." The big mouth spread in an appealing grin. "Come to think of it, that means 'old one' and I am younger than you."

"Yes, *ealdor.*"

"And I have prettier hair." Mockery danced in the green eyes.

"Yes, *ealdor,* very beautiful hair. If times are out of joint when the King of Baelmark is not a Cattering, the entire universe is out of joint when even the Earl of Catterstow isn't?"

Æled grinned bloodcurdlingly. "I knew right away you were a clever man, Gerard! A king's cousin! You are royally born!"

Gerard shivered and decided to get it over with. "Far from it. My great-grandmother was a sister of Queen Enid, the wife of Everard IV. That makes me a third cousin of King Taisson, but I have no royal blood in me. I've never been presented at court. If you demand ransom for me, he'll have to ask the College of Heralds who I am. My father isn't even a baronet, let alone a noble. I wasn't lying about the two hides of land. In your terms I'm barely a thegn—born free, of the class that owns land but is not noble. What do you call that?"

He expected an outburst of maniacal Bael fury, but the tanist just laughed. "You wore a sword! No ceorl would rush into danger as you did. Only a true thegn would have the courage to slay honest Baels going quietly about their business, and now tell me to my face that he lied to me. You were not lying. You were trying to find a way to pay off your debt. I can see you haven't solved all the difficulties yet, but I'm sure you will." He patted his prisoner's shoulder comfortingly.

"No! I can't help you. I'm useless to you. Why don't you just kill me and get it over with?"

The raider shook his head, swinging his copper tresses. "I'm not going to kill you, Gerard. I'm not even going to enthrall you, because then you would be just another biddable body. You must be able to think to make me king."

In order to think, a man needed information. Gerard set to work to learn more of Baelish society. He found it extraordinarily complex, combining many class distinctions with a system of rewarding ability that was completely alien to his Chivian experience. A sharp line was drawn between the free and the slaves, as he had expected, but there was an even more important distinction between commoners and the warrior class. Young Brimbearn's distinguished ancestry had qualified him to bear arms, but he had still required permission from his earl before he could actually do so and be trained in the use of weaponry. Æled had given him a berth on *Græggos*, but he had been required to prove himself to his shipmates. It had been they who voted him into the fyrd, the fighting men of Catterstow, and thus made him a fully qualified thegn.

Æled's rank of ship lord seemed to depend in various measure on noble birth, family wealth, and the approval of his crew. The men served him voluntarily because of his skills as trader, sailor, and fighter. In fact a *werod* was a private war band, as willing to swing swords as oars, and in Æled's case comprised the crews of all four ships. His rank of tanist somehow depended on the approval of the entire fyrd, as did that of the earl himself.

So far so good, but this was a much-simplified picture. If Baels selected all their leaders by such absurd popularity contests, then the system for choosing a king must be even more complicated.

"Look, Chivian! Wake up!" Powerful hands shook Gerard awake.

He made bewildered noises.

"Look! You must see!" Without even unwrapping his blankets, Brimbearn dragged him out from under the awning and stood him upright, too excited to be considerate of his bruises. "See? Light!"

Dawn had not yet come, and *Græggos* battled over high waves in a stormy night. As his warm covers fell away and exposed him to the sea wind, Gerard shivered hard enough to shake out his teeth. When the ship crested, he made out three lanterns shining at mastheads, so the rest of the flotilla was still in close formation behind; and after four days of almost continuously rough weather that must surely be a miracle of seamanship.

"Wrong way!" the Bael protested. "Missed it. Wait."

Many of the sailors were on their feet and chattering, excited about something. As the ship raised its stern to slide down into the next trough, Gerard looked where Brimbearn was aiming him and made out a reddish glow, about where the horizon ought to be.

"Cwicnoll!" the boy crowed. "Æled brought us right home! Straight to the door! What other navigator could do that? No Chivian, yes?"

"What's burning? Signal beacons?"

Before Brimbearn had stopped laughing at this display of ignorance, the salt-scented wind brought Æled's voice out of the darkness. "The mountain. Cwicnoll is the mountain of Catterstow, Gerard. Don't let it frighten you. Cwicnoll's a big softy. He's been doing that for ten years now and never burned a homestead. Some of the other peaks are more sporting. Fyrndagum buried a village on Wambseoc last year." The steering oar creaked on its pivot.

"*Bæl* means 'fire'?"

"And *mearc* means a mark, or boundary, or territory."

"So Baelmark is the 'land of fire'?"

The pirate chief chuckled. "Unless it is a corruption of *bealu,* which means 'evil.' The march of evil?"

"What did your ancestor call it?"

"Catter? He called it *Fyrland.* And he called himself *Hlaford Fyrlandum,* lord of the Fire Lands. When you have helped put me on the throne of my fathers, Gerard of Waygarth, that is the title I will take—*Hlaford Fyrlandum!*"

"I can't help you," Gerard moaned. "How can I possibly do that?"

"You will find a way." Æled did not mention an alternative.

· 4 ·

The sun rose blindingly over the edge of the world to illuminate a landscape of rugged glory directly ahead. Although there were other faint peaks visible to the north and south, at this distance Baelmark appeared to be a single mountainous mass with Cwicnoll's smoking cone looming gigantic above and a montage of pasture and forest below. As *Græggos* rode the whitecaps closer, boiling white plumes of spray marched like guards along the base of what seemed to be a solid wall of cliff, shrouding the coast in mist.

Swathed in a sable-trimmed cloak, Æled leaned against the stern post, having yielded the steering oar to the giant Toðbeorht. Thirty-two rowers sat ready to run out their oars, and the rest of the *werod* stood at their posts, watching intently for the ship lord's signal. The rest of the flotilla was following in file, tracking Æled's course between foaming shoals as he headed to certain destruction under the cliffs ahead.

"Gerard! Come and enjoy the scenery with me. This will be an interesting homecoming."

Gerard obeyed, staggering over the rolling deck and lurching against the rail. "You just want everyone to see how frightened I am."

"A swordsman who takes on two hundred Baels single-handed does not know the meaning of fear."

"I do now. Does *Græggos* have wings?"

Æled smiled. His present good humor was ominous, but his anger would be more so. "No. I hope we shall not need them. The most direct way into Swiþæfen is by Eastweg, so we are going that way. It is a good passage except in a northerly."

Gerard checked the sun and the streamer at the masthead. "Then it's fortunate the wind is heading straight south." He would call it a gale, although the sailors might not.

The ship lord cocked a red eyebrow. "Your first voyage, is it? It has been a fine *færing*. We ransomed two towns in Isilond, rescued three Gevilian coasters from unworthy owners, and harvested some slaves in Chivial. I believe in spreading my blessings and never outstaying my welcome. We lost only one man. And we captured the King of Chivial's cousin." *Græggos* shifted uneasily in the cross swell as the coast broke up into islets around her. "I will make my challenge to Ceolmund soon." He bared his big teeth joyfully.

"Personal combat?"

The ship lord shrugged. "No. Ceolmund is too wise to fight me himself. But I will be earl, and then times will be not quite so out of joint." He barked an order and activity boiled through the ship. Nimble youngsters swarmed up the mast and stays like squirrels while other men hauled on the lines or ran out the oars. In seeming seconds the sail had been brailed into a roll along the yard and *Græggos* was being rowed. The topmen came sliding down. Æled began beating a mallet on the gunwale, giving the rowers the stroke. Then he set them singing, so they could row in time.

He turned to watch the other ships copy. "It is a pity about Wærferhð. Were it not for losing him I would be more confident. The older thegns may use his death as an excuse to side against me. On the other hand, they will be impressed if I lead in King Taisson's cousin in chains. What do you think, friend Gerard? Should I brag about you now or should I keep you out of sight like the knife in my sleeve?"

Gerard turned away from the piercing green stare. He did not think the tanist was at all lacking in confidence. The real question was something else.

"Well?" Æled demanded.

"Why ask me? Why would you trust the advice of a prisoner?"

Æled snapped orders. Another helmsman, even larger, jumped to Toðbeorht's aid and together they swung the ship around a cape and into a gloomy channel between beetling cliffs. Wind howling through the gap made her pitch heavily and forced Æled to shout his reply. "Because you are my *wita* in this—my wise one. Speak!"

"I think you should keep me a secret."

"Then I shall." He laughed aloud, excited by the maelstrom his ship was now riding and the fact that the rest of his flotilla was managing the turn after her. "You have worked out the answer!"

"No."

"But you are beginning to see its shape! This is good!" He honored Gerard with a friendly thump on the shoulder that almost drove him to his knees.

How could a bloodthirsty killer be so perceptive?

Were such a thing as a map of Baelmark possible, Æled had said, it would resemble shattered glass. With a few outlying exceptions, every island of the thousand lay within bowshot of several others. Between them ran uncounted channels, inlets, fiords, bays, harbors, straits, roadsteads, sounds, and gulfs, all interconnected and known collectively as Swiþæfen. Sheltered from waves and tempest, those peaceful waters offered clear sailing in any weather. The trick was to get in there.

Under the eyes of his crew, the ship lord put on a show of nonchalance as he guided *Græggos* through the perilous maze, but Gerard was close enough to see his concern when he watched the other ships attempting maneuvers he had just made seem easy. Driven by a surging tide, the flotilla wound and twisted between towering stacks painted gray with guano, past weed-shrouded rocks lurking in the breakers, and under cliffs of strange columnar structure like gigantic organ pipes. Islets could be flat and fertile or so precipitous that ancient cedars slumbered on hillsides untroubled by the woodsman's ax. Some bore farmsteadings and herds of cattle, while always a blizzard of white seabirds wheeled and cried overhead. Periodically Æled would bellow orders through a speaking trumpet to the double line of sweating oarsmen, and several times he had to add his muscle to the efforts of the two giants heaving on the steering oar. His control over his ship was incredible. He could turn her in her own length, or move her backward as easily as forward, or hold her in place until he found exactly the wave he needed. Then *Græggos* would bound forward on cue, shipping her oars moments before jagged teeth on either side could snap them off.

When death seemed merely probable instead of imminent, he would chat calmly with his honored passenger. "It isn't always this choppy." The tone was disparaging, but the green eyes danced with excitement.

"Would a sane man even try?"

Æled took that as a compliment and loved it. "Of course not. You see the secret of our success, Gerard of Waygarth? You see how we get away with our pranks?" *Pranks* meaning rapine, piracy, slaving, and wanton murder . . .

"Your islands are impregnable."

"Completely. At one time or another every nation in Eurania has sent fleets against us and done nothing but fatten the lobsters. You see how the winds bank off the cliffs? The eddies and shoals? You have to be born a Bael to wend these channels." He laughed aloud. "Gevily managed to land an army on Fyrsieg back in my father's time, but what can an army achieve? Burn houses? The people have already taken their valuables elsewhere, and there are scores of other islands that you can't get to. Meanwhile, our navy has just ambushed yours and sunk it. Invading Baelmark is futile."

"You're like mosquitoes. We must bleed and bear you."

Æled guffawed, brandishing a fist the size of a ham. "Some mosquito! No, we are bees. We bring honey home to the hive and we can sting."

"What happened to the Gevilian army?"

After a moment . . . "A *fyrdraca* got them."

Before Gerard could ask if a *fyrdraca* was the sort of monster it sounded like, the ride again grew too rough for talk. He clung grimly to the rail, thinking bitter thoughts. He ought to hurl himself overboard to drown or be smashed in the surf, because it was true that there might be a way he could help Æled move closer to the throne, if the system worked the way he thought it did. It would be a fearful gamble for the Bael, but he was a gambler through and through, a jungle predator—deadly and irresistible, cunning and beautiful. Knowing neither fear nor scruple, if he did become King of Baelmark he would be a frightful foe to all the civilized lands of Eurania; and if Gerard had helped him gain the crown he would have betrayed everything: honor, family, the fealty he owed his king. Æled denied planning to enthrall him—and it was probably true that such a spell would render Gerard useless for his purpose—but there were other ways to command loyalty or even just cooperation. Hot irons, for instance. Anyone but a coward would leap over the side and die with honor.

He was a coward, then, because he was still aboard when *Græggos* and her three goslings emerged on the calm waters of Swiþæfen. Then the sail was unfurled and the oars shipped. Roaring with an excitement that betrayed the fear they had been concealing, the sailors threw open the chests and stripped in a wild blizzard of clothing. Laughing and jeering, they donned leather breeches and steel helmets, resuming their bare-chested fighting guise, only now they flaunted golden torcs and arm rings, jeweled buckles and clasps. The hilts of their swords and daggers glittered with gems, weapons far too showy ever to be used in combat. When Æled took the steering oar for the landing, he was dressed as befitted a triumphant warrior prince, with golden embroidery on his smock, a fortune in jewels on his belt and baldric, gold trim on his helmet.

Græggos rounded yet another bend and entered a landlocked bay a league across, silver water so smooth that it mirrored Cwicnoll's towering complex of glaciers and black rock in the background. Trailing ripples, the four ships headed for long beaches where land and water met and a settlement spread over gentle meadowed slopes—not the squalid pirates' lair Gerard had expected but a shining city.

· 5 ·

"The trouble with homecomings," Æled said as *Græggos* neared the strand, "is that the men all want to rush home and tell the kids to go play outside for a while. I will be busy. You wait on the beach and if anyone asks tell them you are my prisoner. Say, *Ic eom Ældes hæftniedling*. I'll send someone to take you to the elementary." His eyes twinkled green as he saw Gerard's alarm. "For a healing."

So Gerard found himself standing on the shore in bandages and borrowed clothes, trying to adjust to the idea of being a slave. He had no possessions, no rights. His own garments had been thrown overboard; his rapier and document case confiscated; and his body belonged to Æled, who could still steal his soul with conjury if he wished.

One battered-looking prisoner was of no interest to the multitude that had come rushing down to the sea to welcome the returning heroes—wives, children, parents. Their joy and excitement when they heard the details of Æled's *færing* showed how great a triumph it was. Despite his jest, the sailors did not hurry off home. The captives were herded ashore, the cargo unloaded, and then the gratings were raised to reveal even more booty down among the ballast—bags of coins and bars of gold that must be ransom paid by the Isilondian towns for the privilege of not being burned and looted, plus whatever the hijacked Gevilian ships and their cargo had fetched when traded off in one of the little coastal states. Spirits alone knew what the waiting slaves were worth, but the material wealth heaped on the black sand would have bought an earldom in Chivial. And this was a little more than a month's work for two hundred men and an admittedly talented leader! Piracy paid well for those who survived.

"Gerard?" The speaker was a shortish, plump, and—what else?—red-haired man clad in outstanding finery, a smock of green lawn reaching to his knees and gathered at the waist by a jeweled belt, a fur-trimmed cloak of velvet. A gold-hilted sword hung at his side, his leggings were cross-gartered with golden ribbons, golden buckles shone on his boots. The soft pinkness of his face was very different from the weathered roughness of the sailors'. Four lesser Baels stood at his back, one of them leading a horse and another a shaggy pony on which sat a boy of five or six. The boy stared curiously at Gerard's battered face.

Gerard bowed. *"Ealdor?"*

"Atheling Cynewulf. The tanist did a good job on you, didn't he?" Cynewulf was probably ten years older than his brother and where Æled was blocky, brawny, and pugnacious, he was fleshy, florid, and supercilious.

How was Gerard expected to respond—as a slave or a captive gentleman? Better to aim high and be struck down than to surrender without a fight. "His arguments convinced me eventually, *ealdor.*"

At that moment a great outburst of cheering distracted both of them. The applause was coming mostly from the *werod,* but also partly from the landlubber spectators, and the object of their approval seemed to be Æled.

"May I inquire . . . ?"

Cynewulf scowled. "My spendthrift brother has just waived his right to a third of a third. Unnecessary extravagance! He has no need to buy their loyalty, for he already has it."

But others would hear of the gesture and choose to support a generous leader. Even a Chivian could see that.

Gerard remembered Brimbearn praising Æled as a giver of treasure, and also his odd and unexplained dismissal of his older brother. "May I ask what they are doing now, *ealdor*?"

Obviously Æled was supervising the division of the booty into three roughly equal parts—three heaps of bullion and three groups of prisoners—but the loot had also attracted men who seemed to be important, in that they sported helmets and mail shirts as well as swords. They were busily peering into sacks, looking over the captives, and generally inspecting the take.

Cynewulf had a lip quick to sneer. "I am a thegn, not a trainer of slaves, *læt.*"

"Pardon my presumption, noble atheling. Your brother hoped to gain some profit from me and I cannot advise him without knowing the customs of the country."

The pudgy little man considered the prisoner with calculated distaste. "Yes, he mentioned that. He sometimes has strange fancies, not always to be taken seriously. What you are seeing is tax collection. Æled divides the take into what he considers three equal shares. The King's shire reeve gets first choice. Then the house thegns pick one for Earl Ceolmund."

"And me?" Gerard asked nervously.

"You and all your heriot are excluded. You are wergild for our brother."

Curiously, it was a relief to know that he still belonged to Æled, who at least considered him valuable. "So the men who risked their lives to collect that booty share only the last third?" Obviously, and it would normally be two ninths without the ship lord's cut. "But I believe I now comprehend, *ealdor,* why your King finds it so difficult to suppress piracy."

Æled's smiles were shared mirth, but his brother's were private amusement. "Do the tanist's ambitions make more sense to you now, Chivian?"

"And those men?" Gerard asked in horror. A gang of porters had come shuffling forward to load the booty on their shoulders. They wore only rags and their hair was not red. Even at a distance he could see the strangeness of their gait and the inhuman blankness of their faces.

"Thralls, of course. Don't worry about them, *læt.* The men are long dead. Their bodies have been preserved as biddable tools, nothing more. You will see when we arrive at the elementary." Cynewulf beckoned for his horse to be brought. He frowned at the boy on the pony. "Sit up straight, Wulfwer."

The shore was a long, buzzing market of ships being loaded and unloaded, others being built, slave stockades and warehouses, fish-drying racks and heaps of lobster pots; but the atheling led the way inland. Hobbling along behind his horse, Gerard trod roads paved with hexagonal stone tiles and thronged with pedestrians, horse wagons, and thrall-drawn carts. Chivian cities were stinking, verminous firetraps because they were cramped inside high walls. Only Grandon itself had spread out beyond its ancient fortifications; and even Grandon's streets were dark tracks carpeted with refuse, winding between houses many stories high. Waroðburh spurned walls, sprawling like a thistle patch in the sunlight with all its buildings safely separated by wide streets and even by herb or vegetable gardens and tree-filled parks. He saw numerous water troughs and women filling their jugs. He also saw inexplicable clouds of steam, but the atheling's route did not go close to any of them.

The buildings were the greatest wonder of all, for every surface was carved with fantastic monster images and brightly colored; even the shingles on the roofs sparkled with rainbow tints like dew on a sunny morning. Although none stood more than one story high, the larger edifices were as extensive as minor palaces; and yet they were obviously family residences, with children and washing in view. Some included workshops or displayed wares for sale. In Chivial only very prosperous families occupied more than two rooms, no matter how great their burden of children, but this was clearly not the case in Waroðburh. Æled's protestations that Baelmark was a poor land were about as reliable as one should expect from a pirate.

Gerard would have liked to linger and look. Even more, he would have liked to have walked slowly, for Cynewulf was setting much too brisk a pace for him. His crotch felt ready to burst into flames.

"*Læt!*" Cynewulf waved him forward to walk alongside his stirrup, then peered down at him suspiciously. "Assuming my madcap young brother does not miscalculate and land himself in an impossible duel to the death, and assuming also that he then persists with his insane ambitions to win the throne, just how do you imagine you can assist him?"

Gerard had no intention of revealing that, not to Æled nor this disdainful brother. "I don't know, *ealdor*. I fear he is making too much of my family connections, although I have assured him I am not of royal birth."

Green eyes stared down distrustfully. "You killed Wærferhð. I would have made an example of you. If Æled dies I still may." He rode on for a while without speaking and then, surprisingly, laughed. "Do you know what his name means—*Æled?* It means 'firebrand'!"

"Appropriate, *ealdor*."

"Quite. No wonder he is headstrong. A few months ago he gambled by challenging the tanist, who had grown too cautious for the younger thegns. The fyrd sided narrowly with Æled, and the tanist yielded without even a token fight. In other words, my brother was very lucky. He now assumes that this same brashness will carry him to the earldom itself, and that is another matter altogether. You understand how it works? Any thegn may challenge the tanist, but only the tanist may challenge the earl. Ceolmund is well regarded, a wise and cautious ruler. I am afraid that Æled is in for a very nasty and possibly fatal surprise." His lip settled into its customary sneer.

Curious! Atheling Cynewulf would have been head of the family until his younger brother won promotion. Now he must be outranked. Was he merely jealous of Æled's success, or did he have legitimate worries about reprisals if Æled's insurrection failed?

"Instruct me, I pray you, *ealdor*. If the thegn moot sides with your brother, then the earl must accept the challenge and fight, yes? What happens if the thegns vote the other way?''

Cynewulf laughed contemptuously. ''Then Ceolmund remains earl and names a champion, which means he hires the best fighter in the fyrd to render justice. Æled is good, but far from invincible. Even if by some miracle he survived, he would have incurred blood debt and gained nothing. The odds are staked in favor of the incumbent, naturally.''

''Naturally. The rules for challenging the king are similar?''

''More or less. Only an earl may challenge, and the witenagemot decides whether the king must fight in person.''

''Witenagemot? The witan are the king's chosen counselors?''

Again the sneer. ''Yes, but they just talk. The only ones who vote are the earls, rulers of the twenty-one shires.''

Which was much as Gerard had expected. ''I do not know how your brother expects me to aid him, *ealdor,* but the Catterings have always given Baelmark its strongest kings. As a loyal subject of King Taisson, I can do nothing to restore that state of affairs. It is in Chivial's interests that the present ineffective rule continue.''

The Prince gave Gerard another long stare and then smiled narrowly. ''That assurance might be worth a ticket home, *læt.*''

''You are most gracious, *ealdor.*''

If Cynewulf would betray his own brother so readily, then any ticket he provided Gerard would buy only a one-way trip to the lobster beds. Forced to trust one of the two sons of Fyrlaf, Gerard would choose the raider every time.

At that point they were overtaken by a line of trotting children and adolescents, at least forty of them, all wearing metal collars attached to a long rusty chain. Guards on ponies rode alongside, urging them on with sticks. The youngest captives were gasping from the effort of keeping up, being helped along by larger neighbors. Gerard recognized some of his former shipmates and knew that this was part of the human loot from Ambleport. He assumed that their drivers were professional slavers. The gruesome procession went past and disappeared into a cluster of buildings just ahead.

Moments later he drew close enough to make out faint sounds of chanting, and his gut knotted as he realized that he had arrived at the elementary. There were at least half a dozen buildings in the complex, most of them circular and low for their width, all extravagantly inlaid with mother-of-pearl and brightly colored stones. The central dome was enormous, and the last of the captives were being driven in through its wide doors like cattle to the slaughter. Flunkies came hurrying over to greet the new arrivals.

Cynewulf dismounted gracelessly. Tossing his reins to one of his own men, he went to the boy on the pony. *"Wast þu hwæt þis hus is, Wulfwer? Wære þu her beforan nu?"* He spoke in the plodding tones used to the very young or very stupid, so Gerard could understand: "Know you what this building is, Wulfwer? Have you been here before?"

The youngster gave him a surly look. *"Na, ealdor."*

Cynewulf backhanded him across the face, almost knocking him out of the saddle. *"Hwæt geclipast þu me?"*—"What do you call me?"

"Fæder." The boy blinked back tears. The tip of his tongue crept out to lick his bleeding lip.

"When you behave like a slave you are whipped like a slave. Now listen. This is the Haligdom. Here spirits are conjured. What is it called?"

"The Haligdom, where spirits are conjured . . . Father."

"Again?"

"The Haligdom, where spirits are conjured."

"Correct. Come inside and watch. And try to learn." He turned away, making no effort to help his son dismount.

Gerard limped along behind. The Haligdom was larger than any elementary he had ever heard of, echoing with the doglike howls of the prisoners. Its domed roof was supported by an elaborate system of trusses, a further example of the magnificent Baelish woodworking skills.

Most of the floor was occupied by the largest octogram he had ever seen, tiled in many colors and obviously intended for mass processing slaves, for it contained a ring of eight head-high posts, to which the Ambleport captives were now being secured.

A tubby, bald man in flowing black garments reacted with exaggeratedly amazed delight upon seeing the newcomer. He waddled forward, bowed repeatedly, and gabbled greetings. Although his exact words escaped Gerard, the meaning was clear enough: profuse welcomes to the noble atheling and how might he be served? Cynewulf obviously was demanding an enchantment for the prisoner his thumb was pointing at. The conjurer then tried to lead the honored lord off to one of the smaller elementaries and Cynewulf refused, wanting to witness the enthrallment ritual they were about to perform on the prisoners. Bowing and fawning again, the bald man lauded the prince's gallantry and forbearance.

Gerard fought down nausea as bad as any he ever had known on the ship, trying not to imagine himself in there, chained like a brute. What if Cynewulf decided that the easiest way to stop the cryptic Chivian from aiding his upstart brother's march to the throne was to enthrall him here and now? *Terribly sorry, Æled, I misunderstood.*

The eight conjurers in their black robes took up positions on the points of the octogram and began chanting in Baelish. The prisoners screamed at the tops of their lungs, trying to drown them out, but the spirits heard the summons regardless. As far as Gerard could tell, the enchantment was mainly a revocation of the two elements, air and fire, that were the main components of soul. He did not want to watch, but sheer horror held him frozen like a fascinated rabbit while the victims' screams and abuse faltered, then died away to confused mumbling. Expressions faded from furious to puzzled, and finally eyes drooped shut. Starting with the smallest and ending with the young adults among them, they staggered, sank to their knees, then to the floor, finally lying still. Forty youngsters lay like corpses.

The conjurers paused to catch their breath. Cynewulf

gave Gerard a shove. Gerard very nearly swung a punch, but checked himself in time. *"Ealdor?"*

"Get in there. They are about to be taught the language. One more won't hurt." And probably the enchanters would not dare charge the atheling anything. Shivering, Gerard raised his chin and stepped boldly into the octogram to stand alongside the unconscious prisoners. Conjuration began again, this time taking longer, with air and fire apparently the main elements invoked. He felt nothing, not a prickle, but near the end he looked down and saw to his dismay that the thralls now had their eyes open, staring blankly. As soon as it was over, he moved back to safety outside the lines.

"Rise!" shouted one of the slavers. "Stand up now!" With a great clattering of chains, the slaves climbed to their feet and then just stood, waiting for further orders.

"See?" Cynewulf remarked cheerfully. "Their bodies remain behind unharmed, while their spirits are returned to the spirits." He pulled his son's ear to turn his head. "Look! These are new-caught slaves, Wulfwer. See how much better they behave, now they have been made into thralls? See how they don't talk unless you ask them a question? This is why your mother doesn't speak to you much."

The obsequious conjurer reappeared, lugging a sack of coins he had just accepted from the chief slaver. "How else may we have the honor of serving you, *Ealdor* Fyrlafing?"

Gerard now understood Baelish.

"Heal this *læt* for me."

The conjurer frowned at the prisoner as if surprised that anyone would waste good money on him. "I am forced to inquire as to the cause of his injuries, *ealdor*. He had an accident?"

"Oh, no. He was being questioned."

The conjurer beamed. "That makes things simpler, much simpler! Virtual spirits are hard to influence, you understand. Especially elementals of chance. They are so unpredictable! By definition, of course. Deliberate damage, involving only the manifest elements, is much easier to reverse. How exactly was he tortured?"

"He was given a face wash."

"The noble atheling will forgive me, but I—"

"Nautical term. He was hung upside down over the ship's side and banged about in the wake until he stopped misbehaving."

"Ah! Then a major revocation of water should clear up most of the problem. A minor addition of fire to speed the healing."

"He also had a bad bang on the *beallucas,*" Gerard remarked, with feeling.

"Specific treatments for that injury are complex," the conjurer said cautiously, implying *expensive.*

Cynewulf shrugged. "Then don't worry about it. We do not intend to use him for breeding."

As the young thralls obediently trudged away, the conjurers returned to their stations on the points of the octogram, and now Gerard stood alone in the center. He had experienced minor healing before and he was impressed by the Baels' skill. When the ritual was finished, even the throb in his groin was barely more than an unpleasantness. The only side effect he noticed was a raging thirst.

· 6 ·

With two of his men assisting, Cynewulf heaved himself up into his silver-studded saddle; he had clearly lost interest in Gerard, at least for the time being. "That's done. I must go and see if dear Æled wants me to clean his boots next. He said you were to wait for him at Cynehof. Don't expect him soon, because he plans to visit Wærferhð's mother to break the news. That makes as much sense as lecturing a rack of lamb—thralls can't mourn. A complete waste of time. Guðlac, show him the way to Cynehof and then run home. If you take all day about it, you know what will happen to you."

Gerard watched the atheling depart with his son and the other three attendants. Now he understood young Brimbearn's unspoken criticism of Cynewulf. It took something more than high birth and a strong arm to make a man throne-worthy and that one did not have it.

He turned to find his ginger-haired companion watching him with a sardonic expression. He was of middle years, stocky and weatherbeaten. Why amusement in a man just threatened with a beating?

"Would you describe the atheling as throne-worthy?"

"Would never say he wasn't." Guðlac turned his head and spat.

Gerard smiled for the first time since he killed Wærferhð. "And his brother?"

"Ah." The Bael considered him thoughtfully, as if wondering how far to trust. "There's a stallion for a big herd!"

"Quite. Shouldn't we be on our way?"

"What's the hurry? You fancy a swim?"

Baelmark was a place of infinite surprises. The steam clouds Gerard had observed earlier marked natural hot springs within the town. These were used to supply public bathing pools, some of which were open to the slave classes, and he was soon lolling naked in steaming hot water with a hundred other men. The only payment required was that he tell Guðlac his story, which soon gathered a large audience—slaves' lives lacked entertainment. In the desultory discussion that followed, a strange conversation between floating faces speaking to the steam overhead, he learned that most of his companions had been born in captivity, although some had been captured in other lands when too young to require enthrallment. Very few had red hair.

"I was a thegn," Guðlac asserted, "over on Suðmest, south of here. Five generations, my ancestors bore arms."

"What happened?"

"Killed a man in a brawl." He made this seem a minor misfortune that might happen to anyone. "So I was *witeðeow.*"

"Why didn't your *werod* pay the wergild?" asked a voice somewhere in the steam.

"Or your lord?" demanded another

"My lord wanted my daughters. Liked girls young. He bought them at the sale. My wife was bought by her brothers, but they couldn't afford the kids."

There were no more questions. Gerard was left wondering how much the audience believed the story, at least the last part, and what Guðlac had done to be so unpopular with his mates. He clearly felt no loyalty to his present owner, being happy to waste his time, which of course belonged to Cynewulf. But he did admire Æled, or so he said. "He is considerate of his men. He hoards their lives and is liberal with treasure."

"How will he fare when he challenges?"

Other voices answered.

"Good."

"Yea, the thegns will welcome a Cattering earl again—"

"Who might bring the crown back here to Waroðburh . . ."

"Ceolmund's too cautious."

"Niggardly!"

"An earl's wealth," Guðlac said, making an effort to assert superior knowledge stemming from his warrior birth, "lies in the strong arms of his thegns, not bags of silver in the cellar. He's been relying on his crony Cynewulf to keep Æled under control. Something went wrong about the time the kid started shaving."

"And if Æled succeeds," Gerard asked, "what are his chances of becoming king?"

"Depends on the other earls, of course. Kings are rarely deposed without cause. I don't think Ufegeat is unpopular."

* * *

Even after he and Gerard had dried, dressed, and resumed their journey to Cynehof, Guðlac followed a leisurely, circuitous route. He showed off much of the city, including the markets. The stall keepers could tell at a glance that the two men were not potential customers; they shouted abuse and threatened to ask the next passing thegn to chase them away. Guðlac paid no attention and let Gerard marvel at the many magnificent things on sale—ostrich feathers, exotic metalwork, patterned silks, and dozens of other luxuries from distant lands. He was especially impressed by some magnificent illuminated manuscripts, which must have been looted from much closer to home.

Once, distant thunder announced that Cwicnoll was blowing out fire and smoke.

"He does that every few hours," Guðlac explained offhandedly. "When the wind blows this way, he can spray Waroðburh with ash."

"Don't the houses burn?"

"Sometimes."

"Why not build them of stone, then?"

His guide looked shocked and disbelieving. "Houses of stone? What happens when the earth shakes?" Apparently earthquakes were a much more serious problem than fires.

"What," Gerard asked, recalling Æled's tale of the Gevilians, "is a *fyrdraca*?"

Guðlac shivered and lowered his voice. "You know that each of the eight elements has a special place in the world, a home where the spirits dwell. Baelmark is the home of the fire elementals; Cwicnoll is one of their nests. Sometimes fire spirits mate with those of earth and birth a firedrake, which is monstrous and most deadly, seeking out men to destroy them. The scops sing epic tales of great heroes fighting firedrakes, like Æled's grandfather, King Cuðblæse, who fought one on the slopes of Hatstan."

"I heard that one destroyed an invading army."

Guðlac spat, his standard way of indicating disapproval. "In the days of King Fyrlaf, Cuðblæse's son. Instead of fighting the drake, he drove it against the Gevilians and burned them up."

"Sounds like a smart move."

The former thegn showed a rare flicker of emotion. "Smart can be shameful! Honest fighting men should not be treated as kindling. The witenagemot felt so disgraced that it shipped the survivors home without charge." Apparently there were depths to which even Baels would not sink; and Gerard recalled that Æled had hesitated before mentioning the incident—and had not alluded to his father's part in it at all.

They came at last to Cynehof, whose name meant "king's hall," although for the last twenty years it had been only the seat of the earl. It was a single high-roofed building backed by a fenced compound of many smaller buildings. Those were not truly houses—Guðlac called them cabins—because their occupants were mostly transients and ate in the hall. In ancient times an earl's thegn had been required to sleep in his hall, but nowadays only the *cnihtas* had to. Most thegns owned houses of their own in the city or on estates scattered throughout Baelmark.

Cnihtas?

Guðlac had halted at one side of a courtyard, whose far side was the front of Cynehof, wide stone steps up to a great oaken façade. "Boys with swords. See those over there? Stay away from them if you can, friend!"

"Why?"

All afternoon, Guðlac had been having trouble understanding Gerard's ignorance of what servitude really meant. He stared incredulously. "Because you're a *læt,* that's why! And they're thegn colts."

" 'Fraid I still don't understand."

The Bael sighed. "When a thegn-born's beard starts showing he goes to his earl, and if his birth is good enough, the earl accepts him as a *cniht.* For training. You can tell the *cnihtas* because they wear swords and helmets but not mail. The ones with the chain mail are house thegns. They're the earl's bodyguards and enforcers, his personal *werod,* understand? They keep order in the hall and the town under the command of the marshal.''

Only house thegns and *cnihtas* could take weapons into Cynehof itself, Guðlac explained. ''But *cnihtas* can get uppity with trash like us, friend, so that's where you're going and I'll head off now and find my supper if you *don't* mind.'' Guðlac studied Gerard for a moment. ''Is it true what Cynewulf said—that you could help Æled win the throne?''

''I—I am not sure.''

Even that weak evasion impressed the Bael. ''I suggest you put your mind to it, friend! Any man who helped Æled Fyrlafing mount the throne of his fathers would surely be buried in gold. He would hold lands as far as the eye could see and eat off plate till the end of his days.''

Gerard thanked him for all his help, wondering how he would have reacted a week ago had anyone told him he would take an honest liking to a Bael. Whatever his past, the slave bore his present situation with commendable resignation. His obvious dislike of Cynewulf should also be counted in his favor.

The five bored *cnihtas* slouching on the steps regarded the newcomer with contempt, he being unarmed. At a guess they ranged from fifteen to eighteen in age, and in size from shoulder height to enormous. Each wore a sword and helmet. They heard his story, then their leader sent the smallest to fetch Leofric, whom Guðlac had described as the tanist's closest friend and most trusted helper.

Leofric soon arrived. He was no older than Æled himself, but taller and slender, and although he would have been called a redhead anywhere else, his hair was blond by Baelish standards. A jagged white scar disfigured the right side of his face, the eye socket hidden by a silver patch bearing a single huge emerald. That was either a joke or a challenge, because the remaining left eye was much closer to blue than green—reputably a serious impairment among Baels. It seemed sharp enough as he appraised the newcomer.

He led the way to an outlying cabin furnished with a

cot, chair, and storage chest. Gerard looked around it in disbelief, seeing finer accommodation than the Green Man in Ambleport.

"A slave gets his own quarters?"

Leofric's smile was doubtless intended to be reassuring, but it held more menace than most men's scowls. "Tanist says you are to be treated as a war captive. You were thegn-born in Chivial, and he will not put you among *lætu* and thralls. Do not try to wear a weapon here, though."

"Of course not!" Gerard said hurriedly, wishing he had never touched a rapier in his life.

"Æled left you some gold, for clothes and so on. I will show you where to obtain a woman when you need one."

Thrall woman? Gerard shivered and shook his head at that offer, but he could think of nothing to say about the rest except, "He is very generous!"

"Always!" Leofric said emphatically. Suddenly his smile made him seem boyish and harmless. "A true giver of treasure. One day I could not ride because my mare had foaled, so he *gave* me two horses. It is his way. He is truly throne-worthy, a leader fit to die for."

Or kill for? Gerard thought that Leofric had not been told to make that speech; he really meant it and would back up his loyalty by doing anything at all for his hero.

When he had gone, Gerard peered in the chest to see how much a giver of treasure provided for a man who had killed his half brother. Although he could not be certain of the weight of the coins, they must be worth at least twice what Lord Candlefen had paid him for a week's work and two weeks' travel. More important, they were lying on the lid of his precious document case, which he had never expected to see again.

He took it over to the bed, where the light was best. The contents had been shaken about, which was hardly surprising after that voyage, and a couple of his pens had suffered, but the ink bottles had not spilled and nothing at all was missing. His best sketch of Charlotte, which he had placed at the bottom of the papers, was now on top. He sat and stared at it until his eyes blurred with tears.

• 7 •

Twice in the next two hours Gerard felt the earth move. The second time he was in the city, busily spending his new wealth. He was impressed by the total lack of panic, even among small children. Cwicnoll's antics were ignored like a minor breach of manners in a genteel salon.

At sunset the war horns' chilling wail summoned the fyrd to the feasting. By that time Gerard was ravenous. Dressed in his new Baelish garments and armed with his equally new knife and drinking horn, he headed purposefully to the great hall, but paused when he reached the paved yard to take stock. In Chivial he had visited houses where the main door was reserved for the nobility and even an artist-clerk from the College of Heralds must use a servants' entrance. Here he was much less than a clerk; but the Baels seemed to have no such rule, for all sorts of people were trekking in and out of the big archway, even slaves carrying provisions and barrels of ale to the feast. The only restriction he could see was that thegns had to surrender their swords to the *cnihtas* on duty in the porch. Reassured, he strode over the black flagstones, mounted the wide steps, and was allowed to enter unquestioned.

He paused again just inside the door, letting his eyes adjust to the dimmer light, gaping at the barbaric splendor. In truth the hall was no more than a shed on heroic scale, but its soaring roof was supported by an intricate trellis of spidery smoke-blackened rafters, and the high walls were festooned with antique weapons and ancient war trophies, anonymous under layers of soot and grease. Its only door was the one by which he had entered; its only windows were the two gable ends, left open so wind could waft away smoke. Along either side stood tables and benches for feasting, with a gap in the center for four great open hearths, set safely distant from the walls and manned by sweating thralls turning whole carcases on spits, exactly as the old tales demanded. A low platform at the far end supported another table that must be reserved for the nobility, for it was furnished with stools and a high-backed throne. He felt as if he had been misplaced several centuries in Chivian history; he reminded himself sternly that this was *now* and a slave's wergild was trivial. The advice Guðlac had stressed above all was that annoying a thegn-born could be a fatal mistake; being a *læt* was still better than being just plain dead.

When the scent of cooked meat put him in grave danger of drowning on his own saliva, he headed for the nearest tables. There was plenty of space and the thralls served anyone who sat down. In moments a trencher loaded with thick slabs of bread and crisp-roasted pork and beef was thumped down before him. He began to gorge. A woman filled his horn with cold bitter ale and the world got even better.

He was starting to see that apparent misfortune could be turned into opportunity. In Baelmark an earl's counselor might live very well.

A well-dressed couple entered with an entourage of armed followers, all heading for the high table, but no drums or horns announced them and none of the diners paid much attention. The man took the throne and so must be Earl Ceolmund. He was about forty and had a marked stoop. Put him in a sword fight with Æled and the money would all be on the tanist. His silver-haired companion seemed about twenty years older than he, but that was normal, a sign of many children.

Few people were yet ready to eat, apparently, for the hall remained remarkably empty, far below capacity. Atheling Cynewulf strutted in, nodding in bored fashion to friends, and took a seat at the high table. Æled must belong up there also, but he might be planning a hero's entry for later.

"What is the world coming to?" inquired a voice at Gerard's back. "There's dirt on this bench!"

"And on the table too," said another. A sword flicked Gerard's trencher into his lap, food and all. It clattered down to the flagstone floor.

He twisted around to face a pair of red-haired youths, both armed and grinning. The one who had drawn had not yet sheathed his sword. Now, too late, Gerard registered the slaves and servants sitting on the ground just inside the door and knew where he should be dining.

Guðlac had warned him.

"On the floor, slave!" said the tall one. "Dogs eat down there."

Gerard considered his options, which did not take long. "I am Æled's captive," he said—*Ic eom Ældes hæftniedling.* That was what Æled had told him to say, but now that he knew the language he could see that while *hæftniedling* certainly meant prisoner, it also meant slave. So did *wealh* and *hæft* and *niedling.* Clearly Baels made little distinction between prisoners and slaves, and these two *cnihtas* obviously did not, for their eyes were gleaming at meeting refusal, with its obvious opportunities for sport. Gerard spoke again, at a slightly higher pitch. "The tanist gave me quarter in Cynehof because I am thegn-born in my own land. Do you seek to overrule the tanist? Is that how you treat guests in Catterstow?"

The boys' confidence wavered slightly. "You lie, *niðing!*" said the one holding the sword, but he took a quick glance at the high table to see if Æled was watching.

Æled had still not arrived, unfortunately.

"I slew Wærferhð Fyrlafing, the tanist's brother, and the tanist honors me as a warrior. He appoints me his *wita,* but you insult me. Are you so much greater than Æled Atheling?"

The *cnihtas* exchanged worried glances. Gerard gambled on a chuckle, hoping it would not emerge as a nervous snigger. "I will forgive your ignorance this once. You did not know. See, the thralls have brought food. Come, sit, and, while we feast together, thegns, I will tell you of the fight in Ambleport, when I slew the atheling.''

They clearly disliked the thought of sitting beside a foreigner, but the prospect of hearing his news overcame their scruples. Warily they sat, both on his left and farther away than courtesy would normally dictate. If their friends discovered them, they could deny being with him.

The crisis was over for the moment, but Gerard's hand shook when the ale woman filled his drinking horn; he emptied it in one long gulp. He introduced himself, and so—reluctantly—did Wulfward Wulfwining and Boehtric Goldstaning. Between mouthfuls he told the story of Wærferhð's death, spinning it out, making a fight out of it but not downplaying his own crushing humiliation at the hands—or knee—of Æled. By that time the ale was working its way up under the carroty hair and they found that ending very funny indeed.

But puzzling. ''He really appointed you his wita?'' demanded Wulfward, the tall one.

''Why would the tanist expect wisdom from a Chivian *niðing?*'' asked Boehtric, oblivious of the possibility that a foreigner might resent an insult that would have him on his feet instantly, sword in hand and ready to die.

''When he arrives you can go and ask him. I'll introduce you, Goldstaning. But I am not familiar with your customs. Will scops sing tonight of the tanist's *færing*?''

The ale was potent. The sons of Goldstan and Wulfwin explained as well as they could shout while chewing that to welcome home the victors there would certainly be songs and speeches and distribution of treasure and drinking to oblivion.

''Is it possible,'' Gerard said uneasily, glancing around the hall, ''that the tanist will decide to challenge the earl tonight?''

''Never!'' Wulfward proclaimed. The night after a ship returned was always a night for jollity and feasting.

Why was the hall so quiet then?

''Tell me what happens when he does choose to challenge.''

Then, the *cnihtas* explained, talking in counterpoint, the

tanist would march in bearing arms. He would refuse an offer of mead. He would recite a formula, which they quoted, couched in such archaic Baelish that Gerard's enchantment failed to translate it, although the boys might not have it right. After that, they explained, the earl would set a date for the thegn moot to meet, usually the next day, and then the fyrd would decide whether the earl must answer the challenge in person. The vote was literally a siding, each man going to stand by the man he supported, so a head count could decide the issue.

The boys began arguing over the earl's choice of champion.

The hall was even quieter. Men were moving around—gathering in little knots or even walking out the door. Atheling Cynewulf rose, bowed to Ceolmund, and strutted out. That one would know a sinking ship when he saw one. Others followed.

This was to be the night.

"Thegns," Gerard said, and managed to catch their attention at the second repeat. "You think a Chivian cannot be wita? I offer you wise *ræd*—go now, go quickly. Where is the tanist? Where is the fyrd? I think you should be on the winning side, thegns."

There was a painful pause as the boys worked it out—as they realized that Cynewulf and his companions were almost at the door, with men rising everywhere to follow. Boehtric and Wulfward leaped to their feet and sprinted, dinner forgotten.

Gerard retreated to the underlings' corner, where the coerls and *lætu* had gathered to watch the drama. It was probably very typical of Æled to play by his own rulebook and not wait a few days as custom demanded. Ceolmund handled the situation as best he could—sitting alone with his wife at the high table, chatting peacefully and ignoring the empty benches. When only house thegns remained, he beckoned to them to come up and join him. His wife herself served them ale. The scene had time to grow quite poignant before Æled marched in at the head of his *werod*. He was in full war gear, shining with gold and steel; the rest of the fyrd followed, several hundred of them, filling the hall. Big Brother Cynewulf and the one-eyed Leofric were near the front.

Æled halted when he reached the central hearths. The earl's silver-haired wife stepped down from the dais with a horn of mead, and came to greet him with admirable grace. He returned her smile but courteously refused the horn. She went back to her husband's side. Æled called out the formula of challenge, but in a tone that showed it was only a formula and the personal insults were not intended to hurt.

The stooped earl responded with equal dignity. He did not ask for the support of his fyrd, for the result of a siding would be a foregone inevitability. He straightened up as well as he could, then retraced his wife's path until he reached the tanist. There he knelt to clasp the upstart's hands and swear loyalty. The hall erupted with a noise that Cwicnoll might have envied. Æled's closest followers lifted him shoulder high and bore him to the throne.

Then began cheering and feasting, wholesale drinking and distribution of silver and gold, riotous celebration that went on beyond dawn. The hugely grinning new earl handled himself well, naming his predecessor as his chancellor and loading him with a minor fortune in bullion to salve his wounded honor and pay off his house thegns. Æled made other appointments, too, the only two of which meant anything to the watching Chivian were Leofric as marshal and Cynewulf tanist. Of course an earl and his tanist should be close relatives and there was no one else. Besides—Gerard concluded cynically—if no one liked Cynewulf, he could not be a threat.

After twenty years, a Cattering was Earl of Catterstow again. Now it was up to Gerard of Waygarth to make him King of Baelmark.

III

• 1 •

For the next three days Æled was much too busy to interrogate his prisoner. He had to exchange oaths and gifts with every thegn in the shire, from landowners of enormous wealth to young sailors who did not own even their swords. He had to appoint his witan and enlist house thegns.

Gerard wandered the city at will, thinking hard. He wrestled with his conscience until he wanted to scream or just punch a thegn on the nose and die. He went over the arguments a thousand times. He owed no loyalty to King Taisson! His mother had petitioned her royal kinsman several times, seeking office or advancement of some kind for her son, but the only response had been one terse note expressing His Majesty's best wishes, penned by some anonymous palace flunky. The Waygarth family was not merely not royal, but over the generations it had been tainted by various scandals until the House of Ranulf wanted nothing to do with it.

Æled, though, was offering him the chance of a lifetime. There were only two roads to security in life and a man without inheritance had to rely on the second one, an influential patron. To become advisor and close confidant to a future king of Baelmark would be incredibly good fortune, the sort of opportunity men dreamed of. Æled himself was the sort of inspiring leader they dreamed of, too. Gerard's fortune would be made.

More important—he would be able to rescue the woman he loved.

* * *

On the fourth morning the sun rose into a blue sky and he was shaken awake by a *cniht* sent to tell him the Earl was coming. He had barely time to dress before he heard hooves and went out to watch Æled ride up on a magnificent black, leading a saddled chestnut mare. Should it be a surprise that the Earl was as skilled with horses as he was with ships? He looked down on his captive solemnly, his customary wide grin totally absent.

"Gerard of Waygarth, you owe me wergild for my servant Wærferhð Fyrlafing. In requital of that debt are you prepared to tell me of some feat that will raise me in the eyes of the earls so that the witenagemot will favor my challenge to King Ufegeat?"

Unpleasantly aware of crossing a bridge that allowed no returns, Gerard said, "*Ealdor,* I can think of one such deed. I do believe it has a chance, although the risks would appall any other man I have ever met and I certainly can't promise—"

The raider frowned. "I don't like risks."

Gerard opened and closed his mouth a few times. . . .

Æled's green eyes stared icily down at him. "Stupidity is not courage. Brains are not cowardice. I never take unnecessary risks; I plan my moves and weigh the costs. My motto is *'When you hunt the wolf, beware the she-wolf!'** She is rarely far away. Had you remembered that in Ambleport, you would have realized that Wærferhð would have many she-wolves at his back."

"Yes, *ealdor,*" Gerard said, chastened.

"But I will take risks if the prize is worth it and the odds are reasonable. Go on."

"Thank you, *ealdor.* The hunt I propose may make you king or kill you, but if you fail I don't think men will laugh at you."

Then came the grin, bright as the rising sun. "That is important! Mount up. Let us be on our way, lest the shire reeve come hunting me again, for if I throttle him as I want to, then good King Ufegeat will be seriously annoyed."

* * *

*Wigest wulfe, wylfre ware

At first he set a pace that made conversation impossible, but as they were leaving the sprawling fringes of the city behind, heading inland through grain fields toward the ice-capped cone of Cwicnoll, he let the horses slow to a trot and Gerard was able to draw level.

"Is it safe for you to ride out like this without guards?"

"Me? House thegns?" Æled snorted contemptuously. "Like Taisson the Frail, you mean? A hundred swordsmen around his sickbed?"

"You have won the richest shire in the country. You must have acquired enemies to go with it."

Such talk made Æled smile. "Of course. King Ufegeat, for one. But assassinating me would just start a blood feud. If someone kills Taisson, the Chivians will automatically be stuck with Ambrose. Here we have better ways. When the fyrd of Catterstow decides it wants to be rid of me, there are means available."

Put like that, the peculiar system seemed less barbaric, almost rational. "What about the oaths of loyalty everyone has been swearing to you?"

"What about them? I respond by swearing to be a strong and just lord. If I get greedy or vicious or too decrepit to swing a sword, then I have broken my side of the bargain and they are free to find a better man." The grin flickered back, briefly. "And if I haven't, let traitors beware! I mean to be king, though, and then I will make Catterstow rich and happy. Tell me your plan."

He slowed the pace to a walk as the trail left cultivated plains behind and began climbing through steep pastures. Cwicnoll had withdrawn from view, retreating behind ridges and lesser peaks.

Gerard gathered his thoughts. He had rehearsed this often enough. "You need to do something different, not just another *færing,* because you have shown you can do those better than any. Nor just shedding a lot of blood."

Æled nodded impatiently. "Any fool can make a massacre. Violence usually stores up trouble for the future, so I use it only when I must."

"I will remember, *ealdor.* This should not need violence, or very little. I was in Ambleport that night because

I was on my way back to Grandon from Candlefen. That's on the Wartle, about a day's journey west.'' A shrug told him the raider had never heard of it. ''There are old records of Baels raiding upriver as far as Wartcaster and Tonworth, but back in Goisbert the Third's time they built a highway along the coast there and bridged the Wartle. The fiendish Baels couldn't get their ships up the river anymore.''

Æled raised his copper eyebrows skeptically. ''No?''

''Or they haven't tried. Candlefen Castle has fallen into ruin. It's deserted. The family lives in Candlefen Park, about three leagues inland. That's a very fair mansion, but you could jump the wall. I told you I am—was—a gentleman scholar for the College of Heralds. I do odd jobs for the nobility. Lord Candlefen is marrying his daughter to the Duke of Dragmont, who owns half of Westerth. There will be a huge celebration. I was sent out from Grandon to advise them—who must be invited, who is presented to whom, who sits above the salt, who can bring men-at-arms. How many servants. All that.''

He could have done it in three days. He should have done it in a week. He had spun it out for two.

''Lots of loot at the party?'' Æled said with no great enthusiasm.

''Loot? I suppose the fat ladies will be wearing their weight in pearls. The Duke of Dragmont is a swine. I called him Dreg Mouth behind his back until I was terrified I would do it to his face—his breath will kill a horse at fifty paces. He also has a disgusting rash on his neck and hands, and I assume everywhere else from the way he scratches, and he's *three times* as old as the bride. He has *grand*children almost her age! But he's the king of beasts in Westerth—powerful, spiteful, vindictive. The Candlefens daren't do a damned thing to—'' He was almost shouting and Æled was looking at him oddly.

He took out the tube of paper he had tucked inside his tunic, untied the ribbon around it, and passed it across. Æled glanced at it and handed it back.

''Yes, I saw that. You are very talented. I wondered if she could be real.''

"It doesn't do her justice. Not close even. She's seventeen. She's—she's perfect! Witty, spirited, considerate . . ." And she was to be married to that human sewage. He had promised her he would not go back for the ceremony. "The wedding is set for the fifteenth of Seventhmoon." Realizing that the Baelish calendar might be different, he said, "That's the day of the full moon closest to the summer solstice. I watched you beaching *Græggos*. That bridge would be no obstacle at all. You'd just push your ships around it, across a road. About as far as here to that rock."

"We could do it with rollers." The Earl was not impressed so far. "If the tide's in and the river's navigable and the weather's favorable. We could be back at the coast before any troops get there. It would have to be well scouted in advance. She's very lovely, and I understand why you disapprove of the match, but I can't risk the lives of hundreds of men just to kidnap a rich old duke from his wedding. The fat ladies' jewels are tempting, I admit. It would be a riotous caper and every mead hall in Baelmark would shake with laughter, but—"

He broke off with a frown because Gerard was laughing. Rather a high-pitched laugh, teetering on the edge of hysteria.

"Sorry, *ealdor*! I'm not experienced at this *ræd*-giving. I forgot to mention that Charlotte's mother's mother is Princess Crystal, a daughter of Ambrose II. Charlotte is first cousin, once removed, of King Taisson, and thus second cousin of Crown Prince Ambrose. She is a generation closer to the throne than I am. I'm just connected by marriage. I'm not royal and she is. Charlotte is of the blood. She's seventh in the line of succession."

Æled's grin reappeared. It grew wider and wider and wider. "Let me see that sketch again! Oh, yes! Oh, yes, yes. Speak on, wita!"

"You'd have to marry her," Gerard said in sudden terror. "Just carrying her off and raping her wouldn't do! You *must* marry her!"

"Yes, Gerard. I'd marry her." Æled took a deep breath. "Yes, I *will* marry her! Cousin of the King of Chivial!

And the greatest beauty of the land. To go to the witenagemot with her on my arm . . . This would be truly throne-worthy! You give vintage *ræd,* wita. Speak on!''

''There is one she-wolf lurking.''

''I can see at least six!'' Æled said with the glee of a child counting cakes.

''She is close enough to the throne that they must invite the King to the—''

''*Taisson* will be there?'' Baelish eyes flashed.

''No, no!'' Gerard said hastily, remembering he was trying to steer a killer who might well prefer to go to the witenagemot with the King's head under his arm instead. ''His health won't let him. He wouldn't go anyway, because a reigning monarch eclipses the bride and groom. And don't look disappointed, *ealdor*! Kings of Chivial have Blades! Two or three Blades could cut your whole *werod* into fish bait.''

''Maybe.''

''Truly! The snag is that Crown Prince Ambrose may accept the invitation. He's been doing a fair bit of traveling since he came of age, and he hasn't been to Westerth yet. I warned them that they might have to put up with Tin Trumpet. That's his nickname. He's a young blowhard. And he has some Blades too, so—''

''How old is he?''

''Twenty. Well, he'll be twenty next month.''

''Oh? What week?''

''Er, second.''

Æled's grin returned, bigger than ever. ''Coincidence! We're the same age.'' He rode on, staring down at the grass, while his wita waited breathlessly. Then the Bael looked up with a very, very dangerous gleam in his eye. ''How much ransom would Chivial pay for its Crown Prince?''

''He may not be there!''

''But if he is? How much silver would Taisson pay?''

''How many men would you spend? I told you Ambrose has Blades of his own; and he may bring some of the Royal Guard as well, because they're going crazy guarding a sickroom. You'd lose a hundred men before you could lay a hand on him—and he fancies himself as a swordsman, so he's likely to die in the melee and then you gain nothing. How many of the witan would support you after that kind of massacre?"

Æled chewed his lip for a while, then sighed. "Too few and I would not be one of them. You are right. I give you my word I will not move against the Prince. You sound as if you had fallen in love with the girl yourself." His green eyes raked Gerard. "Did she spurn you, friend? Is this your revenge—to have her carried off by raiders?"

"No, of course not!"

"What is she to you, then?"

"Nothing!" Gerard insisted. "Just a pretty girl. I've only known her a few days, *ealdor,* truly. I pity her having to marry that stinking old goat, that's all."

Æled said, "Hmm? Well, I swear to you I will make her my wife and queen and then any other man who as much as catches her eye will wish he had never been born. You do understand that part of it, don't you?"

"And I swear to you, *ealdor,* that no such thought—"

"Of course. Now there is much to plan, and a myriad things that could go wrong." He looked up at the cliffs ahead. "I am on my way to visit a man who is something of a soothsayer. Whether he will agree to see you or not, I cannot tell, but he can give wise *ræd* on this. I don't think we can pull this off without some spiritual assistance. If anyone can solve the problems for us, it is Healfwer."

• 2 •

Some nights later, just before moonrise, a dory containing three men passed under the bridge at the mouth of the Wartle and headed inland. By dawn it had scouted upriver as far as Candlefen Park and returned to the sea. There Æled ordered that preparations for the *færing* proceed. He and Leofric then sailed away to their rendezvous with *Græggos* and their voyage back to Baelmark, but Gerard walked along the shore to Wosham and purchased a horse, telling tall tales about his own having gone lame and being left with a farmer. Three days later he reached Grandon by stagecoach, having encountered no problems except a tendency to speak and think in Baelish. An *ealdormannes wita* . . . er, earl's counselor . . . certainly need never worry about *sceatt* . . . money. . . .

Gentleman scholars were not expected to toil by the clock like artisans' apprentices, so no one in the college commented on his reappearance or how long he had been gone, certainly not Eagle King of Arms, a kindly octogenarian whose thoughts were permanently several centuries behind the times. Lord Thyme, the ancient archivist who actually kept the college moving at its glacial pace mumbled that Lord Candlefen's latest letter had been most complimentary about Gerard and regretful that he would not be able to return for the wedding itself.

"My other plans have fallen through," Gerard said. "I'll take the assignment if you want." With turbulent feelings, he watched his name being written in the appointment book. For almost anyone over the age of thirteen, marriage was a simple matter of a declaration before two witnesses, but families holding lands or titles usually had their children's unions registered by the heralds. This duty was unpopular in the college because fathers of brides were commonly so close to destitute by the time the celebration arrived that they notoriously failed to reward the registrar, sometimes not even reimbursing his travel expenses.

Gerard had promised Charlotte he would not be the one to marry her to the Duke of Drain Mud. Well, he wasn't going to, was he? *Oh, spirits!* Don't even think about it. He was sleeping badly.

The next few weeks were a prolonged agony of deception. He visited his parents but dared not tell them they would probably never see him again. When he hinted that he might have found a rich patron, they became very excited and peppered him with questions he could not answer—his mother, especially, lived in dread that her son might ultimately sink to the level of *trade.* He made discreet inquiries of Greymere Palace, and received the standard response that the Prince's travel plans were never announced in advance. There was no news from Candlefen and would be none unless the wedding were canceled and perhaps not even then. He dared not trust himself to write to Charlotte. He shied at shadows. He shunned his friends. He lost his appetite.

He found consolation in work. A certain rich merchant had discovered traces of blue blood in his veins and wanted the College to provide him with a complete family tree back to the mists of antiquity. Surprisingly, Gerard identified a couple of quite interesting branches. He prepared a multicolored vellum scroll festooned with armorial crests and blazons, one of the best things he had ever done. It was finished by the start of Seventhmoon and he still had some days to kill, so his fevered imagination began running wild, and he filled in gaps with fictitious links to memorable Chivian traitors and ancient Baelish monsters like Smeawine and Bearskinboots. On the evening of the ninth he left the completed and ruined project on Eagle King of Arms' desk—hoping it would not make the old gentleman die of shock in the morning—and left the College for the last time. The next day he packed a few souvenirs and caught the western stage.

At sunset on the thirteenth, he came riding along the beach under Candlefen Castle. Most of the walls had been quarried away by local builders and sand had drifted into what remained. He could see no signs that anyone had visited it in years, which would mean that Æled had abandoned the *færing*. The wild surge of hope that almost choked him was proof, had he needed any, that he was not cut out to be a spy, traitor, or conspirator. Nevertheless he must make sure of that change of plans, so he rode up the slope, taking care to stay on loose sand where the wind would remove his tracks. When he noticed the tall red-blond man standing in the shadows watching him, his heart almost jumped out of his mouth.

Of course it was Marshal Leofric, the Bael of another color, and his single eye had seen Gerard a long time before Gerard's two had seen him. He was dressed in ragged Chivian garb, nondescript yeoman garments that would normally escape attention, but if he had been prancing around the countryside with that sword at his side, it was a wonder he had not been questioned. At least the patch over his empty eye socket was of plain leather, not silver and emerald.

"Day after tomorrow!" Gerard blurted as he dismounted.

"That's how our numbers come out too. Bring that horse in here before anyone sees it." He had a small camp set up inside the hollow shell of the keep.

"How long have you been here? Has anyone seen you? Has anyone been asking you what—"

"I come and go," Leofric said. "Vagabonds and trash use this place all the time. Not horsemen."

"Æled?"

"He'll be around when he's needed," the thegn said guardedly. "Sit there." He pointed to a fallen stone lintel.

Gerard obeyed uneasily.

Æled's *werod* ranked Leofric a better killer than Æled

himself, because he had fewer scruples. He handed his visitor a slate and a piece of chalk. "Write, 'I have not betrayed Æled.' "

"Why? Is this some sort of test? If you don't trust me, then—"

The Bael folded his arms in a way that put his right hand very close to his sword hilt. "I will trust you when I have seen you write. Are you frightened to write what I told you?"

It *seemed* to be a perfectly ordinary piece of slate, but Gerard's fingers shook slightly as he obeyed orders. *I have not betrayed Æled.* Nothing happened.

"Rub that out. Now write, 'The Crown Prince is not coming to the wedding.' "

Gerard wiped a damp hand on his jerkin. "I won't. I don't know whether he's coming or not."

Leofric shrugged. "Write that, then." He dictated a dozen more sentences before he was satisfied and took back the slate.

"What would happen if I had written a lie?" Gerard asked hoarsely.

The big man smiled. "You will never know." He hurled the slate against a wall, shattering it. The whole thing had been a bluff, then—or perhaps not, because his mood was less threatening now. "I have been wanting to throttle you for months, but Æled says this is the most wonderful *færing* he has ever attempted. You have not been to the park yet?"

"No."

"Lots of wagons in and out the gate all day today. A swordsman in blue livery and one in green—I think those were Blades!"

"Very likely. Advance scouts for the Prince?"

"And a coach containing a woman in white wearing a foolish pointed hat?"

"A sniffer?" Gerald covered his face and howled. "They never said they were going to call in the Sisters! This is the end. We can't do it without enchantment of some—"

"It's a small snag, but we foresaw the possibility."

"I didn't," Gerard admitted. "I should have." Bringing in White Sisters to inspect any building where the King or his heir would be staying was probably the Blades' standard practice. "If she just looks around and then goes before he arrives . . . that isn't very likely, is it?"

"No. And I like the look of the weather even less. Off you go now to the Park, and we will talk again tomorrow night."

Panic! "No, wait! It's impossible! I can't go slinking in and out under the eye of Blades! Nor can I ever smuggle conjurements past White Sisters! Suppose they have inquisitors there as well?"

He saw he was not going to change Leofric's mind on anything. If Æled ordered the marshal to eat a longship he wouldn't ask for salt.

"Why should they?" The man of action sneered at the scholar's timidity. "Listen. At sunset tomorrow take out one of those boats they keep tied up at the waterfront. Take a woman with you if you want—I expect that's what they're for. When you reach the old mill, lose an oar. Drift downstream a little way, pole ashore with the other oar, and then walk back to the park for help. The *right* bank, the one on the *north,* understand? Leave the woman, if any, to wait in the boat. I'll catch you on the road."

"What's the plan? Why not tell me now? What about the enchantments? What—"

"Tomorrow, *laet.* What you don't know you can't let slip."

"I'm not a slave! Not in Chivial."

The tall raider did not even bother to look annoyed, merely contemptuous. "Ceorl, then. I thought you wanted to go up in the world?"

"I promised to help Æled."

"Then do as I say." For the first time Leofric offered a smile, although a singularly unreassuring one. "And win your reward! You should worry less about what Æled will give you than about what I will if anything happens to him."

* * *

Darkness was falling by the time Gerard reached the gates, which were being guarded by men-at-arms in the Duke's livery. Although private armies were forbidden in Chivial, such rules never applied to royal cronies like Ditch Muck. To Gerard's extreme annoyance they would not take his word for who he was; he had to unpack one of his bags and bring out his herald's tabard before he was allowed to ride on up the driveway. His anger faded when he realized that many of those men were doomed to die when they were hit by the horror of the Catterstow fyrd. And not only they—the grounds had become a small city of tents and pavilions, in expectation that the three hundred guests would certainly bring at least twice that many servants, plus horses and guards. Trying to imagine the chaos when several *werodu* of Baels came charging through, he was appalled, nauseated. To think that all this sorrow had flowed from his folly with the rapier in Ambleport, a single stone of evil becoming a landslide! It was too late to back out now, for Æled's fleet must be somewhere close and if he found the wedding guests fled he would seek out other prey. It would need a real army to stop him, and there was no army within call.

Gerard had expected to be billeted in a tent himself, but he was shown to an attic room. It was considerably less imposing than the quarters he had occupied the last time, understandably, but considerably more than he felt he deserved. He was going to betray his hosts' hospitality, and few crimes ranked lower than that.

Nor did it help his feelings that Lady Candlefen was one of the most charming persons he had ever met, straight-backed and yet warm, witty but dignified, a silver-haired ideal of what mothers should be. That she and her husband were marrying her daughter to a toad must distress her deeply, but the toad had forced their hand. She did not discuss such matters with strangers. She greeted Gerard in the great hall, which he recalled as an echoing empty place and yet now was bustling with people, for numerous impoverished Candlefen relatives would not miss a chance to arrive as early as possible, stay as long as possible, and eat as much as possible. She ought to be almost frantic at this stage in the preparations, but her greeting was serene and cordial.

"Charlotte was so pleased that it would be you recording the vows, Gerard!"

He doubted that very much. "I am happy to have the honor, ma'am. She must be very excited."

Lady Candlefen was well aware that her daughter and the gentleman scholar had fallen hopelessly in love within ten minutes of their first meeting. She sympathized, it was unfortunate, but chance was elemental and such things happened. They had to be kept under control, that was all.

"I think she is too busy to know what she is feeling. You will join us for dinner, sir herald."

He tried to refuse and was overruled. College recorders were annoying anomalies, neither servants nor gentry, but most noble families expected them to eat in the kitchens.

"If you'll excuse me," Lady Candlefen said, glancing around, "I'll tell them to set one more place. . . . Ah, Sir Yorick, Sir Richey! Have you met Master Gerard?" Callously abandoning him to two predatory Blades, she departed.

Richey wore the blue and silver of the Royal Guard and Yorick the Crown Prince's green and gold. Yorick was fresh-faced and eager, while Richey in his late twenties, nearing the end of his service, seemed more cynical. Apart from those details, they could have been brothers, both to each other and to any of the other dozen or so Blades Gerard had met in the past. Until that moment he had never considered Blades as anything more than exotic flunkies, but suddenly he was very much aware of their stealthy menace and the dangerous swords they wore.

The Blades politely wanted to know who he was and why he was there and they were going to get answers. When he told them, they thawed a little, and he was reassured that he must not seem one thousandth part as guilty to them as he felt. Perhaps he could discover how badly his plans were collapsing—

"Can I assume from your liveries that this house will be honored by both your principals tomorrow?"

It was the young one who answered. "No."

"Oh." He hoped his smile conveyed amusement and not panic. "I can't or it won't?"

"Yes."

The older Blade chuckled softly. "He means neither. You can't assume, but no, His Majesty is not coming."

Yorick snorted. "There you go, giving out state secrets to all sorts of suspicious characters. The College of Heralds is probably riddled with subversion."

"Rheumatism mostly," Gerard said. "Spirits! Is that a White Sister?" It was an idiotic question, because her tall white hennin loomed over the tallest heads and no one else wore those anymore.

"Either that or the family ghost." Was Yorick's interest in Gerard increasing or was that notion just a figment of his terrified imagination?

"They never told me they were going to bring in a sniffer!" He tried to sound like a petty bureaucrat with an out-of-joint nose, which ought not to be difficult. "What are they afraid of?"

"The Candlefens?—nothing," young Yorick said. "It's a piece of antiquated hocus-pocus that the King insists on. Sniffers can find a conjuration if it's in plain view in an empty field. In a crowded building like this one, they wouldn't recognize a love spell if there were naked bodies writhing all around them."

"Oh, come," Richey objected. "The King is too fond of his treasury to throw away money. He wouldn't have the White Sisters patrolling his palaces at all unless they did some good."

Gulp. "You mean they actually do uncover conjurements directed at His Majesty?"

"Certainly," said Yorick. "All the time. Are you finding it over warm in here, Master Gerard?"

"What? No! No, if anything I think I'm a little chilly. The damp, you know . . . Why, there's the bride and I haven't paid my respects yet . . . do please excuse me. Been great fun chatting with . . . do it again some . . ." Gerard fled like a hare.

• 3 •

"By the way, Charlotte darling—while I remember—an army of rapists and slavers will invade the house on your wedding day to carry you off, but their leader is a dashing young fellow with lots of muscles and while he's a bloodthirsty monster he does have a big smile and he says he will marry you and make you Queen of Baelmark one day. So don't worry, you'll be much happier with him than with that disgusting old duke."

That was what he ought to say, but of course family and admirers were fussing around the bride like midges, and even if she had been alone, the message would have had to be passed with more tact. *Considerably* more tact!

She was taller than most women but still as slender as a child. Blue was always her best color and tonight she wore a rustling dress of sapphire silk, whose voluminous skirts accentuated her tiny waist. Her thick and high-piled hair shone in the rich tones of honey fresh from the comb, she had the amber eyes that so often showed up in the House of Ranulf, and her neck was the longest he had ever seen on a woman—she favored low necklines to display it. He could stare for hours at the perfection of her ears and nose and delicately pointed chin. She had the fragility of a porcelain doll and rode to hounds like a hussar. A word of praise made her blush hotter than a smith's forge, yet he had heard her blaspheme worse than a blacksmith hitting his finger.

He lingered on the fringes of the swarm for some time before she acknowledged him with a brief smile, and all the time she kept up the required pretense of happiness and cheerful chatter. He had seen her in a myriad moods: Charlotte festive; Charlotte wistful; Charlotte reflective; Charlotte elated as she put her horse over gates and hedges, daring him to catch up; Charlotte laughing as she chased the spring lambs; Charlotte witty; Charlotte mischievous at cards; Charlotte graceful as moonbeams in minuet or gavotte—a woman of constant variety—and yet he had never seen Charlotte somber, not even when she spoke of her abhorrent future with the repulsive duke. "One makes the best of things," was as far as she would ever go to admit unhappiness.

At last she introduced him and brought him into the conversation. "It was Master Gerard's inspiration to hold the ceremony in the rose garden." The gentry nodded without pretending any interest in a mere heraldic scribbler.

"I distrust the weather now, my lady," he said. "We may be forced indoors."

"Oh, I am certain it will be glorious on the day." She would never stoop to pessimism.

Then came the summons to dinner, and her brother Rodney offered his arm to lead her in. Of course Gerard was seated far below her during the meal. He did contrive a face-to-face meeting later in the evening, but only when they were back in the crowded hall, amid scores of possible onlookers, so their faces smiled while their whispers were bitter.

"Why are you here?" Smile, smile. "You promised you would not come."

"I was terrified you might have changed your mind. If you have, then there is still time. We can run away together."

"*Gerard!* Oh, Gerard, have you forgotten that you are about to marry me to one of the wealthiest landowners in Chivial?"

"I have thought of nothing else for months. You don't have to go through with it. We can flee to Isilond or Thergy and be together always." Æled's money would just cover the fare, with nothing left over.

She laughed as if he had just made a joke, but her eyes

denied the mirth. "Living on what, Master Gerard? I do not know how to mulch pigs or brew gruel."

"I'll find work! I'd work myself to death for you, Charlotte."

"That really does not sound very practical. Perhaps I can learn to clean fish on the docks. Will you take my family with us? Or how will you defend them?"

Alas, there was the root of all the trouble! As seventh in line of succession, she was so close to the throne that she needed royal permission to marry, and the Duke of Dung Murk was a lifelong pal of old King Taisson. That was where the pressure was coming from. If Charlotte refused the match her whole family would be ruined; and if she eloped with Gerard, both he and her father might die under the headsman's ax. Only outside Chivial could she ever find happiness—with Gerard in poverty, or as a future queen of Baelmark. Her family could not be blamed for a Baelish raid.

"Oh, poor Gerard!" she said. "I do understand, I really do! We just mustn't think of it."

"Of course you mustn't think about sharing your"—he almost said "bed"—"*life* with a diseased old—"

"Fourteen major estates and castles, Gerard. Of course we shall live in Grandon most of the time, and I shall be a frequent visitor at court. Jules has the King's promise that I shall be Mistress of the Revels next Long Night!" Her brave smile invited him to share her happiness, and yet he had seen her be physically ill after an hour of being pleasant to the disgusting lecher. He dared not explain the alternative he had devised.

She turned away to greet an ancient uncle.

He tossed and twisted the night away in his attic, but his aching conscience was not his only torment. With his nose almost touching the roof he could hear the rain and the wind, and he kept remembering Leofric's prophecy of bad weather. The Baelish fleet might have been driven halfway home already or piled up on rocks. Uncertainty only added to his woe; he worried that he might be worrying unnecessarily.

By morning the midsummer storm showed no signs of departing, and even the wedding was in jeopardy. Roads would be impassable, bridges washed out, horses injuring feet in water-filled potholes; and out in the grounds tents were collapsing by the dozen. Guests would start arriving by noon, soaked or cold or both, and this could only add to the confusion in the already overcrowded mansion. He offered to sketch Charlotte in her wedding gown.

"A splendid idea!" her mother said. "That will be a nice peaceful interlude for her. It has been so hectic around here, and the next two days are going to be very stressful!"

Lady, you cannot imagine. . . .

An hour or so later, Charlotte stood in an upstairs drawing room, staring out the rain-streaked window as Gerard had posed her, while he chewed his tongue and struggled to make pencil lines convey the subtleties of fabric. Her brocade outer dress of midnight blue swept out from narrow waist to a wide hemline; it was open at the front to reveal the scarlet satin of the inner dress just as her neckline was cut to the waist to show her pearl-encrusted bodice. She seemed even taller than usual, so she must be wearing platform shoes, and her voluminous headdress hid her hair. The face was no problem. He could draw that in his sleep, with all the fine bone and the perfect skin, teeth, lips. . . . Yet all of those were lit from within by fires of vitality faceted like diamond, and there his skill failed absolutely.

Her mother, being understanding—too understanding—dispatched the servants on various pretexts, but she herself remained, fussily checking lists at an escritoire, not quite out of hearing. The conversation was stilted, naturally, and Gerard did have to concentrate on what he was doing. Elopement being now out of the question, all he could hope to do was drop some comforting hints, but the minutes flew by, his allotted time dwindled fast, and it seemed he would have no chance. Then Charlotte gave him the cue he needed.

"So where have you been since you left us?"

"Abroad," he muttered.

Her cry of wonder made her mother look up in equal surprise.

"What?" She had turned in alarm, forgetting her pose but no doubt recalling his mention of Isilond and Thergy. "How exciting!" she added more cautiously. "Where to? What were you doing?"

"Oh! I shouldn't have mentioned . . . but if you will promise not to tell anyone . . . and you also, my lady? Absolute secrecy! Even the Prince may not be privy to what is happening." *He had better not be!* "And even if he is, he will not wish to discuss it. We heralds sometimes get called upon to initiate discussions with foreign governments. Of course I am not yet trusted with any major assignments." He was babbling, but he had told no lies so far.

"You are modest, Gerard! Can't you drop us just a teeny hint?" *Charlotte teasing.*

"Well, I had occasion to pay a very brief visit to . . . Baelmark."

The ladies chorused their horror.

"Those monsters!" Charlotte said. "You must have heard! Just after you left us—they raided Ambleport and kidnapped scores of children and young people. Men slaughtered! Brutality! It was unthinkable!"

Gerard nodded soberly. "My visit was not unconnected with that event."

"Oh!" Lady Candlefen clapped her hands. "How wonderful! You were negotiating ransom for those unfortunate captives?"

"I cannot reveal the substance of my discussions, ma'am. But it was a very memorable experience. I was truly surprised. Of course I only saw one city, Waroðburh, but a most beautiful place! I expected naked savages living in caves, and found a prosperous, cultivated people. Their houses and clothes are richer than most of Chivial's." He smiled at their incredulity. "I met a young prince, for example, about the same age as Crown Prince Ambrose. Honestly, he is one of the most charming people I ever met. He may well become the next King of Baelmark."

"He is welcome to it." *Charlotte icy.*

"I do think the Baels have been rather slandered. I admit they are aggressive at times, but so few foreigners ever visit their country—"

"Why would anyone want to? Gerard, you are talking about slavers, killers, pirates, men who assault defenseless women." *Charlotte angry.*

"The violence is not all on their side. Chivians can be slavers too, although we never hear about that. A Baelish vessel was seized at the quay in Ambleport and the entire crew hanged! Did you know that?"

Mother and daughter exchanged disbelieving glances.

"No. When did that happen?" Lady Candlefen demanded.

"About fifty years ago. The Baels have long memories." Gerard saw he wasn't making a great deal of progress.

By noon more guests were arriving, and Crown Prince Ambrose was one of the first. He brought more Blades with him, making a total—although it took Gerard some time to establish this—of six from the Royal Guard and ten of his own. Unless his father's health improved he would likely take most of Ironhall's output in future. He set up court in the great hall in front of the fireplace, dominating everyone. He was loud, he was big, and he had a young woman with him who was very obviously his mistress—the two of them sniggered and made eyes at each other. Compared to Æled he seemed a vastly overgrown and spoiled child.

Gerard retreated to his attic and worked on his sketch while the roof creaked in the wind. The Blades would have been a sickening problem if the weather had not already ruined everything. Even Baels could never land an army in this storm, not with the split-second timing that would be required. He had failed to rescue Charlotte and failed to satisfy the man he had hoped would be his new master, so he would sink back into obscurity where he belonged and abandon dreams of being a king's counselor.

The Blades were irrelevant. Love was irrelevant. Everything was irrelevant.

By sunset the overcrowded house had become such a bear baiting that merely going out for a walk in the mud would not be seen as evidence of insanity. Taking a boat would be, for the Wartle was a racing brown flood licking the tops of its banks. Gerard set off into the rain, pausing only to chat with the men on the gates and see who could curse the weather hardest. There was no one else on the road. As he approached the old mill he began to whistle, but when a voice hailed him it came not from the mill but from a hedge on the opposite side of the road. He climbed over a stile, where a path trailed off into the woods.

"Down here." Leofric was sitting on the ground under a spruce.

Gerard scrambled in beside him like a child playing king's men and outlaws. The ground was dry close to the trunk, and the air pungent with the aromatic tree scent. "It's all off, isn't it?"

The silver patch was back, a giant's eye burning in the gloom. "Not that I've heard. Report."

"But Ambrose is there already and Æled swore he wouldn't move against him!"

"He won't, but he may move around him. What else is happening?"

Gerard groaned. "Everything is going ahead as planned. There may be fewer guests than they expected, that's all. Half the tents have collapsed and the rest are awash. If this rain keeps up, he'll be able to sail *Græggos* right in the front door. You're not seriously expecting him to go through with it, are you?"

Leofric showed his fangs. "I've known him as long as anyone, and never seen him fail at anything yet. He took you through Eastweg in a howling northerly, didn't he? No one else would dare try. Keep talking."

"The ceremony is still to be held mid-morning in the great hall. Then the banquet, and I expect that'll go on long into the night. The Prince has *sixteen* Blades with him! Blades are invincible when they're defending their ward, Marshal!"

"No they're not. All men are mortal. How many sniffers?'

"Just one." And now Gerard realized that he had not seen the White Sister since he had been on his way to breakfast. "She may have left. I'm not sure."

"You should be sure, but we have to risk it anyway." The Bael reached under his cloak and produced a flat package wrapped in oiled cloth. "There are two sheets of paper in here. One bears a watermark of a heron, the other of a ship. Write something on them so that you know them at a glance. If you put them in with your other papers, you can always claim you don't know where they came from, but Healfwer doesn't think a sniffer can detect them while they're not active, not without actually handling them. Keep your distance from her and you should be all right. To release the enchantment, you tear the sheet in half."

"Tear it in half? And what happens then?" More than the water trickling down Gerard's neck was making him shiver.

"The one with the heron will scare all the birds within half a league, maybe farther."

"And you will notice. What's the message?"

"That the wedding party has entered the hall. That's our signal to move in. If Æled hasn't come, then nothing happens. The birds go back to their nests and you just carry on with the marriage."

"And if the White Sister is still there?"

Leofric shrugged. "She probably has a fit. At close range she may be too stunned to know who did what where."

"Your confidence is really comforting!" Gerard yelled.

The Bael lunged forward and caught Gerard by the throat, half choking him and dragging him forward until wolf teeth snarled right in his eyes. "This was your idea, *niðing*! You knew what would happen if you threw an idea like that at Æled. If you didn't, you should have. And I swear if anything happens to him because of you, you *burbyrde bædling,** I will see you take a month to die! Understand?"

Gerard made choking noises, and the thegn hurled him away one-handed as if he weighed nothing. He rolled on some painful roots, banged his head on a branch.

"Ready to listen some more?"

Gerard sat up and dusted dirt off his palms. "Yes, *ealdor.*"

"You tear the paper with the ship at the last moment—either just before you complete the marriage or when there's enough noise outside that the meeting's about to break up in confusion. Understand? This is important. Too soon and we won't be there yet."

"How long do you need?"

"As much time as you can give us. You'll probably hear when we are getting close. A Blade or two going out to see won't matter, but we don't want panic. The last possible moment!"

Gerard groaned and nodded. "And then what happens?"

"It will create a diversion. Everyone presently in the room will be frozen to the spot. It's harmless and it won't last more than two hundred heartbeats, so Healfwer says. By the time it wears off, Æled will have control of the hall. We hope."

"Or there's a free-for-all."

"That's true." Leofric smiled as if his earlier anger had never been. "It may be quite a ruckus."

"Suppose something goes wrong? What if the sniffer detects the conjurements?"

Leofric shrugged. "I told you—you protest that you had no idea those pieces of paper had been enchanted and you cannot recall where they came from or how they got in among your effects. If they haven't beaten the truth out of you or chained you to the rafters, then when the ceremony is about to start, run out the front door and keep

*Low-born weakling.

going down the drive to the gates. We'll do the best we can without you. Repeat your orders.''

''Heron means come to the house. Ship means come into the hall.'' Gerard could hear the swish of the headsman's ax already.

· 4 ·

An abduction would have been much easier out of doors, although that had not been the reason Gerard suggested, back in Fourthmoon, that Charlotte be married in the rose garden—he had merely concluded on his first glimpse of the great hall at Candlefen Park that it was an exceedingly ugly barn. She had supported the proposal enthusiastically. So had her mother but, knowing the climate of Westerth and lacking her daughter's perpetual optimism, Lady Candlefen had suggested they make backup plans to hold the affair indoors just in case—fortunately so, because sheets of mist and rain were still marching relentlessly in from the ocean.

That morning everyone was going around wrapped in the warmest clothes they had brought with them, complaining of being cold. Gerard was more chilled by the realization that the gale had dropped to a bitter breeze, so the *færing* might well be possible again. Rain and fog without much wind were ideal Bael weather; and unless Æled had been driven to the farthest corner of the world, he could probably bring his ships right up to the paillemaille lawn before anyone even noticed them. Even the ducks would be staying indoors today.

The hall was about eighty feet long, with the great main door at one end and the minstrel gallery and the staircase up to it at the other. No musicians ever played there, the Candlefens admitted, because the sound echoed so badly. Admittedly the hammer beam roof had some merit, but throw in the fake armor and make-believe banners on the walls and you still had a very ugly barn. So be it—the true artist made the best of his materials and Gerard had devised a workable plan, indeed several of them, depending on whether or not Prince Ambrose came or even the King. At the time he drew those up, he had not contemplated inviting a Baelish army also.

As the guests filed in, they had the windows on their left and two kitchen doors plus the monumental fireplace on their right. The first third of the hall was filled with tables, which servants were hurriedly setting for the banquet, and the center held rows of seats facing the gallery. Gerard was the last to enter, resplendent in his multicolored tabard. The bone-jarring thump of the great doors closing behind him was a signal to the principals that it was almost time to appear, but two Blades had done the closing and remained outside to guard. Another four were standing at the far end, keeping an eye on everything, and a fifth in the gallery replaced the servant Gerard had stipulated. Blast pompous young Ambrose! At least there was no white hennin in sight, no White Sister.

He dodged between the domestics, walked along the narrow aisle between the rows of chairs, and came to the small table that had the last third of the hall to itself. He turned briefly to bow to the guests, then opened his document case and laid out the items he would need. When everything was ready he looked up and nodded to the Blade in the gallery. The Blade went out to send in the wedding party.

Gerard had never married a duke before and would have been nervous even without his knowledge of impending doom. As it was, when he took up the paper with the heron watermark, on which he had written some meaningless notes, it trembled so hard that he had to clutch it to his belly. Either the Bael fleet had been driven hundreds of leagues away or it was on its way upriver at this instant.

The first to appear on the gallery was the odious Duke

of Dog Meat himself, who had elected to come alone, although he could have squired any of three daughters or several granddaughters. The audience rose to its feet. *As much time as you can give us,* Leofric had said. The ceremony had started. Gerard ripped the paper in two. Between the fog and the rain streaming over the windows, his view of the trees in the park was too vague to show anything smaller than eagles and he sensed nothing at all happening—unless that had been a slight breath of wind on his face? He had never been sensitive to spirituality, but he was very close to a powerful conjurement and birds were creatures of air.

As the groom was descending the staircase, the sixteen witnesses began to parade in along the gallery. Ambrose led the way, of course, escorting ancient Princess Crystal, Charlotte's grandmother and his great-aunt. So far everything was going perfectly. They had all been rehearsed less than an hour ago, and even aristocrats couldn't forget anything so simple in that time. Uncles, brothers, sisters, children . . .

Had Æled allowed for the rain, or were his ships wallowing helplessly in the flood?

The Duke in his fancy silks arrived on the far side of Gerard's table, with the Order of the White Star blazing like a sun on his hollow chest and his hose padded to disguise spider-thin shanks. The leprous folds of his neck were hidden inside one of the high jeweled collars that were the latest fad among young dandies in Grandon. He looked over the assembly with satisfaction, ignoring Gerard. Oh, what a surprise he had coming!

The witnesses lined up in a row across the hall, Prince and aged Princess in the center. Charlotte appeared in the gallery on her father's arm, the Blade coming in behind her and closing the door. Again there were five Blades in sight, which meant eleven prowling the house or the grounds, unless some were off-duty—but Gerard had a nasty suspicion that Blades never went off-duty. Blades weren't really human. Charlotte was cautiously descending the stairs in her cumbersome gown—*take all the time you want!* This was not the magnificent entrance parade he had designed, but it was not bad under the circumstances. It would have been more imposing if they had let him rebuild the staircase as he wanted.

Charlotte arrived at the Duke's side and released her father's arm. She was taller than the bridegroom; she barely acknowledged his smile of welcome, staring fixedly over Gerard's head. She would not descend to hypocrisy by pretending to enjoy herself.

He waited as long as he dared. The spectators fidgeted, the servants clinked dishes. *Æled, where are you?* Eventually both bride and groom were frowning at him and he had to begin.

"Your Royal Highness, Your Highness, Your Graces, my lords, ladies, and gentlemen . . ." If Æled could take just this collection of blue blood witnesses and hold them to ransom, he could *buy* the throne of Baelmark. Perhaps the brawny lad was planning to do exactly that, or worse. He had not necessarily confided his true intentions to Gerard. "You have gathered here today to witness the"—*rape of*—"marriage of Jules Claude de Manche Taisson Everard, Duke of"— *get it right!*—"Dragmont, Companion of the White Star . . ." and on and on, a huge list of honors and titles and estates. The Dragmont family fortune sprang from a notorious robber chief two dynasties back, a man probably worse than Æled. It had been ruthlessly increased by generations of peasant-grinding barons. " . . . to the Lady Charlotte, eldest daughter of . . ."

Charlotte had demanded the shortest possible ceremony. He was making it the longest possible. Were the Baels disembarking yet? When they were sighted and the alarm went up, how long would it be before the racket was detectable inside this stone mausoleum? What if nothing at all happened and he had to complete this awful farce? The next item was supposed to be the taking of the vows but that was the actual marriage and he must not let things go so far. The alternative was to name the witnesses first.

" . . . in the presence of His Royal Highness, Crown Prince Ambrose Taisson Everard Goisbert of the House of Ranulf . . ." and so on. Charlotte was glaring at him. The Duke of Dirt Muck was scowling. And so it went. Without a flaw, unfortunately. And it could not last forever. He came to Charlotte's youngest sister and the list was over. He must proceed now to the actual rites.

"Repeat after me: I, Jules Claude de Manche Taisson Everard, Duke of Drain Mouse, Viscount . . ."

The smelly old man did not seem to notice the slip. "I, Jules Claude de Manche Taisson Everard, Duke of Dragmont . . ."

Panic! Somewhere in among his notes, Gerard had lost the paper with the ship watermark. He gathered the whole bundle and tried not to let them shake.

The groom repeated the final words of his oath. Pity.

"Repeat after me. I, Charlotte Rose—"

There was a noise in the kitchens.

Gerard stopped and frowned in that direction.

Nothing more happened. Sigh. "Where were we? Oh yes. Repeat after me, I, Jules Claude—"

"We already did that!" Dragmont flashed fire at him.

"We did? Oh, I am sorry. Well, my lady, repeat—"

There was another noise in the kitchens, louder. Now everyone looked that way.

The door in the minstrel gallery flew open and two Blades came running in to join the one already there. *"Baels!"* they shouted. *"Raiders!"* Two of them raced for the stair and one leaped over the rail, landing like a cat. The four against the wall surged forward, all frantic to reach their ward. The audience screamed. Gerard ripped the sheets he was holding—

—and froze.

He could not even move his eyes. He could barely breathe. The moving Blades pitched headlong, with the two on the staircase rolling and sliding horribly all the way to the bottom. Ambrose and many others were caught off balance and toppled over. From the servants at the far end of the hall came a fearful crashing of glassware. In the resulting silence, faint screams and metallic clatters drifted in from the rest of the mansion. A low, stifled moaning arose from the congregation, the best that frozen throats could do.

The Blades broke free. As a duck's plumage repels

water, so their binding resisted the conjuration. Like men fighting their way out of molasses they struggled to their feet and in moments they were all active again, except for one of the two who had fallen down the stairs. The rest swooped on the petrified Prince and lifted him bodily.

"The window!" one shouted, but they moved only a few steps before they came to a cursing halt. Gerard could not turn to see what they were seeing, but he assumed the grounds were filling up with redheaded raiders. One of the kitchen doors crashed open and three more Blades raced in, swords drawn. They, too, converged on their ward; through the doorway behind them came sounds of chaos and slaughter.

The giant Toðbeorht came marching out on the minstrel gallery, huge and terrifying with his shield and battle-ax, his steel helmet concealing his face, his great chest and shoulders matted with wet red fur. Behind him came half a dozen men armed with crossbows.

"Blades!" he roared. "We intend no harm to your ward." Æled must have chosen him for volume, because his voice reverberated like thunder. "We have not come here to molest Prince Ambrose. Stand him in a corner—"

Two of the Blades raced to the stair to get at the threat, leaping over their fallen comrade. The first was already halfway up when a crossbow cracked and put a bolt through him and into the steps. He fell forward on top of it. The other one stopped where he was.

"I said," Toðbeorht bellowed, "to stand your ward in a corner and no harm will come to him. The bowmen will stay up here. Look to your injured, Blade."

Glowering, the Blade on the stair sheathed his sword and bent to examine his comrade. The rest rushed their ward into the safe ground under the gallery and surrounded him with a human shield. Their faces were ashen with fury. In a moment two more rushed in from the kitchens, one of them limping and trailing blood, but they went to be with the others. Æled had foreseen this—the Blades would be no threat to him as long as he left their ward alone.

"As for the rest of you," Toðbeorht bellowed, "we did

not come here to hurt or kill or enslave anyone. You will be released from the conjuration very shortly. Stay where you are and you will not be harmed. If you do as you are told you will keep your lives and freedom." He glanced around at the couple who had just appeared in the gallery and then boomed out like a herald, louder than ever: *"Her Majesty the Dowager Queen Maud of Baelmark!"*

Her escort was Æled, of course, in smock, leggings, and cloak, a sword at his side. Gerard had not met the tall woman on his arm before, but he recalled hearing talk of her.

The enchantment vanished as suddenly as it had come, leaving a momentary giddiness. Gerard staggered and leaned on the table for support. Others less fortunate reeled and grabbed at neighbors, in some cases dragging them down with them. Those who had fallen earlier struggled to their feet, and a huge wail of alarm reverberated back from the roof. The witnesses rushed together into family groups—Charlotte going with her parents and brothers and sisters, and the Duke with his children. Scores of armed Baels had taken control of the hall, herding the servants into a compact huddle, blocking all the doors, and even lining up at Gerard's back to block any effort by the wedding party to join the main congregation.

Ambrose was on his feet, scarlet and cursing, but firmly jammed into the corner by a living wall of Blades, who would not let him leave that spot as long as the bowmen remained on the gallery overhead. Baels gathered up the wounded Blades and delivered them to their comrades. Gradually an uneasy quiet fell, as everyone waited to hear what their captors wanted.

Gerard caught Charlotte's eye. What he saw in it was fury, although she was sickly pale. She knew who had been babbling about Baels. She could not know what was going to happen next. He hoped that she would feel better when she did; actual forgiveness might have to wait a long time.

Æled and his mother descended the staircase together. Although it was centuries since Chivial had seen such garments, their quality and richness were obvious. Queen

Maud was not young, but flowing veils concealed her hair and neck, and her height and grace made her the equal of any woman in the hall. Her son, of course, was capable of dominating all men. His belt, sword hilt, baldric, and shoulder brooch flamed with gold and jewels. His copper braids hung to his shoulders. On reaching the bottom of the stairs, he paused and looked to Gerard.

"Herald!"

Gerard's heart lurched; he hurried over and bowed. "Highness?"

"You may present these nobles to my royal mother."

After one glance at the seething knot of Blades, Gerard chose to go no closer. Who took precedence? He bowed to Queen Maud. "Your Majesty, I am honored to present His Royal Highness, Crown Prince Ambrose of Chivial."

She cocked her head expectantly. Ambrose just glared. His bodyguard had not left him enough room to bow anyway, but he showed no signs of wanting to.

Gerard tried again, although the college's texts on protocol contained little guidance for such a situation and the titles did not translate exactly—an atheling was less than a prince, an *ealdormann* more than an earl, about a duke. . . . "Your Royal Highness, I have the honor to present His Highness, Atheling Æled, Earl of Catterstow."

Æled bowed.

"Pirate!" Ambrose bellowed. "You will pay for this outrage with your head."

The pirate grinned. "I was twelve when I learned not to make vain threats."

Apparently he wanted the charade to continue, so Gerard turned to the Candlefen group, which contained the next in precedence, Princess Crystal. He proclaimed her titles. Bless her!—the old lady curtseyed solemnly to the visiting Queen.

Maud smiled. "We are honored by your respect, Your Highness."

"We are grateful to you for enlivening a most boring morning, Your Majesty." The old lady's eye twinkled.

Æled was presented and bowed low to her. Then it was the Duke's turn, but his diamond-studded star had disappeared and when Gerard tried to present him to the atheling, he turned his back.

Æled bared his teeth. "If those are Chivian manners, I will teach you Baelish. Goldstan, take that man outside and throw him in the cesspool. Empty his pockets first." As two burly Baels hustled the screaming Duke from the hall, the Earl raised his voice and the echoes. "I came here on personal business. It is my intention to marry—and take home to Baelmark as my wife—the fair Lady Charlotte."

In the resulting chorus of screams and wails, he led his mother over to the bride and bowed to her. For a moment they just stared at each other. Then Æled bowed again.

"Word of your beauty has crossed the oceans, my lady, although words cannot do it justice. I understand that this hasty wooing must be a shock to you, but I swear that my intentions are to treat you with all the honor due the wife of an earl, to cherish you all my days, and—if the spirits of chance favor me—to make you queen in my land."

Charlotte, still ashen pale, looked again at Gerard and the accusation in her eyes needed no words. He nodded and she turned her face away.

Releasing his mother's arm, Æled produced a ring and held it up. The setting was gold. The incandescent stone was a ruby the size of a plump raspberry. "I offer you this for a betrothal gift, my lady."

Charlotte spoke for the first time since she entered the hall. "And where did you steal that from, pirate? Was it you who raped Ambleport last spring?"

Her show of fire summoned back Æled's widest grin. "It was, my lady. But the ring has been in my family longer than this house has been in yours, I suspect."

Lord Candlefen's face, always florid, was dangerously inflamed. He had trouble speaking, gasping for breath. "This is outrageous! You force your way into our house to abduct my daughter?"

"I would marry your daughter. There's a difference. I abduct people all the time."

"What choice does she have?"

"What choice did she have before? Why did you not defend her then?" Æled's quiet questions silenced the peer. "Recorder, come here."

Gerard moved closer. Charlotte was not looking at him now. He started to whisper, "You can trust—"

"Perform the marriage!" Æled snapped.

"Yes, *ealdor.* Your Majesty, Your Royal Highness, Your High—"

"I will have no part of this rape!" Ambrose roared from his cage.

Gerard ignored him and completed listing the witnesses. "Repeat after me: I, Æled Fyrlafing, Earl of Catterstow, of the House and Line of Catter, take this woman, Charlotte Rose . . ."

Æled repeated the words in a voice that rang from the hammer beams.

Now Gerard had to look her in the eye again. Now was heartbreak time. Now he must bind the woman he loved to the lord he had chosen to serve. She was biting her lip, staring at the floor, fighting back tears. "Repeat after me: I, Charlotte Rose . . ."

Silence.

Whispers in the audience . . .

"The record can show," Æled said softly, "that the groom claimed his bride by right of conquest. If that is what she prefers."

Still no reaction.

Into the silence crept the words of Queen Maud, so gentle that only those very close could hear. "I had even less choice than this, my dear. I was carried off by force, just like those young people from Ambleport. I was fortunate in that their leader took me for his own and did not have me enthralled. But I was his slave. I had no choice, neither in bed nor anywhere else. I bore him a son before he acknowledged that he loved me and made me his wife. I gave him other children after that, although only Æled survived. I came to love him dearly, for he was a noble man within the limits of his breeding. I warn you that Æled is sawn from the same timber as his father and will let nothing deflect him once he has set a course. He will carry you out of here over his shoulder, screaming and weeping, if you choose that way. But he is offering you the choice of accepting the inevitable with grace and maintaining your dignity. It is no victory, but it may soften the bitterness of defeat. And he will be beholden to you. That is important, for he learned from his father to pay his debts."

Charlotte glared at the older woman for a moment, then at Gerard . . . at the armed brigands that had violated her ancestral home . . . and finally she looked Æled over as if she had not really seen him before.

"Beholden?" she whispered.

He nodded. "Very much so, my lady. Grant me this and you can demand almost anything of me for evermore."

Even softer: "King?"

"I will win the crown of Baelmark or die in the attempt. If I fail, you will be sent home. If I succeed, you will rule at my side as my queen."

She drew a deep breath and then looked to Gerard again. "Start over."

"Repeat after me: I, Charlotte Rose . . ."

She raised her voice, high and clear, almost as loud as Æled's had been. "I, Charlotte Rose . . ."

The audience gasped.

" . . . do solemnly and most willingly swear . . ."

" . . . do solemnly and most willingly swear . . ."

She did not hesitate once.

"Then I declare you man and wife under the laws of Chivial," he said.

Slops!

It was not legal. Even without her need for royal permission, a sword-point wedding could never be legal. He did not bother asking for signatures on the certificate, knowing that Ambrose would refuse and no one else would then dare to comply.

Æled was beaming. "Also under the laws of Baelmark, as my *werod* is witness. Thegns, hail Lady Charlotte of Catterstow!" The Baels roared approval, beating swords on shields, setting up a reverberating racket. "Thus the betrothal." He placed the great ring on her hand. "And the wedding gift.'' From his sleeve he produced a shimmering string of rubies and set them around her slender white neck. ''And the kiss.''

She did not refuse him. Nor did she seem to encourage him, but when he released her he looked wondrous pleased. ''You honor me greatly, my lady.''

Without a word, Charlotte turned to his mother and the two women embraced. It was magnificent. Even Æled seemed impressed. He drew a long breath and looked around the hall as if wondering whether so great a triumph could be real.

''Wife, we must leave quickly, for every minute we delay increases the chances of bloodshed. Your family may follow us to the ships to make their farewells there if they wish. I give you my word they will not be harmed or restrained. If you have ladies or attendants who will risk this journey with you, I give them safe conduct on my honor as a thegn and swear that you will have means to reward them richly and send them safely home.'' He raised his voice to fill the hall. ''When my men leave, they will take hostages, but they will be released unhurt when our ships cast off. Only my wife will be taken aboard, unless any of you wish to accompany her, in which case I promise you safe return. I admit that the rest of you will be asked to make donations to a wedding gift, but I rely on your natural generosity to avert any unpleasantness.''

He paused to look over at the Crown Prince raging impotently behind his shield of equally furious Blades, and all his teeth showed in a grin. Gerard guessed what was coming and thought, *Don't do it, Æled!*

Æled did do it. It was out of character for him to be petty, but he was exultant, ablaze with victory on a scale few men would achieve even once in their lives, and he could not resist the chance to gloat. If he forgot the she-wolf once that day, it was then.

''Cousin? You don't mind if I call you that now, do you, Cousin? Now we're related? We were born in the same week, did you know? Some boys grow up faster than others, of course. *Dear* Ambrose, my wife and I will be delighted to entertain you if you wish to come and visit us. But do let us know in advance, won't you? Our coasts are well defended."

"I will come!" Ambrose roared. "I will bring a fleet and burn out your nest, pirate. And you I will hang from the highest branch in Baelmark!"

Æled bowed. "Words are for braggarts. Princes should be men of deeds. Fare thee well, Cousin. I like your Blades. They're very pretty."

He offered his arm. Charlotte took it, and again the hall gasped in disbelief. Smiling, he steered her toward the main door, walking within a double line of thegns. Gerard, following, found himself escorting Queen Maud. Studying her profile, he saw no resemblance to Æled in it. Hard years and many troubles had engraved deep lines, but they gave her face such character that he longed to sketch it.

"That is no easy voyage, mistress," he said as they left the hall. "Your presence here does you great honor."

She glanced at him and then away. "No one comes out of this affair with honor. The girl displayed incredible courage while being publicly raped, that is all."

As they passed through the outer door, nervous footmen fell into place alongside to hold umbrellas over them, being encouraged to do so by Baelish swords. Æled and his bride were leading the procession along the terrace path, Charlotte now swathed in a hooded, floor-length robe that looked as if it might be ermine, in which case its value was incalculable.

"Lady Charlotte could find no better husband than your son."

"You think so?" Maud said. "He treats women like livestock and men like tools. So did his father. I do not find this behavior admirable. It is to my shame that I did not manage to talk him out of this plan or bring him up to know better."

Two dead Blades lay in full view on the lawn, but marks on the grass showed where other bodies had been dragged away, more than two. Already the rain had faded the bloodstains.

Gerard protested. "She detested the thought of being married to that ancient, slimy Duke!"

"There is shame enough for your King to share, yes. My son behaved like a brute today, but what about you, Master Gerard? You tell a woman you love her and then you sell her?"

They rounded the rose garden hedge and saw the fleet ahead, eight long vessels tied up at the bank of the Wartle. Dragon ships seemed a nightmare delusion in the peaceful heart of Chivial.

"Never! I did what I did for her happiness! She had been given no choice before. I found a better man for her, that's all."

"What right had you to make that choice? Why did you not let her decide? Yes, you could! You could have told her this morning what was going to happen. Then she could have fled or stayed, whichever she wanted. She could have been waiting at the river mouth when the ships arrived—but that wouldn't have worked, would it? That would not have provided the drama, the romance of the handsome pirate chief arriving in the nick of time to steal the royal maiden from the lecherous old aristocrat under the very nose of the Crown Prince. Oh, no! Think not that you did this for Charlotte. You wanted to be the little gray spider. Your ambitions do you no credit."

Unfair! "He is a third the age of that old degenerate. He offers a greater title, probably more wealth. Charlotte will learn to be happy with him, just as you learned to love his father. I found her a better future." Now that the tension was over he was starting to shake, but his own future seemed most wonderfully bright, too.

"Of course we foolish women will love whoever warms our beds, won't we?" said Queen Maud. "No brains required as long as you have a *pintel.* I have heard blind people laugh. Even the maimed can learn to be happy again. But Charlotte might have been happier in a bed of her own choosing, Master Gerard. Nothing can excuse what you have done. Fortunately, I see no profit in it for you."

The procession had reached *Græggos,* whose gangplank

had demolished a fine rosebush. Charlotte stopped and turned to look back.

"I fear that your family has chosen not to come and see you off, mistress," Æled said.

"Did you ever think they would?"

He shook his head, studying her face with wonder. "Not really. And thus I am even more grateful to you for your acceptance. Your courage astounds me. I swear again that I will strive evermore to be worthy of your love, my lady."

She was recovering her color, unless that was only the chill wind burnishing her cheeks, or the contrast of the snowy fur framing her face. The robe was indeed ermine. "Beholden? Is that the word you used, my husband?"

Æled smiled. "Ask for anything in the world and it is yours, mistress."

"Divorce?"

"Anything *except* that!"

"I shall remind you of this vow in future, perhaps often."

He laughed. "You will never find the need." Then the atheling's green eyes turned on Gerard and their merriment chilled into cold appraisal of unfinished business. "What of that one, wife? He is a friend of yours? A close friend? I am thinking that his friendship is strange."

"Too strange for the name!" Charlotte said quickly. "You wound me by suggesting it. The man deceives himself. He is a flunky, a lowly scribbler who mistook courtesy for affection and could not be misappraised of his error. My lord husband, I swear to you that I never gave him the slightest encouragement."

"Then you do not wish to take him with us?"

"I should much prefer never to set eyes on him again. Is he not in your pay?"

Æled's smile was back manyfold. "I promised him nothing. He owed me wergild for a thegn he slew, but he has requited his debt and now we are quits."

Horror and disbelief had kept Gerard paralyzed through this exchange. Now he lurched forward. "No! You said I would be your wita. You are a giver of treasure!"

Æled shoved him so his feet slipped away and he

crashed on his back in the mud. The pirate looked down with contempt. "I never promised to take you as my man. You are already traitor to one king, so how could I ever trust you? Your life was forfeit in Ambleport. You have won it back, so begone and be grateful." He looked around. "Osric, keep watch that this Chivian does not board. By your leave, my lady . . ." Effortlessly, he scooped Charlotte into his arms.

She smiled at him for the first time. "You are very strong, my lord."

"You are very fair, my lady." He carried her up the plank.

IV

"How I Got Here?" Raider said thoughtfully. "I suppose the greatest blame should be laid on Gerard of Waygarth. A nice enough young man, I understand, yet sadly misguided. He was of no real importance in himself, but back in 337, during your father's—"

"Never mind him! You need not go that far back."

Wasp felt peeved. Why would the King not let Raider tell the whole story? What could have happened twenty years ago that he still wanted kept secret?

"I was merely going to explain how I caused the war—"

Raider was interrupted by a tap on the door. Commander Montpurse took delivery of a pitcher of water and another receptacle that led to some embarrassing moments. When that one had been removed and both Wasp and Raider had enjoyed a drink from the other, Raider began his tale.

• 1 •

"The witenagemot is like your Privy Council, sire, in that the witan are the king's advisors, appointed by him. But it is also like your House of Lords, a formal summoning of all the earls. The earls are the only ones who vote and the only vote that ever matters, or is binding on the king, comes when one of them issues a challenge. If the others support him, the king must abdicate or fight. If he wins the vote, then woe to the upstart!

"My father's exploit in carrying off Your Majesty's cousin from Candlefen was hailed throughout the land as the finest *færing* in generations, full worthy of a Cattering, but it did not automatically make him king. Far from it! First of all, many of the earls had unpleasant memories of the strong rule Catterings had imposed in the past and preferred the looser hands of a Nyrping monarch. Second, it is almost impossible for the witenagemot to assemble without the king's summons. King Ufegeat was in no hurry."

Raider seemed perfectly relaxed, enjoying the conversation. Wasp now understood his friend's interest in politics, and Ambrose was listening intently.

"His hand was forced in Tenthmoon of that same year, when the Chivian ambassador presented an ultimatum. On pain of war, he demanded that the Lady Charlotte be returned immediately and her abductor handed over for trial in Chivial. You will forgive my mentioning, sire, that in Baelmark everyone assumed that the trial would be brief and the execution leisurely. It seemed an excessive response to an amusing caper, but since the alleged pirate was the most powerful earl in the country, Ufegeat had no choice but to summon the witenagemot. My father took Mother with him to Norðdæl, which was Ufegeat's city on Wambseoc and the then capital of Baelmark. She took me, although not from choice, I suspect.''

Wasp's expanding grin shrank rapidly when the King noticed it.

''Boy, that caper you are talking about cost the lives of five Blades and some men-at-arms.''

''I am aware of that, sire,'' Raider said somberly. ''I have heard their deaths described in the Litany. If you will pardon a momentary digression, what is not known in Ironhall is that the other side lost twenty-five men in that fight, all of them slain by Blades. This was repeatedly charged against my father in the debate. Perhaps Commander Montpurse could have that fact added to the record.''

''I will see to it myself,'' the King growled. ''The Commander will repeat nothing he hears in this room.''

Neither, Wasp suspected, would Wasp.

''Thank you, sire,'' Raider said. ''As for Gerard of Waygarth, I recall hearing my mother speak of him. I think she eventually repented of her anger and decided that he had acted from nobler motives than she had at first believed, but I never did hear what happened to him.''

No one questioned a monarch, and that comment darkened the royal countenance. ''I really cannot recall at the moment.'' The King's show of indifference was very unconvincing. ''Do you remember, Commander?''

''Before my time, sire,'' Montpurse said. ''According to Guard tradition, he died while resisting arrest. Bled to death from a large number of wounds, I believe.''

The threat might be moonshine, but it made Wasp shrink a little deeper into the corner of the settle. Raider hastily resumed his story.

''Four earls found excuses to stay away and send their tanists. The ambassador presented his demands, the wise men mumbled cautions, the young firebrands thundered. My father made a masterly speech. With his life at stake, he somehow managed to convert the debate into a challenge and then won by the narrowest possible margin, eleven to ten. King Ufegeat was still throne-worthy, a man of strength, and he chose to fight rather than yield. The scops still sang even in my day of their battle. Father never claimed it was an easy victory, but in the end he managed to bring Ufegeat down. He spared his life, which was condemned as a piece of foolhardy sentimentality.

"Had my father lost either the vote or the duel, he would certainly have died. He maintained—and I do not think he was entirely joking—that it was I who made the difference. I had been conceived in the dragon ship, on the voyage home from Chivial, and by the time of the witenagemot my mother's condition was known. Visible to the women, not the men, he would say; but it was common knowledge, and he drew attention to it in his speech. If the witan chose to knuckle under to the Chivians' demands, they would be handing over an innocent, unborn Cattering to hereditary foes. How could Baels ever descend to such shame? I suspect the earls were more worried about an outbreak of civil war than about me, but perhaps I made a difference. If I carried even one vote, I changed history, because of course the new king's first act was to make the Chivian ambassador eat his ultimatum in public, seal and all. Trade between our two nations ended and random piracy became all-out war."

· 2 ·

To the Baels, it was always Prince Ambrose's War. They believed he had fanned the indignation in the Chivian Parliament and bullied his ailing father into launching a conflict he had been resisting ever since he came to the throne.

Ironically, King Taisson's health soon rallied and he reigned for almost a dozen years more. Long before he died, the Chivians were cursing him for what they called Taisson's War.

There was never any serious prospect of the Crown Prince being allowed to see action, so the fleet he had promised Æled he would bring sailed without him. It raised the peaks of Baelmark on the first day of Fourthmoon 338, and that night it was blown onto the reefs called Cweornstanas, the Millstones. Only a tenth of the men aboard ever made it home to Chivial. The rest drowned or went to the slave markets. From then on Baelmark had no fear of invasion and Chivial was fighting a defensive war.

News of the disaster—or good fortune, depending on point of view—was proclaimed in Waroðburh on the very day Queen Charlotte gave birth to Atheling Radgar. Her labor was hard and he was never to have any brothers or sisters, but the babe was healthy and the mother survived. The omen of the timing was widely noted and Baelmark rejoiced that her King had an heir to continue the line of Catter.

Like many thegn-born, Radgar grew up speaking Baelish to his father and another language to his mother without realizing that there was anything unusual about that arrangement. His mother was beautiful, and his father wore a sword—little else mattered.

His first world was his parents' favorite country home at Hatburna, a sheltered glen on the southern slopes of Cwicnoll, and especially their private cabin, which stood a little farther up the valley than the main buildings and which his father forbade anyone else ever to approach. It was no larger than a ceorl's hut, a single room with a stair up to a sleeping loft. The boy's earliest memories were a composite of many late, gloomy dawns with rain beating on the roof louder even than the distant drone of the waterfall and his parents' voices drifting down, while he lay snug in bed wondering whether it was safe to climb out into the chill air and totter upstairs on his short legs. If all went well they would pull him in between them and all three would cuddle together for a long time, for life ran slow in a Baelish winter. Rarely he would be sent away again. If they were talking, the decision rested on his mother's voice, which might be happy or angry, for his father's was always the same deep, reassuring rumble. If they were playing tickling games, as was frequently the case, he could be certain of a warm welcome if he waited until they had finished.

Even when living in Waroðburh, in the royal quarters on the north side of Cynehof, King, Queen, and atheling slept in close proximity. Mother had an adjacent cabin where she entertained friends and where her maids lived; Father had one on the other side where he held private meetings. Uncle Cynewulf, the tanist, lived in the largest with Cousin Wulfwer and a varying succession of women, and others nearby were occupied by Chancellor Ceolmund, Marshal Leofric, and numerous house thegns. Leofric's son Aylwin was Radgar's age and became his best friend as soon as they were old enough to admit friends into the scheme of things.

In summer he ran wild, growing brown as old leather, and every summer his world expanded. At three he had a pony. At six he was sailing boats with Aylwin and a dozen others, all amphibious as frogs. About then he began to realize that he was different: he was royally born. They were sons of thegns, coerls, *lætu,* or thralls, but he was an atheling. The only difference that made, his father explained frequently, was that he must be the best at everything. This he staunchly believed and not infrequently achieved. Around then, too, he began recording distinct incidents, single events that would remain with him when he left his childhood behind.

There was the time he fell off a cliff and broke both legs so badly that they took a week to heal, even with the best enchantment.

There was the time he almost killed Aylwin, although Aylwin outweighed him handily. He was not to recall what had caused the fight nor even the fight itself, but he remembered his father's terrifying anger. "You are an atheling!'' the King said. ''You must learn to control that temper of yours. You cannot even save it for battle as other men may, because you will be a leader and leaders must be able to think clearly at all times.'' Radgar never forgot the beating that followed—not the pain, but his father's tears when it was over, when they embraced and wept together. ''Promise me, son, that you will never make me do that again!''

He did, though. Older boys who tried to pick on the King's son discovered that they had roused a dragon. On three separate occasions his opponents had to be taken to the elementary for healing and one lost an eye in spite of it. Eventually the unwisdom of provoking him became known, and his father realized that beatings were not going to solve the problem.

There was the time he and Aylwin took a sailboat out through Leaxmuð and back in through Eastweg in a nor'wester. They had just turned eight. Their hysterical mothers insisted they be punished for that stupidity and so they were, if a few halfhearted slaps on the butt could be counted as punishment. *Somebody* told Sigebeorht the scop the story, and that night in Cynehof he sang it to the fyrd as if it were an exploit of legendary heroes. The thegns put the pair of them up on a table and cheered and pounded the boards as if they had just come back from a great *færing* with half the wealth of Chivial. That was worth all the beatings in the whole world. Mother was not amused. Father got very drunk.

Then there was the first time he met Healfwer.

• 3 •

It began when Aylwin outgrew his pony and was given a horse. Radgar complained to the highest authority about the unfairness of this. Obviously an atheling should be better mounted than his thegn, although by then he knew enough not to put his grievance in those terms. He just said, "Father, I need a horse."

King Æled did not even look up from the dispatch he was studying. "You can have a horse when you can read."

Radgar withdrew to consider the terms. They seemed irrational—what had reading to do with horses? On the other hand, there was no trap involved that he could see. Anyone could learn to read; he had just never tried, that was all. He found his mother writing letters. Despite the war, she still corresponded with friends in Chivial, sending the mail through Gevily.

He said, "Mother, teach me to read . . . er . . . please."

"Yes, dear. Bring me a book."

She was not surprised? That made him suspicious, but he brought a book. Soon she was surprised. For three days he gave her no peace at all, and in the end she squeezed him in a big hug and said, "You are a wonderfully clever boy. Go and show your father."

He marched into Cynehof, where the King and Uncle Cynewulf and Chancellor Ceolmund were conferring with the Gevilian ambassadors. He went to the high table where the men sat, deep in conversation. He waited.

After a few moments his father frowned at him and said, "What do you want?"

"A horse."

The King passed him a sheet of paper. He read the first paragraph aloud, slowly but without a mistake. The King took it back.

"Which horse?"

"Cwealm."

"He'll kill you!"

This reply opened dazzling prospects, because Radgar had been so certain of outright refusal that he had a list of six backup choices ready. "You asked me!"

"I should know better by now. Show me you can manage Steorleas and you can have Cwealm."

Steorleas had been his third choice. Radgar yelped, "Yea, lord!" and sprinted for the door, wondering why the men were suddenly laughing.

He showed that Steorleas, despite his name, could be steered. Again he demanded Cwealm, this time as a matter of right. To his astonishment—and his mother's horror—Father consented. To everyone's astonishment and relief, Cwealm also failed to live up to his name, in as much as he did not murder Radgar, or at least he had not done so by the end of the first week when he and Aylwin went riding up into the hills. He was considerably bruised, but alive. Undoubtedly his string of successes had made him overconfident and he was looking for another challenge.

As they climbed, distant peaks came into view—Seolforclif, Hatstan, and Fyrndagum—and also other major islands, Hunigsuge, Þærymbe, and Wambseoc. The land grew ever more rocky. When at last they reined in, they had reached Bælstede, a bare shoulder of mountain where men had kept watch for invaders in the days long past. Ruins of their shacks stood there still, but one glance showed that there was nothing there worth exploring.

Aylwin was pointing. "Eastweg!"

Some of the glints of open water in the maze of islets below certainly represented parts of the channel, although there was room for argument as to which. Ten-year-olds could not resist exploring any room for argument, but before the discussion could become heated they became chilled.

"We'd better move the horses," Aylwin said.

"Yes."

They turned to study the prospect they had been ignoring. The ground was a rubble of sharp black clinker, falling away sheer on two sides and rising vertically on another, but there was a defile in that cliff. They could go back down the trail they had just come up, or they could go into that defile—they had no other choice. The gap, which was visible from the town far below, was called Weargahlæw and it was one of very few places in the whole shire forbidden to them. There was no room for argument on this—Weargahlæw was off limits. Even a few months ago, that would have been the end of the matter, but there comes a time when a boy realizes that some restrictions apply only to small boys and he has outgrown them.

The wind wailed through the cut, a sound to make a scalp prickle; but the more Radgar stared at the gap and the very faint track leading to it, the more he managed to convince himself that he had gone there once, maybe more than once, a long time ago. He realized that Weargahlæw was why he had come.

"Let's go and look."

Aylwin had been waiting for this. "They'll take Cwealm from you!"

"Why? There aren't any wolves near here."

"Then why is it called that?" Aylwin said ominously.

Hlæw could mean "cave" or "grave." *Wearga* meant either "of the wolves" or "of the outlaws"—intriguingly vague. It was true that there were scary stories of Chivian outlaws lurking in the hills, either prisoners who had escaped before they could be enthralled or castaways still at large since the Great Wreck in the year Radgar was born. It was also true that rank disobedience like this might lose him Cwealm and the sun was not far from setting, but when Aylwin put the matter in terms of danger he was left with no choice—for an atheling must never show fear, no matter how dry his mouth.

"Go home and learn to spin then."

"No. We both go. *Now*, Radgar! My dad says you're *always* getting me into trouble and if I didn't follow *you* around all the time he wouldn't *always* be having to switch me!"

"Oh, it's a sore butt you're afraid of?"

Aylwin's face crumpled. "No."

Radgar shrugged. "If I'm not back by dark, tell Father where I went and why you did not come with me."

Aylwin shuddered. Better death than that! When Radgar rode forward, he followed. He always did.

They were wearing only breeches, so the torrent of air they met in the ravine made their eyes water and threatened to freeze the tears on their cheeks. If no one ever went to Weargahlæw, then why were there horse droppings on the trail to it? Why was there a trail at all? It wound up and down and in and out in a labyrinth of fallen boulders, but when it suddenly descended to the mouth of a cave at the end of the ravine, Radgar was not surprised. He knew of many caves around Waroðburh. They were usually long pipes, with no branches or bigger chambers, just tubes that eventually ended in rock falls. Some were used as animal shelters; others made good play holes. But now he had another misty memory of a dark tunnel leading through to daylight somewhere else, and none of the familiar caves did that.

Aylwin howled. "You can't go in there!" His teeth were chattering.

"Why not? Only girls are scared of bats!"

"Weargas!"

"Weargas?" Radgar said scornfully. "How can there be outlaws in there? What would they eat?"

How would they see? He dismounted, handing his reins to his trusty retainer, and stepped cautiously into the cave. There was a draft blowing out of it, so his vague half memory of a tunnel was probably correct—but he would not tell Aylwin about it in case he was wrong. The entrance was black as an icehouse and littered with jagged pieces of rock fallen from the roof. Cwealm wouldn't go in there. If this were Radgar's front door, he would keep a tinderbox handy . . . somewhere easy to reach, out of the rain. . . . He found it in few minutes, also some old-looking horn lanterns and a box of candles.

"How did you know those were there?" Aylwin squeaked.

Radgar shrugged. "Had to be. Do I light one lantern or two?"

"Two," Aylwin said miserably.

"You sure?"

"Course I'm sure!"

So was Cwealm, when he was granted some light. He let Radgar lead him into the tunnel as happily as if it were the palace stables. Even with this example of model horsiness to follow, the normally docile Spearwa gave Aylwin a lot more trouble. The passage was more than high enough to walk along. Fallen rocks had been cleared aside and the worst holes filled in with gravel to make a level path.

"What happens if Cwicnoll shakes while we're in here?" Aylwin demanded, his voice quavering oddly in the echoes.

"Perhaps the cave'll close behind us." Now there was a skin-shivering thought! On the other hand, it could be that falling rocks were all that parents were fussing about and there weren't any *weargas* at all.

The way curved into total darkness and then brightened, returning to daylight at the top of a short scree slope within a small, almost circular, valley enclosed by high black cliffs. The cave was at treetop height, providing a view over a wild, shaggy forest. Here and there steam clouds promised hot springs, but there were no signs of buildings.

"This is the real Weargahlæw!" Radgar explained as if he had known all along what to expect.

Again it was almost-sort-of familiar, especially the precipitous path down the slope in front of his toes—and he would not even try to imagine what might happen to a horse caught on there by a tremor. If he injured Cwealm, he would *never* get another horse, not *ever*. And just inside the cave mouth stood three sacks of meal, two unopened, one still half full, and also a small stack of empty sacks weighted down with a rock. The explorers exchanged shocked glances.

"Somebody's feeding the *weargas*!" Aylwin squealed.

Four lanterns stood in full view on a ledge, plus what was certainly another tinderbox. *Fresh* droppings. Cwealm whinnied and was answered. Down in among the first trees stood a horse. It had been hobbled and left to graze, and the pack saddle was still on its back!

"He's still here!" The fear in Radgar's belly was an agony and also a glorious excitement. His mouth was so dry he could hardly speak, and wonderful shivers ran up his arms. "Whoever brought that horse is still here!"

Aylwin was sickly pale. "Let's go! Now, Radgar! *Please!*"

"You go. My father must know about this. You go and tell my dad—or your dad, I suppose. Bring the house thegns! I'm going to stay here and keep watch, so we know who the traitor is."

His trusty thegn put up a few more protests, but his heart wasn't in them. It was *very important* to take word back, Radgar said; and Aylwin would not be running away when he was ordered to go. For once, Aylwin didn't even question his right to give such orders. He led Spearwa back into the tunnel.

Radgar scrambled up on to Cwealm's great back. Feeding outlaws was an *unfrið*, a breach of the King's peace, so he was right to investigate. It was a wonderful chance to do something interesting and not be punished for it; but even without that excuse, curiosity ate at him like a plague of mosquitoes. He still had the lingering sense of having been here before, so there were two mysteries or even three—because Cwealm had obviously known the tunnel too. Cwealm had been one of Dad's own mounts, but other men in Cynehof had ridden him—the hands who exercised him, for example. Suppose the traitor turned out to be someone in the palace itself!

The precipitous track down the scree brought him to the tiny meadow where the packhorse had been left to graze, but beyond that stood real forest—huge cypresses and cedars hiding the sky. Very little undergrowth could flourish in that gloom, but the ground was so hummocky that he could rarely see more than two or three trees ahead. The path was clear, going up over rocky knolls and down into mossy, squelchy hollows. Whenever it divided, he let Cwealm choose, hoping he would follow the scent of the traitor's horse—Dad said horses went by scent much more than people did—and that seemed to work, because sooner or later he would find another muddy patch showing hoof marks. There were too many marks for just one horse and all going the same way he was. He wished he could muffle Cwealm's hooves like heroes did in stories, like Dad and his men carrying the scaling ladders to the walls of Lomouth. . . .

The heavy, soporific smell of the trees was achingly familiar, but there was no forest like this anywhere close to Waroðburh. No one would log here because there was no way to drag the trunks out. It was creepily silent, without wind or birdsong, only rarely a distant tattoo from a woodpecker or the harangue of a squirrel. A couple of times his nose caught the stink of hot springs, and once he was close enough to see wisps of steam drifting through the trees.

Then he reined in his trusty steed on one of the hillocks, looking down into a puddled hollow with no tracks in the mud. "You made a mistake, big one! We should have gone the other way at the last fork."

Cwealm raised his great head and twisted his ears. The trees muffled sound, but then Radgar heard, too—hooves! On the trail he had just left.

"Don't whinny, big one! Please, *please,* don't whinny!"

Amazingly the big fellow did not whinny. Perhaps the heavy tree smells confused the scent, but whatever the reason, he stood in silence as a horse went by the junction. A fleeting glimpse of the rider was enough to let Radgar recognize Uncle Cynewulf.

His initial anger was followed at once by dismay—there was no great secret after all! Dad would not be amazed and grateful to hear the news that somebody was feeding the outlaws in Weargahlæw if Uncle Cynewulf was the one doing it, because Dad must have ordered him to. As tanist he was Dad's main helper and ran the shire whenever Dad was away *færing* or just being king somewhere else. That might even explain how Cwealm knew the tunnel, although the tanist was notorious for always choosing docile mounts.

So perhaps Dad himself fed the *weargas* sometimes! Obviously there was a secret here that nosy boys were not meant to know. He would be a brat, not a hero. Aylwin would tip the fish out of the creel the moment he got back to Cynehof—unless Uncle Cynewulf caught up with him on the road, in which case it would happen sooner. Either way, the result would be sore-butt time and perhaps even take-Cwealm-away time, which did not bear thinking about; but when a man found himself in this much trouble, he might as well satisfy his curiosity. Radgar turned Cwealm around, kicked in his heels, and said, "Move, monster!"

He had ridden about three bowshots along the other track when Cwealm let out a whinny that could have been heard at the top of Cwicnoll. Radgar had not even started to curse him before the answer came, and round the next great rock he found a treeless hollow wide enough to admit some sunlight. It contained a pile of firewood, a very small stream, and—at the sunny end—a tumbledown thatched shack of poles and wattles that blew war horns in his memory. Yes! He had seen that shack before, when he was very small.

The solitary horse tethered there was Sceatt, Cousin Wulfwer's usual mount. That was *really* annoying. At seventeen, Wulfwer grew pink hairs on his lip and had almost completed his *cniht* training; but he was still only the tanist's son, and if he was trusted to keep a secret then an atheling should be. Radgar slid to the ground and hitched Cwealm alongside Sceatt. They were good friends, which explained the whinny. Their owners were not. Relations between the cousins had never been warm and had recently become extremely strained.

Wondering why no one had appeared to greet him yet,

Radgar headed boldly for the shack to announce himself, then stopped in his tracks as he realized that what was going on in there was very probably *forlegnes.* That was a word he was not supposed to know, the name of a game that grown-ups very much disliked having interrupted. About a month ago Radgar and some friends had caught Wulfwer doing the *forlegnes* thing in the barns and had raised the traditional uproar and pandemonium, inviting everyone to come and watch. Boys being boys and youths being youths, this was not an uncommon source of amusement around the palace; but in that case it had turned out that the woman was another man's thrall, so Wulfwer had not only been exposed to ridicule but also required to pay a sizable compensation.

Worse, having guessed that his young cousin had been the ringleader—always a safe bet—he had waylaid him one evening to administer justice. Radgar, who would hold still for a beating from Dad but no one else, had flown into one of his infamous temper tantrums and managed to kick Wulfwer in the eye before a band of house thegns came to investigate the uproar and pull them apart. For days after that Wulfwer's spectacular shiner had prompted his fellow *cnihtas* to mock him for being beaten up by a child half his size. He was probably still hankering for revenge. Out here in the wilds of Weargahlæw, discretion would be advisable.

As Radgar mulled over his options, he heard a voice. It was not a *forlegnes* sort of sound from the hovel. It was chanting, and it came from somewhere in the woods nearby. Forget about discretion! He went up the bank like a squirrel.

He approached with care, slipping from trunk to trunk until he could peer around one of the closest and see what was going on. The open space where the enchantment was taking place was a flat clearing ringed by trunks like enormous pillars. No sunlight reached the ground, and had he wandered through the dim space by chance he might not have noticed the tiny octogram marked out there by lines of black pebbles half buried in the loam. At the moment it was obvious because a small horn lantern marked fire point, with a pottery jug two to the right of it for water point, and a rock opposite for earth. There was no easy way to designate air or any of the four virtual elements, and Dad had told him that even marking those three was just a convenience for the mortal operators, not something that influenced the spirits.

What was an octogram doing here in the wilds and out of doors? It was minute compared with the one in the Haligdom, where prisoners were enthralled, smaller even than the ones the healers used. There was one person inside it and he was neither chained up nor lying flat like a patient—he could not have stretched out inside the lines of rocks anyway. He was squatting on his heels with his head down and his arms wrapped around his shins as if trying to scrunch himself as tiny as possible. He had no clothes on. From the redness of his hair he was obviously a Bael. A very big one.

Much more surprising was the chanter. First, he was all alone, although conjurations were always performed by eight conjurers, one for each element; and second he was running around the outside of the octogram instead of standing inside it. Third, he was a very scary-looking person indeed, tall and misshapen, although he would not stay still long enough to be studied properly. Nothing of the man himself could be seen inside a long drab robe; he wore a baglike hood of brown cloth over his head. He must have considerable trouble seeing anything at all through the eye holes; and yet there he was, lurching wildly around the clearing, wielding a staff as tall as himself and shrieking out the invocations and revocations in a voice as shrill and discordant as a knife on steel. Back and forth he flapped, sometimes pivoting on his staff from one point to the next adjacent, sometimes lurching halfway around the clearing, all the time calling out to the various elements and raising puffs of dust as the hem of his robe swept the dirt.

Could this be a real conjuration? What good did Cousin Wulfwer think he was doing being shouted at by a maniacal scarecrow here in wild Weargahlæw? Radgar's skin rose in goose bumps. He had watched enthrallments often enough to know that this was a much longer and more complicated conjuration than that, if it was a real conjuration at all. *What was going on?* Wulfwer's father had brought him here and then gone away as if he did not want to watch. Radgar was not alone in not liking Cousin Wulfwer much—nobody did. His mother had been a thrall, and he was surly and sullen, although not as witless as most of the thrall-born. It was common knowledge that he was having trouble finding a *werod* willing to take him, in spite of his royal breeding and his size. Could this ritual be intended to un-thrall him somehow? Make him more talkative and likable? Smarter? Could conjuration give a man a sense of humor? Radgar had never heard of such an enchantment, but neither had he ever heard of one person managing a conjuration all alone.

Perhaps that was dangerous and the spirits might escape? Or was this all just some crazy fake? *Could* one man perform an enchantment? The light dimmed and Radgar prickled all over with shock until he realized that it was just the sun dipping behind the cliffs. He must leave right away if he was to have any chance of reaching home before dark. He didn't.

Sudden silence. The conjurer had stopped his chanting, leaning limply on his staff and gasping for breath. Now his deformity was obvious. He had no right arm and the hang of his robe suggested that he was missing most of the shoulder also, which was why he seemed so lopsided. But he had not finished the ritual. He drew a deep breath and let out a huge, cracked bellow: *"Wulfwer Cynewulfing!"*

Wulfwer moved for the first time, lifting his head. He was blindfolded, yet he turned his head as if looking for something.

"Wulfwer Cynewulfing!" roared the hooded cripple again.

The big *cniht* unwrapped his arms and swayed to his feet. He seemed confused, peering in all directions but making no effort to remove the cloth tied around his head. That rag was the only thing he was wearing, for his boots, clothes, and weapons lay in a heap on the edge of the clearing. Wulfwer's face was much improved by being covered up, but Radgar did envy his muscles. Although he would certainly never admit this to anyone, he secretly hoped that he would have a chest and shoulders like his cousin's when he grew up. And some hair on his chest, too.

Again the conjurer roared out his name; and this time Wulfwer turned to his left and took a step, then stopped, irresolute. If he was drunk, he was very drunk, barely able to stand. Had the enchantment stolen his wits? Again and again the tall conjurer shouted his name as if summoning him from a far distance; but the more he called, the more bewildered Wulfwer seemed to become, reeling around with arms outstretched, ever more frantic, either trying to escape or just hunting for the source of the summons. It was absurd that so huge a man could move so wildly and yet remain within so small a space; at times he even seemed to be running, his long limbs flailing, and yet he went nowhere.

Then he did. He spun around, tripped on the pot that marked the water point of the octogram, and pitched over it, landing flat on his face, right at Radgar's feet. Only then did Radgar realize that he had left his hiding place and walked out to stand in full view of the hooded conjurer.

· 4 ·

For a moment shock kept him rooted to the spot as firmly as the trees—whatever had possessed him? Wulfwer sat up, cursing and reaching for his blindfold.

"No!" the enchanter screeched. "Death and fire! Wind and waters, wait! Look not yet!" He cradled his staff in the crook of his elbow and flapped his solitary hand in a go-away signal. The eye holes of the hood were directed at Radgar. Needing no further invitation, Radgar vanished behind the nearest tree.

Then he peeked.

"All right, you can look," the old man croaked. He came lurching around the octogram; and now his deformities were clearer, for only one horny foot showed under the hem of his robe. On the right side he was balanced on a wooden post and the hang of the cloth showed that he had only a short stump of thigh left. He had been doing all that dancing on a wooden leg!

Wulfwer hauled off the rag. He twisted around to study the octogram, his brutish features screwed up in a scowl. "Water? Water! You can proof against water!" He stood up. He was taller than the tall conjurer and twice as wide.

"Stupid *earming*!" the old man mumbled. "Yes, I can proof against water. Death and maggots, is water the answer? Wind gusts, wave crests, weird will follow. . . . Who is sure?" Even when he was not chanting, his voice was discordant, muffled by the hood. "Water or blood? Or wine, even?"

"That's water!" Wulfwer kicked the empty pot and then cursed because he had no shoe on.

"But you knocked it over, you clumsy goat. Fate, is that significant? Ah, death! From the time it took you to find the way out, Slow Wits, there's no urgency. I'll chant the *hlytm* again next time you come . . . and no great loss if you die before then anyway."

"Do it now!" The big youth's growl usually got him what he wanted around Cynehof, but it did not frighten the old man.

"It's too late, brainless! See not the sun its setting nears?"

"Why does that matter?"

The conjurer lurched at him and screeched right in his ugly face: "It matters if I say it matters!"

Wulfwer recoiled, tripped over the pot again, and went down like a falling cedar, almost causing Radgar to burst out laughing.

The conjurer struck him across the thighs with his staff. "Do as you're told, *niðing,* or I'll leave you to drown. Put your clothes on before the lice starve and get out of here—you stinking *ocusta.*"

"Yes, Healfwer! Sorry, Healfwer!" Wulfwer scrambled up, but his clothes lay at the base of the very tree Radgar was hiding behind, so when he hobbled over to get them he came close enough for Radgar to hear him muttering, "Stupid old goat," and other less polite descriptions. His next move would be to go and collect Sceatt and there he would find Cwealm. Radgar vanished into the forest.

Bats flitting through the trees were shrilling their impossibly high calls as he walked back to the cabin the next time. Bats did not scare him; he just wished he could see as well as they did, because he was having to rely on memory to find the right paths, and the forest was very dark. The walls of the crater cut off the long midsummer twilight; there was no moon. Hidden in the trees, he had watched Wulfwer lead Sceatt and the packhorse into the tunnel. Radgar had unsaddled Cwealm and left him in the little meadow where the packhorse had been. The big chump wouldn't stray from all that juicy grass.

Once Radgar showed up at the palace he would never

be allowed back into Weargahlæw, so he must satisfy his curiosity about it now, and especially find out more about the mysterious conjurer. Anyone who called Wulfwer a stinking armpit and hit him with a stick must be admired for his good judgment. *Healfwer* meant "half man," obviously a name bestowed after he lost his arm and leg. He had sounded old, although he had been nimble enough. Radgar could run very fast when necessary. All the same, there was still enough danger in this *færing* to produce that delicious sick-creepy feeling in his belly again. While Dad probably did know whatever it was that Uncle Cynewulf and *ocusta* Wulfwer were up to with the conjurer, he might not; and in that case Atheling Radgar would be back in hero territory. It was good he had sent Aylwin home to say where he was. If he didn't show up by morning, reinforcements would arrive.

He had never stayed out all night before. Mother would scream two octaves higher than a skylark. If he wasn't in hero country, if he was just a wayward brat snooping where he had been forbidden to go, then the reckoning was going to be terrible—good-bye to Cwealm, hello to mucking out stables with the thralls for months and months and months, and sore butt on an epic scale the scops would sing about for centuries. He'd be better off plugging up the tunnel with rocks and living like another hermit here in the valley.

The forest was so still that he heard thumps before he even saw the lights. The cabin's doors and shutters fit so badly, and there were so many chinks in the walls, that it glowed like a starry sky. Smoke was pouring out of it just about everywhere except the proper smoke hole. Someone had cut the old man's firewood for him, because obviously one hand couldn't manage that great ax stuck in the chopping block; but the periodic bangs coming from inside proved that the old man was hitting something. Radgar tapped on the door.

Then he heard nothing except the fire crackling.

After a few spooky-long minutes, he tapped again. Now the harsh voice cried out, "Who wakens the dead? Here are rotting bones and ancient hatred. Flee while you still can!"

Radgar pushed the door open, squeaking on its leather hinges. Smoke gushed out white in the darkness, making his eyes sting, so he dropped and crawled in on hands and knees, knowing the air would be clearer down near the dirt floor. The hearth was just a central circle of stones. The scarecrow conjurer sat on the ground with his back to the entrance, his real leg outstretched beside the wooden one, but the bag over his head was caught up at one side, revealing wisps of white beard, as if it had been pulled on in haste. A small hatchet and heap of kindling near his hand explained the earlier banging.

"Begone!" the old man croaked, "lest my curses rot the flesh from your bones."

Radgar kicked the door shut and moved some baskets and a bucket so he could move closer to the fire and sit down, legs crossed. "I need to know when I'm going to kill Wulfwer." He also needed something tasty to eat, of course, and a comfortable place to sleep. The blackened crock steaming and bubbling in the embers emitted fine savory scents, but comfort was in short supply. Even a thralls' barn had more of it—no chairs or stools or tables, and the bedding just a layer of branches with some mangy old furs on top. The rest of the furnishings were crude clay pots, a couple of oaken chests, no shelves on the walls, although there *was* a sword hanging up opposite the door—and a pretty fancy one too, as far as he could tell through the smoke. Some scrolls and books shared the top of one of the chests with an inkwell and a heap of goose quills . . . how did the cripple sharpen a quill one-handed? The conjurer must live entirely at ground level, like an animal. Certainly with only one arm and one leg, he would have trouble standing up and sitting down. Now he had turned his head to look at his visitor, but only darkness showed inside the eye holes of his hood. At least there were two eye holes, not only one, as there would be if the half man had only half a face. *Shiver!*

"Spawn of slime, who sent you to torment a dead man in his infliction?"

"No one sent me, *ealdor.* Your *hlytm* summoned me, didn't it?"

"Torment, torment! Who told you of the *hlytm,* Atheling?"

Aha! Suspicions confirmed! If the conjurer knew who he was then Radgar must have been here before. "No one told me, *ealdor.* It was obvious."

"Don't give me titles. I am a dead man, but if you must speak to my corpse call it Healfwer." The conjurer's voice sank to a disgusting phlegmy rattle. "Women wile with whitened arms . . . What was obvious?"

Uncertain which women had entered the conversation, Radgar decided to ignore them. "From what you were doing, what you said. A *hlytm* is a casting of lots, yes? You were casting lots among the elements to see which one will kill Wulfwer. When you had summoned them you stood at death point and called him, and in the end he went to water point so—you told him he would drown, but really he knocked over the water pot, didn't he, so it didn't count, and he was coming to me! He came to *me* and fell down before *me.* I am Wulfwer's bane, his weird!" Not many ten-year-olds could have worked that out, but an atheling had to be more clever than others.

"Does that make you happy, pig-toad?"

"You shouldn't speak to me like that."

"I'll speak to you how I want. Answer me before I make you scream with agony. Their white arms . . ."

"And don't threaten me, either. I'm the King's son."

The old man raised a gnarled hand to his hood. "Answer my questions, Æleding, or I will show you my face and then you will never sleep again."

That was a new threat to Radgar, one that would need some thought. "No, I don't really want to kill Wulfwer, but I will if I have to. We're going to be rivals to succeed Dad when he gets old. I'd rather kill him than let him kill me. If he stays out of my road I won't hurt him."

The horrible old man shrieked with mirth. "Earth and water! He could crush you with one hand, little grub. Fire and fish so fair the song . . . Everything smells of music now. Why came you here?"

"Because I'm only ten years old." That piece of impudence had worked on Dad once—only once and the second time had turned out to be unwise, but Healfwer had not heard it before.

The old man growled in exasperation. "You may never see another winter. You expect to eat my supper and sleep by my hearth?"

"Oh, thank you, *ealdor*!—I mean Healfwer. A share of your food and a place by the fire would be very kind of you."

"Explain, worm! Weird and woe the *wylfen* brings."

"It was too dark to go after Wulfwer left and if I'd gone ahead of him he'd have seen me."

"I mean why did you come at all?"

"Your conjuration summoned me, didn't it?"

"You just want me to agree so Æled won't whip the skin off your ass, boy."

"Partly," Radgar admitted. It would be a very good defense: "The *hlytm* made me do it."

"How could it have summoned you when you came before I started it? When you didn't know about it? What really made you come?"

Radgar shrugged. The smell from the pot was making him drool so much he was drowning. There was meat in there, which Wulfwer must have brought, for how could a one-armed man catch game or even skin it?

"I went *færing* on my stallion, Cwealm, taking only my trusty follower Aylwin Leofricing. I decided to explore Weargahlæw and saw that someone was feeding the *wear-gas*. That is an *unfrið*, so I sent Leofricing back to tell the marshal to send some house thegns. And I came on ahead myself to investigate."

The enchanter made a strange choking sound that became a racking cough. He threw more sticks on the fire. "Filth and death! Has not your father a hundred times forbidden you to come here?"

"Not that often. And the tanist brought Wulfwer—will you chant the *hlytm* for me, too? I want to know my weird."

"Weird?" the old man screeched. "Your weird is to

die as I did! Die now, brat, and save yourself suffering!" He snatched up a log and hurled it at Radgar.

It struck him on the forehead. Fortunately it was a very small log, already split for kindling, but the impact and shock were enough to knock him over. He fell on his back, crying out at the pain.

"You almost hit my eye!" He clapped a hand over the injury and felt blood running.

"More than that will I hit!" Healfwer shouted. One-handed he grabbed up his staff and struck as if swatting a fly. Fortunately the fire between them made that a difficult shot; and Radgar saw the pole descending in time to roll clear. The end struck a heavy stone crock and shattered it. His head would have been smashed like an egg.

"You're crazy!" He jumped to his feet. "I'm the King's son!"

"You're *dead*! Dead like me!" The old man tried another swipe with the pole, but Radgar could dodge now. "Die, curse you!" Releasing his staff, the conjurer hurled another log, then a third, each larger than the last. By the time he reached for the hatchet, Radgar was opening the door. As he leaped out, the hatchet passed through the space he had filled a moment earlier and slammed into the wall—and stuck there.

He was out in the night and running.

He crossed the clearing in a dozen strides and stopped in case he ran into something. Far behind him the door slammed, cutting off the glimmer of the fire and leaving him in total darkness. Cold and shock together made his teeth chatter, and he hugged himself tightly as he waited for his eyes to adjust. The horrible old man really was crazy! Those had been real attempts at murder. A man had tried to kill him! He shivered at the memory of that hatchet sticking in the wall.

It seemed Weargahlæw had been put off-limits for good reasons; his *færing* had not been brave or clever, only very foolish. His head throbbed. The cold began to bite, making him shake more violently. A man could freeze in the nights up here, and he wasn't properly dressed. He could light a fire with the tinderbox at the entrance tunnel if he could get there—and if Healfwer had not gathered up all the loose deadfall in the forest. Getting there would be the problem. There might be other lunatics wandering the valley. Or animals. Wild boars, bears . . . Dad could never wipe out wolves because they swam from one island to another.

He soon realized he wasn't going anywhere; he couldn't. Filmy clouds obscured all but the brightest stars, so even within the clearing he could barely see his hand in front of his nose. The track through the trees was as dark as any cave, quite impossible to walk. He was stuck here until dawn. His head still hurt and seemed to be still bleeding, because it felt wet when he touched it . . . but it was an honorable wound, an honest attempt to kill him. It might leave a good scar and then people would ask him where he got it. His teeth chattered. He was freezing! He jumped up and began walking back and forward across the clearing, from almost the door of the shed to the point where overhanging branches hid the sky at the other side. He cursed Healfwer under his breath.

Why did the madman have to go and react like that? Just because Radgar had asked to learn his weird? Wulfwer had been told his. No, Wulfwer thought he had, but the answer had not been clear. When Healfwer had called him to death point, Wulfwer's weird had drawn him to water point instead—or else to Radgar. Obviously Radgar could not be anyone's bane if he was destined to freeze to death here in the woods before morning. What sort of answer would the *hlytm* give a man if his weird was to be frozen to death? This was something to think about while he did just that. Cold was not one of the eight elements, although it felt like the only thing in the world that mattered at the moment. The opposite of fire in the octogram was earth. So if Healfwer had chanted the *hlytm* for Radgar before Radgar froze to death, would Radgar have been summoned to earth point? Who would guess that earth point meant freezing? If the *hlytm* had told him earth was his bane, he'd have thought that meant a sword or a house falling on him in a quake. Except people buried by earthquakes often died of lack of air and the opposite of air was water. Could air be a man's bane? If he was hanged, maybe, so he had too much air underneath him.

It was all stupid! There were too many ways to die and not enough elements.

Spirits, it was cold!

The manifest elements were bad enough—so he decided as he stalked to and fro, slapping his back to keep warm—but the virtual elements might be worse. Suppose a man went to time point? How could you die of time? Hmm—you could die of old age, too much time. And chance would mean an accident. So maybe the virtual elements actually made more sense as predictors than the manifest elements did. . . . How about death point itself? If Wulfwer had gone straight to death point when Healfwer called him? Suicide, maybe? Yes, that could mean suicide, or death very soon. Love? A weird of love would have to mean treachery. If you were doomed to die at the hand of a loved one or someone you trusted, then love was your bane. So the virtual elements actually did make more sense than the manifest ones! Hanging, fever, drowning, falling—almost any sort of death he could think of could be reduced to an excess of a single element! Except freezing. He cursed Healfwer under his breath again.

How long until his fingers started dropping off from frostbite?

And while he froze to death that madman was sitting there in his hovel all cozy by his fire, and now doubtless eating that juicy-smelling meat stew. Next time Radgar's progress brought him near the wall of the shack, he crept closer and peered in one of the crevices where the smoke was coming out. Yes, there he was. Healfwer had taken the crock from the fire and was vigorously shoveling stuff into his mouth from it with a big horn spoon. He had removed his hood, of course. At first all Radgar could see was the back of his head, but that was quite enough. On the left side wisps of silver hair hung from ordinary pink scalp, but on the right the skin was all white scar tissue with no hair at all, as if he had been flayed or terribly burned, and the line dividing the two was straight as an arrow, right down the middle. His right ear, even, had gone. When he turned slightly to toss another log on the fire, Radgar caught sight of a long silver beard on the left of his face.

The spy must have made a noise then, for the monster twisted around to stare at the wall right where he was. Despite the two eye holes cut in the hood he'd worn earlier, he did have only one eye. One side of his face was that of a haggard old man; the other was white ruin, like cheese. Even his mouth was half gone.

Radgar recoiled from the horrible sight, remembering the conjurer's threat that he would never sleep again. Well, he wouldn't if he froze to death! He crawled away and resumed his pacing, although his legs shook with weariness. Short as summer nights were, dawn must be hours away yet. No matter that he had seen the madman's mutilated face, he would fall asleep on his feet and freeze. There were hot springs in Weargahlæw—he had seen the steam from them and smelled the sulfur—and even an eelbrain like Healfwer would surely have chosen a site near a hot spring for his home. The first problem would be to locate it in the dark, the second would be finding a safe shallow place to lie in so that he wouldn't drown if he fell asleep. Some hot springs were mere seepages in the beds of streams, but others were shafts going down to the bottom of the world. Wading into one of those in the dark would not be a pleasant fate. Sadly he discarded the idea of soaking himself in hot water all night.

He lost count of time. It seemed half his life had been spent walking in that clearing, blowing on his hands, sometimes running on the spot. Ears, fingers, even toes ached. The cold would not give up—and it must win in the end, because his strength would not last until morning. What a stupid, stupid way to die! He was not used to thinking of himself as stupid.

Eventually he noticed that the lights twinkling from the chinks in the conjurer's hovel were growing fainter. If Healfwer was letting the fire burn down, that meant he had gone to bed, or was about to. Why should that evil old cripple be allowed to sleep in peace when he had refused succor to a worthy traveler? All peoples everywhere respected the laws of hospitality, even savages in far-off Afernt—so Dad had told him. He hurried to the woodpile and selected a stout branch, seasoned but not brittle. Back to his spy hole again . . . Although the interior was darker now, the conjurer was visible as a shapeless heap in the area of the bedding.

Radgar crept around to that side. He swung the branch as hard as he could. *Bang!* Had the cabin been built of heavy logs, the impact would have been barely audible, but it was only a ramshackle construction of withes and plaster. The wall shook. He heard a few fragments fall and could guess that more had showered down on the inside. Again—*Bang! Bang!*

"Healfwer!" he yelled. "Wake up!" When he heard shouts of anger in reply, he stopped banging and took another peek. The cripple was sitting up, faint light from the embers of the fire glinting on the leprous-white side of his head.

"You're not going to sleep tonight!" *Bang! Bang!* "Dance, cripple! Chant your spells!" *Bang! Bang!* The wall was losing the fight, flaking off in chunks. At this rate he could wreck half the cabin before morning. He paused to listen to the screams of rage.

"Worms and waste your weird shall be! Boy, I will kill you!"

"No you won't!" *Bang! Bang!* "You had your chance earlier and failed." *Bang! Bang! Bang! Bang!*

He stopped then, partly to catch his breath—for he had been putting all his strength into the exercise—and partly to sneak a look at his victim. As might have been predicted, Healfwer seemed to be strapping on his wooden leg. He had poked up the fire and added sticks to it. Radgar set to work again, battering at one of the shutters. Just as it collapsed into ruin, he heard the squeak of the door.

By the time the enchanter came lurching around the cabin, cursing and raving, his tormentor had disappeared. When the old man completed the circuit and reached his door again—and was silhouetted against the fire—a jagged lump of black rock streaked out of the darkness and struck the back of his head. Another bounced off the cabin as he stumbled inside. A third hit his back before he could slam the door.

Now both sides had drawn blood and the score was even. Radgar, having been raised on battle songs and the bragging of drunken thegns, had an innate grasp of tactics in such a situation and knew the value of pressing an advantage. Screeching every threat and rude word he could think of, he resumed his attack on the shack, smashing away chunks. This time the old man tried fighting back. Firelight was streaming from so many holes in his walls now that he could see Radgar almost as well as Radgar could see him. Wielding his staff like a spear, he lunged through one of the gaps at the boy outside, but with only one hand he lacked control. Radgar saw the move coming. Healfwer screamed as his precious staff was snatched away and vanished out into the woods. Caught off balance, he fell heavily, narrowly missing the fireplace. Moments later, a renewed attack on his walls showered him with plaster.

"Stop! Stop! What do you want!"

"A blanket! Two blankets!" Radgar considered asking for a pot of stew and decided not to push his luck. If he miscalculated now and let the old man get within grabbing range of him, his weird would be settled very swiftly.

"Then you'll give me back my staff? I can't live without my staff!"

"Yes, I'll give it back. Hurry!"

"I need it to get the blankets."

"You think any son of Æled Fyrlafing would be that stupid? Push them out through the wall here."

Mumbling furiously, the old man did as he was told—he was only crazy when it suited him to be! Radgar dragged the blankets out through the wall and gloatingly wrapped himself up. They smelled terrible but they were warm on his skin.

"You can have your staff back in the morning!" He marched away from the conjurer's wails and howls, crossing the clearing to the place he thought the path should start. He found it by waving the long pole to and fro, then managed to go along it a little way without walking into any trees. When he could no longer see firelight, he lay down and rolled up in a cocoon. He fell into sleep almost immediately, gloating over the fact that Radgar Æleding, the future great warrior-king of Baelmark, had just won his first real fight.

· 5 ·

Morning was bad. He awoke at first light feeling cold, stiff, hungry, thirsty, sore everywhere, and dizzy from lack of sleep. The wound on his head was swollen like an egg and throbbed worse than anything. Scops never sang about heroes feeling sorry for themselves on the day after the battle.

Having given the matter thought, he did take Healfwer's staff back to the cabin—a thegn could be magnanimous to a beaten foe. He lost his way in the forest because the sky wasn't light enough yet to tell him which way was east, and when he finally did reach the little meadow, Cwealm perversely refused to be caught. Either he liked having a valley all to himself or he didn't trust the pale bloodstained waif in the smelly blankets. Radgar chased him and chased him, pleading, threatening, and finally almost weeping; and Cwealm merely swished his tail and kept his distance. Just about the time Radgar was ready to give up—but fortunately hadn't quite done so—he saw a horse and rider coming down the path from the tunnel. It was Dad, riding Wiga.

The sun rose over the crater walls and the world brightened.

* * *

Dad jumped down from the saddle and gave him a hug to break his bones, then a kiss, and finally held him at arm's length to look him over. He shook his head and said, "Oh, if your mother could see you now!" in a man-to-man sort of way.

Radgar, shamefully, started to cry.

Fortunately Dad did not seem to notice. He swung up into Wiga's saddle and hoisted his wayward son up behind him. "Hot bath and breakfast?" he said, kicking in his heels. "Fresh clothes? And a long talk?"

Radgar blew his nose, wiped his fingers on one of Healfwer's blankets, and said, "Yes, sire." Whatever punishment was in store for him, he would feel more able to bear it when he had some breakfast inside him.

"Strip and jump in," Dad said. "I think this is my favorite hot spring anywhere. Very hot this end, very cold over there. About there's usually just right."

The pool was small and shallow, steaming quietly in the middle of a rather swampy clearing. The little surface stream that varied its temperature had also given it a sandy bottom to lie on, which was unusual. Radgar obeyed orders eagerly, submerging until only his face showed, feeling all his joints melt in bliss. He resumed his story, telling about his fight with Healfwer.

While listening and sometimes shooting questions, Dad tethered Wiga to a stout bush, removed the bit so he could graze, loosened the girth, and then began unpacking the saddlebags. He seemed to have thought of everything: towels, fresh clothes for Radgar, and especially food—cheese and bread and hard-boiled eggs and some meaty ribs, all of which he laid out on a handy tussock. Then he laid his sword there also, pulled off his clothes, and came to lie in the pool alongside his son.

He made no comment about Radgar's folly, or at least not yet. He certainly wouldn't wait long. Justice should be quick, he always said, or it wasn't just. He chose a beef rib and pointed it at the sky as he chewed his first bite.

"See that eagle? There's always an eagle over Weargahlæw, sometimes two."

"Cwealm knew the way here."

"We keep the inmates fed," the King explained with his mouth full. "Usually a house thegn brings the rations, but I may come if I have business, or your uncle, and now Wulfwer. Weargahlæw isn't secret, but it isn't widely talked about, either. Grown-ups know better than to come here. Small boys must not, but few of them have horses capable of the ride."

Oops! Radgar thought he knew one who wasn't going to have such a horse much longer and wasn't going to want to sit on one for quite a while either. "There's more people live here?" He eyed the sword, left within reach.

"It varies. Only six at the moment. Some are witan who just want to be alone to study. They're hermits by choice and can leave if they want to. Others are *weargas,* banished by royal command—dangerous, crazy people, or thieves and murderers I chose to exile instead of enthrall, for one reason or another. They must stay here or pay the other penalty. There have been people so ugly that other people cannot tolerate them, and some with strange diseases the healers can't conjure. Other earls have their own places of exile, prison islands."

Radgar swallowed the remains of his fourth egg and reached for bread and cheese, trying not to get them wet. Eating in a hot pool was trickier than he'd expected. He knew of nothing in the world more fun than going a-*færing* with Dad, who always seemed to have new places to show him and new things to do, and he would be enjoying every second of this bizarre picnic enormously if he didn't have his unknown punishment hanging over him. *Good-bye, Cwealm!*

"Healfwer isn't the worst," Dad said. "He's only crazy some of the time, and he never threatens a strong man like Wulfwer. Children or vulnerable people seem to enrage him, and yet I know he's truly sorry afterward. He's the most brilliantly clever enchanter anywhere. No one else can conjure elementals the way he does, all by himself. If I need something special in the way of enchantment, he can almost always manage it for me. He can't help being crazy—wouldn't you be if you were crippled the way he is? He must have a lot of pain, too."

"What happened to him? Who was he before he became Half Man?"

Dad chewed for a moment, and the copper stubble on his jaw glinted in the sunlight. "That's his business and one day perhaps you can ask him. You're not going to talk about Healfwer or Weargahlæw at all, understand? To no one."

"Yes, my lord. I promise!"

"On our best behavior suddenly, are we?" Dad chuckled and cracked an egg on his elbow. "Your job, Son, is the same as any other boy's of your age, and that is to make as many mistakes as possible while you're young enough to be either forgiven or walloped. You're ten, and that's the age the law starts treating you as an adult, so you're almost out of time. Soon you will be judged wicked instead of ignorant. What have you learned recently?"

Here it came. "I knew Weargahlæw was out of bounds, so I was disobeying when I came here."

There was a pause, then Dad said, "That's all?"

"Well, the *hlytm* that Healfwer—"

"We'll get to that. About Weargahlæw itself."

Radgar thought. "I broke the rules."

"Nothing wrong with breaking rules, provided you know why the rule is there and what will happen if you do break it. I've broken lots of rules in my time. Rules are usually made to protect either you or other people, and the king's law is there to punish people who hurt other people by breaking rules. But if a rule is unfair or wicked, then it is your *duty* to break it! I'm really proud of the way you broke this rule, riding in through the tunnel, then sending Aylwin back and staying yourself when you thought there was something wrong."

Radgar released a long sigh of wonder. "You are? *Proud?*"

"I'm proud of your courage. Your stupidity is another matter altogether."

"Oh."

"You didn't know why the rule was there, but you broke it anyway. I've always told you to remember the she-wolf, but you didn't even look for the wolf. That was stupid! Staying inside the crater was stupid—you could have waited outside to see who left with the packhorse. What else have you learned, if anything?"

Radgar decided he was full and didn't want to eat any more. "The *hlytm*? Healfwer was trying to find out what Wulfwer's weird is."

Dad sighed. "Yes. What about it?"

"It doesn't give clear answers."

"Sometimes it does. Did you notice what point Wulfwer went to?"

"Water."

"That's not a bad one. Some elements can mean so many things that the *hlytm* is no real use. It doesn't help much to be told that chance is your weird, for instance. And it only works once. If Wulfwer's weird is water, then Healfwer can ward him against water. Then he probably won't drown after all, but he's going to die someday anyway, just as we all are. He'll meet another bane and the *hlytm* can't warn him against that one. It won't work once he's warded. You can't be warded against a second element, either."

Then Radgar had to explain how he had walked out in the open and Wulfwer had maybe come to him, not the water. Dad did not look pleased.

"Wulfwer doesn't know that?"

"No, lord. Healfwer signed me to go away before he let him take off his blindfold. And I don't see how the *hlytm* could have summoned me up to Weargahlæw because they hadn't even started it when I came in through the tunnel."

"It's time to go. Wash that blood off your face." Dad stood up and waded over to the towels. "I can't see it either, but conjury is very strange at times. If I were Wulfwer I might make sure of things by running a sword into you. So the rule about not telling anyone about Weargahlæw applies doubly to the *hlytm,* understand? *Please* don't mention it to your mother!"

"Yes, lord." Radgar began drying himself. He was limp as string after the long soak. He wanted to sleep for a month. "Healfwer said he'd chant the *hlytm* for Wulfwer again some other day."

"Good. I may keep you tied to your bed until he does." Dad smiled to show he didn't mean that. But what else did he have in mind, apart from taking away Cwealm?

"Do you suppose he'd chant it for me? After what I did to his house? Has he ever done it for you—chanted the *hlytm*?"

"If you caused him half as much trouble as you've admitted, young man, I won't let you near the old horror until you've grown twice as big as Wulfwer. The *hlytm* may not work for you anyway, because stupidity is not an element, although it ought to be. There's more pure stupidity in the world than almost anything else." Dad's grin disappeared as he pulled his smock over his head. He emerged frowning. "I expect one day he'll chant it for you, if I ask him to. And, yes, I know my weird, and, no, I won't tell you what it is. I don't tell anyone that. Gather up that food and I'll take it to Healfwer as a peace offering."

Radgar was dressed now. He was fed and warm—and very sleepy. Why was Dad making him wait for the bad news?

"Bring that," Dad said, taking the other bag and heading for Wiga. "I'll take you to Cwealm and see you mounted and into the tunnel. I want you to go straight to the elementary and ask Conjurer Plegmund to heal that cut on your face before your mother sees it. I'll have the money sent to him."

"And you?"

For a moment Dad didn't answer, being busy tightening the girths. Then he said, "How badly did you damage Healfwer's cabin?"

Radgar hung his head. "Dad, I really smashed it up. It'll have to be rebuilt, I think, but it was the only thing I could think of to—"

"Good!" said the King. "I've been trying to get him to move to a better place for years, the stubborn old loon;

and now he'll have to, so that's what I'll do now. There are some fine, solid log cabins nobody's living in. Tell Leofric and your mother that I won't be back until tomorrow." He swung up into the saddle and held out a hand. "Up?"

"Tell me!" Radgar yelled. "Please, please, don't keep me waiting any longer!"

Dad stared down at him in surprise. "Waiting for what?"

"What are you going to do to me? I don't mind sore butt, as many whacks as you want, and I'll muck out stables or cut corn with the thralls or do anything, anything at all, but please, please, please don't take Cwealm away!"

"Oh!" Dad pursed his lips and studied the cliffs for a moment. "Well, Son, you were very foolish, weren't you?"

"Yes, lord. I'm sorry, really I am."

"I'm sure you are. I've warned you never to catch more than you hunt, yes? You went hunting a little mischief and you almost froze to death, you almost got murdered. You had to go a whole day without eating, and you were more frightened than you've ever been. Yes?"

"Yes, lord."

Dad grinned. "So you punished yourself. See, grown-ups don't have dads to paddle their butts, but they do have to pay the penalty, whatever it is. I can't do anything to you worse than what you did to yourself and I should never want to. Cwealm's yours, Son. I won't take him away."

It was absolutely shameful, but as Dad pulled him up on to Wiga's back, Radgar began to cry again.

6

Little more was said, except by Aylwin. He had not been punished for the Weargahlæw escapade either—much to his surprise—but he did want to know what had happened. When Radgar wouldn't tell him, there was a certain amount of shouting, shoving, and punching. The coolness passed in a few days, as it always did, and the friends found new trouble to fall into together.

It was more than a week later that Dad inquired whether Radgar would like to go surf fishing, just the two of them—a very foolish question for a king to ask. So they sailed over to Blodenclif, and while they were standing on the rocks with their lines out and the waves foaming all around making so much noise that it was almost impossible to hear, Dad suddenly shouted over to Radgar—

"Healfwer chanted the *hlytm* for Wulfwer again."

Radgar had something on his line just then, probably a fat bass, so he wasn't much interested in the affairs of his ugly cousin. "And what?"

"And water was his bane again. So you were just an accident."

"Good," Radgar said and concentrated on the more important matter of landing that bass.

The matter came up again very briefly when they were sailing home that evening. Radgar had the tiller and the setting sun was painting scarlet ladders on the ripples of Swiþæfen. He had caught more fish than the King of Baelmark and the world was as perfect as could be.

"I was thinking," the hero remarked, "about the *hlytm*.

I think the worst weird of all would be love! That would be terrible—to know that you were going to be killed by someone you loved!"

After a moment Dad said, "I'm sure you're right, Son."

· 7 ·

When Radgar was eleven, the Chivian King Taisson died and Crown Prince Ambrose succeeded. This seemed like a good opportunity to end a war that had dragged on far too long, but Grandon sent no overtures for peace to Waroðburh. Next spring, therefore, King Æled launched the heaviest offensive of the war, harrying the Chivian coasts and strangling its trade. Month after month the booty and good news flooded back to Baelmark, but casualty lists came, too. Wives need husbands and children fathers. A land frets when all its young men are absent for prolonged periods, and by fall the mood of the country was growing sour.

It was then that Atheling Radgar went on a royal procession, accompanied by Aylwin and a few other twelve-year-old boys and girls, all dressed in court finery of purple and ermine. Their armed escort was made up of *cnihtas* only a couple of years older. They visited eleven shires, not counting Catterstow, and in every capital were made welcome by the Earl or his tanist. The celebrations included a feast, of course, and other sorts of pomp, such as singing, horse races, and martial competitions between the visiting *cnihtas* and the locals.

This zany performance was the brainchild of Queen Charlotte, organized by her and the earls' wives. When the idea was first proposed, Regent Cynewulf turned it down flat, but he had never been noted for his sense of humor. Æled, appealed to in a letter, wrote back overruling his tanist, and as usual his judgment was sound. The sight of children traveling the land unmolested was a fine contrast to the news from war-savaged Chivial; the mockery of the ways of royalty exactly fitted the spirit of the time. The nation laughed uproariously.

"That atheling looks just like his father," everyone said admiringly. "Never know what he's going to get up to next, either."

The jester king and his train sailed home to Catterstow from Twigeport on the thirtieth day of Ninthmoon, arriving in a chill, misty drizzle. Had theirs been a genuine royal progress, it would have ended with a parade and a welcome-home feast in Cynehof, but Uncle Cynewulf had refused to play along. The juvenile courtiers muttered about the regent's sourpuss attitude, but in fact they had tired of the game and were not sorry that the joke was over. Being polite and gracious for almost a month had proved to be unbearably wearing. And when Waroðburh came in sight, they saw the beach covered with longships and more than half the population teeming around them. The campaigning season was over also. Joyful turmoil acclaimed the return of the fyrd, and there would be feasting after all.

Radgar was the first to leap ashore. A shouted question told him that Dad was safe. He ran all the way to the palace, which was in an even greater state of uproar, but the only welcome he received was a thorough licking from Brindle. He had to ask several people before he learned that Dad had ridden off to Hatburna, his favorite home. That was very strange, because he must have huge amounts of business to see to. Normally when he returned from a *færing* he would just send word and Mom would come hurrying back to the capital to greet him. It was only when Radgar asked more questions that someone mentioned the firedrake in Wambseoc. He yelled for Cwealm to be saddled up, ordered Brindle to stay behind, and took off for Hatburna as fast as he dared push his horse.

* * *

He was as well mounted as any man in the kingdom and weighed less. The rain had softened the track, but sure-footed Cwealm made record time and would certainly have caught up with the royal party had the road been just a little longer. As it was, the horses were still being walked when he thundered and splashed into the stable yard. Radgar leaped from the saddle, thrust the reins into the hands of a ceorl, and ran into the main house without even taking off his mud-caked boots, an omission that Queen Charlotte regarded as a capital offense in athelings.

Hatburna was a rambling, ramshackle old place, much extended by successive generations of Catterings but still far too small to house a ruling monarch. A king could go nowhere without a train of thegns, house thegns, ministers, clerks, and miscellaneous courtiers trailing at his heels. Æled usually made things worse by inviting friends to stay also. When he was there, the walls bulged, and massed snoring scared away all the wildlife in the south half of the island—so he claimed, and everyone laughed when a king made a joke. He refused to have the place rebuilt or repaired, not even to close up the chinks in the notoriously unprivate walls. If he made it more comfortable, he said, then more people would find excuses to come.

The herd of courtiers and officials was busily settling in, but from the racket they were making—demanding attention and ordering servants around—Radgar knew at once that Dad was not there. Again, he had to ask several people, but eventually he learned that His Majesty had gone in search of the Queen, who was thought to be at the private cabin. He sprinted out the door in a spray of mud and headed up the hill. The trail was not long, but it climbed steeply through a forest of oaks, maples, and sycamores, a canopy of leaves shining gold, bronze, and copper in the rain. He arrived panting.

The little cabin by the waterfall was the center of his world, the place he kept his heart. It had never been formally given to him, but his possessions had taken over the main room completely and he slept in the big bed in the loft. When Dad was away Mom always stayed in the main house, and last winter Dad had done so, too. Radgar assumed that they were less concerned about privacy now that they had grown too old to do the *forlegnes* thing—Mom had turned thirty now and Dad was even older. And whatever they did or said, he would hear them here just as well as neighbors in the main house would.

He exploded in through the door, bringing a blast of fine rain with him. Dad was sitting on the couch, leaning back with his legs outstretched, all spattered with mud and looking as weary as a man who had just spent three hours in the saddle, which he had. Mom was standing by the fireplace, wringing her hands.

Radgar yelled, "Dad!" and launched himself at his father, who yelled in alarm, but caught him expertly and rolled him into a hug. "Dad, Dad, you're not going to go and fight the firedrake, are you?"

Queen Charlotte took three strides to reach the open door and slammed it with an impact like thunder. "Radgar! Just *look* at this!"

Her tone caused her menfolk to break out of their clinch and sit up in alarm. "What, Mom?"

"This *pigsty*!"

Bewildered, he peered around. It was true that the hearth was full of cold cinders and everything else had a visible coating of gray dust. The bedclothes on the couch had perhaps been there too long, but he had changed the sheets upstairs only a few months ago. Dad had always forbidden anyone else to come to the cabin, even the house thralls. She didn't expect an atheling to do *housework*, did she?

If she didn't mean that, then perhaps she meant untidiness? Admittedly there was rather a lot of *stuff* about, more than the table and stools could hold. More than the floor could, either. A lot of it actually belonged to Aylwin and other friends and he should tell them to take it away, but everything there that belonged to him was important: his fishing spears, various rods, tackle, waders, creel, and nets; his horse gear, blankets and saddles, riding boots; two archery targets, three—no four—bows, a lot of arrows and the makings of many more, because he had taken up fletching last winter—staves, goose feathers, glue, straighteners. . . . There were also his practice spears, swords, shields, helmets—just the toy stuff that boys were allowed to play with before they became *cnihtas,* but quite a good collection. . . . Other boy things: balls, wooden puzzles, skittles, climbing boots, his bird nets and throwing sticks, animal traps, two sets of antlers, a couple of hunting knives, a very smelly bearskin that had not been properly tanned. . . . That could go, but he must keep his collections of shells and birds' eggs, and the model longship that he had never finished. . . . Too many books. A thegn didn't need all those books. A thegn didn't need a box of paints and a lot of brushes, either, but it was Mom who'd encouraged him in that, and Dad thought that some of the thirty or so sketches piled up over there in the corner were quite good; she was more doubtful. Yes, those could be thrown out, but not the skis, skates, paddles, or oars! He wasn't very good on the lute yet, but he really was going to practice more this winter and he could certainly throw out a lot of those clothes and shoes he had grown out of. Most of that rope was good enough to be useful someday. Brindle's basket could go because he always climbed into bed with Radgar anyway and just used it to store chewed bones.

"Well?" demanded the Queen. "What have you to say?"

Why on earth was she talking about this when Fyrndagum had erupted and there was a firedrake loose on Wambscoc? "I need a bigger room," he said. "Dad, you're not going—"

But the look in his father's eyes was answer enough.

"No, he is not!" the Queen said. "If Ufegeat has a problem, let Ufegeat handle it himself."

"He can't," Dad said softly, rising. "He has no conjurer capable. A firedrake is the king's problem, always. I must deal with it because I am *Hlaford Fyrlandum.*"

"And leave me a widow?" Mom screamed. "Radgar an orphan? You know the odds when heroes go against firedrakes. You imagine a boy of Catter's line can survive in this awful country without a father to defend him? You think that fat brother of yours can hold the throne when you die? Someone else will kill him and take it, and whoever it is won't leave any young Catterings around to be a threat."

Radgar stood up also. He was shaking, but that was all right after such a long ride. Men could shake when they were very tired. It wasn't fair, though! Other boys had gotten their fathers back today, but his had to go away again, and into worse danger than ever.

Dad looked at him wistfully, as if measuring him against future manhood. "We Baels don't make war on children."

"Yes, you do!" she yelled.

"Well, not our own children. Not usually. I survived."

"You had an older brother!"

Dad shrugged. "Yes I did, and maybe now you understand my loyalty to him."

"You're exhausted," she said. "I haven't seen you in months. That volcano's been erupting for weeks. Surely you don't have to rush away and—"

"Yes, I do, Charlotte. Eruptions don't matter. Eruptions happen all the time. This is a *firedrake* we're talking about. It's a monster. It's evil. It will ravage all of Wambseoc. Every hour counts, every minute." He flashed Radgar a half smile and then held out his hands to his wife. "Listen, both of you. I haven't told you this before. Years ago Healfwer chanted the *hlytm* for me, *and my weird is not fire*! The firedrake can't kill me, understand?"

But it might mutilate him horribly, Radgar thought. Firedrakes had killed his father, Fyrlaf, and his grandfather Cuðblæse. Why wasn't Mom going to him?

"I am *Hlaford Fyrlandum,*" Dad repeated. "Earl Ufegeat has appealed to me for help against the firedrake and I cannot refuse. Radgar, I am going to Weargahlæw now. I'll leave in about an hour . . . don't want to ride alone . . . was going to take Leofric, but since you're here, will you come with me? I want to hear all about this wonderful progress. I'm so proud of you."

Mom's mouth opened and shut without making a sound, but Radgar's heart burst into flames of rapture. "Then I won't have to tidy my room?"

Dad guffawed. "Get out of here, you insolent young horror! Tell them to saddle up Spedig for me and one for you. . . ."

"He's as tired as you are!" Mother snapped. "He's only a child! He's—"

"A thegn's son," Dad said. "Have a warm soak. Dress warmly. Bring a full day's food because I'm starving and I expect you are. Blankets, change of clothes. We'll probably have to spend the night there. Think what else we'll want. You've got time to eat, so eat well after you dress. Meet me here in an hour with the horses."

Bliss! "Yes, sire!" Radgar said, saluting like a thegn. He went out and then poked his head back in to say, "I will tidy it, Mom!" He shut the door quickly, before she could answer. If he bent down to tighten his garter, his ear would be level with the knothole. . . .

". . . need you?" Dad said. "I'm going crazy. It's been half a year. I have howled for you every night."

"What?" There was something strange about Mom's voice. "No raping? No campfire orgies? No voluptuous Chivian virgins in—"

"Not by me. You know me better than that. I may be going to die, dearest. You know that, too. The firedrake will be far more dangerous than the war ever is. Don't refuse me now, please! I beg. I plead. I offer anything."

"Give up the firedrake."

"Anything except that."

"I heard that first on our wedding day. It's always been anything—except. Whenever you want to play stud horse, you promise me the whole pasture except the bit you're standing on."

"If I refuse this I won't be the man you married. I'll be counted craven. New king in Baelmark, new Earl of Catterstow. Is that what you want? To be the wife of a disgraced thegn?"

"Oh! You . . . !" It sounded almost like Mom and yet not Mom. "Isn't that better than being the widow of a hero? But you know perfectly well I can never refuse you.

Never once since you first . . ." Her voice became muffled and then stopped.

They must be going to do the *forlegnes* thing after all! At their age? How dis*gust*ing!

Radgar strode off down the path.

· 8 ·

So Radgar went to meet Healfwer a second time. Hatburna was actually closer to Weargahlæw than Waroðburh was, Dad said, but it would be a steep climb and misery in this rain. He went in front on Spedig, leading the two packhorses; and Radgar brought up the rear on Steorleas, because Cwealm had already earned his oats that day. He'd forgotten how Steorleas tended to walk sideways, stupid mule! In fact the weather wasn't too bad under the trees, and once they reached the moorlands they could ride side by side and talk. Then time passed more quickly and a man didn't mind so much if the wind and rain froze his nose and ears off.

Although he said he was in a hurry, Dad made a detour over to where a group of his ceorls were repairing sheepfolds, preparing for the winter. He sent them all home, saying that they didn't have to do that sort of work in this weather, and they were to tell the reeve he had said so. That was typical of Dad, the reason everyone in Baelmark loved him, from the *lætu* to the earls.

On the ride in, he'd heard stories about the progress, and now he demanded a full report—"Like a ship lord gives me when he comes back from a *færing*." He asked questions, but finally he said something that made Radgar's face burn hot enough to steam in the rain. "If you can handle yourself as well as that in public at your age, Son, then you've got most of what it takes to be a great king."

"Dad! That's crazy! Flattery—"

"No, I mean it! Impressing your own people is far more important than banging your enemies. Obviously you made them laugh as you wanted; they didn't take offense, which they easily could have done. I am really proud of you. I'll bet all the earls were accusing you of building up support for a challenge to your old man?"

"I swore that would never happen, sire, no matter how long you kept switching my butt."

Dad laughed and said that was a very good response. Radgar had actually heard more comments about Catterstow getting a much better tanist in a few years, but he didn't repeat those. It was none of the other earls' business who Dad's tanist was.

As they climbed higher the mist closed in, until there was nothing to see, but Dad had grown up at Hatburna and knew every coney track in the hills.

Radgar wanted to hear about firedrakes.

"You probably know as much as I do, Son. This one appeared last night and seems to be heading for the coast. Healfwer must know more about what makes a drake than anyone, but he usually won't talk. Fire elementals, yes. They're an essential ingredient. Plus spirits of earth—or perhaps air. And there may be more to it even than that. The one that Hatstan spawned sixty years ago, that killed your great-grandfather Cuðblæse, looked like a great bird. And this one's like a bull, they say."

"It looks like a bull?"

"Or behaves like a bull. I hope I can head it off before it destroys the Norðdæl town."

"And drive it into the sea?" That was what the songs said.

"Or *lure* it into the sea." Dad laughed oddly. "I'm sure I'll run faster away from it than toward it. I'll see what Healfwer suggests."

"Is that why you're going to see him? For advice?" The man was madder than a pondful of loons. Radgar still had nightmares about that hideous old cripple, and it was more than two years since he and Aylwin went *færing* into Weargahlæw.

"Partly. Mainly because I want him to ward me against fire." Dad pulled a face. "Let's talk about something else! I think we'll reach Weargahlæw before sunset. You want Healfwer to chant the *hlytm* for you?"

Was *that* why he had been invited along? Why was Dad suggesting it now?—because he thought Radgar was grown-up enough to handle the knowledge of his doom? Or because this might be his last chance to ask Healfwer on Radgar's behalf, his last visit to Weargahlæw?

Did a man really want to know his weird? It might make him a coward in some circumstances. But it should make him braver in others. Radgar swallowed and said, "Yes, please."

The trail narrowed to cross a steep face then, so the conversation was interrupted. He had the uneasy feeling that he had missed something and tried to puzzle it out while the rain dribbled down his neck and soaked through his hat; and all the time he was wishing he was riding Cwealm, who was as surefooted as a squirrel. Steorleas definitely wasn't. Eventually Radgar remembered Dad telling him that warding only worked once and you couldn't be warded against more than one element. So . . . ?

So if Dad wanted Healfwer to ward him against fire now, then Dad had never been warded against whatever his bane was, because he'd said his weird wasn't fire. Why in the world not? Well, there was one element of the eight that a man would probably not *want* to be warded against, even if he knew it would be his bane.

The drizzle had turned to whirling snowflakes by the time they reached Bælstede and the defile leading into Weargahlæw. By then Radgar would have been falling asleep in the saddle had he not been so chilled that his very bones were shivering. Of course he had to dismount when they reached the tunnel, so then Steorleas decided to be awkward and the packhorses joined in. Dad told him to lead Spedig on ahead as an example and managed to coax the rest of the train into following by luring them with oats. There wasn't anything Dad wasn't good at.

There was no snow or rain falling inside the crater, but everything was hidden in bleary white fog. Without wind the air seemed warmer, so Radgar felt better but also sleepier. He helped Dad unload the supplies that Leofric had sent along for the hermits, but after that he just sat his horse like a meal sack and paid no heed as the trail wound through the great forest. Healfwer's new cabin was farther from the entrance than the old one had been.

Dad reined in on the shore of a bean-shaped pond that curved away into the fog. "You look to the horses," he said, dismounting. "The old villain needs time to get ready for visitors." He strode along the edge until he reached the bend, then cupped his hands to bellow, "Healfwer! It's Æled. Healfwer?" He went on out of sight and the sound of his hailing was soon muffled by the trees and mist.

Radgar began unloading, unsaddling. The high, thick branches would shelter the horses from any real rain if it came, but in this clammy valley there was nowhere really dry to stable them—except the tunnel, of course, and that was too far away. He checked their feet and gave their backs quick rubs with a pack of coarse grass, but they needed proper rubdowns and proper shelter to ward off chills. Dad would surely have come back by this time if Healfwer was not at home. . . . The fog obscured the sun; he couldn't tell what the time was; he felt as if he'd been riding for weeks. He fed the horses their oats and let them go off to drink and graze. Spedig and Steorleas hobbled and the packhorses free to roam. Then, cold and sore and weary, he sat down where he could lean back against a tree with an apple and a hunk of cheese from the provision bag. Dad and the wita must be having a long chat about firedrakes, or perhaps the crazy old man was being difficult. Dad would handle him. Would there be fish in that pond? Would there be a fire in the conjurer's cabin?

"Radgar?"

He awoke with a start and a very sore neck. "Dad? Oh, I'm sorry!" He scrambled to his feet. Fire and death!

Sleeping on picket duty was a capital offense! How could he have done such a terrible, childish, stupid—

Dad smiled, knowing what he was thinking. ''Nothing to be sorry about. You've done everything I told you to do and I didn't order you to keep watch. Healfwer says he will chant the *hlytm* for you.'' He eyed his son skeptically. ''Sure you're up to it? You look beat.''

So did he, more tired than Radgar could ever remember seeing him. Radgar squared his shoulders. ''Course.''

''Come then. Leave the rest of the stuff for now.'' Dad set off with long strides, carrying one of the bags on his shoulder. ''You're going to have to take your clothes off. Don't ask me why—and don't ask Healfwer, either! He's grumpier than ever today. He doesn't require nudity for other enchantments.''

Once around the curve of the pond, they were in sight of the cabin, a solid construction of tree trunks that would withstand any assault by an angry ten-year-old. If smoke was rising from the fieldstone chimney, the fog concealed it. Dad turned off into the woods and in a moment reached a shadowy open space, not really large enough to be called a clearing. It was carpeted with a mulch of soft brown needles and bore the expected octogram picked out in black rocks. A larger cobble marked earth point and already a glimmering lantern and a pottery flask had been set at fire and water. The gaunt old conjurer was standing there, leaning on his staff, and staring out from the anonymous eye holes of his hood. One real eye hole and one fake.

Radgar walked around the octogram to him and bowed. ''*Ealdor,* it was very wrong of me to spy on you when I came here last, and wrong of me to force my company upon you. I am sorry.''

After a moment's silence Healfwer mumbled, ''You've grown.''

''Yes, *ealdor.*''

''What you are asking for is very frightening. Grown men may scream in terror when they see their weird. I have known battle-tested thegns soil themselves or weep like women. I want no hysterical children disturbing my peace."

Nasty old man! Radgar took a firm grip of his temper. "I am Radgar Æleding of the line of Catter. I will shame neither my father nor my forebears. I have never let fear stop me doing *anything*." That was far from true, of course, but he had heard the thegns boasting in Cynehof on the eve of a *færing*, and he knew that once a man said something like that, he had left himself no way to back down.

"Then you are a hopeless fool. You will die so soon that there is no point in chanting the *hlytm* for you."

"With respect, *ealdor*, I try not to confuse cowardice and prudence."

"Didn't I tell you not to give me titles?"

"I forget. I am sorry, Healfwer."

Dad laughed. "Give up, old man! He's at his very worst when he goes on his best behavior like that, and stubborn as a limpet too. Strip, lad, and let's get this over before we all freeze." He held out a towel.

Radgar pulled off his wet clothes, rubbed himself briskly but hastily, and then scurried into the octogram. He crouched down as small as he could in the center—which was what he had seen Wulfwer do, and the only sensible position to adopt if one really must do such unsensible things at this time of year. He felt like a chicken trussed for the oven, gooseflesh and all. He faced toward the conjurer, who had taken his place—somewhat surprisingly—at fire point, where the lantern was, and not at death, which would have seemed more logical.

If brute Wulfwer could do this, then Radgar Æleding certainly could.

"Blindfold him," the old man growled. "Stay there, brat, and don't move a muscle for as long as you can."

Dad tied a cloth over Radgar's eyes and presumably then stepped back out of the octogram.

"Hwæt!" the old man cried, like a scop starting an epic song, except no mead hall would tolerate a voice so discordant. He launched into his chant. It was very long, coming from first one side and then another, around and

around, back and forward, invoking all the elements in turn. No, not all. The manifest elements, yes—air, fire, water, earth. But not all the virtuals, just love, chance, time. Did shivering count when one was supposed to be not moving muscles? Death had not been invoked, but neither was it revoked, and gradually Radgar began to see the logic. He was also seeing strange lights moving in darkness, as one did when blindfolded. Death had not been invited, but death must be there, so the *hlytm* would discover which element was hiding death.

He couldn't help his teeth chattering. He just hoped Dad would understand it was only the cold making them do that. As his eyes adjusted to the darkness, so the vague colors became brighter and more meaningful, shifting and repeating their patterns. The chanting had moved farther away, as if the clearing had grown much larger, and there was a curious echo now, reminding him of Stanhof, the big hall in Twigeport where he'd been yesterday. Flames! Was that only yesterday?

Eek!

There was something behind him, something that shouldn't be there—he wasn't sure if he'd heard it or how he knew, but he knew. Yes, he knew. The back of his neck prickled and he struggled against the need to leap up and tear off the blindfold. Dad was here. Dad wouldn't let anything creep up on him. He had sworn not to give in to fear. But he did feel horribly vulnerable with no clothes on! *There it was again!* Flames and death! *Cold* and death. Never had he felt so cold. Cold as a corpse. And the chanting had stopped. Was it over? In the reverberating hollow silence, something was coming, slithering. It was trying not to make a sound as it slithered closer. . . .

"Radgar!" Dad screamed. *"Look out!"*

He jumped like a frog and spun around even as he landed.

There wasn't anything there at all. The empty dark floor stretched away to the walls. He turned again, quickly. The chamber was as big as Cynehof, but more round than oblong . . . eight-sided, of course. Dark, shiny stone or metal. And eight empty doorways, dark archways. The glowing lights moved faintly here and there, things of mist going about their own business. It was the doorways that mattered.

"Radgar!" Dad shouted again. "Come here! Quickly!" He stood in one of the doors, not very well lit, but definitely Dad.

"What's wrong? Where is this place?" Radgar ran over to him. "How did we get out of the—" The floor was too smooth for proper footing. He grabbed at the edge of the opening to stop himself before he plunged through, and even then his feet slid. There was no Dad. There was a raging, roaring sea outside. *"Dad?"*

"Over here, silly. Quickly, we haven't much time."

He ran across to the proper arch, but this time he was a little more cautious. And right to be so. Again he had gone to the wrong door, and if he had fallen through he might have fallen forever—there were *stars* down there!

Where now? The hall seemed to be getting smaller.

"Radgar!" This time the shout came from two directions at once. "You must get out!" shouted one dad. "Don't listen to him," cried another. "Come to me. Hurry!" But as he approached the nearer dad, he vanished and appeared in two more doors, so there were three dads calling him. "Faster, Son! I can't wait. You have to get here before I go. Quick!"

He ran from one archway to the next. Dad was never there when he arrived, always calling from somewhere else. A roaring fire, yes. A warrior leaping forward with bloody sword raised and his face hidden in a battle helmet. The hall was growing smaller and smaller, Dad's shouts more urgent. Then another voice, calm and amused—

"Oh, Radgar! Don't let this stupid *hlytm* frighten you. Can't you see that's what they're trying to do—confuse you and frighten you?"

He found the source. "Mother!" All the Dad voices had stopped.

She held out her arms. "Come, love! It's a very foolish, cruel thing they're doing to you and you don't have to play this game anymore. Come."

He walked over to where she stood in the archway and

Dad was right behind her, not speaking but grinning rather sheepishly as if he'd been caught out doing something foolish. "Mom? Is it really you?"

She laughed. "It's really me."

"Sorry if we upset you, Son," Dad said. "I love you too, but this was necessary."

There were other shapes behind them, people he felt he ought to know. Nice people, good friends, dear people. "Come!" they all cried at once, all holding out their arms. "Dearest!"

"Yes, I love you," he said. "You won't mind if I just take a last look in all the other doors first?" He backed away a step. Arms grabbed for him, the hands become talons. He screamed and leaped out of reach. The other doors were closing in on him, all shouting for him, in Dad's voice, Mom's voice, even Aylwin's and other friends' voices. Hands beckoned, the hall shrank smaller.

"Dad!" he screamed. "Dad, where are you really?"

"Here, Son," Dad said quietly. "All right. It's over."

Radgar jumped into his arms.

Dad caught him in a blanket and hugged him tightly. He shivered so hard he thought he would fly apart, and his heart was racing. Then he realized that he still had the blindfold on and he could smell the pine trees, so he dragged an arm free and uncovered his eyes. The dark and foggy forest had not changed. Healfwer was leaning on his staff, still panting. Dad's stubbly face was right next to his, smiling.

"Dad? Did you call me?"

His father smiled. "No. Did you hear me? I didn't say one word. I just ran around after you, trying to guess where you were going to come out."

Then Radgar remembered the purpose of the ordeal and looked down. He had kicked over the lantern.

V

• 1 •

A burning log collapsed in a spray of sparks and a waft of smoke. Wasp, being closest and most junior, glanced inquiringly at King Ambrose. Receiving a nod of permission, he knelt to stoke the fire, which had wasted to glowing embers.

"So I knew my weird," Raider continued. "And all the voices I had heard had just been a single shout from the conjurer. That wasn't how it had seemed to me; but both he and my father insisted that I had barely hesitated—just jumped up and run around the octogram once before I jumped out at fire point. That meant, Healfwer said, that my doom was not far off."

"The college would like to hear about this conjuration," the King growled. "We shall instruct Grand Wizard to discuss it with you."

"I shall be happy to give what information I can, sire, although after so many years I remember very little of the ritual itself."

Sir Janvier stepped forward, and Wasp handed him the empty scuttle—passing it around the back of the settle, of course, and not in front of the King. Wiping his hands on his jerkin, he resumed his seat to hear the rest of Raider's story. It was still incredible to him that his best friend had turned out to be one of the Baelish monsters, the savages who had burned his family to death, callously driving women and children back into the inferno. Raider was a wonderful, caring person, not an inhuman fiend. Yet the loving and well-loved father he was describing had been the chief monster. These things would need much thought.

"I think my father would have liked to ride off again that night, so anxious was he to tackle the firedrake, but Healfwer insisted that warding against fire could only be done at sunrise. I was exhausted and I doubt my father was in much better shape. I even doubt that the old hermit could have managed three conjurations in so short a time, but as it was we spent the night in his cabin and at dawn my father and I stood and held hands in the octogram, and he warded us simultaneously. That was a much simpler and shorter conjuration. That is how I became fireproofed, Your Majesty, as I demonstrated to Your Grace earlier this evening."

"Tell Grand Wizard whatever you can about that one, too."

"I shall try, sire. All I can recall is that it almost never mentioned fire itself. I had the impression that all the other elements were being invoked to repel fire. It was a long time ago and I was young."

King Ambrose adjusted his bulk in the leather chair. "You're still not exactly old, yet you have tucked a lot of living into your years." That was the first half-agreeable remark he had made since Raider had refused binding. "Tell us about the firedrake."

Raider smiled ruefully. "I was allowed nowhere near it, sire, warded or not. When we reached Waroðburh, my mother was there. She put me straight to bed and I slept the sun 'round. Dad—my father took ship to Wambseoc right away. The next two days were very anxious for us, as you can imagine. My mother was distraught. But he came sailing back a hero, even more of a hero than he had been before. The experience had taken toll of him, though. He went off to Hatburna with no one but my mother and did not return to the capital for almost a month. He rarely spoke of his ordeal.

"According to others' accounts, the drake materialized high up on the slopes of Fyrndagum during an especially violent eruptive episode, and this is standard for the horrors. As you might expect, firedrakes have no fixed form, changing shape continually. They may stay in one place for weeks or waste the countryside for miles around, and yet are capable of terribly swift movement, hunting people down to kill them. They are spiteful—they routinely destroy empty buildings, for example. They seem to be vulnerable to wounds, yet no unwarded man can venture near enough to their fiery heat to inflict harm upon them. The Wambseoc drake had destroyed three villages and was closing in on Norðdæl itself. My father rode out with Earl Ufegeat—a nephew of the king he deposed—but when they came within sight of the monster, he went on alone. At first he wore sandals and some light linen garments, but he had to shed those when they began to burn. He carried a two-handed broadsword and several times during the battle he had to provoke the horror by stabbing at it. The trophies hung in Cynehof include some that show the touch of firedrakes. As a child I was fascinated by a gruesome half-melted breastplate that had belonged to my great-grandfather Cuðblæse. It still contained a few charred fragments of him.

''My father's purpose was to lure the monster to the sea, and after two days' hair-raising effort and ordeal, he was successful. The witnesses were insistent that the thing resembled a bull. At times it even looked like a bull, they said, but it was always bull-like in its behavior. It soon learned to beware of my father, but as he crept closer it seemed to watch him. It tore up the ground as a bull does, throwing rocks around. It blew jets of smoke and fire and made deep bellowing noises. And then it charged him. Just because he was warded did not mean he was invulnerable—far from it! The firedrake could have crushed him like an empty eggshell or swallowed him up, burying him in its own flaming mass. But water is the firedrake's bane and it is curiously unable to see even large quantities of water, although it can certainly see people. In the end my father dived from a rock into the surf and swam for his life. He was a powerful swimmer and he had rescue boats standing by offshore. The drake plunged in right behind him and perished in great explosions of steam and boiling water.''

Silence. Raider took a sip of water, waiting for the King's comments or questions. A faint tap on the door announced the refilled log scuttle. Sir Janvier accepted it and brought it around for Wasp to put by the hearth.

"Well, that explains your trickery with the candle," King Ambrose said. "What you still haven't told us is how you came to be here, in Ironhall." He flashed Wasp a calculating look. "You must have arrived while the war was still on."

"Right at its end, sir," Raider agreed. "It was 351 by your calendar, Eighthmoon to be exact. . . ."

· 2 ·

Radgar's first chance to steer *Græggos* came when he was thirteen. He almost died of pride. Had he tried it in the open sea, of course, the steering oar would have flattened him against the side or thrown him overboard like an apple core, but on the gentle swells of Swiþæfen he could manage—just barely manage, for the channel was narrow and the headwind eddied erratically off the cliffs on either hand. Low as her freeboard was, if he let her flank swing even a couple of points she would turn her bow to the rocks despite anything he could do.

Radgar steering, big Toðbeorht beating out the stroke. Radgar knew he was mostly decoration, with Dad standing ready to grab the oar if he fouled up, but he had done all right so far and very few men ever had a chance to steer a dragon ship, let alone lead a fleet of them. King Æled and his lady queen were journeying in state to Twigeport with Atheling Radgar as helmsman! It was a glory he had never imagined happening until he was grown-up and the most dreaded ship lord on the seven oceans. *Græggos* sported her dragon-head prow, which no ship except Dad's was allowed to do in home waters. Her sail bore the fiery crown emblem of the Catterings, and eight other ships followed behind. Oars creaked, gulls cried, and the familiar tang of the sea tingled in his nostrils. He could imagine nothing finer happening in his life if he lived to be a hundred.

Mom sat nearby on an ornate chair, smiling as if she were impressed. Both she and Dad were already dressed in regal splendor. She had spent almost as much time prettying up her son as herself, but the instant Dad had offered him the chance to steer he had stripped off everything except his breeches. The day was warm for late summer and he was working his heart out in his struggle with the oar—port or starboard as the wind shifted, up and down in time to the swell, breath gasping, bare feet slapping on the deck.

He wasn't working one-hundredth as hard as the rowers, though; all big men, all bare-chested, red-faced, running sweat. There was no real hurry, but when the King's ship was being escorted by the whole fleet of Catterstow, they were on their mettle to row every other crew to death. Hard as they strained, they were still able to grin at their helmsman's puny efforts and the desperate struggles that followed every gust. He wondered wistfully when he would have muscles like theirs. Why did growing up have to take so *long*?

"Take a breather, Son." Dad laid a red-hairy hand on the oar. He did not seem to exert himself at all and yet instantly it began obeying him instead of Radgar.

"I'm doing all right!" he gasped. "Aren't I?"

"You're doing very well. I'm really proud of you, but I want to tell you something. There won't be time when we arrive. Can you listen and steer too?"

"Yes, lord!"

Dad removed his hand. "Then do so. There may be trouble at Twigeport. Lots of trouble. And it could involve you."

"Me?"

His father grinned. "Imagine! You've been doing so well at staying out of trouble lately that I decided to start some for you.'' The grin faded. ''No joking, Son. You know why I called the moot. It will be a stormy session.''

''Yes, lord.'' Peace! The moot was going to hold peace talks with an ambassador sent by King Ambrose. They were going to end the war that had started before Radgar was born, and it would all be over before he was old enough to fight in it. Dad had ordered the witenagemot to assemble in Twigeport, which was the port city of Grætears, the shire at the north end of Fyrsieg.

''Don't repeat to anyone what I'm going to tell you.''

''No, lord!''

''I'd really prefer you just call me 'Dad,' Radgar.''

''Yes, Dad.''

''The country's badly split. Some shires are doing very well out of the war, and others would do better from trade in peacetime.''

''Don't you decide? You're the king!''

Dad smiled. ''Yes, I'll decide, but it helps to have all the arguments out in the open. There are going to be days and days of wind and waffle, too! This is how these things are done: Chivial asked for terms, in secret. We sent our list of demands, and I put in everything I could think of—the Chivian crown jewels and King Ambrose's head pickled in vinegar and—''

''No!'' Radgar squealed with laughter and then hurriedly directed his attention back to *Græggos.*

''Well, not quite, but close. Now the ambassador has arrived with authority to negotiate, but of course he's going to start by rejecting just about everything we demanded. He may even add a few demands of his own, like my head on a pike or sending your mother home.'' He said that loud enough for her to hear. ''We'll refuse that, of course.''

''Oh?'' Mom raised eyebrows. ''Suppose I want to go back?''

''What?'' Radgar howled. ''Go and live in Chivial? You couldn't possibly—''

''Of course I could. And I'll take you with me.''

''Look out!'' Father snapped.

Græggos shivered and began to swing to port. Radgar

heaved all his weight against the oar until he thought every bone would break. Reluctantly she turned her bow back on course again. Close one! He managed to snatch one hand free for a moment so he could wipe sweat out of his eyes.

"If she wants to go, she is free to," Dad said as if nothing had happened. "She told me last night she didn't want to. That was in bed, of course. She had other things on her mind at the time."

Mom pouted and looked away. She never enjoyed Dad's teasing on that subject. For some reason it made Radgar uncomfortable too, although he knew all men made such jokes.

"Will the war end?" he asked wistfully. Everyone had been debating that for days, but he had not heard Dad offer an opinion.

"I honestly don't know, Son. We haven't heard the ambassador's terms yet, but Ambrose wouldn't have sent your uncle if he wasn't serious."

"But you decide, lord?"

"Yes, I decide. The earls will talk and talk, but none of them will vote against a reigning king unless they have a good challenger ready and are sure that he's going to gather a majority. I would know if that was in the wind and it isn't—I'm not falling apart from old age yet! When the vote comes, they'll all side with me whatever they really want." Dad grinned his big grin, but Radgar sensed the menace in it. He knew an angry king could arrange a lot of trouble for any earl he didn't like, even tanist trouble.

"And do you want peace or war?"

"I didn't start this war!"

"No, lord!"

"That's important, because the worst sort of fight is the one you start and then lose—it makes you look stupid as well as weak. The best sort is when the other lad attacks you and you beat him anyway. Then he's the fool as well as the loser, and if there is guilt it belongs to him, understand? That's why winners always make losers confess that they started the fighting. And if they obviously didn't, then they have to admit that they forced the winners to attack them, so it's their own fault anyway. Of course in this case it's perfectly obvious that Chivial did begin the war. King Taisson sent an insulting ultimatum. Honor left us no choice but to reject it, and they lost so badly that his son is suing for peace, at last. But we are not going to sign any treaty unless it begins with King Ambrose admitting that his father was wrong to start the war. He'll squirm like an eel before he agrees to that."

"Good!" Perhaps peace wouldn't come after all and Atheling Radgar could grow up to be the dreaded Ship Lord Radgar, flail of the Chivians. . . .

Dad chuckled and tousled his son's sweaty hair as if he could hear him thinking. "You may suppose it doesn't matter much whether King Æled or King Ambrose accepts the blame, but it matters a whole lot! It especially matters in a country like Baelmark, where the king can be deposed. A king who admits to a mistake is starting to list. Two mistakes and he sinks."

"You didn't make a mistake! They started it and you won!"

Dad grinned again. "That's right. Point to starboard, helmsman. Now listen! There's going to be a lot of argument in the witenagemot. About half the earls are like me—they'll listen to the terms and then make up their minds. But the war-forever party has at least five sure votes, and so does the peace-at-any-price party. I call them the Bloods and the Wines, but don't repeat that."

Radgar nodded, keeping his eyes firmly on what his ship was doing. "Yes, lord." It was exciting to be trusted with state secrets like this.

"And although I'll make the decision, I can't ignore the witenagemot completely. I will canvass the earls in private before we vote, and in the end we'll probably all vote the same way. But the talk isn't all fake and there will be a lot of menace and bribery going on. The Bloods have enough wealth to buy some Wine votes. The Chivians will have brought sacks of gold and bales of promises. Twigeport's the heart of the Bloods, a hotbed of hotheads.

I won't be surprised to see butchery before this moot is over."

Shocked, Radgar glanced at his father and did not like the grim look in his eye. The witenagemot met at least once a year in Waroðburh and he could not recall there ever being violence worse than the inevitable drunken brawls.

"Swordplay?"

"Swordplay, cudgels, knives in the back. Perhaps even poison or enchantment. If a tanist and his earl don't agree, then a knife in the kidney is a quick way to switch a vote. Swetmann is head of the Bloods. He's violent and unscrupulous. He'll play very rough if he has to."

Swetmann was Earl of Grætears. He was new, young, and heartily distrusted. A few months ago he had challenged one brother for the post of tanist and then another for the earldom itself. Both had chosen to fight and had died in the resulting duels. That sort of fratricide was legal, but it did not bring a man much respect. Worse, as far as Radgar was concerned, was that Swetmann was a Nyrping and the Nyrpings were the second-ranking royal house after the Catterings. Swetmann might be a threat to Dad one day.

"Then why did you summon the witenagemot to meet in Twigeport?"

Dad's eyes twinkled brighter than the emeralds in his shoulder brooch. "Because Stanhof is larger than Cynehof. Because it's traditional courtesy to a new earl. Because I can keep the Chivians in one city and stop them spying too much. The one thing I don't want to hear is that you or your mother have been taken hostage."

Radgar squealed, *"What!?"*

"It's possible. That's one way to change *my* vote, which is the one that really matters."

"But . . . !" Radgar spluttered as he realized the implications, and *Græggos* almost got away from him again. This time Dad had to lend a hand—just one hand, and he did not even move his feet. He made it seem so easy!

"Yes, but you're a special person and very important to me and to Baelmark. I had to bring you, because you should meet your uncle, but I've told Leofric to keep extra guards around me and your mother. I've assigned Wulfwer to look after you."

Wulfwer? Had Dad gone crazy? Radgar glanced aft. Today his cousin was helmsman on *Ganot,* bringing his father as part of the royal escort. Wonderful!—*Ganot* had dropped back in line, unable to keep up. *Græggos* had pulled three or four lengths ahead. So that was why the rowers were grinning! No credit to his steering.

Cousin Wulfwer was twenty and a thegn now, one of the largest men in the fyrd. He had gone a-*færing,* boarded Chivian ships, swung a sword in battle, sprayed Chivian blood. He still wasn't popular, but he was much esteemed as a fighter. A madman, men said admiringly, and the scops compared him to a killer whale. It was obvious that the cousins must eventually contend for the earldom. It was true that Healfwer's second *hlytm* had decided that water and not Radgar would be Wulfwer's bane, but that did not mean Wulfwer might not hanker to be Radgar's. Mutual dislike was going to become deadly rivalry in a very few years.

"Is he the best choice, lord?" Radgar said, trying to keep his voice matter-of-fact.

Dad frowned. He disliked family disputes, even when they were kept private. "I think so. He's a surly brute, but he's not stupid, and he's worth six other men in a fight."

"I mean can you trust him not to cut my throat?"

Mom said, "Radgar!" He hadn't realized she was listening.

Dad shrugged. "He's being realistic, Charlotte, and that's good. Yes I can, Son. I know that one day your ambitions and his are going to clash. I just hope the two of you can come to an amicable agreement, as your uncle and I did, and don't have to resort to steel. Kin slaying is a crime most foul, even when it's legal. That's why I not only charged Wulfwer with keeping you safe, but I also made sure many people heard me doing so. If anything happens to you in Twigeport this week, he will never clear himself of suspicion. Even if he isn't suspected of having had a hand in the crime, it will always be whispered that he did not try hard enough. Or took a bribe. He knows that, so he knows that whatever ambitions he has to succeed his father or me depend on bringing you home safe this time. Understand?''

Radgar nodded. Then he grinned.

''What's so funny?''

''I have a very clever dad.''

Surprisingly, Dad did not return the smile. He shrugged. ''I hope you do, Son.''

· 3 ·

Just before the long fiord opened to the sea, an ancient lava flow blocked it from side to side to form a plain now occupied by the city whose name meant ''two harbors.'' To the south it had access to Swiþæfen, while the north side provided the only anchorage in all Baelmark that foreign ships dared approach without a local pilot aboard. Twigeport was both a major port and a logical site for invasion, and thus the site of many historic battles.

When the King's fleet approached the shore, Radgar reluctantly yielded the steering oar to Toðbeorht and began putting on his clothes again. He judged the timing perfectly, so that he finished just as the gangplank was being run out. Mother frowned at the state of his hair and the cross-gartering on his leggings, but she had no time to do anything about them—which would have been an unbearable humiliation in front of the crew. He wondered if being continuously nagged was an affliction common to all athelings.

Earl Swetmann was on the quay to greet his king, accompanied by eight other earls who had arrived early for the moot—in time to do a little preliminary conspiring, no doubt. Swetmann was astonishingly boyish, with an easy, infectious laugh and a guileless smile that did not match his gruesome reputation. He knelt to Father to take the oath of loyalty; presented Mother with a luxurious sable cloak as a memento of her arrival in his earldom; and when Radgar was introduced, returned his bow with a lower one.

"Atheling, you are indeed welcome, and your reputation as a horseman has long preceded you!" He beckoned without turning and a groom led forward a snow-white stallion of at least sixteen hands. "I know you will find our talk boring, so pray accept Isgicel now to amuse you while you are our guest. He will be shipped to Waroðburh when you depart, of course."

Radgar had become blasé about formal gift giving. Anything of any real value he received—gold-hilted daggers or jewel-encrusted belt buckles—he had to surrender to the royal treasury as soon as he went home or the guests departed, whichever the case might be. But a horse he might well be allowed to keep, and he saw at a glance that if there was a steed in the whole world to match his beloved Cwealm, this Isgicel could be the one. He had no trouble putting enthusiasm into his voice as he thanked his host, however disloyal that made him feel.

At this point in the speeches, smiles, and embraces, fat Uncle Cynewulf rolled in on a wave of hypocrisy, congratulating the new earl on the support his fyrd had given him and stopping just short of commiserating with him on his sad bereavements. Radgar, fighting a strong urge to leap onto Isgicel's back, found himself suddenly shadowed by the looming shapes of Cousin Wulfwer and his two closest cronies, Frecful and Hengest, who were almost as large as he was. Radgar could not look any of them straight in the nipple. They closed in around him, scowling and fingering their sword hilts.

"I'm supposed to play nursemaid to you, brat," Wulfwer growled. "Give me any trouble and I'll beat you black and blue."

"If you have trouble," Radgar retorted, anxious to establish their new relationship on a sound footing right away, "it's because you don't have enough brains for the job."

"That's one!" said Hengest. His name meant "*stallion,*" which was not what his parents had named him at birth, of course. It was his nose and teeth. . . .

"One what?"

"Smart-ass remark," snarled Frecful. "Two more and the pounding starts."

"When did you learn to count that high, Freckles?"

Frecful did have freckles and was notoriously touchy about them, being as boyishly beautiful as Hengest was horse-faced. No warrior should be so pretty or blush so easily. He raised a threatening fist, but then Mother turned and loosed a glare that cowed even Wulfwer's private army.

Being confined between two waterfronts and two cliffs, Twigeport had necessarily grown taller than other Baelish towns. Radgar enjoyed exploring its cramped and narrow streets, but it seemed unlikely that he would get the chance this time.

The procession to the hall was led by Dad and the earls on horseback, followed by Mother and Uncle Cynewulf in a carriage. Radgar had been scheduled to sit with them, but Isgicel provided a wonderful excuse not to. Even better, his bodyguards had to hurry along on foot beside his stirrup, sweating like pigs in the heat.

"Hold your heads up, lads!" he said. "Smile at the nice people. Remember you're an atheling's escort now. You can't help being ugly but try to look worthy." And so on. The streets were very narrow and although Isgicel was responsive, he did not like strangers close to him. With very little encouragement from Radgar, he managed to nip Frecful, kick Hengest, and twice slam Wulfwer against a wall. It all helped improve the afternoon.

Although built of stone and very large, the earl's hall was otherwise a traditional one-story barn, concealed by a forest of living quarters and other outbuildings that had sprung up all around it. Radgar wanted to see Isgicel stabled and then go exploring on foot—preferably without his unwilling guardians—but as soon as they reached the palace he had to escort his mother to an important preliminary meeting.

A *cniht* led them to a small room two stairs up. It was stuffy in the heat and stank as if it had been used as a thralls' dormitory for centuries, although at the moment it was furnished with only a faded carpet and two chairs. The paneling was old, split in places. Overhead it was open to the roof of the building—rafters and the undersides of the shingles. Mother surveyed the place with great distaste.

"I did ask for somewhere private. I can't imagine anyone coming here voluntarily, so we shouldn't be disturbed." She sat down and arranged her skirts, trying to appear composed, but he knew her too well to be fooled. He went over to the poky little dormer window. It was unglazed and the shutters stood as wide as they would go, so it was doing the best it could to provide fresh air. He leaned out, feeling a hint of breeze on his face and smelling the sea. He could see over many shingled roofs to the fortified north harbor. There were dozens of ships and boats tied up at the quay or anchored offshore.

"Just remember, Radgar, that Chivians are taught to expect all Baels to be barbarian brutes. Try and behave like a gentleman."

She had said this a hundred times in the last two weeks. "Yes, Mother."

They were awaiting the arrival of His Excellency the Chivian ambassador, who was Mom's brother Rodney, now Lord Candlefen, an uncle he had never met. What Father had said—just once—was, *"Be polite and respectful if he is. Be considerate of your Mother, because this will be difficult for her. You need not tolerate insults to you or your family."* "Family" in that case meant Dad himself, of course.

Most of the craft out in the bay were longships, but some were cogs with two or even three masts—decked craft that could carry a lot of cargo but would roll abominably in the slightest sea. They would be slow, too.

"Remember this is a family meeting, dear. We'll have no nonsense about princes taking precedence. You are a boy meeting his uncle, that's all."

"Baelmark doesn't have princes, Mother," he said patiently. "I'm just an atheling." Not all of those merchantmen need be Chivian or even non-Baelish, of course.

"As far as your Chivian family is concerned, you are a prince." She was not being very logical.

"Very well, I'm a prince." But he could not hope to become Dad's successor until he had proved himself throne-worthy, and that would be much harder to do if the war ended. So many roofs packed together! No wonder Twigeport had bad fires.

"This is a very moving moment for me, dear. Please don't do anything to spoil it! I *can* trust you, can't I?"

He turned. "Trust me with what?"

"Trust you to be polite!"

"Have you ever known me be anything else, Your Grace?"

She gasped. "Once or twice!" Then she laughed. "You get more like your father every day!"

He bowed. "You flatter me, mistress."

She smiled approvingly. "Just keep that up and—" She stiffened at a tap on the door. "Come!"

A man entered. Radgar was impressed at once. The newcomer had dark hair and dark eyes, which seemed bizarre in Baelmark, and so did his hose, jerkin, and the white lace around his neck, but something about the way he moved, the way he scanned the room, suggested that he would be a dangerous man to cross. The pommel of the sword at his side was a gleaming golden gem. He wasn't old enough to be Lord Candlefen, though . . . a bodyguard? He stepped back out of the room without closing the door.

"Was that a *Blade*?" Radgar whispered excitedly. "Will Uncle have *Blades* guarding him?"

"Perhaps." She seemed amused, suddenly. "He probably thinks we have wolves and bears wandering the streets here. But if the King did assign Blades to him it would have been just recently. That man was too old."

Of course! Radgar should have thought of that. Blades were sort of enchanted house thegns. They had a special *cniht* school of their own somewhere, but then they were spiritually bound to their lords. So a Blade couldn't transfer from one to another, and any newly bound Blade would have to be young. It was extremely annoying that Mother had seen that before he did.

A tall, very bulky man stumped into the room and the door closed silently behind him. His hair and beard were brown streaked with gray, his face was bright red, and his breath rasped from the climb. On a hot summer day, he was absurdly overdressed in multicolored fur-trimmed cloak and padded, slashed, embroidered jerkin, doublet, and spirits-knew what else. He looked like a festival decoration. Someone must have warned him that Baelmark had a cold climate.

"Rodney!" Mother cried, leaping up.

The Chivian ambassador bowed stiffly. "Madam!"

She flinched as if he had slapped her. Losing her balance against the chair she had just left, she fell back onto it. Her brother turned fishy eyes on his nephew.

Radgar bowed and said, "My lord," which was less than he had intended to say.

"Hmm. You look very like your father."

"Thank you, Your Excellency."

Mother rose, more slowly this time. "What way is this to greet us, Rodney? It has been so long!" She advanced with hands outstretched.

He ignored them, scowling at Radgar. "I understood we were to have a private meeting, Charlotte. That boy will tattle everything we say to his father."

"And what if he does? His father is my husband."

The ambassador's scowl made his meaty face seem sulky. "His father is the pirate who carried you off. We have never recognized your abduction as a marriage."

A tremor at the hem of her dress suggested that Queen Charlotte had started tapping a foot, which had been a danger signal all through Radgar's childhood. In this case, for once, he was neither the cause nor the anticipated victim. When she spoke it was in her most baleful tone, which even Father shunned.

"I accepted him in front of witnesses!"

"Do not remind me." Uncle Rodney eased his bulk down on a chair and flapped pudgy fingers at his sister. "Sit, woman. Those words you spoke that day were the ruin of your family. We have been cast out, vilified, impoverished, and disgraced because you acquiesced in a public rape." He was a taller man than Uncle Cynewulf, and probably weighed a lot more, but his flab seemed to be spread evenly all over him, muscle gone bad. His Chivian silk stockings were stretched over enormous calves. Uncle Cynewulf had very skinny legs and a belly like a lobster pot, which he followed everywhere.

Mother took her time sitting, fussily adjusting her skirts. Radgar went to stand beside her and put his hands behind his back because they were shaking. It was two years since he'd thrown one of his mad temper tantrums and he'd hoped he'd grown out of them. Now he was not so sure.

"I was merely," Mother said quietly, "making the best deal I could for myself under the circumstances. I did not understand that it was my responsibility to defend the Park against raiders. I do not recall that you made any effort to come to my aid when my wedding turned into a public rape, as you so charmingly describe it, although I am certain you were wearing a sword. If you made any sort of protest at all it has slipped my mind. I do not even remember your expressing regret in your letters. Of course the first one said little more than, 'Father is dead.' And the second much the same: 'Mother has died. Weather continues fine.' There was a third about poor Rose and the cesspool. Just three brief notes, in fourteen years! But you did admit that you received mine."

Radgar contributed a quiet snigger to help the fight along. This Chivian fop didn't have a chance. Even battle-blooded thegns were lucky to escape with their balls if his mom went after them.

The ambassador's florid face had turned almost purple. "Every one of those letters was opened by the Dark Chamber before we ever saw it. Anything we wrote in reply was also intercepted, of course. There was war, woman! We were suspected of treasonous activities. Do you honestly think your husband did not have his agents open your correspondence likewise?"

"*Yes!*" she snapped. Then, softly again: "Æled would never stoop to such a thing. I freely passed your letters to him to read, else he would not have touched them. Now enlighten me. Am I to understand that the whole unfortunate scene at my marriage was all my fault? Is that why you have virtually ignored me all these years? *Disowned* me?"

The ambassador scowled at Radgar, as if contemplating ordering him out of the room. "It was not your fault originally, but by failing to defend your honor you shamed us all."

"Oh, did I?" Mom was *dangerously* mad now, foot tapping audibly on the rug. "I'd say it was my menfolk who failed to defend it for me. Who tried to sell me to a leprous, lecherous old goat. Who failed to take adequate precautions only a few weeks after the sack of Ambleport. Who lacked the *beallucas* even to send me good wishes on my birthdays in case the inquisitors thought they were some sort of treason in code."

For a moment there was silence. The ambassador had apparently been struck speechless.

"I do hope," his sister continued, "that I am not to be held responsible for the war itself? Like What's-her-name being carried off in a thousand ships and the siege of Wherever-it-was?"

"Go outside, boy," the Chivian said.

"You stay right here, Radgar."

"Yes, Mother."

"Anything you have to say, Rodney, may be said before my son. He is somewhat involved in this discussion of his legitimacy."

Her brother was growing redder than ever. "Am I to understand that you have no wish to be returned to your family?"

"You understand correctly. However would you stand the disgrace of having a pirate's castoff slave underfoot?

Æled has been a model husband, loving, faithful, and generous. I do not approve of the manner of his wooing, but I have come to admire him and love him dearly, and my only regret at this stage is that I was unable to bear him more sons as fine as this one.'' She was sailing close to the wind now, because he had heard her describe Father in much less flattering terms right to his face. Quite frequently, in fact. Nor had Radgar ever been a model son before. ''The last time anyone asked me that question was when your predecessor came bringing threats of war unless I was packaged up and shipped home. Æled offered to let me go and give me a chest full of treasure to take with me. I refused because it—''

''I should hope so!'' the ambassador wheezed. ''Having raped you, he would give you money and make you a whore?''

''Had I accepted it would have meant his death and we both knew it. I had learned by then what manner of man chance had given me. You may not be able to understand the concept of greatness, but I assure you—''

Lord Candlefen hauled himself to his feet. ''There is nothing more to discuss. Clearly I need not consider your plight during the negotiations.''

''Plight?'' Mother yelled. ''You sit down, Rodney. *Sit!* I have not finished correcting your contorted and misguided illusions. We shall also discuss the matter of my inheritance now. Radgar, wait outside.''

His Lordship did not sit down. Radgar still had hold of his temper, but only by the tip of its tail. Perhaps Mother had guessed that. He was not lucky with uncles.

''As you wish, mistress,'' he said. ''Your Excellency, I wish we could have met under more favorable—''

''Radgar!''

''Let me finish, Mother. My lord, if you had thought to ask in the streets here you would have learned that my mom is cheered wherever she goes. I've seen warriors who sacked Chivian cities, seized its ships, waded in blood''—he was trying not to shout now—''watched them honor her most humbly and willingly, my mom, because she's the honored queen of this land and any treaty that says she has to go home won't get a single vote in the moot, not one! You ask anyone! All over Baelmark when they say, *seo hlæfdige,* which means 'the lady,' they mean my—''

''Radgar!''

''Yes, Mom.'' He made a leg and stalked to the door. When he shut the door behind him, he leaned back against it for a moment, shaking violently. He had *not* lost his dragon temper, although he might be going to have the sick reaction that always followed it. He thought he had done quite well under the circumstances. Not a bad speech! He struggled to calm his breathing.

Oh!—he had an audience.

· 4 ·

The corridor was gloomy and stuffy, the only window being at the far end. On his right, the top of the staircase was hidden behind Frecful and Hengest, Boehtric and Ordlaf—his bodyguards and Mother's—who together represented enough meat to feed all the wolves of Skyrria for a month. On his other side, the ambassador's swordsman leaned against the wall with his back to the light and the unruffled confidence of a cat looking down at four hungry dogs from the top rail of a safely high fence.

Radgar bowed. ''I am Radgar Æleding. Welcome to Baelmark, my lord.''

The foreigner returned the bow gracefully. ''Geste is my name, Your Highness. I am honored indeed to be greeted by the King's son, for I am a mere knight, no lord.'' He smiled but his eyes never left the other men.

''Don't worry about them. They're only dangerous

when they're sober. You're a Blade? I've heard about Blades." He could believe the stories when he looked at this soft-spoken tiger. He was small by the standards of the Catterstow fyrd and yet there was an unmistakable aura of menace about him.

"Ah, well, I *was* a Blade. Now I'm not, not in the way you mean, just a knight in the Order. I'm no longer bound to a ward, that is."

"But that's a cat's-eye sword? May I see it?"

"Some other time, very willingly, Highness. At the moment it's on duty." Still the dark eyes watched the four bulls.

"Please call me Radgar. We don't have Highnesses in Baelmark, just lownesses like those four." He was amused by the scowls of frustration on the thegns' faces. They must know just enough Chivian to tell he was making fun of them.

"Pity. I was hoping the next king of Baelmark would be half Chivian."

"The present king already is. I'm three-quarters, a mean and nasty mongrel. I think you're going to be out of a job very shortly."

For the first time Geste glanced right at him. He was amused. "And why is that?"

"Even as you stand here, my mother is tearing your ward limb from limb."

The Blade chuckled. "She's outside my jurisdiction."

The door flew open and his jurisdiction came lumbering out, almost knocking Radgar over. He paused to glare down at his nephew.

"So you're Radgar?"

"And you're Uncle Rodney." The dragon temper twitched again.

"Well, lad, I'll say this—I was quite pleasantly surprised. Your mother has taught you some manners."

"You may be more surprised in future. My father is teaching me to fight."

Sir Geste uttered a loud guffaw. Even the four walruses chuckled, probably judging more by actions and reactions than words. Lord Candlefen glared and marched away. They stepped aside to let him pass.

The Blade sighed. "Duty calls. My respects to your royal parents, Prince Radgar." He bowed, less deeply than before, and strode off after the ambassador. The glowering watchdogs let him through and he did not spare them a glance.

Radgar went back into the room. "Mother?"

"Go away." She was standing at the window, looking out. He realized that she was weeping.

"But, Mother—"

"Go away, please, Radgar." She did not turn to him. "I'll be all right."

He wondered if he should run and find Father, then decided it would be very foolish. He'd seen her weep often enough before. "Yes, Mother."

He stepped out into the corridor and closed the door. "The Queen wishes to not be disturbed!" he informed Boehtric and Ordlaf. Being two of Dad's house thegns, trained and run by Marshal Leofric, they were good men.

Frecful and Hengest, being Wulfwer's cronies, were not. Whatever else might happen that afternoon, no one would need or want Radgar Atheling for anything until at least sundown and the feast in the hall, probably not much even then. He opened the door opposite and went in, slamming it behind him confidently. Wulfwer knew his cousin's little ways, but Beauty and the Beast should not be a problem.

Fortunately the room was not presently occupied, but he almost gagged at the reek. A dozen bunks were stacked in the tiny space and the owners had not washed their blankets in generations. He plodded over a thick litter of discarded clothing to the window, which was exactly like the small dormer he had inspected earlier, except that it faced south, of course. The vertical bar dividing the opening made it a tight squeeze even for him, but he pulled himself up and wriggled out feet first, having to turn sideways to get his hips and shoulders through.

He sat on the sill with his feet on the shingles and wondered how much of a splat he would make if he slipped and fell all the way to the ground. Would he just splatter blood on the road or up on the walls of the houses too? He must ask someone. Thegns should know because topmen must fall out of rigging sometimes. Heights had never bothered him and he would be a great topman on his first few *færings,* before he became a ship lord, and although Mother would certainly shriek if she saw him now, he was in no danger—his toes were at least two feet from the edge.

He had a fine view southward to the long North Channel where he had sailed *Græggos* earlier, and he could see more dragon ships approaching the port. In the distance Cwicnoll was a hazy mass, looking more symmetrically cone-shaped than it did from Waroðburh. He worked his way sideways, clear of the dormer, then scrambled on all fours up the roof to the ridge. There he found a slight breeze at last. Now all the world was spread out all around him under a cloudless blue sky—the tiny dots circling high up must be fish eagles, and gulls watched him curiously as they floated by. The town, the cliffs, two harbors, Swiþæfen's shiny waters, and the grayer expanse of ocean northward . . . The shingles were hot under his hands and buttocks, but smoothed and silvered by many years of weather, speckled with bird droppings, even mossy in places. A few buildings away some ceorls were repairing a roof. He waved to them and they waved back. Last year there had been a big hole in the town where a dozen houses had burned, but it seemed to have been rebuilt already.

If anything in life was certain, it was that Hengest and Frecful could not work their shoulders through that window; not even far enough to put their chins 'round the corner and see where he was now. When they discovered he had eluded them, their tiny minds would expect him to head for the stables and Isgicel, so he wouldn't. He had been assuming he would have to wait out here for them to leave, but now he saw that another of the palace buildings abutted this one at right angles, its roof only a few feet lower and equally well supplied with dormers. All the shutters would be open on this sweltering day, so he could go and find another staircase. He walked along the ridge to the end, scrambled down almost to the eave, and stepped over onto the other wing. Then it was merely a matter of finding an open window and slithering inwards, although that proved to be trickier than coming out. The room he had found was a sleeping chamber with some fairly decent furniture in it—and he had a sudden worry that the door might be locked, but it wasn't.

He trotted downstairs, passed the guards on the gate without challenge, and set off to explore the town, starting with the north port. Despite Dad's warnings about kidnapping, he was certain no one would take that risk just yet. Once everyone saw where the talks were headed, then the weaker side might resort to violence. Not today.

It did not occur to him that there might be more than two sides.

• 5 •

As the sun dipped down behind the western wall of the canyon, he came trailing back to the palace compound. He was admitted when the Catterstow house thegns among the guards on the gate vouched for him; they gave him directions to the royal lodging. He was hot, weary, and more than a little nauseated. An hour earlier he had discovered a woman peddling marvelous honey cakes with raspberry custard in them, and had offered a silver sceatt for as many as he could eat on the spot, which had turned out to be eight. While wondering what excuse he could give to stay away from the coming feast, he managed to get lost in the maze of high buildings. He knew he had found his destination when he saw Leofric himself standing outside a door talking to house thegn Ordlaf, who looked like a giant lobster in chain mail and steel helmet. Except lobsters didn't sweat.

The marshal acknowledged the atheling with a nod and a studied frown. "You feeling all right, lad?" There were times—many times—when Aylwin's dad seemed to see better with one blue eye than other men did with two good green ones. When the boys had been small, they had believed his claim that the emerald on his silver patch let him read their thoughts. Even now, Radgar sometimes wondered.

"Ate too many cakes, *ealdor*." Minor sins were best confessed right away, especially those that had brought their own penance.

The thegn was less amused than expected. "Wulfwer was looking for you."

"Wulfwer couldn't find his face in a mirror. Can't think why he'd want to, of course."

This time the frown was more serious. "I have seen the thegn soaked in blood within a circle of dead Chivians he has slain. I've seen him turn a battle around single-handed. What feats do you set against those? Have you wounds to show, loot to flaunt? Is your birth so much more noble than Wulfwer Atheling's that you are entitled to mock him?"

Yes! Wulfwer was thrall-born. Besides, since dumpy Cynewulf had never fathered any other children, plenty of people thought hulking Wulfwer couldn't be his spawn anyway. But Leofric was Dad's best friend, the only man in the kingdom who could give the King's son a thorough thrashing and be sure of the King's blessing on it. He'd done it before and was capable of doing it again, by force if need be.

"Sorry, Uncle."

The eyepatch glinted. "Are you still a child that you call me uncle and play stupid tricks?"

"No, Marshal. I was foolish. I will go to Atheling Wulfwer at once and set his mind at rest." Shouldn't be difficult—his mind was never very active.

Leofric set his jaw for a moment before he decided to

accept that apology without further comment. "Top floor. We found you a room to yourself."

"I am honored." It would be in character for Wulfwer to snore like a pig.

"With very small windows."

"Oh."

Leofric hesitated, glancing briefly at the listening Ordlaf. He did not want the story generally known, obviously. "I should report to your father."

"He has a lot on his mind just now, *ealdor.*"

"Yes, so I won't if you give me your word."

Radgar managed a bow, which his overfull belly did not enjoy. "I promise I'll be a good boy."

"I suppose there's a first time for everything," the marshal said dryly.

They both knew that direct orders were red rags to Radgar but he would not go back on his word when he had given it freely. Take orders from Wulfwer? He went indoors feeling sicker than ever.

With the town full to bursting, even the house assigned to the King must be packed like a fish barrel. Four rooms and a staircase led off the lobby. The ground floor would be reserved for the guards and probably some of the elderly witan. Probably Uncle Cynewulf, too, because he hated stairs. So did Radgar at the moment. Mom and Dad would have one of the rooms on the next floor, and the rest of it would be reserved for the queen's ladies-in-waiting and perhaps the wives of those earls who preferred to sleep in Stanhof with their house thegns.

Phew, but it was hot! Another flight brought him up under the roof, servant territory. Here he had the choice of only two doors. Hearing his cousin's braying laugh from behind one of them, Radgar opened it and walked in.

The chamber was surprisingly roomy and not as breathlessly hot as he had feared, because it ran the full width of the building and the dormer windows on either side made a cross draft. It contained two chairs, two narrow beds, and a straw pallet, but it also contained Wulfwer, Frecful, and Hengest, who were lounging on the beds, stripped down to their breeches. They pretty much filled it to capacity. Originally it had been larger, but the far end was closed off by a crude plank wall with a door in it, and that must lead to the private quarters Leofric had promised Radgar.

"Don't bother to kneel, lads," he said, heading purposefully in that direction. Had he not been feeling so queasy, he might have sensed his danger in time. As he reached the door, a leather belt slammed across his shoulders like a kick from a mule, hurling him forward against the wood. He yelled with pain and spun around, registering too late the flushed faces and empty wine bottles. The one who had struck him was Wulfwer, still holding his baldric and leering. The other two rolled on the beds, convulsed with laughter.

Radgar's only hope was speed. He dived forward, feinting to the left, then dodged right and actually won past his much larger opponent, who was unsteady on his feet. Alas, Hengest stuck out a foot and sent him sprawling. By the time he sprang up again it was too late—Wulfwer was blocking the door. The other two closed in on their victim from behind, driving him forward.

"Strip!" Frecful said. "We'll start with twenty lashes from each of us."

"You just dare!" On principle, Radgar never appealed to his father's authority, but he knew that this time he had bitten off enough to choke on. "My Dad sees welts on me, he'll find out you didn't watch me and I got away!"

"That's true!" Hengest growled. "Absolutely right. We mustn't put welts on him, warriors. No bruises, either."

"Stand aside!" Radgar squealed, wondering if the guards downstairs would hear a cry for help.

Wulfwer leered again, revealing a gap in his teeth. "You're not going anywhere. This won't leave a bruise."

He swung. Radgar dodged the first blow successfully and tried to block the second, but the thegn's brawn knocked his puny hands aside and slammed a massive fist into his abdomen. *Punch!*

Nothing had ever hit him like that before. He would have gone flat on the floor if Frecful had not caught him.

He hung in the thegn's grip for a moment, gasping, gagging, too shocked to speak.

Then his temper exploded at the unfairness, and from somewhere he found the strength to break loose and swing a killer kick at his smirking cousin. It very nearly connected, too. Wulfwer snarled and swung his fist again. *Punch!*

Frecful caught him again and held him. "Good one. Try again."

Wulfwer did. *Punch!*

Hengest said, "My turn," and gave him two on the chest, right and left, knocking all the air out of him. *Punch! Punch!*

Radgar found himself on the floor, knotted up in a black mist of pain and bewilderment, croaking in his efforts to breathe. He thought they had finished, but horny hands hauled him upright for more—it was fun to straighten him out and then curl him up again. *Punch! Punch!* He lost count of the blows. *Punch!* Most hit him in the stomach, some on the chest or back. They stopped only when all the honey cakes exploded out of him.

"Yuck!" Wulfwer yelled. "You clean that up right now, brat!"

But Radgar was too far gone to hear—vomiting and choking, turning purple. He heard voices shouting, felt hands working on him, all in a swirling mist. He began to bring up blood. Suddenly his assailants were far more frightened than he was. They thumped his back and got him breathing again, but he continued to vomit bloody mucus. He heard voices from far away—

"Idiots, you ruptured his spleen, he'll die!"

"Got to get him to an elementary!"

"Quiet, fools, there's women below us."

"Then mop up that blood before it starts dripping on them."

"Got to get him to an elementary—gotta conjure him before he dies."

"No! You want to hang for this? Æled finds out he'll hang all three of us whether the brat lives or dies. . . ."

Die it would be . . .

* * *

Well, not quite. Radgar became aware that he had been stripped, washed, and wrapped in a scratchy, smelly blanket. Wulfwer was kneeling beside him, steadying his shoulders with a thick arm, offering him a drink of wine. He sipped some to rinse the awful taste from his mouth.

"You gonna be all right, Radgar?" the big brute muttered anxiously. "Got a little carried away there. Played rougher than we meant to. Men games."

Radgar didn't speak—breath cost too much pain to waste—but he nodded. He wasn't sure where he was or how he got there . . . must be hallucinating. Outside the door Hengest was down on hands and knees as if washing the floor. Thegns did *not* wash floors!

Wulfwer lowered him gently to lie on the pallet. It hurt horribly to straighten and more to pull his knees up. Everything hurt. He moaned and rolled on his side and managed to curl up that way.

"Don't suppose you feel like going to the feast?" Wulfwer mumbled.

Radgar closed his eyes. He was afraid the brutes had broken something inside him. It was all he could do not to weep aloud from the pain as he continued to retch and cough, but he would not give them that satisfaction.

"Course you got nothing to wear," Wulfwer said. "Frecful's rinsing out your things, but I don't expect they'll dry in time."

Later, as he lay with his face to the wall, he became aware of Mother arriving in a flurry of anger that quickly turned to alarm, a cool hand on his forehead, a tattoo of questions: What had he been doing? eating? *drinking?*

Wulfwer's voice came from somewhere high above. " 'Fraid he got into the wine, Aunt. Sneaking it behind our backs."

"Radgar! How could you! How much did you drink?"

Nursing the throbbing furnace in his gut, Radgar just wanted to be left alone to die. "Too much," he moaned.

He wished Dad had come instead. He didn't think he could fool Mom. But apparently he did, because she stood up with a jabber of *serves you rights*, and turned her wrath on Wulfwer.

"You, young man, have failed in the task the King set you. The boy would not have taken up drinking all of a sudden unless you and those loutish friends of yours encouraged him. Since he is in no state to go anywhere tonight, you will stay here and guard him every minute, is that clear? And if I have any more trouble with you, Cynewulfing, I'll have you demoted to ceorl and out of the fyrd so fast your feet won't touch the ground. If you can't watch a thirteen-year-old for an afternoon, you aren't fit to hold a sword. Do you understand? Clean up these rooms properly. They stink." She stormed off to go to the banquet.

Wulfwer kicked him. "Now I *really* want to break your neck."

"I wish you would," Radgar whimpered.

· 6 ·

By morning he realized that he was not going to die soon, although he feared he might never again be able to stand up straight. The room Leofric had assigned to him was probably meant to be a storage area, a narrow gap boarded off at the end of the attic. At its best it was less than four feet wide and only half that in the center, where it was narrowed by the stonework of chimneys from the lower floors. The two windows were mere slits and he remembered Leofric's sneer about them.

He took a long time getting to his feet, every move a fresh agony. The outer room was a litter of clothes, bedding, and three snoring, naked guards. The girls Radgar had heard there in the night had now gone. He hobbled over to the door—holding himself almost, if not quite, upright—and there found dear Cousin Wulfwer spread across his path. Deliberately, of course.

Radgar kicked him as hard as he could, which wasn't very. It undoubtedly hurt him more than Wulfwer. "Wake up!"

The resulting growl would have done credit to a bear roused from hibernation by an attack of gout. It began with a *What?* that became an agonized scream as daylight burned tender retinas and tapered away into a murderous whimper of *Gobacktobed!* The thegn covered his head with a blanket.

Radgar kicked again. "No. The first thing my mother is going to do this morning is come looking for me. This time I'll tell her what happened." He wouldn't, of course. He would die first, but Wulfwer could not count on that.

Radgar used the other foot, harder. "Move! I need to go pee."

Wulfwer groaned piteously. "Just a minute. Find my clothes." He had realized that—today at least—Radgar had him exactly where he wanted him.

Stanhof was bigger than Cynehof, although not so high, and its walls were of stone as its name implied. It displayed no awesome array of battle honors, but for some reason voices were easier to hear in it, and its sheer size turned a witenagemot into an imposing spectacle.

Stools and benches had been set out in a triangle. Northern earls would sit on one side, southern on the other, with the moot reeve presiding on a throne at the apex. The witan proper—mostly elderly deposed earls and a couple of former kings—would sit along the base of the triangle. Today some stools had been placed in the center for the Chivian emissaries. Dad rarely acted as his own moot reeve. If there was anything serious to be discussed, he would appoint someone else to keep order while he took his place among the other earls. They liked that, he said, and since he was now the longest-reigning of the northern group, his seniority put him next to the throne anyway.

Cnihtas and pages trotted around the outside, carrying messages. Tanists, wives, sons, and other spectators sat or stood wherever they could find room at the far side of the hearths.

It took a long time for everyone to assemble and find correct places. There were open mutters of disapproval when Uncle Cynewulf took the throne. Dad's most frequent choice for moot reeve was Chancellor Ceolmund, his predecessor as earl. Although the old man's back was so bent now that small boys followed him in the streets shouting insults, his wits and honesty were widely respected. Perhaps Dad thought Ceolmund would have enough to do in the negotiating to come, or perhaps he was showing his support for his tanist. Uncle Cynewulf was little respected, because he had only gone on one *færing* in his whole life; now his age and potbelly and bulging red nose did not fit the picture of a Baelish thegn. His only qualification was being the earl's brother. Wulfwer looked mightily pleased to see his father take the chair, because there was open talk around Waroðburh that it was time to find a new tanist. The most talked-about alternative was Brimbearn Eadricing, who was probably the best ship lord of them all—after Dad, of course—and also a Cattering, albeit on a very minor branch, one not considered royal. Radgar liked Brimbearn and would not mind him holding the office until he was ready to take it over himself.

He had managed to avoid close contact with Mom, merely waving to her from the far side of the hall so she would know he was alive. The rest of the time his bad-tempered, bloodshot bodyguard clustered around to keep him from public view lest anyone report back to the Queen that her son was a walking corpse. He wanted only to go back and die quietly in his bed, but they found him a stool and closed in on him like battlements. He settled for that, leaning against Hengest's bulk and paying very little attention to the proceedings.

A herald called for silence and eventually got it.

The moot reeve informed His Majesty that the witenagemot of Baelmark had answered his summons, as if he were blind and could not see that for himself.

Dad rose and explained to the assembly that the King of Chivial, having realized that his nation had lost the war, was humbly suing for peace and he, King Æled, being ever mindful of the advice and counsel of the noble earls, wished to hear their views on the terms he should impose on the warmongers. There was much cheering. A herald then read out the text of the safe-conduct that had been granted the Chivian suppliants. This was really a list of Baelmark's terms for peace, and if it did not require the delegates to bring with them the head of King Ambrose pickled in vinegar, it hinted that this might be a good idea. Wulfwer and his friends were bored already, while Radgar just wished he felt well enough to follow what was going on.

The Chivian criminals having then been summoned, half a dozen very grandly dressed delegates followed Ambassador Lord Candlefen in and took their places in the center of the triangle. Radgar, rousing himself to see how Uncle Rodney was doing, was amused to notice that the stools provided for the honored delegates were considerably lower than anyone else's, leaving the honorable gentlemen sitting almost on the floor.

Lord Candlefen, having been given permission to address the throne, announced that His Glorious Majesty King Ambrose IV of Chivial had responded to the pleas of the defeated Baelish pirates by extending them most lenient terms. A herald read out the Chivian counterproposals in both languages. It was obvious that the two sides were a long way apart, but Dad had warned Radgar that this would be the case.

When Uncle Rodney sagged back down on his absurdly low stool, Uncle Cynewulf rose from his chair and pointed out that the two opposing lists of terms, although differing widely in detail, did follow the same subject order and hence he would make that the agenda. He suggested that the meeting begin at the beginning and called for discussion of the Preamble. Several earls sprang up, but one of them was Earl Æled of Catterstow, who was recognized at once.

"Honored ambassadors and colleagues," Dad said. "Is it not obvious that the issues that have been addressed first in the exchange of notes are the most contentious? Reasonably so, of course. The final points all deal with matters of less significance, and some are completely routine. Why do we not then begin at the end and work forward, hoping that early agreements on minor matters will hasten a sense of progress and a spirit of compromise to aid us when we come to the more difficult negotiations?" He sat down.

Uncle Cynewulf called for discussion, but no one was going to argue with the King over a mere point of procedure, so it was declared agreed that the provisional agenda would be followed in reverse order. Witan and diplomats shuffled their notes rapidly.

"Clause Twenty-eight," the moot reeve proclaimed, "mutual recognition of passports."

Standing up was easy; straightening was not, but eventually Radgar could square his shoulders enough to let him meet Wulfwer's glower. "Nothing is going to happen for hours, if not days. Let's get out of here."

"There are times this brat makes sense," said Frecful.

Most people had not yet realized that there would no interesting shouting until tomorrow at the earliest, and the throng was still thick enough that Radgar would have made little progress through it on his own. His escort plowed it aside like hay for him, but just as they reached the great doors—

"Radgar the Terrible! All hail!"

Radgar stopped and his bodyguard reluctantly opened a gap so he could blink at the speaker. "Huh?"

"What's the matter with you, Youngling?" It was the Blade, Sir Geste.

"Hangover."

"Oh?" The dapper little swordsman could convey more disbelief with one eyebrow than most people could with a complete face. "You look as if a horse kicked you in the belly."

"It was three mules."

Most people would have taken that remark as a mere joke. Sir Geste said, "Indeed?" and looked over the Wulfwer private army. "Any particular three?"

"No. Just some bad mead."

Amusement shuffled the Blade's narrow features into a wry sort of grin. His fingernails drummed a tattoo on his scabbard. "Sure? If you need your initials written in scar tissue on anyone's forehead, Youngling, you have only to ask. Happy to oblige. Antique scripts a speciality."

Wulfwer and Hengest decided to glare menacingly, which was one thing they did well. They did not ripple Sir Geste's sails at all.

"In hard cases," he added, "I have been known to include a dedicatory message or brief poem."

Radgar considered laughing and decided it would hurt too much. He did manage a smile. "I'll keep your kind offer in mind, sir. Shouldn't you be over there defending your ward?"

"Nothing I can do. They're going to laugh him to death and I can't fight ridicule." He glanced thoughtfully at the three tame bears. "Any of these lunks know Chivian?"

Something in his tone sent a tremor of interest through Radgar's curtain of pain and nausea. "They can't speak it. They may understand some of what you say, though."

"Then I'll talk quickly and look innocent. The moot and the Chivian commissioners will argue back and forth on every single point, right? Eventually, they will come to a compromise somewhere between what your father demanded and what King Ambrose conceded in his reply, right? Your father can yield as much as he wants, but Candlefen can only go as far as his instructions allow him to go. He was given limits. You with me so far?"

"Er . . . yes, sir."

Geste flashed a piratical grin and lowered his voice to a whisper. "I can tell you what those limits are, Youngling! I can tell you exactly what and where and how much, and your dad would give a private harem for that information. Too young for harems? A private dragon ship with crew? Whatever you want. Interested?"

Radgar glanced around him in disbelief, half expecting the hall and its inhabitants to dissolve in mist. He was encircled by four swordsmen and everybody else was intent on the proceedings and not close enough to listen anyway. "Who're you trying to sucker, Chivian? A Blade betraying his ward?"

The strange dark eyes flashed anger. "Never! Candlefen's no ward of mine, Youngling. The old king was. I spent five years on Starkmoor, learning to be the sixth best swordsman in the known world. Taisson himself bound me, so I spent another ten years in his Royal Guard—defending a sick old man who never went anywhere, bored, bored, bored! A waste of a life, that's what it was! Then he dies and his son takes the throne, so it's 'Arise, Sir Geste!' and *that's* that! Unbound. Dismissed. Not a single word of thanks. I mean that—not one! After fifteen years!"

"Doesn't sound fair."

"It wasn't. Even aging swordsmen have to eat. Your precious uncle ranks no Blades of his own, so he hired me and one other to guard his backside on this trip. If I hadn't been ready to starve, I'd have spat in his eye for what he's paying me."

Radgar's brain was not working as fast as usual today, but even so he could sense that there could be vital information involved here. "You betray your King because you don't like the master you chose to serve?"

The look on the Blade's face made Wulfwer and Frecful grab for their sword hilts, but he ignored them.

"Don't push me too far, Youngling! All I'm offering to do is to speed things up a little. Chivial desperately needs peace. It's bled white. Ambrose has given Candlefen incredible limits, but that disgraced uncle of yours is desperate to make a name for himself by driving the hardest bargain he can. He'll drag this out for weeks and weeks, and meanwhile the fighting goes on; men and women are dying."

Dad should know about this offer. "What's your price?"

Sir Geste grinned and ruffled Radgar's hair—a move

that normally drove him to fury but this time seemed quite fitting, conspiratorial. "I like the look of your old man. I think he'd be fairly generous under the circumstances. And I trust you to tell him where you got the information."

"It could still be a trick."

"It could. So your father won't believe you." The Blade sighed. "Well, it was worth a try. . . ." He began to turn away.

"Wait! It still is. Tell me."

With all the *cnihtas* coming and going, nobody noted Radgar when he shimmied up behind Dad and tapped his shoulder. One of the silver-haired witan was on his feet, droning out an appraisal of the wording.

"Radgar!" His father looked around and frowned, then took another look. "What's wrong with you?"

"Hangover. Listen, lord! I've got a spy in the Chivian camp."

The frown became a royal glare capable of melting steel. "Radgar!"

"It may be a trap, but you can test it. Clause Twenty-five: You demanded a waiver of all import duty on salt fish for ten years. The envoys will offer one third for five years, but they can go as far as waiving all of it for five years and half for the next five." He was young and his memory was fresh as dew. He could parrot back what the Blade had told him word for word, even the bits he did not understand. "Clause Twenty-three: Chivial will pay an indemnity of ten thousand gold crowns every year for eight years and five thousand for another four. Clause Twenty-two: No prejudicial treaties with other states for the next fifteen years without reciprocity." And so on—fishing rights, harbor fees, consular privileges, clause after clause.

Dad's eyes grew wider and wider, his face redder and redder. At the end he said only, "Where did you get this?"

"Told you—I got a spy! Oh, Dad, Dad! He says to test it. If you can beat Uncle Rodney down on Twenty-five and Twenty-four to the limits I said, then you'll know the rest is right, won't you?''

''You little fiend! What comes after? You stopped at Fifteen.''

''He says you won't get that far until tomorrow, and he wants to talk terms before that. I think he wants land!''

''I bet he does,'' his father said softly. ''Yes, it could be a trap, but the gamble is worth it. Go away. Stay away unless I send for you. Don't talk about this. But tonight I'll either abdicate in your favor or make your butt so sore you won't sit down for five years. Fair enough?''

He grinned so widely that Radgar laughed and immediately wished he hadn't. Until then, he had forgotten his aching gut.

''I'll make you my chancellor.''

The King beckoned a *cniht* and sent a message. In a few minutes, when the meeting had finished with the trivialities and reached Clause Twenty-five, the item that was sure to start serious wrangling, Earl Æðelnoð of Suðecg rose to insist that Chivial must waive all custom duties on imports of Baelish salt fish for at least the first ten years of the peace, which was exactly what King Æled had originally demanded, giving no ground at all. Earl Swetmann and the other Bloods cheered and stamped their feet.

The ambassador protested, but after consulting with his advisors he stated that he would agree to a total waiver for five years, with a lesser reduction of half for the next five, as a token of his desire to speed the negotiations to a favorable conclusion, and so on. Those were the numbers Radgar had prophesied. Dad was already sending more messages.

His Excellency stopped smiling when he heard the demands on Clause Twenty-four. This time he tried to bargain, but the Baels refused to budge. When he conceded, it was time for Twenty-three. Several times the talks seemed about to break down and always it was the Chivians who yielded. All through a long, hot day, the hapless ambassador twisted and squirmed in the center of the triangle, pleading, threatening, sweating, and progressively retreating, while his nephew watched from the sidelines with no pity whatsoever.

Radgar had abandoned thoughts of taking his injuries back to bed, preferring to stay and watch the results of his meddling, surviving on a diet of goats' milk fetched on demand by his hulking nursemaids. Even the agonizing cramps that tied up his gut periodically had a bright side, in that they sent his bodyguard into sheer panic. He did embellish them a little, but not much. The fact was that Wulfwer, Frecful, and Hengest had almost killed the King's son and in the sober light of day they could appreciate that one word from their victim could ruin them utterly. By afternoon he was feeling much better.

At one point Queen Charlotte appeared with a small flock of noble wives and daughters in attendance. "Are you all right?" she demanded suspiciously.

"Of course I'm all right. I'm all right, aren't I, lads?"

Yes, yes, they said, Radgar was all right.

"You enjoy watching over me, don't you?"

They agreed they did. They admitted it was an honor to guard the atheling. They even conceded there was nothing they would rather be doing. He considered this more fun than watching them being flogged. He still had that option in hand.

An hour or so later, during one of the brief adjournments, a pock-faced *cniht* summoned the atheling to his father, who had gone outside for some air and was now lurking in a shadowy corner near the kitchens. He grabbed his son in his arms and gave him an almighty hug. Caught by surprise and forcibly straightened, Radgar cried out.

"What's wrong?"

"Bit my tongue." That was true.

Fortunately the King was too exultant to question. He set his son down and thumped his shoulder. "It worked! Everything you said was right! Magnificent. Who told you?"

Radgar peered around, but there was no one close enough to eavesdrop except his faithful minions, who were staying well back. He switched to Chivian anyway. "The ambassador's bodyguard, Sir Geste."

Dad frowned. "A *Blade*? I didn't know he'd brought a— You're saying a *Blade* betrayed his ward?"

"A retired Blade—he's not bound anymore. He doesn't care much for Uncle Rodney. Or King Ambrose. He says he trusts you to reward him. He . . . What's wrong?"

"Nothing, nothing. Just seems odd that . . . I'll be glad to reward him. You'd better keep away from him. He may be in danger, because the Chivians must be on a traitor hunt by now. We need to talk terms so he'll tell us the rest of the secrets. How do I get in touch with him?"

"He said he'll be at the Blæc Hors Tavern for an hour after the ambassador returns to his ship." Radgar sniggered. "I told him I'd send Hengest to fetch him. He agreed that he couldn't mistake that face."

The King did not seem as amused as Radgar expected him to be at the implications of sending Stallion to the Blæc Hors. He beckoned Wulfwer forward. "I'm about to have your father adjourn the moot for the day. I want Hengest to report to me then. Meanwhile, don't let your guard down. The Bloods can see where this is heading. If there's going to be trouble, it will come tonight."

Wulfwer growled, "All right."

"What?"

"Lord, I mean! Yea, *lord*!"

"You're on duty, thegn," Dad said icily. "That means you and your men stay sober until I say otherwise. There will be one of you awake at all times, and *no women*! You will not be warned again."

An expression of pure agony twisted Wulfwer's brutish face grotesquely. "Yea, lord. Happy to serve, lord." As soon as Dad had gone, he added, "Now I *really* want to kill you, brat. No drink, no *girls*? Oh, by the eight, do I want to wring your neck!"

"You should address me as Your Royal Highness," Radgar said.

• 7 •

Many things must have happened that night unbeknownst to the impudent atheling—secret meetings in which the various factions bargained, conspired, and betrayed. One illicit act that the King had expressly forbidden happened right outside Radgar's cubbyhole and, although he was aware of it, he was not old enough for the thegns' lechery to disturb him unduly. It gave him one more hold over them, in fact. He certainly wouldn't let girls make a fool of *him* like that when he grew up! He pulled a pillow over his head and went to sleep while the absurd nonsense was still in progress.

He awoke at dawn feeling almost his old self. The witenagemot did not convene until noon and several earls appeared much later. The mood was grim. Lord Candlefen was clearly determined to refuse the sort of humiliating concessions he had made the previous day, while the Baels had the smell of blood in their nostrils. Numerous thumping headaches did not improve the prospects for compromise or reasoned debate.

When the moot reeve called for discussion of the next clause, it was Earl Swetmann who rose to speak. The spectators murmured in surprise, for none of the Bloods had participated in the debate the previous day. From the Chivians' point of view the change was no improvement. The baby-faced thegn bargained like a blacksmith's hammer, ignoring all arguments and leaving the envoys no choice except to take it or leave it. Reluctantly they took it. Swetmann smiled contemptuously and sat down.

On the next clause another Blood took over and did the

same thing. Radgar noticed that his Baelish uncle—the one on the throne—was openly smirking, while his Chivian uncle—the one in the cockpit—was aghast, his normally florid face pale as a fish belly. The clash of the fat uncles!

Being more aware of the background than most people, Radgar soon realized that King Æled must have taken Swetmann and his supporters into the plot and given them the pleasure of making the enemy bleed. But if the Bloods had accepted that enjoyable task, they must have agreed to support the treaty that would result. It would be sufficiently lopsided to satisfy even them.

For a long time it did seem that the Chivians would balk. Proceedings became exceedingly boring, an endless drone of speeches. The limits the ambassador had been given were fallback positions; he was not supposed to retreat that far on every point. Lord Candlefen's diplomatic career was in ruins. Several times the moot was adjourned to let him consult his advisors. Radgar daydreamed, wondering if his bruises would permit him to take Isgicel out. Dad just sat and listened patiently, revealing nothing.

Hour by hour, clause by clause, the Chivians conceded. They tried a desperate last stand on Clause One, which dealt with the end to hostilities and the return of prisoners. Many captured Baels languished in Chivian jails or labored in Chivian mines. Baelmark was demanding that they all be sent home at once, no matter what they had done or were accused of, yet it absolutely refused to give up its far more numerous collection of Chivians. Most of them had been sold into slavery in distant lands and those still available had been enthralled—so what use would their families have for them anyway? Nothing could have been more unfair or one-sided, but if Dad was going to insist on his position, then he must know that the other side had authority to grant it.

As the light began to fade, a haggard Lord Candlefen rose and mumbled almost inaudibly, ''We could probably accept something resembling those conditions if a satisfactory text for the Preamble can be negotiated.''

Some of the spectators started a cheer, but it soon faded

into puzzled silence. Uncle Cynewulf ordered the two conflicting Preambles to be read out in both languages. Radgar, for one, knew that these innocent-seeming introductions contained what Dad had warned would be the most deadly sting of all, the admission of guilt. Had Lady Charlotte's marriage to King Æled been legal under the laws of Chivial? If so, then the late King Taisson should not have implied otherwise and launched a war. If not, then Baelmark should have returned the lady and handed over her abductor. What was Lord Candlefen's fallback position on that?

A hard one, apparently, because for the next hour he fought like a cornered badger to have his nephew Radgar declared a bastard. Baelish speakers by the dozen insisted that the lady had consented. As the sun drew close to setting, it became clear to everyone that the ambassador's instructions on that point left him no room to yield. Earl Swetmann and his cronies brightened considerably.

King Æled rose to be recognized. He had not spoken since he made the first speech the previous day.

"Your Excellency," Dad said—his voice was soft, forcing silence on the hall—"clearly we can never agree on this matter. It is a vital point in honor and yet in practice a very small one. Why prolong the bloodshed and suffering because of something that happened almost a generation ago? Everything else has been agreed. Your Excellency, let us just omit the Preamble altogether. Say yes and we can end this war now, this minute."

Ambassador Candlefen did not consult his advisors, he just sat, hunched over, thinking awhile. Then he struggled wearily to his feet and said resignedly, "I have repeatedly explained that my instructions require me to see that the Preamble includes those assertions of fact that I previously—"

"Then ignore your instructions!" King Æled roared. "Because I will not negotiate shame on my wife and son. I will waive confession by the guilty, but farther I cannot go. Take what I offer now, or I declare this witenagemot dissolved and give you until noon tomorrow to quit my realm!"

For a dozen breaths nobody breathed. Then Uncle Rodney sighed and nodded. Even when the King strode forward to clasp his hand and Stanhof erupted in thunder, the ambassador continued to hang his head morosely, as if he was expecting to lose it when he got home. No matter, the war was over.

The peace could now begin.

Even in Twigeport, that hotbed of hotheads as Dad had called it, the treaty was greeted with exaltation. This was not merely peace, it was victory, and the bloodiest of Bloods could not quibble over the terms. The feast in Stanhof that night was stupendously raucous. The Chivian delegation dined with Dad and the earls at the high table, leaving no room there for wives, so Mom and the earls' ladies had to sit at another. Radgar, to his bottomless disgust, was put with them, which was unutterably dull and humiliating. In one more year he would be a *cniht* and wear a sword instead of just a stupid dagger.

There were lots of good speeches to listen to, though, and not the usual militant bragging and promises, but true tales about past battles and triumphs. No one would stop talking long enough to let the scops sing—not, that was, until one of them started up *''Hlaford Fyrlandum,''* that rousing marching song about old Catter. At once everyone joined in and eventually Dad had to stand and take a bow. Some of the earls hoisted him shoulder high and bore him around the hall until it seemed the volcanoes themselves must soon start complaining about the noise. Radgar was so proud he thought he would burst. Had any king of Baelmark ever been so popular? Yet there was even better to come. Swetmann and another young earl swooped down on him and lifted *him* up also and marched him around behind Dad as the next Cattering. The crowd cheered itself hoarse. The honor was Dad's not his, of course, but it felt so good he had to fight back tears.

He saw even Wulfwer, Hengest, and Frecful laughing and singing and waving to him. They were as drunk as any, because Dad had declared their guard duty ended. No one could gain anything by violence now. One person he did not see anywhere was Sir Geste. If the Blade's treachery had been discovered, he was probably at the bottom of the fiord.

When everyone had tired of *"Hlaford Fyrlandum,"* when both king and atheling had been returned to their places, then the young men of the fyrd began singing the sort of song that Mother would never stay to hear. She had already endured much more of this feast than she did of most, and now she announced that she was ready to retire. Some other women murmured agreement. She nailed Radgar down with a warning glare, because he had been known to disappear under tables at this moment, but in truth he was weary enough to behave himself for once. After being carried shoulder high around a mead hall, what more could a man ask of a day? And so the first ladies of Baelmark—or most of them—rose and curtseyed to the King and their lords, indicating that they were departing.

"I hope," Mother said with a disapproving glance around the hall, "that we can find a sober man or two to escort us." Most of the earls were past caring what happened to their wives in the next few hours, although Dad had noticed her problem and beckoned for a *cniht* to carry his orders to someone.

"Indeed the very best." Uncle Cynewulf strutted out of the throng. "I have a pounding headache and can stand no more of this. You will permit me the honor, mistress?"

"The honor is mine, Atheling," Mom said.

Ha! What could *he* do if some drunken young thegns got uppity? Knock them down with his belly? Mom had very little use for her brother-in-law at any time, but she never revealed her feelings about him in public. She accepted his arm with a smile of thanks. Radgar followed them out of the hall, into the cool night wind and comparative quiet, although the din in the hall was still quite audible out in the alleys. He managed a quiet chuckle when they reached the royal quarters, seeing that, while Dad had let down his guard, the ever-cautious Leofric had not. He was there in person, with two staunch house thegns beside, both looking very glum at having missed the festivities.

"You display a commendable dedication to duty, Marshal,'' the tanist remarked with barely a hint of sarcasm, although he and Leofric rarely said anything good of each other.

"A job worth doing is worth doing right,'' the one-eyed man answered sourly. "That treaty is not signed and sealed yet.''

Radgar said a polite goodnight to his uncle inside the front door. Almost asleep on his feet, he trudged up the stairs behind Mom and endured her hug and kiss outside her room. Then he could escape to his private aerie under the eaves, too tired to care that the cubbyhole was still breathlessly hot from the day. Without removing his tunic or leggings, he hauled off his boots and flopped down on his mattress, expecting to be asleep in seconds.

It took longer than that. Too much had happened. He would have to adjust to the idea of peace, for he could not guess what changes it might make to his life. Rowdy crowds went past the building, celebrating. Soon he heard women's voices sifting up through chinks in the floorboards, but that was not surprising when Mom's ladies-in-waiting were billeted directly below him. Later a rumble of male voices joined in, but that, too, must be expected. The younger thegns could always find better things to do than drink and sing and quarrel all night.

• 8 •

He was dragged up from bottomless sleep by shouting a long way off. He muttered angrily and turned over. The noise faded. . . . Good! Why did he feel something was wrong? He resisted, reluctant to waken, but eventually he sneezed. Smoke, he thought. Smoke drifting up through the floorboards.

Smoke? He sat up, coughing. *Spirits!* He was on the top floor of a wooden building and his room was full of eye-stinging smoke. The night was very dark, with nothing visible except vague outlines of the two slit windows and not even his slender form could squeeze through those. He could hear voices a long way off, but whether inside or out, he could not tell. He scrambled to his feet, banged his head on the gable roof, lunged for the door. It was bolted. He screamed and tried to kick. Bare feet. Dropping to hands and knees—and yelling as loud as he could between coughing fits—he found his boots. Then he was back at the door, kicking it, pounding fists, screaming.

Fire was his bane.

"Wulfwer! Hengest! Frecful!" Why bolt the door? They had not done that the last two nights, even when they'd had girls out there. Part of his education, they'd said, laughing; come and watch. *"Wulfwer!"* Why not answer? *"Frecful!"* Kick, kick, kick! Had they all drunk and *forlicgen* themselves into stupors—or had they gone off somewhere with their women and left him? He realized with a shudder of terror that there might be no one out there. They might have all gone away and left him. *"Hengest!"* The shouting that had wakened him had stopped. The house was horribly quiet. Had it already been evacuated? *"Mom! Dad!"* He was sobbing now.

The smoke was worse; the room was getting warmer. Fortunately the door was not a close fit, so he could locate the bolt with the point of his dagger. Then he began attacking the jamb. He dug and pried and cut, flaking away wood. Slow, so slow! Chinks of light were showing through the floor; the distant noises were growing louder but no closer. He knew how fast a house could explode—trickles of smoke one minute and a ball of flames the next. His eyes were streaming tears, every breath was a cough. Healfwer had fireproofed him, but if the house collapsed in a heap of red-hot coals, he might well be buried under the ruins or break his back, and his body wouldn't burn until he was dead. . . .

Dad! Oh, Dad, please come! Dad was fireproofed, too. Why didn't he come?

Chip, pry, dig . . . so slow! He was too late already, because he could see light around the door, the fire had reached the outer room, but he had to keep going. Working by touch, he uncovered the bolt until he could push it back with the dagger point and throw the door open. He plunged out into worse smoke and a heat that would have blistered other people. The light was coming from the stairwell beyond the outer door. There were no drunks asleep there and the bedding was neatly stacked where the thralls had left it. Wulfwer and the others had never returned from the feast.

The stairs were ablaze. He was fireproofed. It would hurt, but he had no choice. If he ran fast he should make it. He discovered his error at the top step, too late to turn back—*pain!* He toppled into the inferno and rolled down with a scream that emptied his lungs. Clothes blazing, he thumped into the wall at the bottom, right beside the entrance to his parents' rooms, whose door had already collapsed in glowing embers. *Painpainpain!* Everything was so bright that it was hard to see anything. In an ocean of light he was almost blind, and there was nothing but fire agony in the whole world. Even his boots had disintegrated but it hurt no more to run naked and barefoot over the burning floor into the room.

Where everything was blazing yellow, his father's body seemed almost dark. All his clothes had gone, of course. Framed in flame, he lay on his back amid the crumbled remains of the bed. He was unburned, although his hair was starting to smolder and the tips of his ears and fingers to turn black. The blood covering his chest was still shockingly red. He was obviously dead, because his throat had been cut across to make a ghastly parody of a grinning mouth. *Surprise!* it said. *Burning is not the only way to die.*

· 9 ·

Radgar never really remembered what happened next, although the accounts of others formed a reasonable pattern. Details of his escape were driven out of his mind by extreme agony and the shock of what he had seen. He may have fallen through the floor when it collapsed, but he suffered no broken bones or even major bruising, so it is more likely that he simply found the stairs and ran or slid down them. He retained no recollection of that, or of how and when he left the inferno. Long as his ordeal had seemed to him, it is likely that very few minutes elapsed between the first alarm being raised and the collapse of the floors and roof. Men were still pouring out of Stanhof.

With its narrow streets, Twigeport was more prone to disastrous fires than any other city in Baelmark. It did have procedures for dealing with them, although they were seldom effective. The night watch sounded the tocsin, summoning all able-bodied men to assemble with axes, ropes, and buckets. A building already burning could almost never be saved, so priorities were to rescue residents and keep the blaze from spreading. If the site was near one of the harbors, a bucket chain would try to wet down adjoining roofs, but that rarely did much good.

A brisk wind blew along the fiord that night. Even before the tocsin rang, the building had become an inferno, with floors collapsing and flames pouring out through the roof. By the time Wulfwer and his friends arrived on the scene—shocked almost sober by the magnitude of the disaster—the crowd's attention was entirely on the two adjoining houses, where thrilling rescues were in progress.

The three thegns had left worldly possessions in their room, so they looked the other way.

Thus they were the ones who saw the boy coming staggering out of the furnace, naked but physically unharmed, mere moments before the building caved in. Wulfwer jumped forward and bundled him up in his cloak.

Radgar became aware of being carried swiftly through the dark streets. "Dad!" he wailed. "My dad is dead!" At first he had no room in his head for any other thought, but eventually he gasped out, "Mom! Want my mom!"

"Don't know where she is." Wulfwer was panting. Big as he was, he was carrying no mean load in his arms and running with it. "Don't know where my old man is, either. Don't know who's after us. Gotta get home."

Men were hurrying by, all heading the other way, most of them carrying axes or wrecking bars or empty buckets. None paid heed to the man and boy going seaward. Footsteps echoed strangely in the night.

Radgar whimpered for his mother again. Then, "Where are we going?" Where were Frecful and Hengest, normally inseparable from Wulfwer? He had a fuzzy idea they had been sent on ahead . . . somewhere . . . where? Dad was dead. Mom had disappeared. Was she dead too?

"Home. Catterstow." The big man was panting. "Gotta get away from here, brat. Swetmann'll kill us all."

"Who? What?" Dad had been murdered!

"Swetmann. Torched the house. Wants to block the treaty."

It was hard to think. Mom too? The Bloods taking revenge? Wulfwer must know, because he sounded very sure of himself. At that moment he ran under the stone arch of the gate to the harbor and Radgar screamed.

"This is the north port! This isn't the way home! Where are you taking me?" He began to struggle. Dad was dead. Help, someone! *"Help!"*

"Shut up, brat!" Without even breaking stride, Wulfwer shook him like a rag. He was running along the front now and the brightening eastern sky cast enough light to show the forest of masts—small boats moored to the piers, larger ones anchored farther out, all swaying in stately measure as their mistress the sea moved them. But everywhere in the harbor sails were being unfurled, lines cast off, anchors raised as the sailors made haste to depart. A bad fire might mean men being conscripted to fight it or even desperate refugees swarming aboard; it was time to go and leave Twigeport to its own troubles.

"Let me down!"

"Stupid! Stupid brat! There's blood feud here. Swetmann and his gang get hands on us, brat, it's sunset, understand? You believe that fire was an accident?" The big man ran up the ramp to a pier and then his boots made heavy hollow noises on the timbers.

Dad had said that Wulfwer was not stupid. Radgar had not yet worked out what had happened—how Dad had been killed, what had caused the fire, whether Mom had died too. Radgar was not thinking very clearly at all, but he knew that Dad had not cut his own throat, nor bolted him in his room and fired the house. If a Cattering had been murdered, vengeance belonged to other male Catterings. Blood feud automatically put Cynewulf and Wulfwer in danger also and Radgar himself as well, because boys grew up and became men.

Swetmann was a Nyrping, royally born.

Another man was running with them, guiding them. It was Hengest. Everyone else was too busy preparing to leave port to notice them.

"We're going home?"

"Home, back to Waroðburh," Wulfwer panted. "Be safe there. If my dad's still alive . . . be earl now, make me tanist."

And cats ate grass! The thegns tolerated Cynewulf only because Dad wanted him. They would never accept him as earl and who else would want the surly Wulfwer as his tanist? Cynewulf might be dead anyway, along with Mom, and perhaps Leofric and Dad's house thegns, who were his main supporters. There would be a flurry of claims and challenges, but whoever finally held the earldom would be no friend to Radgar Æleding. Maybe Wulfwer was the best hope he had left, his only surviving relative. The last of the Catterings must stick together.

They arrived. Frecful was down on the deck of a boat, making it ready. That was wrong! Granted that the harbor patrol had been drawn away by the fire, no boat owner would ever trust the watch to guard it. There should be men aboard, but perhaps there had been and weren't anymore. In this confusion a man might get away with anything. Wulfwer jumped down to the deck, making the little craft plunge and rock, and then thumped down three steps to the gratings, where he deposited his burden ungently. "Keep out of the way, brat."

The craft was a coaster, only six or seven spans long, single-masted, with a small deck at bow and stern. Radgar had seen a dozen like her when he toured the docks. There were some barrels stacked in the waist, not cargo enough to stop her rolling badly. She stank of fish. The small deck at the stern probably covered a tiny cabin—a kennel for sleeping or sheltering from the weather—and the hold in the bow would be reserved for perishable goods. A raked mast bearing a lateen sail was a rig simple enough to be handled by a minimal crew, perhaps just the owner and a couple of strapping sons. Big oceangoing ships brought trade goods into Twigeport from the far ends of the world, and then little craft like this one carried them to outports all over Baelmark, returning with their products of wool, hides, or salt fish. In winter she would ply the safe waters of Swiþæfen, braving the open sea only in summer.

Hengest untied the painter and followed Wulfwer aboard, clattering down the little ladder into the waist. Seeing that he had left the way unguarded, Radgar clutched his wrapping tight around him and started up, but he stubbed his toe, the boat plunged again, and he completely lost his balance, toppling onto the deck hard enough to knock the breath from his lungs. Hengest and Frecful were wielding long sweeps, pushing the boat out from her berth and fending off from another, larger, ship, so he was too late to climb up on the pier, even if he could have done so without help. Already there was open water between the stern and the weed-encrusted piles. He had no boots, no clothes. No friends. No dad. Perhaps even no mom. If it had been Wulfwer who bolted the door, then now he would do the job properly, making sure his cousin never set foot ashore again.

The rig was unfamiliar, but Wulfwer and his cronies knew boats as well as Radgar did. They hoisted the yard and set the sail as if they had done it a hundred times. The wind filled it and the coaster leaned over. Hengest headed aft to take the tiller—and stopped, mouth agape.

"A fine night for a cruise," someone remarked approvingly.

· 10 ·

Remembering that last plunge of the boat before she was pushed out, Radgar turned his head to inspect the boots that should not be there and then looked up. Sir Geste was standing between him and the tiller with his arms folded, a picture of confidence, although he was hatless and breathing hard as if he had been running. A somber, full-length cloak hung loose from his shoulders, swirling and roiling in the wind, over standard Baelish tunic and leggings; his sword hung on a plain black baldric. Radgar had not known that the Blade spoke Baelish, but the question had never arisen.

No matter, he was a very welcome sight, and Radgar scrambled up to stand beside him, shivering and clutching his wrapping.

"Not too close, Youngling," he said, keeping his eyes on the three men. "Can you steer this thing?"

"Yes, sir!" Radgar fumbled an arm loose to take the tiller and lean on it. After *Græggos,* she was easy. He caught the wind, pulled her away from the merchantman she was about to ram, and headed her out into the harbor. The wind spitefully tried to unwind his cloak and he had no hands free. He fought it to a draw, leaving him steering half naked.

Wulfwer found his voice—lots of it. "Flames!" he roared. "Where did you come from?"

"Same place you did, thegn," Sir Geste remarked cheerfully. "I'm not sure we're all bound for the same destination, though."

"What do you want?"

"I want no trouble with any of you lot, to start with. I give you fair warning—I'm a King's Blade. I'm not as good as I was at twenty, but I'm still capable of cutting all of you into fish bait. Against three I won't take any chances. I'll play for keeps. Is that clear? No fancy flesh wounds." He smiled, face lit by the fast-brightening sky. "I heard my young friend shouting for help and thought I'd follow to see what the problem was."

"Did you so?" Wulfwer growled. He bent to pick up one of the sweeps. Hengest, at the other side of the mast, took up the other. Frecful just fingered his sword hilt. "We're on our way home to Waroðburh and we don't carry passengers."

"You go north when Catterstow is south?"

Wulfwer took a pace forward. He was a few feet lower than the stowaway, but the length of the oar he held more than made up for that disadvantage. He could not swing it easily without striking the mast or stays, but he could throw it. Or he could thrust it like a lance and push the Blade over the stern without ever coming within reach of his sword. With the boat pitching as she was, that would be safest. "Too obvious. Swetmann would have been watching the south port."

"Swetmann?" Geste said scornfully. "What has the earl got to do with you abducting the King's son? Does he think Radgar tried to burn down his palace? Steady as she goes, Youngling. You're doing fine. I'm relying on you."

Rolling abominably but showing a surprising turn of

speed, the lightly laden coaster had already passed through the anchorage and set her course for the open sea, easily outdistancing most of the other fleeing craft. It took Radgar a moment to work out what the Blade wanted. He turned her bow a few points westward, making her pitch so as to keep Wulfwer and Hengest off balance.

Wulfwer's brutish face scrunched in a scowl. "Wasn't abducting. Swetmann's leader of the war party. He wants to block the peace treaty."

"I still don't see why you are kidnapping the King's son."

"The King's dead! That's what the brat says."

"Does he?" Sir Geste glanced briefly at Radgar, too briefly for his opponents to react. "Not just guessing, Youngling? You're sure?"

"Yes, sir. I saw him. His throat was cut."

"That's tough. Sorry to hear that." The Blade returned his attention to the thegns as they all continued to edge forward. Now both Wulfwer and Hengest were close enough to strike him with their poles. "So Cynewulf becomes king? That's how it works?"

"My father's king now," Wulfwer agreed, "unless they got him too."

"They didn't," Geste said. "I saw him in the crowd. He won't last long, though, will he? He'll be challenged."

"And the fyrd won't have him as earl," Radgar said. "They'll throw him out as soon as he sets foot in Catterstow." His uncle might be allowed to keep his throne long enough to lead the funeral service. There could be no balefire for King Æled. He'd burned already, his fireproofing gone when he died.

Wulfwer shot him a glare, shifting his grip on the sweep as if he were just noticing how heavy it was. "Watch your mouth, brat, unless you want to have an oar growing out of it. Who killed the King if it wasn't Swetmann? How about a certain Chivian swordsman?"

"Not *too* very likely," Geste said easily. "No motive. And just how would a Chivian swordsman get past the guards at that time of night?" He paused a moment as the coaster shifted her gait, feeling the open sea under her keel. "My money goes on you, thegn. You and your father. Either of you could get into the house. He may not be able to hold the throne for long, or even the earldom, but King Æled was rich, wasn't he? One third of all the booty taken in fourteen years of war. He owns more land in Baelmark than any three other landowners put together, so I've heard."

"Wulfwer bolted my door!" Radgar yelled. "Locked me in my room to burn!"

Wulfwer snarled and hefted the sweep as if about to swat him. Everyone spoke at once.

Hengest was the loudest. ". . . never left the hall! He was with us all the time! Not him!"

"It was Swetmann!" Frecful said. "There's only two royally born earls just now. Thegn Wigferð's a Scalthing, but he's over thirty and no Scalthing's been king in more than a century. Swetmann's a Nyrping and they rank next to the Catterings. He can make a challenge and he has all the earls in town already, ready to vote on it. He did well cutting up the ambassador yesterday—it was real stupid of Æled to set him up like that. The witan wouldn't have supported him against Æled, but they won't give Cynewulf the dirt off their boots."

Wulfwer roared angrily. Hengest shrugged and said nothing.

"They won't support Swetmann if he murdered my dad!" Radgar shouted. But who was to know if he had? There would be suspicion, of course, but no proof. And the witenagemot would certainly want to dispose of King Cynewulf as soon as possible. *Oh, Dad, Dad!* Swetmann it would be. Would he sign the treaty or would the war go on?

The boat had cleared the mouth of the fiord. Her westerly course had given her the sea to herself, because that way lay only the dreaded Cweornstanas. The rest of the fleet was hull down to the northeast with murky shapes of outer islands just visible against the dawn beyond.

"Stand by, Youngling," Geste said quietly. Then louder, "So Swetmann had motive. But how could he do it? You saying he had help from someone in the house—

the house thegns, perhaps? Were there traitors in Æled's fyrd?''

The three thegns bellowed their fury at this insult.

''Or was it his brother after all?'' the Blade continued. ''Cynewulf for king and his son for tanist? Motive and opportunity.''

It was light enough now to read the doubting expressions on Hengest and Frecful. *King Cynewulf* just didn't carry conviction. Fat King Cynewulf. Cynewulf the Great. *Dad! Dad! Dad!*

''So now we catch you taking the unwanted kitten down to the harbor. How about you other two? *How do you two brave warriors feel about helping to murder a child?''*

Geste's question hit Hengest and Frecful just as the deck tipped, but he was slightly higher than they and facing forward, so he had seen the ocean swell coming. Even so, his timing could not have been better. The two men holding the sweeps staggered off balance, and that was all Geste needed. His sword flashed into his hand and he leaped down into the waist. Hengest screamed and fell back with his arm streaming blood. He fell back too far and vanished overboard, the sweep he had dropped clattering on the barrels. Frecful managed to draw and Geste skewered him, faster than a whip. Wulfwer, seeing his target now alongside him, instinctively tried to bring his sweep up and around to defend himself, but Radgar leaped, hurling himself at the blade. Wulfwer, with his hands too close together to resist the leverage, found himself unexpectedly overpowered. The sweep swung in his grasp until the far end caught against a stay and then Radgar had even more advantage. The pole took Wulfwer under the chin, the side of the ship behind the knees. Now his height worked against him, so he and the sweep went over together. Radgar staggered and almost followed.

He didn't though. The coaster went on her way bearing Geste and Radgar. Two thegns were gone to the lobsters and Frecful's corpse lay in the waist.

VI

• 1 •

Candles were guttering; the fire had burned down to glowing ash. Still, the two Blades stood like obelisks at the doors, untiring and ever vigilant, while King Ambrose had slumped to a monumental heap in Grand Master's chair, his foxy little eyes shadowed by his hat. Clearly Raider's tale was almost done.

"So I killed my cousin," he said placidly, "and without a word of regret! I'd hope any normal boy would have hysterics and fits of contrition under those circumstances, but by that time I was incapable of feeling anything except ghoulish satisfaction that a slip of a lad like me could discontinue such a hulk. I didn't even suggest we go back and look for him. It would have done no good. If the cold didn't get him right away, the Cweornstanas reefs did. There were no other ships close."

Wasp wondered how any thirteen-year-old could have survived what Raider had endured that night. He knew he couldn't—not even now, when he was more or less a grown man. He was also a very hungry man, and a worried one.

The King grunted, the first sound he had made in some time. "Commander! Send for Grand Master. Also Archives and Rituals." As Montpurse passed the order out through the door, the royal frown returned to Raider. "You have not explained *why* you came to Chivial."

"Sir Geste made that decision, sire. I went down into the poky little cabin to find some clothes. I fell on the bunk and slept until dark. Nature will have her due. I couldn't take any more. When I reappeared, Geste was still holding the tiller. He said, 'I'm assuming you can sail this tub to Chivial, Youngling. I've kept it pointing southeast all day.'

"At that age I would promise anything. In light winds she was easy to handle." Raider shrugged. "I didn't tell him she wasn't rigged for the high seas and heavy weather would sink us. Of course I asked why we were going to Chivial and he told me what he'd worked out. I trusted him . . . I had to, but he was a proved friend and all I had left. We couldn't go back to Twigeport, he said—not with a stolen boat and blood on the deck, three men missing. Quite apart from that, I knew my father had been murdered, so I had a blood debt to call when I grew up, and the killers, whoever they were, would want to act first. So Twigeport was out and that meant I couldn't go and ask help from Lord Candlefen, even if I wanted to.

"Nor could I risk Waroðburh, because while Uncle Cynewulf was in charge there he would certainly have questions to ask about his son. When the fyrd deposed him, his successor might decide to tidy up any atheling problems left around.

"The key was my mother, Geste said. He'd heard the crowds around the house moaning that both the King and Queen had died, but he stressed that we couldn't be sure about Mom, since I hadn't seen her body, only Dad's. If she had survived, being widowed she might well decide to return to Chivial with her brother. Even if she didn't, I had more family in Chivial than I did in Baelmark and fewer potential enemies. He promised he would look after me for a few weeks, until we learned the outcome—whether the treaty held, who succeeded my father as king and earl, what had happened to my mother, and so on. I did not have an automatic claim to the throne like a Chivian prince would, but I was the last of the Catterings and that would make me an important token in Baelish politics when I was old enough to be counted throne-worthy. The trick would be to live that long. So we were Chivial bound.

"Food was a concern, and the water keg was almost empty. Fortunately the luxury imports in the bow included some edibles like olives and nuts—and also fine white wines. Our course may not have been the straightest, but we made it to Chivial.''

A faint smile touched the royal lips at that point, the first sign of approval King Ambrose had shown all night. Shifting his position on the hard settle, Raider crossed his legs. He must not be aware he was doing so, for such informality was gross presumption. Being allowed to sit at all in the King's presence was a signal honor.

''The war was officially still on, but I kept my hair out of sight and we had no trouble. Geste raised cash by selling some of our pirated cargo just like an honest trader, and we worked our way around the coast to Prail. We didn't meet any Baelish pirates, which I was secretly hoping we would, boys being boys.

''In Prail he rented a couple of horses and we rode here to Ironhall. It would be a perfect hiding place for me, he said, while he went to court to pick up the news. Of course the idea of hiding among the Blades appealed to a brash thirteen-year-old. We came in through that door there, but I was sent out while he spoke with Grand Master. He may or may not have told the truth, but the story we had made up said I was an orphan from Westerth, because that was the accent I had picked up from my mother. Grand Master tested my agility and accepted me into the school.

''Geste's argument had been that, if the worst came to the worst, I would receive five years' superb training, and with that I would be able to make my way in the world, but he promised he would return for me.'' Raider shrugged. ''He never did. He sent one brief letter saying that both my parents had died, my uncle had not been deposed yet, and he would let me know as soon as he had more news. He never did. After five years, it seems unlikely that he will now.'' He paused as if waiting for a comment from the King, but none came.

''The peace treaty was announced in the hall and then fog closed in on Baelmark. It seems to be of no interest in peacetime. I think it was mentioned only twice in our political classes.'' Raider asked wistfully, ''My uncle still rules?''

Ambrose nodded. "My sources claim he's ruling well. Someone tried a challenge not long after your father's death, but the moot backed your uncle handily. He's secure, it seems. The land is at peace."

"Only one challenge? I misjudged him. But if he had not had talent, Father would not have tolerated him. That's my story, sire."

Silence. Wasp, too, had lost his family in a fire, but he had not seen his father with his throat cut. He had not walked through the furnace and had the clothes burned off his body. A prince being the Brat . . . that explained some of the stories of how Raider had won his name—stories that could be laughed at now but would not have seemed funny when he was fighting a dozen fights a day, waging a one-man war.

"A remarkable tale," the King admitted. "You are a remarkable young man—Cousin."

"Thank you, sire."

Good for Raider! He was in, accepted, royalty, one of the nobility. What would he do now? Go home and hope to succeed his uncle? Try to discover who had murdered his parents? He had mentioned blood feuds more than once.

Never mind. What was going to happen to Wasp, who had affronted his king and now would never be Sir Wasp? The laughable thing was that he'd thought he could be a help to Raider in whatever he was planning to do. He had never dreamed that Raider's fortune lay in savage Baelmark. Realistically, what earthly use would a kid with a rapier be there, among the barbarians? Would he even have the courage to draw it? Blades had no problem with courage because their binding drove them, but Wasp was never going to be bound. Even if King Ambrose let him go rather than throwing him in jail, in Baelmark he would be a liability, a foreigner, no help to Raider at all, probably too scared to stand up to any angry Bael. . . .

"Rodney Candlefen died last winter," the King said.

"I heard that, sire. I only really met him that one time, very briefly." And thought very little of him—in his time of troubles, Raider had not sought help from his Chivian relatives. ''His son succeeded to the title, I heard. Rupert. About my age?''

''Mm. You must be about twelfth in line for the throne,'' King Ambrose mused. ''Not that Parliament would ever allow a Bael to succeed.''

''Er . . . yes, sire.'' Raider had been about to say something else. He would have calculated where he stood in the succession—the royal family being a topic in political classes—but whether he put himself at tenth or fifteenth, one did not contradict monarchs, especially not on that most delicate of topics.

''Candlefen must be informed that his cousin has returned to life.'' Ambrose scowled at this upstart relative of his. ''And so must King Cynewulf. We do not wish to jeopardize our good relations with Baelmark.''

That barely veiled threat caused Raider's legs to uncross. ''Of course not, sire. I will certainly be guided by Your Majesty.'' He had to say something like that. Prince or not, he was as much in the King's power as Wasp was. ''I have no illusions that I would be considered throne-worthy. Not yet, perhaps never.''

''Hm?'' His Majesty seemed skeptical. ''But you do not intend to renounce all ambitions . . . No matter. You are our relative and potentially a future ruler of a nation with whom we are bound by treaty. Those are two reasons why we shall extend you our friendship. And your tale of hardship has won our sympathy.''

''Your Majesty is most—''

''Yes. Nevertheless your reappearance must be announced with tact. As you said earlier, if you turn up at court with that conjuration of yours, you will scare all the White Sisters out of their wimples.'' The little amber beads of eyes turned to gaze at Wasp, as if their owner had just recalled his existence and was not convinced it was really necessary.

His skin crawled. And the King went on talking to Raider while continuing to stare at Wasp, no doubt trying to devise a suitably ghastly fate for him.

''This Geste . . . I sent no Blades to Baelmark with

Candlefen. I just wonder whether the man was even more of an imposter than—''

Knuckles tapped on the door. With a grunt the King heaved himself to his feet; the two youngsters leapt up. In came the masters who had been summoned, almost tumbling in, as if they had just been wakened. They would not have dared go to bed before the King did, so perhaps they had fallen asleep wherever they had been waiting. Master of Rituals was still buttoning his jerkin and Grand Master running fingers through his flyaway white hair. They lined up and bowed raggedly to the King. Under less trying circumstances, Wasp would have found their performance comical.

''Ah, Grand Master,'' the monarch boomed, ''sorry-disturb-you-this-time-of-night. . . . I have listened to Candidate, um, Raider's explanation and agreed that owing to some very exceptional—extremely exceptional—circumstances, his refusal to pursue a career with the Order can be justified.''

Grand Master's face twisted in an expression somewhere between relief and amazement. ''I am indeed happy to—''

''Quite. One point requires clarification.'' Ambrose's authority filled the room like a whirlwind. ''He claims that he was brought to Ironhall and recommended to Grand Master by a Blade calling himself Sir Geste. Neither Commander Montpurse nor I can recall any Sir Geste in the Order.''

He had made the statement a question. He had also indicated quite clearly how he wanted it answered.

Grand Master raked his hair again. ''I do not recall the name. Nor my predecessor commenting . . .'' His voice trailed away as he and everyone else turned to Master of Archives.

Master of Archives had not been in his post very long, either. He was a tall, spare man of about forty with ink stains on his fingers, already developing the stoop and bemused, shortsighted look that went with the job. He wilted under the King's frown. ''We keep no records at all of the candidates' previous circumstances, Your Majesty. Um, forbidden by the, um, Charter . . . nor the names of who bring them. Geste? Not familiar . . . I shall of course make a search. Approximately how old?"

"I am sure if he existed you would remember, Master. I fear the man is fated to remain a mystery." Ambrose did not seem displeased. No one remained who could shed light on the unknown Sir Geste. The previous Grand Master, Master of Archives, and Lord Candlefen were all dead. "He must have been an imposter."

Wasp wondered how an imposter could have known every detail of the ambassador's instructions. Those were major state secrets.

"He bore a cat's-eye sword," Raider said softly. "He *looked* like a Blade."

"He's dead, then!" That royal glare was reputed to flake plaster off walls.

But Raider was royal too, and he had donned his stubborn expression. "The original owner of the sword may well be, of course, but the sword itself was called *Fancy* and it has not been Returned in my time here."

Then it seemed a winter wind rippled through the room, raising eyebrows and pursing lips. Eventually even Wasp worked out what Raider was hinting. By custom, on the day a Blade was to be bound he chose a name for the sword he would receive. Master Armorer inscribed the name on it for him, and almost certainly Master Armorer also saw that the name was entered in the archives, along with the date and the name of his ward. Those records were supposedly secret, but could they have remained secret for five years from a determined young man like Raider? It would take very few minutes to skim back to the appropriate years and hunt down a sword named *Fancy*. He might know a lot more about Geste than he had revealed.

"No matter!" barked the King and turned his fearsome attention on Wasp again. "How much of his story had he told you?"

"N-n-none, sire!"

"Hmm?"

"Not a word, sire," Raider murmured.

The royal lips pursed. "Hmm? Then perhaps you are not quite such a fool as I took you for, Will of Haybridge. It does seem your friend may have need of a trusty swordsman or two, as you guessed. I am inclined to give you a second chance. I also want to keep your mouth shut. So, Candidate Wasp, for the last time: *His Majesty has need of a Blade. Are you ready to serve?*"

Joy! "Yes! Oh, yes, Your Majesty!" Wasp fell on his knees. "*Thank* you, sire! Yes, yes!" He kissed the royal fingers.

Raider was gaping at him in dismay, but he had said the words. He would become Sir Wasp after all.

Now. Right away.

• 2 •

Master of Rituals was currently the only teacher in Ironhall who was not a knight in the Order. A large, bluff, sandy-colored man resembling a sturdy farmer, he had been an adept with the Royal College of Conjury when his predecessor was elected Grand Master and lured him away to Ironhall to be his replacement. He had very little experience of dealing with princes and none at all of resisting His Majesty King Ambrose IV in full pursuit of an objective. Royal enthusiasm reverberated through the little room like an earthquake in a glass factory.

"It is not long past midnight, is it, Master? Close enough that we can proceed directly with the binding?"

"But, sire . . . the fasting, meditation . . ."

"The two principals have been fasting—and meditating also—for several hours now. So there should be no problem. I do not wish this night's events to become known beyond the eight of us here, Master. Is it not fortunate that eight is exactly the number we need?'' The King advanced a couple of steps, and his unfortunate victim automatically gave ground.

The unequal struggle would have been funny to watch had the stakes not been Wasp's life. It was his heart that was going to be nailed, and if anything went wrong with the ritual, the damage would be extremely fatal. He remembered Wolfbiter describing how he had seen that happen when he was the Brat, very few years ago.

''. . . swords, sire . . .'' Master of Rituals bleated, ''. . . have to get Master Armorer to identify the right—''

''I can do that.'' Commander Montpurse's voice was quiet, but it cut like steel. ''I spent some time with Master Armorer earlier and he showed me the swords he has been making for the seniors. Candidate Wasp's is very distinctive.''

The King's smile was a more fearsome sight than most of his frowns. ''Then we can proceed at once. Grand Master?''

Grand Master still had a little backbone unbroken. ''Such haste in a potentially mortal ritual is highly inadvisable, sire. Strict order of seniority is enjoined by—''

''We *asked* them in order of seniority! This one changed his mind, that's all. Nothing in the Charter against that.''

''But we shall need a Second and Third, and the Brat normally signifies the element of chance. . . .''

''Sir Janvier and I,'' Montpurse said, ''will be happy to play whatever roles are needed. We could chant the words in our sleep, I'm sure. As it happens, neither of us has eaten since morning.''

''And I,'' boomed King Ambrose, ''will handle the role of the Brat. I am notoriously unpredictable.''

The night was blustery, cool, and very dark. The wind's turmoil was more than matched by the legions of butterflies flapping inside Wasp, but he wasn't going to admit to a single one of them. In fact, he thought he was managing to appear admirably composed. Beside him, Raider sounded much more agitated than he did.

"This is insane! I don't need a Blade! I am not going to poke a sword through you! I want you as a friend, not a guard dog."

He was rarely so tactless. They were walking from First House over to the Forge, following the bobbing lights of lanterns carried by the Masters of Archives and Rituals. Grand Master was escorting the King, and it was ominous that Montpurse and Janvier were not close to Ambrose, as they would normally be. Instead, they were right behind Raider and Wasp, which suggested that the Commander now shared Janvier's distrust. They were close enough to have heard themselves classed as dogs.

Wasp staggered in a gust. "You are so going to bind me, you barbarian Bael!" he shouted. "If you don't, Ambrose will drop me in the deepest dungeon he's got and pave it over."

"Why should he?" Raider was arguing to soothe his conscience. He knew that neither of them had any choice but to obey the King. "Why not just kick your cute little ass out the gate and be done with you? Why go to all the fuss of binding you? Why waste a Blade on me? I'm not a close relative, nor important enough. It makes no sense."

It made a lot of sense if candidates who refused to be bound were wiped from the collective Ironhall memory as if they had never existed. It made sense if the King was planning to use Atheling Radgar as a pawn in international politics and needed to make sure Wasp kept his mouth shut in the meantime. This unorthodox, improvised binding might well shut it permanently and Ambrose must know that. Possibly he was even counting on it. *Oops! What a pity . . .*

"Another thing," Raider grumbled, "I know you have cause to hate Baels for what happened to your family and I don't blame you for being bitter. Now you know my evil secret, how can you possibly bear the thought of being *bound* to a Bael? I've heard you curse every Bael ever born. I've heard you classify us as the filthiest scum on Earth and wish infinite eternal torment on all of us."

Wasp shuddered, remembering just a few of those remarks. How many terrible things had he said in the last five years? "How did you stand it? I can't ever say how sorry I am. I still can't think of you as one of them. . . . I expect Chivians can be just as brutal."

Raider jabbed a friendly punch at his arm. "You don't really believe that, but it's true. I could tell you stories that would make you lose three days' meals. You'd better decide, though—can you really spend the rest of your life guarding one of *them*?"

"You're not 'one of them.' You're different."

"Not as different as you think! Ironhall's given me some Chivian manners and I'm mostly Chivian by blood, but I'm a Bael underneath, Wasp. All your life, you'll be bound to a *Bael*!"

"There isn't anyone I'd rather be bound to." Wasp could foresee a wildly exciting future. "I do want something from you tonight, though, Your Piratical Highness. A promise. Promise you won't keep me waiting. Be fast! Strike the instant I speak the oath!"

Raider groaned. "I still think we'll both regret this. You'll be stuck, you know."

Gulp! "That's the whole idea."

"I meant being a private Blade is a lifetime commitment."

Right then Wasp would settle for a lifetime of life.

The Forge was a cavernous chamber, half underground. The eight-pointed star inlaid in the floor was surrounded by eight hearths, eight stone troughs of spring water for quenching, and the eight anvils on which the splendid cat's-eye swords were wrought. The ninth anvil, the great metal slab in the center, was the innermost heart of Ironhall, the place where human Blades were bound to their wards. Usually at bindings the flames danced while more than a hundred men and boys stood around the octogram and sang their hearts out in the choruses. Tonight the coals merely glowed and yet the crypt seemed brighter, for there were only the eight participants present—seven chanting in one key and the King in several. No one could fault Ambrose on volume, but the overall effect was unconvincing.

Wasp had watched a hundred or so bindings without ever being a participant. His tenure as Brat had been unusually short, only six days. Normally he would have played Third for Mallory and Second for Raider before his own turn came, but chance had given him lead role on his first appearance. Although he was not especially sensitive to spirituality, being inside the octogram made a real difference, raising the hairs on his skin when the powers began to gather. A skeptic might say that he was just cold, of course, since he and Raider and Montpurse had all been required to bathe in four of the water troughs successively and he had not been allowed to put on his doublet and jerkin again afterward.

In shirt and hose he shivered at death point, directly across from Raider at love. Montpurse was singing a fair tenor on his right and Janvier a resonant bass on his left. He was a worry, that one, with his hostile stare constantly fixed on Raider. He had little to do in the ritual, but the balance of the elements in a conjuration as complex as a binding was very delicate, easily upset by any discordance. Janvier had always been an odd character; his binding last year seemed to have made him even more so. The whole idea of a Blade "instinct" for danger to his ward was pure goose gobble, based on no real evidence. A few hard-to-explain incidents were only to be expected in a tradition that went back more than three centuries.

Nor was Janvier the only potential tangle in the thread. A binding should begin at midnight, but now it was nearer to dawn. The very slight change in the oath Wasp was planning *shouldn't* make any difference, but one never could tell. So there were several breaks in the pattern and when Grand Master had been Master of Rituals and teaching the course on—

His sword! Rumbling out the words of dedication normally squeaked by the Brat, King Ambrose marched forward to lay the sword on the anvil. There was the weapon the armorers had made especially for Wasp, and of course it was a rapier. But what a rapier! The cat's-eye glowed like molten gold; the metal gleamed a spooky moonlight blue. He could drool over a sword like that, for it was to be his, his very own sword for all the days of his life, and when he died it would hang in the sky of swords as his memorial. He could hardly tear his eyes away from it as he turned to face the scowling Janvier. He kept sneaking glances as Janvier unbuttoned his shirt and helped him out of it and even after he had turned around and Montpurse was counting ribs and putting a charcoal mark over his heart. He barely registered the Commander's encouraging wink. He meant well by it, probably. . . .

But now, at last, he could step over and take up the rapier, a three-foot needle. *Never* had he felt one so light! It floated in his hand. . . . Alas, proper examination would have to wait. He jumped up on the anvil and spoke to Raider, whose face was haggard with worry.

"Radgar Æleding!" Variations of this scene had filled his dreams for the last five years, but he had never expected to see his best friend down there—and certainly never a *Bael*! "Upon my soul, I, Candidate Wasp in the Loyal and Ancient Order of the King's Blades, do irrevocably swear in the presence of these my brethren that I will evermore defend you against all foes, setting my own life as nothing to shield you from peril. To bind me to this oath, I bid you plunge this my sword into my heart that I may die if I swear falsely or, being true, may live by the power of the spirits here assembled to serve you until in time I die again."

Raider had noticed the omission. His eyes widened, but he strode forward. Wasp tossed the rapier to him, jumped down to sit on the anvil, raised his arms. Montpurse and Janvier should have been there to hold them so he would not hurt himself in his struggles, but they were not ready for such unseemly speed.

Raider was. "Serve or die!" he cried, and ran the whole length of the rapier through Wasp's heart until the side rings struck his chest.

Oh shit!

He had not expected such agony. He could not scream with a sword through his chest. His teeth ground; his back arched. Before Janvier and Montpurse could grab him, Raider whipped the blade out again and the pain stopped. He looked down in time to see the wound close. All over.

At this point in an orthodox binding, the spectators cheered to hail the new Blade. There were no spectators in the echoing cavern that night, but the new Blade sprang up with a yell and his ward let out a Baelish war howl. The two of them embraced, then joined hands and cavorted all around the octogram in a frenzied victory dance while everyone else jumped back from the wildly flailing rapier Raider still held. This was not an orthodox binding.

Sir Wasp, companion in the Loyal and Ancient Order of the King's Blades! Raider's Blade. Oh, it felt good!

Now at last he was free to take back that wondrous weapon, the perfect sword, matched to his hand, his arm, his style. He feasted his eyes on the diamond-shaped blade—still bearing streaks of his lifeblood—the silver quillons and finger rings, the leather-bound grip, and above all the cabochon cat's-eye of the pommel. It was large, to bring the point of balance well back, but on a weapon so light it need not be large enough to seem clumsy. Incredibly, the bar of light that gave such jewels their name was in this case twinned, *two* streaks of shining gold brightness. Distinctive, Montpurse had said.

"Look at this!" he whispered. "I never saw one like this!"

Raider was inspecting his friend's weapon just as eagerly as he was. "Of course not. It's made for you. Those are your stripes, Sir Wasp! Oh, she's a beauty! What will you call her?"

"Nothing."

"Nothing? That seems very—"

"Not nothing, *Nothing.*" Wasp had thought of this when he was only a fuzzy and had been savoring the idea in secret ever since. "Always remember, you are my ward and *Nothing* can save you!"

Raider howled out a laugh. "And Master Armorer's fast asleep, so he will write *nothing* on her blade!"

Mirth died as they became aware of six unfriendly glares fastened on them. Montpurse and Janvier were closest, obviously disapproving of an armed man in the King's presence. No one looked more furious than the King behind them, though.

"Congratulations on your binding, Sir Wasp."

"Thank you, sire."

"Did we hear correctly?" His Majesty snarled. "It seemed to us that you left out part of the standard oath for private Blades."

Wasp attempted to look bewildered. "I don't think so, sire. Did I?"

The words in question were *"reserving only my fealty to our lord the King,"* and he had omitted them because no man could serve two kings and one day his friend and ward was going to be king of Baelmark. It was done now and there was absolutely nothing fat Ambrose of Chivial could do about it. Which was why he was chewing his beard in fury.

"Hmm! Atheling?"

Raider spun around. "Your Majesty?"

"I want you to get that smart-ass brat out of here before I wring his neck. We offer you hospitality at our palace of Bondhill. You will remain there for a few days until we consult our Privy Council. Is that agreeable to you?"

Wasp blinked. There was something wrong with his eyes.

Raider bowed. "Your Majesty is most generous. I shall gladly await your pleasure at Bondhill."

Wasp tried rubbing them.

The King grunted. "Commander?"

"My liege?" Montpurse said, never taking his pale stare away from *Nothing.*

"You said you and Sir Janvier missed dinner. I suggest you take our new Blade and his ward to the kitchens and see what you can scrounge. Then send them off with Sir Janvier to Bondhill."

"A larger escort could easily be spared, sire."

"He will suffice. It is our pleasure that this affair remain known to as few persons as possible. I trust, *Cousin,* that you will not feel slighted if we board you in the Guards' quarters at Bondhill for the immediate future?"

As Raider was bowing and spouting gratitude, Wasp rubbed his eyes again and took another look. No change. The center of the Forge now was not the anvil, it was Raider. The same red hair, fair skin, freckles, the same faded jerkin and patched hose, and yet that lanky young man burned brighter than any of the hearths did, brighter than they ever could. He was Wasp's ward, the center of Wasp's world, of the entire universe. He mattered more than life itself. *Spirits!* This was what it was like to be a Blade.

But there was another anomaly present. One man seemed to glow with darkness, a sinister aura of menace. He had not worn this shadow cloak a few minutes ago, but apparently those Blade instincts for danger to a ward did exist after all. Wasp had them too. Now he knew what Janvier experienced, but he was seeing the exact reverse. He, also, could scent danger to his ward, and the threat raising his hackles was King Ambrose.

· 3 ·

An hour or so later the newest Blade was riding toward Blackwater with a full stomach and a heavy heart. Although the quarter moon had risen, it kept burrowing into silver clouds. Starkmoor looked even bleaker than it did by day, with the rocky tors appearing and disappearing like gray ghosts. Bogs, lakes, and stony ground all seemed much the same.

The road was too rough to allow any speed, and Raider soon began complaining about all the jockeying going on. Instinctively, Wasp was trying to stay between his ward and Janvier's sword, whereas Janvier wanted to keep

Raider between himself and Wasp. He did not trust Wasp, which was wise of him. In the end they settled on Janvier out in front with Raider behind him and Wasp in the rear, where he could watch.

Back at Ironhall Commander Montpurse had seen them off and wished them good chance, but Commander Montpurse was most assuredly nobody's fool. If he was not on their heels himself, he had some good men close, no matter what the King had ordered. Everyone was an enemy, every rock an ambush. Wasp had never thought this way before. He did not like it much, but there was nothing he could do about it now. His ward was in danger—he didn't know how or why, but that didn't matter. There were no ethics to being a Blade. One of the first things they taught the sopranos in Ironhall was that a Blade had no moral choices to make. Most of the time he was a good and peaceable citizen, because to be otherwise might endanger his ward, but in the face of danger he was ruthless. Ruthless it must be.

When the light was good, Raider would let Janvier draw ahead while he fell back to chat with Wasp. He told some of the story that Ambrose had not wanted to hear—how his father had abducted his mother from her wedding and how he was thus the King's second cousin, once removed.

"There's a huge collection of historic weapons hanging on the walls of Cynehof—Bearskinboots' helmet and Smeawine's battle-ax and so on. Point to any item and the scops will sing you its story. Whether they know it or not. In among all this junk is a shoddy, cheap-looking rapier. That's the one Gerard of Waygarth used to kill Wærferhð. That's what started all this. My father pointed it out to me and told me that if it wasn't for that rapier, I wouldn't be. I said, 'Wouldn't be what, Dad?' and he said, 'Wouldn't be at all.' "

Very funny. *Nothing,* dangling at Wasp's belt, was another rapier—at least he'd never have to handle another lousy saber again! But *Nothing* would have to earn her keep, and he suspected that very few swords had ever faced quite such a career as she did. If this bizarre instinct of his was correct, no other Blade in history had ever faced a potentially mortal threat as soon as he had, right at the moment of his binding. Almost none of the Royal Guard ever had cause to use his sword in ten or more years' service. An instinct was only a sort of hunch. Could he kill a man on a hunch?

"Why did you stay so long?" he asked. "Once you decided Geste was never coming back to Ironhall for you, why not just go?"

Raider shrugged. "Go to what? I had no family left that I cared about. You and the others were my friends. I had friends back in Baelmark, of course—but I also had enemies, and no obvious way of getting there. True, I was stealing the world's finest training in swordsmanship from King Ambrose, but we barbarians never worry much about theft from foreigners. I had no cause to go home until I was old enough to think of asserting my rights."

"You can certainly do that now."

"Can I? I suppose with a good sword I can handle any Bael in the world now, one on one. But, Wasp my buddy, truly Baelmark is not a snake pit where men kill each other all day long. It has laws. Different, but not necessarily less civilized. The tricks Ironhall has taught me won't let me march in and slaughter every man who stands between me and the throne. And you are going to be a mountain of a problem."

They rode on for a few minutes in the dark and the wind, tackle jingling, horseshoes clinking on stones.

Finally Wasp said glumly, "I was hoping to be an answer."

"Don't misunderstand me—I'm sure you are a terrific answer to the right sort of question and it's wonderful to have you with me. I know we'll have great times together. But suppose I become a thegn and challenge the tanist. Can you stand aside and watch me fight a duel?"

Wasp supposed. He bit back a scream. "*No! No!* You mustn't!"

"See?" Raider said. "Thegn, ship lord, tanist, earl, king—that's the road, and there are no shortcuts. I don't see how I can ever try to claim the throne with you around.

I wonder if that's why King Ambrose decided to deed me a Blade?"

"May have been one of his reasons." Anyone who thought he understood that royal fox was madder than a hare in Thirdmoon.

Just as the road descended into a shallow valley, the moon peered out to see how they were doing. They were almost at the Narby turnoff, which was as far eastward as candidates were allowed to ride. Of course, they all went on to Blackwater or Narby itself at least once, just on principle, but having no money they rarely had much success at getting into mischief.

Mischief? Somehow Wasp must get rid of Janvier. Soon. For once he could almost regret he was so much a rapier man. If he'd been an all-rounder like Wolfbiter or Fitzroy, or a woodchopper like Bullwhip, *Nothing* would have had an edge as well as a point. She didn't. She was subtle and lightning-fast but she just could not hamstring a horse. Not in the dark, anyway.

"It's almost dawn." Raider yawned sensuously. "I don't know how you two stay so bright."

Janvier heard that and looked around. "Because we're Blades."

Wasp peered at him suspiciously. "You mean we need less sleep?"

"We don't need sleep at all. We *can* sleep, if we are quite certain our ward is safe, but you never will. In the Guard we spell one another off. The King very rarely appoints a solitary Blade, you know. Twenty-four hours a day, twelve and a half moons a year—you will probably never sleep again, Sir Wasp." He did not sound very sympathetic.

"What about the outhouse?" Raider asked.

Janvier laughed coarsely. "If there's room for two, he'll be in there with you, at least for the first few weeks. Solitary Blades often go mad."

They had reached the stream and the moonlight was fading fast. Wasp went first. His horse made it safely down to the water and splashed its great hooves across to the other side with no trouble, but the far bank was undercut.

He scouted downstream a few yards until he found a better slope, but even there the crumbling soil made for tricky footing. He reined in at the top and called out a warning.

He fidgeted like a mother with a newborn babe until Raider had followed him safely. Then came Janvier. As his horse scrambled up the bank it stumbled. He was a fine horseman and recovered instantly, but instantly was not quite fast enough when dealing with Wasp. All the Ironhall instructors had agreed that his footwork was inelegant and his technique erratic and often foolhardy, but that no one—maybe not even the great Durendal himself—could top him for speed. The fraction of an instant when Janvier presented his left side to Wasp with his elbow raised out of the way was time enough. For the second time that night *Nothing* plunged into a human heart, only this time not as part of a ritual. This time for real.

· 4 ·

There were precedents. It was inevitable that in the three and a half centuries of the Order wards had sometimes come into conflict, so Blade had slain Blade. Those parts of the Litany were known as the Horror Stories and seldom repeated.

Raider had not seen the crime. He heard the scream of Janvier's horse, and when it shook itself free of the corpse, he rode after it to catch it. Dawn was not far off; already there was a horizon. By the time he came back, Wasp had stopped throwing up, but he still felt ready to die. Murderer! Traitor! Brother killer! Not even an honest fight—just an assassin's underhand stab.

He had straightened out the body and relieved it of its

sword and scabbard. After agonizing over the fancy ring on Janvier's finger, he took that too. The Royal Guard was not paid enough to buy expensive trinkets but it might be worth a few crowns, especially if it was a gift from a woman.

"How bad is he hurt?" Raider demanded, sliding from his saddle.

"He's dead."

"No!"

"I killed him."

Raider stood in stunned silence for a moment, then said faintly, "What?"

"I killed him. Ever since we left Ironhall I've been . . . he knew it. Didn't you see how he was staying away from me? Here."

He held out the dead man's sword. His ward backed away, bumping into the horses.

"Take it!" Wasp yelled. "That's your ticket back to Baelmark. And hurry, because I'm mortally certain that Montpurse has sent men after us, just to see if you do go to Bondhill."

"The King said—"

"Never mind what the King said! Montpurse trusts you no more than Janvier did. The King may have set this up with him anyway, don't you see? Or without him, more likely, because Montpurse wouldn't throw away a man." He was shouting now. "So I may have fallen into a trap and put you in worse danger than before. The King is a sly, scheming rodent—and when he insisted on sending you off with only one guide, he may have hoped that this would happen, because now he can call you an accomplice to murder. Come to think of it, in law a ward is responsible for his Blade's actions, so you're the culprit. Didn't you hear him *explaining* how he wanted to keep you a secret? Since when did Ambrose ever explain his orders? He could guess Montpurse would disregard—"

"*Wasp!* Wasp, stop! This is craziness!"

"So I'm crazy! It happens to solitary Blades, remember?"

"Not in two hours it doesn't," Raider protested. "Ambrose dealt with us more than fairly, considering what we did to his pride. He gave you a second chance, gave me a Blade, hospitality in a palace. . . . He doesn't deed Blades to his enemies or—"

"Ambrose was lying!" Wasp screamed. "He wasn't deeding a Blade when he gave me to you, he was putting out the trash. He knows a lot more than he said he did. The moment you refused to be bound, he guessed who you were, remember? He hailed you by name—Radgar. He called you the missing atheling. But there was no missing atheling! You burned to death with your parents five years ago. Then he said he'd sent no Blades to Baelmark with Candlefen—doesn't that make you suspicious? He'll deed three Blades to Bannerville when he goes to Fitain, but an ambassador to wild, savage Baelmark doesn't get any?" His voice cracked. "Take this accursed sword and let's go before Montpurse gets here."

Still Raider ignored the sword. "He was suing for peace. It would have been a provocation to send Blades."

"Yes it would, because your father had killed five Blades, right? It's all there in the Litany, the Massacre at Candlefen Park. But bound Blades would be all right. They wouldn't jeopardize their ward by causing trouble, so Ambrose *could* have given the ambassador Blades. If he didn't, it was probably because he'd promised your father he wouldn't, a condition of the negotiations. But a *knight* in the Order, one with no ward to worry about—he's free to think of revenge. He's far more dangerous! You *must* have thought of this!"

"Yes! Of course I've thought of it. I've thought of it every day for more than five years. My father was surprised when I told him there was a Blade around. But Geste could not have slipped past the house thegns on the door. The killer had to be someone known and trusted—and if I hadn't been fireproofed, no one would ever know there had been a killer, remember? To the rest of the world it's still just an accident." He shrugged. "You really think Ambrose was playing a double game with me tonight?"

"I'm certain of it." Why were they standing here chattering when the Guard was on its way? *"Take this accursed sword and let's go!"*

Raider accepted it reluctantly, as if it might jump at him. "This ought to hang in the hall, Wasp."

Wasp exploded in fury, screaming as loud as he could. "Burn the hall! *Mount up!* Raider, Radgar—whatever you want to be called, you bastard Bael, you're my ward now and I'll give my life for you if I have to. *Mount!* Mount *now,* burn you! I give you my life as long as I live and I'll follow wherever you go and be your watchdog and never sleep, but when it's a matter of security, then *I'm* master, understand? I don't care if you're rightful king of Baelmark or the Emperor of Skyrria's grandmother, you'll do as you're told until then, and right now we have to get out of here."

He had made a fool of himself. For a painful moment Raider just stared at him, then he put the baldric on and adjusted the angle at which the sword hung at his side. "Sorry. I haven't quite adjusted to being a ward yet. You've changed."

"I'll change a lot more if they cut my head off. Mount."

"Shouldn't we hide the body? Drop it in a bog? They may see it there when daylight comes."

"I want them to find it! Let's go."

"Wasp! You want them to find it? They'll be after us like—"

Raider was never stupid. Why couldn't he see? "No! No! No! If they miss it, they'll just keep going to Blackwater and Bondhill. But if they do find it, they'll know we're certainly not going to Bondhill, but they won't know what road we've taken—Blackwater or Narby or doubling back. It'll depend how many men Montpurse sent. They'll have to get word back to him, and they can't cover all the roads unless there's at least six of them—but leaving the body where it's sure to be found would normally make them chase after us eastward, so they'll assume that it really means we want them to assume that we must be planning to double back and therefore in fact we have gone east after all."

"And where are we going?" There was not enough light to see Raider's expression clearly. His voice sounded mightily puzzled.

"We're going to double back anyway, because if they think we want them to think that, then they'll assume we're trying to deceive them." Flames! Who was he to think he could outwit Montpurse? The entire Order would be hot on his trail like starving wolves. They'd have every junior in Ironhall out riding the moors. "We're going to Prail. We're going to steal a boat there. Or maybe Lomouth and buy passage, but one way or another we've got to get out of Chivial."

Raider tucked a boot in a stirrup and swung lithely into the saddle. He said no more for quite some time.

After living on Starkmoor for five years a man knew every tuft of heather within three leagues and every tor and tarn within ten. By the time the larks were caroling in blue sky, the fugitives were circling well to the north of Ironhall. Wasp had seen no signs of pursuit so far, but all ports within reach would be alerted by nightfall, so he absolutely must get his ward out of the country before then.

He wasn't up to being a Blade. It was his fault that Raider was now a fugitive instead of the King's honored guest. Janvier's death gnawed at his conscience. Dumb kid had panicked and made a good situation incredibly bad. He should have had the courage to refuse the binding. Raider would be infinitely better off without him; and even if they did manage to escape from Chivial, Wasp was going to be a lead weight round his neck when they got to Baelmark. Baelmark was full of Baels. . . .

"You are quite right," Raider said suddenly, addressing the sky. "Ambrose was being devious."

"You said Geste's sword was called *Fancy*?"

Raider glanced around with a grin. "You caught that? Yes, they do write the names of the swords in the archives. They'll write *nothing* for you."

Not funny anymore. Nothing was funny anymore when a man was a murderer, a Blade who had failed his ward within an hour of being bound. "How did you get in there?"

"Wasn't hard. Hid behind the door. I was still the Brat and it's not uncommon to find the Brat hiding in weird places. I wasn't caught, though."

"So whose sword was Fancy?"

"Sir Yorick's. Admitted in 328. He must have been good, because he was the first Blade to be bound by Crown Prince Ambrose. That was in Fifthmoon, 333—a present from Daddy on his sixteenth birthday, I suspect. He lied to me about more than just his name. He was commander of the Prince's Guard until King Taisson died in 349. Then he was dubbed knight and Montpurse was promoted to command the combined Guards."

"So he was at Candlefen that day. Must have been! It was his men who died when your mother was carried off?"

"Undoubtedly."

"And years later, when he's a free agent without a ward to worry about, he turns up in Baelmark on the very day, or almost the very day, your father is murdered. Was your father a good swordsman?"

"Not by Ironhall standards."

"Sixteen years with Ambrose. Do you know the name of Montpurse's sword?"

Raider looked at him in surprise. The rising sun made his stubbled chin shine like polished copper. "*Talon.* Why?"

"Just that we all know that." Wasp rode on for a few minutes, thinking it over. "Hoare's is called *Wit* and Durendal's *Harvest.* Not important, but we all know. Montpurse must have served under this Yorick. Do you believe that neither he nor Ambrose recognized the name of Yorick's sword tonight?"

"I'm just a stupid Baelish pirate," Raider said.

· 5 ·

Rich and secure inside impregnable walls, Lomouth had been the greatest port in Chivial until the third year of the Baelish War. Then King Æled had taken it in one of the lightning raids for which he was famous and had held it for almost two months against every force King Taisson had been able to send against him. During that time he had looted it down to the last spoon and shipped out prisoners by the thousand. Then he had burned it and sailed away unscathed. Lomouth was a great port again, but it was not what it had been.

"The only thing I ask," Raider remarked as they rode in the south gate, "is that you don't mention whose son I am."

"Why not?" Wasp asked bitterly. "You have me to defend you."

His ward gave him a quizzical glance. "You are doing very well so far. I mock you not, friend. I am hugely impressed." He had always been a source of comfort in time of troubles, but Wasp had never realized what a good liar he was.

Inside the gate the streets were narrow and full of people, horses, voices, carts, fascinating storefronts, noise, abuse, stenches and fragrances, hawkers' cries, flapping pigeons, wagons, scavenging dogs, and children liable to get under the horses' feet. A few minutes of Lomouth were enough to make Wasp want to scream and drag his ward away by the scruff of the neck.

Raider's red hair attracted some scowls, but no one took any real notice of the visitors. The rare exceptions were a few young *women,* whose eyes were certainly caught by the rangy, Baelish-looking horseman, if not by his boy companion. Apart from miners' daughters in Torwell—who were always extremely well guarded—those were almost the first girls either of them had seen in five years. Girls had been of no interest back then. They had changed. Raider's head was swinging like a weathercock, and even Wasp felt the distraction.

"First thing we— Pay attention!"

"You're too young to understand. And you should speak more respectfully to your ward and *oh wow!* look over *there*!"

"Die, then. See if I care."

"After you. What do we do next?"

They were both saddlesore and starving—especially Wasp, who had lost his last meal when he murdered Janvier—but Raider had already given his opinion that, from the look of the estuary, they had only two hours until the last ship sailed, so time was perilously short. The King's warrant would have arrived by the next tide and then the sheriff's men would be hunting for a redheaded man and a boy bearing cat's-eye swords.

"Sell the horses?" Raider suggested.

"They have the King's mark on them. That gets you hanged from the battlements."

"We can't just abandon the brutes in the street!"

They could have done that, but it was as easy to dismount in the stable yard of an inn and tell the boy to look sharp there and see to the nags. Then Wasp led his ward into the inn itself and out the front door.

At ground level, the crowds were infinitely more menacing. Every man, woman, and child was a potential knife-wielding Bael-hating fanatic. Every door held an assassin. Every mangy dog was rabid. How did *any* Blade stay sane?

"Now we sell the sword?" Raider asked, staring at a buxom blonde plucking a goose at a butcher's stall.

"No. Anyone wearing a cat's-eye sword in Chivial gets questioned sooner or later. It'll fetch a lot more money abroad. Next we find a goldsmith and you sell this ring."

Raider tore his eyes away. "Why me?"

"Because you're tall and handsome and romantic. If I try, they'll think I stole it from my mother."

Apparently Raider had inherited an ancestral skill at fencing stolen goods. The goldsmith was a crabbed, suspicious little man who conducted his business behind an iron grille in a well-lit garret. He barely glanced at the ring being offered. "Two crowns and I'm being generous."

"Two thousand," Raider responded. "So am I."

The goldsmith took a harder look at these shabbily dressed young men and then a much closer one at the ring, holding it to the light, peering at it with a lens. "It's a fake, of course, but quite a good one. Eight crowns. Take it or leave it."

"Two thousand five hundred. You're wasting my time."

A little later, when the goldsmith had gone up to a hundred and Raider was back to two thousand, Wasp remarked helpfully, "She's going to skin you, you know."

His accomplice did not even blink. "There's lots more cuddly stuff where she came from."

It was an article of faith in the Order that the Blades' binding made them irresistible to women. There did seem to be enough truth behind this belief to make it widely known among—if not necessarily shared by—the general population of Chivial. The goldsmith was allowed to notice the cat's-eye pommels.

For the next half hour, as the argument ebbed and flowed and the tide inexorably ebbed, Wasp died in agony. But he must have done a good job of concealing his impatience, because Raider was able to bargain the price up to 1,145 gold crowns. As they clattered down the rickety stairs, he grumbled that the *Baelish-obscenity* miser was going to make thousands on the deal.

"I'd have taken his first offer," Wasp said. "How did you know it was a real emerald?"

"I saw his eyes. The pupils went as big as wine casks." Raider paused on the doorstep. "Now we find a ship to somewhere?"

"Not yet," Wasp said. Time was precious, but they did not look right—two youngsters in threadbare clothing wearing silver-hilted swords had *thieves* written all over them. If they tried to buy passage out of the country they would be branding themselves fugitives and the fare would sextuple at least.

He took Raider over to a cordwainer's shop across the street and made him buy the fanciest pair of boots they had that would fit him plus a gilt-buckled, embossed leather belt for each of them. Then next door for blankets that could be made up into a bedroll to hide Janvier's saber.

"One Blade's enough," he explained. "Two Blades wouldn't go overseas without a ward. But now we look like rich folk trying to travel incognito."

"Aren't I a bit young to need a Blade?"

"Not if you're your cousin, Rupert Lord Candlefen. We're close enough to Westerth that a lot of people will know of him. I don't suppose anyone will have met him or know he doesn't rank a Blade."

"Who's going to ask?"

"I hope nobody!" Wasp snapped. "But now you have a name ready if you need one. You're a prince. Stick your nose in the air and act the part."

Raider's admiring stares were becoming more convincing as he practiced them. "Where did you learn all this admirable duplicity?"

"By keeping bad company." The binding was making Wasp think as he needed to think. He wasn't Wasp anymore, he was only Raider's Blade and would never again be a person in his own right.

The docks were bustling as vessels cast off and sailed on the tide. Playing arrogant aristocrat, Raider sauntered along the quay reciting every ship's readiness, cargo, destination, seaworthiness, likelihood of accepting passengers, and the captain's honesty.

"How can you know all that?" his henchman complained.

"All sorts of things—the state of the rigging, what

they're loading, what it smells like. That one's just a coaster, not going anywhere we want. That one would scare away rats. And . . ."

Baels! A whole shipload of the brutes! The longship was unlike anything else in view—longer, sleeker, and infinitely menacing. Of course the gang of half-naked sailors swarming over her could not be the monsters who sacked Haybridge five years ago, slaying everyone Wasp had ever known, but the sight of all that red hair buried him in memories so vivid that they blurred his view of the harbor. He saw again the big house, whose stout stone walls had blocked efforts by the raiders to take slaves or booty; the ghouls dancing around it; the flames pouring from its roof after they torched it in their anger. He heard the screaming and laughter as mothers threw their babies out the windows and the Baels threw them back in again. He even smelled the reek of roast flesh on the wind. Then the shouts as the monsters hunted *him,* the cold embrace of the soil as he squirmed frantically down into the badger's sett. . . . They were back and now he had a sword—

For an instant he stood paralyzed, rent by conflicting urges to flee, screaming in terror, or leap down from the dock and lay about him. He was fast. He would get five or six of the monsters before they overpowered him. . . .

"Wasp? *Fire and pox,* man! Are you all right?"

His ward needed him! Sir Wasp felt his binding grab him like a fist. The memories faded. He blinked. "Belly cramp. I could eat rats raw."

"They taste better warmed," Raider said cautiously. After a moment he resumed his progress. Wasp followed, trying not to look toward the Baels again but aware that his ward was sneaking worried glances at him.

"Ah! That's Thergian rigging or I'm a Thergian. Looks like she's been loading lumber—good cargo, that; keep her afloat even if she springs a leak." Raider headed for the gangplank, arriving just as it was being hauled in. "You there, my good man. Tell your captain to come here, will you?"

The hefty, hairy man thus addressed replied with some guttural words that Wasp was happy not to understand.

Just their tone was enough to make his sword hand twitch, but Raider's cavalier demands did eventually bring an officer, even larger and more villainous. He confirmed in heavily accented Chivian that the ship was bound for Thergy and could carry two passengers: "Twenty crowns each. You sleep where the crew sleeps."

"Including meals."

"Meals are a crown apiece and you eat what the crew eats."

"I expect the food will kill us if the fleas don't." But Raider paid up and stalked aboard with his Blade at his heels—and his nose in the air.

Wasp insisted they stay on deck until the *Zeemeeuw* had spread her sails and was heading down the broad waters of the Westuary. No shouting Blades on lathered horses came charging along the quay at the last minute. At last, he could begin to relax a little. It went without saying, of course, that all the hands and officers were planning to cut his ward's throat at the earliest possible opportunity, but from now on he would have to live in a world of monsters.

He took pity on Raider, who was staggering from lack of sleep. They retired to the fo'c'sle—dark and evil-smelling, with barely enough headroom for a man to sit upright, let alone stand. A sailor tried to rent them hammocks, but Raider had Baelish contempt for such decadence aboard ship and just rolled himself up in a blanket, without even a pillow. Putting *Nothing* within reach, Wasp leaned back against the ship's side to wait for his ward's awakening. He would never sleep again.

As the hours passed and *Zeemeeuw* put ever more water between her and Chivial, he began to feel better. He had successfully smuggled Raider out of the country. Now they were fugitives, liable to be hanged if they ever returned, but they were alive and free. He had only his peculiar Blade instinct to reassure him that this was a safer situation for Raider than being King Ambrose's guest at Bondhill, but that instinct had not changed its opinions. If this freak ability of his was more than just the ravings of a fevered imagination, then it was a wild card in the game, one that Ambrose could not have anticipated. Whatever the Fat Man had planned to do with a captive Baelish atheling, he would roar when he learned that the man had escaped.

Counting the hours, Wasp concluded that he had completed half of his first day as a Blade

· 6 ·

Alone among the coastal nations of Eurania, Thergy never suffered Bael trouble. This was partly because its own extremely efficient navy made it dangerous to bully, and partly because it did not let ethics interfere with business. Baels could bring anything into port there and sell it without having to explain the bloodstains. Except slaves. Thergians did draw the line at slaves. So the Baels shipped prisoners south to Morq'a'q or Afernt and marketed inanimate loot in Thergy.

The capital, Drachveld, was a great port, a place of clean streets, neat houses, tiled roofs, and excessive dullness, insipid even for two young men who had not set foot in any city since their childhood. But its very dullness was an advantage. Wasp needed time to adjust to his new status, and Raider—according to Raider—was not going to make any decisions until he had more information.

He began by finding modest lodgings for them at an inn. The bed was small, but he was the only one who slept in it, and his Blade liked the potential escape route over the rooftops outside its window. Raider spent most of one day hawking Janvier's cat's-eye sword around armorers' shops. The price he finally accepted was more than five thousand gilts, which the admiring Wasp mentally translated into almost seven thousand crowns. Most of it went on language conjurations at an elementary—temporary working facility for both of them in Thergian and a costly permanent fluency in Baelish for Wasp.

Thus Sir Wasp became Wæps Thegn and was not at all sure he approved of the change. "What's *Radgar*?" he demanded. "I thought Baelish names all meant something."

"Most do, but they rarely make sense. My father was Firebrand son of Fire-relic son of Famous-blaze. Cousin Wulfwer was Wolf-man son of King-wolf. *Gar* is a poetic word for spear. *Rad* could be the same word as *raid* in Chivian, but my name is quite old and probably came from *ræd.* So Wisdom-Spear."

"Very appropriate."

"Thank you."

Wisdom-Spear also spent enormous sums at men's outfitters, dressing himself and his Blade sumptuously: shirts, jerkins, doublets, hose, breeches, fur-lined cloaks, boots with silver buckles.

"I had no idea you had ambitions to be a dandy," Wasp remarked, pirouetting in front of the first full-length mirror he had ever seen. A starched ruff scratched his neck, but he loved the feel of silk next to his skin.

"My good looks deserve to be well displayed." Radgar had his reasons—he always had reasons. For himself he spurned the haberdashers' suggestions of greens and blues, staying with browns that made his hair less conspicuous, and choosing a hat with the broadest brim he could find. He shaved every morning and wore a short sword, a weapon fashionable gentlemen sported because it would hang vertically and not bang into things. In fact it was very little shorter than Wasp's rapier and would be almost as deadly in a Blade's skilled hand.

He soon located Hendrik's Bierhuis, an elitist waterfront establishment within whose cosy rooms and secure courtyards burghers and brokers met with ship captains to quaff ale and negotiate contracts. Its value to him lay in its boardroom, where clerks chalked up the names of vessels currently in port, their masters, and destinations. Common sailors and other riffraff were not welcome, but two young nobles were.

Baelish vessels arrived and departed on every tide, and these he unobtrusively inspected. Every one seemed to be an honest trader, but it was understood that the longships among them all had a red sail and dragon's head posts stowed under the gratings. Seeing Baels in bunches remained an ordeal for Wasp, for his heart still knew that they were vicious animals even if his head could accept that these were only seamen like any others. He sweated a lot, but his binding kept him under control. One day Radgar undertook to educate him about Chivian behavior and some of the ghastly things that had been done to Baelish prisoners of war.

"If they'd stayed home they wouldn't have suffered," Wasp retorted. "I'm sure they deserved every bit of it." He sulked for the rest of the evening.

In general he was happy to wait upon events. A good Blade never interfered in his ward's affairs unless they seemed likely to be dangerous, and Thergy was certainly a safer place for Radgar than Baelmark. But about the tenth day, as they strolled the docks in the morning sun, he demanded to know what Radgar was planning. He got the usual answer.

"Can't decide until I know more about the weather back home."

"But what do you *want* to do? Go home?"

"If I return from the dead, I will change everything. The Nyrpings, Tholings, and even the Scalthings will unite against me—and my uncle will put me on trial for Wulfwer's murder."

Wasp shivered. Few Blades lived to see their wards go on trial. "You really mean you may choose not to go home?"

"If I learn that whoever killed my parents has been identified and suitably punished—fatally punished, I mean—then I will have no reason to."

This news was too good to believe. "What about your

inheritance? What about the crown? You won't make a play for the throne?''

Radgar pointed to a group of bare-chested youths swaggering ashore and strutting off in search of a grog shop. ''Baelish thegns. See the rowers' arms and shoulders?''

All Wasp could see were necks that ought to be throttled in hemp. ''Frog scats! Those muscles came from an elementary. The older men don't have them. They're conjured.''

''I'm sure they are. But that just shows how different I am, because I can't imagine wanting to look like that or wasting good money to do so. While I've been sleeping on sheets and eating regular meals in Ironhall, those men have been sailing and fighting together all over the known world. They've fought side by side a dozen times—trading and raiding, slaving and whoring. Every one of them has half a hundred friends tested in battle. When the time comes to side, he'll vote for his friend or his friends' friend.'' He watched the raucous, quarrelsome gang disappear into the city with a wistful expression Wasp had never seen on him before. ''I am not one of them, Wasp! I'm a stranger, three-quarters Chivian, unknown, untried. Adolescence is when men forge their truest friendships and I spent mine in a far-off land. At my age my father was a ship lord with his own *werod.* I am already too late to think of a political career in Baelmark.''

''Ironhall was bad for you, you mean?''

''I made good friends there, didn't I?'' Radgar flashed a toothy grin to change the mood.

Wasp returned it. ''So did I.''

''And it kept me alive when I needed refuge. But as for claiming my father's throne . . . My only qualifications for that are my Cattering lineage, which won't carry much weight with the thegns, and a skill at fencing that they will consider a fancy way of cheating. Who wants a tanist or earl who can never be beaten? You're stuck with him until he dies of old age. No, my waspish friend, you will never be a king's Blade in Baelmark.''

* * *

His patience paid off. The next morning, stalking along through the dockside crowds toward Hendrik's, he halted so abruptly that Wasp almost ran into him. He said, "Aha!" and pulled his Blade aside to the shelter of a line of market stalls. A group of young Baels came parading toward them, arguing loudly in a dialect other than the one imprinted on Wasp and paying no heed to the citizens they were shouldering aside. They had the sweaty, thirsty look of men who had just unloaded a cargo and felt they had earned a drink or two.

Radgar let them go by. Then he said, "Better!" but let the next two follow their companions. In a moment he added, "Perfect!" and stepped out in front of a solitary youth hurrying to catch up. "Aylwin Leofricing!"

The thegn thus addressed was no older than he was and no taller than Wasp, but wide as a wagon and all massive muscle. He slapped a hand on his sword hilt and glared up pugnaciously at the dandy who dared accost him. He was bare-chested and filthy and his breeches were indecently tattered; his red-gold mane was a floor mop that had just washed out a stable. Then came recognition. The killer thegn swayed like a highborn lady about to stage a dramatic faint and neither tawny beard nor heavy wind burn hid his sudden pallor.

"Radgar?"

"Of course Radgar, you great ugly sight for sore eyes!"

"Alive!"

"Just as alive as you are!"

With howls of joy, fop and ruffian grabbed each other in bear hugs, pounded each other on the back, leaping around and generally appalling all the straitlaced Thergians in the vicinity. Wasp felt danger rumble like thunder.

Throwing a brawny arm around his long-lost friend in a way that set Wasp's teeth on edge, thegn Aylwin hustled him along the dockside, babbling questions even as Radgar tried to answer them.

"It wasn't an accident," Radgar said. "My parents were murdered and—"

"What? But how can you—"

"Whoever did it tried to murder me too."

"But my dad was—"

"Wulfwer and those two thugs of his dragged me off down to the harbor like a—"

"Then how did you manage—"

The Bael's destination proved to be Hendrik's. He shouldered the door open and propelled Radgar inside, ignoring Wasp. The entrance hallway was dim and probably kept that way to put intruders at a disadvantage. The doorkeeper who loomed forward to challenge the unseemly newcomer was taller than Radgar and wider than Aylwin; he had the battered features and crooked knuckles of an alley thug, although his gilded livery had been crafted by skilled tailors and would have passed in any ducal mansion. He hesitated when he noticed the lout's companions.

Aylwin poked this grandee in the chest with a stout finger and demanded, "*Faroðhengest*—is its ship lord here yet? Tall man with a silver eyepatch?"

Not comprehending Baelish, the bouncer frowned and looked around for help. Another, equally well dressed and almost as intimidating, rolled forward to take over. "We have seen no one by that description, *ealdor*."

"When he gets here tell him to see me at once. Beer for two."

The doorkeepers exchanged frowns. Radgar solved their problem by flashing gold coins. "A quiet table for three, if you please, and when the captain of *Faroðhengest* arrives, will you be so kind as to inform him that his son wishes to speak with him on a matter of some urgency?"

The flunkies doubled over in courtly bows.

"Isn't that what I said?" Aylwin muttered.

They were led through to a small cobbled courtyard secure inside worn brick walls. They had it to themselves, either because few other customers had arrived yet or because those that had should be spared the sight of Aylwin. Tastes vary—he won flashing smiles from the sapphire-eyed, golden-haired serving maid who brought them beer in painted steins. Wasp ignored his because he detested the stuff and the other two ignored him in the joy of old friends reunited, both still chattering like magpies.

By the time Radgar had completed a quick summary of his experiences, his burly friend had fallen into an amazed, slack-jawed silence. It seemed that something about the story bothered him considerably, perhaps several somethings. "What's *he* for?" He gestured with a thumb.

"He's a friend, Wasp. Wasp, Aylwin Leofricing."

Aylwin scowled. "I didn't ask his name, I asked what he's for. It'll look bad, you turning up with a Chivian. Don't want to remind people where you've been. Leave him here."

"I can't leave him. He's my Blade. And don't tell me Blades are un-Baelish, because I know." Radgar gave Wasp a grin, cheerful but not completely convincing.

"King Ambrose tricked him into accepting me, Aylwin Thegn," Wasp said. "If you and Radgar's other supporters want rid of me, you'll have to kill me. I shall understand your reasoning, but I will defend myself." *Oh, let them try!*

Aylwin quaffed beer thoughtfully.

Radgar said, "Wasp has already proved his worth. Ambrose was planning to use me somehow. Chivians think in terms of inheritance and rightful heirs, so he may have hoped to use me to blackmail Cynewulf. Wasp saw the danger and got me out of it and I am very grateful to him. I don't intend to be anyone's pawn, understand?"

"I wish you luck, Atheling." The sailor grinned skeptically.

"You'll see," Radgar said. "My turn to ask questions. Your dad's your ship lord? Inward or outward bound? Trading or raiding?"

"*Færing* to Skyrria for the winter furs . . . not that we turn down anything that looks profitable. You want a safe ride home, Dad'll put her about. We'll all rally behind you."

Wasp doubted that any master of a trading vessel would cancel a voyage just to oblige his son's young friend—or even his old friend's son. Pirates, on the other hand . . . an atheling might be worth a sizable ransom. Ambrose had seen some value in him. If Radgar could be used to mount a revolution, there could be profit in it. How did a Blade defend his ward against his friends?

Radgar did not comment on the offer. "How's that fat uncle of mine managing to stay on the throne?"

Aylwin drummed black-rimmed nails on the table. "Because no one challenges, of course. Seems no earl can win enough support. The only one who pushed it all the way was Swetmann, not long after your dad died."

"What happened to dear Earl Swetmann?"

"What d'you think? By the time the moot voted everyone knew he was going to lose, so the only vote he got was his own. That must'a felt good! The King sent up Big Edgar from Hunigsuge against him—and paid him a bonus for a messy death, it's said. Even Swetmann didn't deserve that."

Radgar pouted. "Maybe he did. How about in Catterstow itself? How does the fyrd feel about Cynewulf as earl?"

The thegn turned sulky and took a long drink. "We put up with him because he's king. It's good for the shire—brings in gold, lets us lord it over the others. Not that the others don't laugh at us for having a gray-haired tub of whale blubber for an earl, but he's their king too."

"Catterstow stays loyal as long as he can hold the throne? Who's his tanist?"

Aylwin scratched his tangled mop with both hands. "You're not going to like this, Radgar."

"Try me."

"Wulfwer."

Radgar winced as if he had been punched. He took a moment to consider the news, glanced briefly at Wasp as if to judge what he was thinking, then said, "I told you, the last I saw of my beloved cousin, he was heading for the Cweornstanas. What did he do—walk on water?"

"Never heard anything about that." The thegn screwed up his face in thought. "And if he looked any cleaner than usual, I was too upset about you to notice. Don't recall seeing him at your funeral, but Cynewulf swore him in as tanist very soon after. Two days maybe."

"And how many ambitious thegns have challenged dear Wulfie?"

Aylwin looked more abashed than ever. "Give him his due, Radgar. If you believe the tanist should be the shire's best fighter—and lots do . . . I don't say we don't have one or two that could beat him. . . . He's nobody's pushover."

"He would be for me."

His friend blinked. "Truly?"

"Guaranteed. And Wasp here could take him with both feet in one boot. Couldn't you, Wasp?"

Wasp said nothing.

Aylwin belched luxuriously. "Challenge is usually done with swords, but incumbent gets choice of weapons. How would your little *cniht* friend do with axes? Or bare hands?"

"Ah! Forgot that." Radgar grinned ruefully. "Not well."

Aylwin emptied his stein and wiped his mouth with a tattered sleeve. "Your cousin isn't married. He's sired a few thrall-born, but no usable heirs—wise of him, maybe? He and his father are the last of the Catterings, and when they go Catterstow may never produce another king of Baelmark again."

Wasp slid his untouched tankard across to the Bael and took the empty one. He was torn. At times he could see the sailor as Radgar's childhood friend and appreciate his good qualities—loyalty, probably tenacity, a certain naïveté, eagerness to please. His bovine manner was affectation, the pose of the warrior who regards thinking as unmanly. Despite the width of his neck, he had brains above it, although his interests would always be practical, never philosophical, and he would value courage well ahead of moral insight. He was sorely in need of a bath, but he had probably been working like a mule for days. He was not unlike Bullwhip, in fact—dull but utterly reliable.

Without warning the view would make a bewildering shift and leave Wasp looking at an animal. Loyalty became ruthlessness, tenacity greed, and that eagerness to please just rank ambition. How many rapes, thefts, and murders had this ape committed? If asked, would he deny them or brag of them? Worse, Wasp could see Radgar's fascination—there but for the grace of Ironhall went the son of Æled. He wanted to scream a warning, and he knew that any word from him would only increase the danger.

Radgar was obviously making adjustments to the conclusions of five years' brooding. "I underestimated Healfwer's skills. He must have proofed Wulfwer against water just as well as he proofed me against fire. Maybe the brute did walk home! How often do I have to kill him?"

The serving maid strolled meaningfully across the yard to flick a cloth over another table and Radgar nodded to her to refill the steins.

"Tell me again," Aylwin growled, "exactly what happened that night."

"Someone killed my parents, bolted me in my bedroom, and set the house on fire."

"My dad was marshal," Aylwin said with enough menace to raise Wasp's hackles. "You're saying he let a murderer in?"

Radgar flashed his most appealing grin. "Looking at all those expensive muscles of yours, old friend, I would never say anything so suicidal. I think I can narrow it down to four people. One was Swetmann, or someone in his war party. It was too late to stop the peace treaty, but he was ambitious and he must have known that the witan would never back him against Dad. I don't have a clue how he could have got past the guards."

"No strangers got past my dad!"

"Then how about Wulfwer? His bootlickers were ready to swear he never left the hall. Did they return too—Hengest and Frecful?"

"Haven't seen them in years." Aylwin scratched his scalp busily. "Don't recall any scandal or accusations. Someone must have paid off their families."

"Cynewulf, I'm sure. But Wulfwer's an excellent suspect, because he hated me and he knew which was my room. We were sure to be rivals when I got older—why let me get older? He got to be tanist, so he gained from Dad's death too."

"We can ask my dad if Wulfwer went in. Who's next?"

"Good King Cynewulf. He escorted my mother and me home, so we know he was in there. He gained more than anyone—he got to be king."

"He also . . ." Aylwin said and stopped.

"Also what?"

"Later. Who's the fourth?"

"Good King Ambrose."

"Not personally, I hope?" Aylwin said skeptically.

"Not personally," Radgar agreed.

At that moment the serving maid returned with three foaming steins. The thegn lifted the one Wasp had given him and drained it in one incredibly long draft, his throat working like a smith's bellows. The others watched in fascinated disbelief. He hardly seemed short of breath when he finished and handed the empty tankard to the girl. She fluttered her lashes at him and he awarded her a smile and a slap on the rump. Her obvious approval of this form of approval made Wasp wonder if it would work for him or if it required conjured muscles.

"Then how?" Aylwin inquired. "Ambrose?"

"He sent a Blade along with the embassy, although I suspect he'd promised not to—and a Blade who was very close to him, who used the name Geste. The Blades had a score to settle with my father. Have you heard anything about such a man?"

"No." Aylwin's former menace was back. "Just how do you say a *Chivian* would have gotten in?"

"He may have had ways."

"Such as precisely?"

Radgar looked to Wasp to see if he wanted to comment, but Wasp was as much in the dark as Aylwin. "Invisibility."

"Whale shit." Aylwin took another drink.

"I think I agree," Wasp said.

"Possibly." This time Radgar spoke to Wasp. "The night before Wolfbiter was bound, I had a long chat with Snake and picked up all the court gossip. There's a rumor going around that the college has perfected an invisibility cloak. Granted, even if they have one now they may not have had it five years ago. But there was something very odd about the way Yorick crept up on us in the coaster that night. He appeared on deck almost as if he— Well, no matter. Just say that Ambrose has access to very powerful conjurements. If anyone could have smuggled an assassin past the house thegns it would be the King of Chivial, yes? I can't see what his motive would be except personal spite, which is not usually a reason for a triple murder. Why include me in it? Kings usually like having relatives among foreign royalty. But those are the suspects—Swetmann and the Bloods as my father called them, Wulfwer, Cynewulf, or Sir Yorick with the connivance of his King."

"I'm really glad you're alive, Radgar Æleding."

"Thank you, Aylwin Leofricing."

"There's something I must tell you. You've got one thing very wrong about that night. Wench! More beer!"

"Have mine." Again Wasp pushed his stein over.

Thc thegn spared him another brief look of contempt and again drained the tankard in a single draft. He seemed to have unlimited capacity.

"What did I get wrong?" Radgar demanded.

Somewhere—it seemed to Wasp—a hunting horn played a warning call, as if danger approached. It was only a hunch, of course, but he sprang to his feet an instant before a swordsman strode into the yard.

· 7 ·

From his silver-buckled boots all the way up to the white plume in his hat, he was an imposing figure, and two of the establishment's male flunkies came fawning in his wake. The hilt of his sword was gilded and bejeweled—from the look of the scabbard it was a falchion, a broad blade with a sharp taper at the end, possibly handy enough in a shipboard melee but not long enough to pose much threat to a good rapier man. The silver eyepatch bearing a sizable emerald identified him instantly as Aylwin's father, Ship Lord Leofric, formerly King Æled's best friend and marshal. He came marching toward his son with a disapproving frown that only deepened when his glance took in Wasp.

"What are you doing in here? I told you to—"

Radgar turned around on his stool.

"Æled!"

"Remember me, 'uncle'?"

"Radgar! Oh, Radgar! Atheling!" The big man started to fold down on his knees. His sailor's tan showed like paint over his pallor, and his one eye seemed ready to jump right out of his head. Before he could kneel, Radgar leaped up and caught his arms, pulling him into a hug.

The hunting horns trilled again, and now Wasp could hear the baying of hounds as well. Either Leofric was the traitor who had opened the door to the assassins—although just looking at the man made that seem beyond belief—or he was the best advisor and helper Radgar could have, his father's most trusted confidant. If he seemed a threat, it was because he would try to lure Radgar home. Friends were more dangerous than enemies at the moment.

Aylwin glared at the waiters. "Wine!" he shouted. "Red wine for the ship lord! And three more beers."

Radgar reluctantly let Leofric kiss his hand and tell him several times how like his father he looked. The big man did not know whether to laugh or weep with joy. He could not *possibly* be faking that emotion!

Then they all pulled up stools and Radgar told his story all over again. The ship lord sat in rocky stillness, staring at him fixedly, showing no reaction whatsoever. Aylwin had sunk into smiling, beery bliss. At the end of the tale, when Wasp was explained, Leofric nodded acknowledgment. Unlike his son, he approved of a Blade.

"It sounds as if you had no need of binding to make you loyal to your friend, Sir Wasp. You may have your work cut out for you in future, I fear."

Wasp bristled. "Will you be more specific, please, *ealdor*?"

The older man took his first sip of wine. "Political ambition in my homeland has become a dangerous business. I will quote you cases later, Sir Wasp." The blue eye and green jewel turned to Radgar again. "You're taller, slimmer. But astonishingly like Æled!"

"I am a lesser man all 'round, uncle."

Leofric shook his head. "Not 'uncle' now, Atheling. Please call me *thegn,* for I dearly crave to be your man as I was your father's. I was never entirely convinced that his death was an accident and now your tale brings back my grief tenfold. I shall know no peace until we have avenged my lord and friend and put you on the throne of your ancestors."

"Well said!" Aylwin proclaimed, somewhat loudly. "This sou'westerly keeps up, we can make lan'fall in four days."

"Three!"

Radgar was shaking his head. "I am not ready for such talk, *ealdor*. No, let me call you that, for you must be my wita as you were my father's. Continue your *færing* to Skyrria, I beg you. If you have room for a couple of green hands, then I should be grateful, although neither of us will pull his weight. You can drop us off here when you return and pick us up on your next voyage, perhaps." Seeing protest brewing, he became insistent. "I have been entombed these last five and half years, *ealdor*! I need to get some living in before I show my face in Baelmark. I am young. There is time."

No. Closer came the danger—horns, hounds, drumming of hooves. . . .

Bright spears of sunlight lanced from the silver eye patch. "You do not have that luxury, lad. Four people were mourned after that fire—four in that house, I mean, for it spread and claimed other lives. Two of the dead were house thegns, who refused my orders and forced their way by me. It was a hopeless quest, because if the *Hlaford Fyrlandum* had not survived, then what could mere men do? But you know the code of a house thegn."

"Four?" Radgar had become very still.

The single eye glinted. "Aye, lad. The other two were you and your father. We thought he'd gone to save you. The heat was so intense after the house collapsed that we found hardly a bone."

Aylwin trumpeted another fanfare belch. "Your mom escaped. Unharmed. She's still alive."

That was it!—the danger Wasp had sensed approaching. The hunt had closed on its prey, slobbering jaws and flashing swords. . . .

Radgar made several attempts before he managed to speak. "Where is she?"

Father and son exchanged glances. Aylwin said, "In Catterstow. She's still queen. She married your uncle."

When Wasp could stand the silence no longer he said, "Can you think of any reason why dear Ambrose didn't mention this to you, Radgar? He must know. She is still his cousin."

VII

· 1 ·

That was a good question. The air was full of good questions, but four days passed before Wasp received answers to even one of them. By then *Faroðhengest* had entered the sheltered lagoons of Swiþæfen through the Leaxmuð narrows. The blue-green sail with its white horse emblem hung limp in a dead calm, and he could lean back against the side and enjoy watching sixty Baels streaming sweat while they heaved on oars and bellowed out lewd rowing songs.

They did not bother him now as much as they had at first. He had come to think of them as just dangerous animals—wolves or wild boars. No matter that his eyes told him they were men, no better or worse, no more clean or filthy, crass or cultured, than could be expected of any other gang of healthy, mostly young, sailors confined in an open boat. Even knowing that they were all well-disposed toward his ward, he still felt only contempt for them as people. The contempt was mutual. Leofric had warned the whole *werod* that the Chivian *cniht* was a Blade and any roughhousing with Radgar Atheling might trigger fatal reactions. He had made Wasp sound like a poorly trained guard dog.

Fishing boats sat on reflected hills and islets; green slopes bearing farms and villages swept back to wooded hills. It was an idyllic scene, but over it brooded the smoking peak of Cwicnoll—white against a sky of perfect blue, whose only cloud was the one over the mountain itself. Before dawn it had glowed red; by day it was almost too white to look upon. Periodically it rumbled.

In an hour or so Radgar would be reunited with his mother, and that idyll was overhung by worse dangers than a mere volcano. Just by being alive, and even more by being married to King Cynewulf, she changed the battlefield. Would she push her son forward as heir apparent under the crazy Baelish rules of succession? The sinister Cousin Wulfwer was alive, too. Radgar still protested that he had no royal ambitions, but even Wasp found that hard to believe. His friends and his family and his father's killers must all have plans for his future—or lack of one.

But had the assassin been a Bael? Ambrose had known more than he should or less than he should. He had let slip that odd remark about a missing atheling. If he had sent Yorick to assassinate Æled and kidnap Radgar—although that last feat was more likely just an opening that chance had offered and the expert fencer had exploited—then why had Yorick not told his royal master where the boy had been hidden?

Why had King Ambrose not mentioned that Queen Charlotte still lived? He must have known that Radgar would learn the truth very quickly now that he was free to ask questions. Only very hard work by the ever-mischievous spirits of chance could have kept him ignorant for so long, for although the Ironhall curriculum ignored Baelmark, it included detailed study of the House of Ranulf. Wasp could remember sitting beside Radgar when Master of Protocol drew diagrams of its many links to foreign royalty. There had been growls of anger when he mentioned the shameful Baelish connection and the Blades who had died at Candlefen—but he had not thought to add that the abducted lady was still Queen of Baelmark.

Web of errors, tapestry of questions. If Yorick-Geste had been the assassin and acting on his own, how had he entered the guarded house? If he had been a Chivian agent and Chivial had so much wanted peace, then why kill Æled before the treaty was formally signed? Why rescue Radgar, lie to him, then abandon him? Had Queen Charlotte been involved in the murder? She had married her brother-in-law less than a month after the horrible death of her first husband—and son, of course, for everyone except Yorick had believed Radgar dead. And Wulfwer. He had survived and knew that his cousin probably had. What would the tanist do now that Radgar had returned? How did King Cynewulf manage to keep the throne of Baelmark at fifty-one when no previous king had been tolerated past forty? Why . . .

Wait! That last question might have some answers!

Ship Lord Leofric was nearby, holding the steering oar easily with one hand, although he had let younger men do the hard work on the open ocean. In shabby smock and leggings tattered at the knees, he looked no grander than his crew. Only his shiny eyepatch marked him as a man of wealth.

"*Ealdor,* you promised to tell me of political dangers in your homeland."

The thegn grimaced. "Flames! It is a shameful matter to discuss with a foreigner and not one I would dare mention in Radgar's presence if I did not know him so well. But you should hear. Pass the word for him."

Presuming that this meant, "Fetch him," Wasp turned and headed aft. Radgar was pulling his weight with the others, stripped to his sunburn and making hard work of it. The *werod* had tried to shame the Chivian *cniht* into joining in also and had mocked him when he refused. Wasp caught Radgar's eye and beckoned him. Of course the sailor brutes started jeering when the atheling shipped his oar, so Radgar arrived at the stern with his face redder than ever. He was still wearing only breeches, wiping sweat off his ribs with a bundled shirt. *"Ealdor?"*

"Show me your hands." Leofric scowled at the display of bloody blisters. "I told you to stop before you got to that stage. Have Aylwin dress them for you before we beach—that's an order, *wer*!"

"Yea, *ealdor.*"

The ship lord smiled. "And may that be the last order I ever give you, Atheling! Now, listen." His expression grew grim. "I hate to sing this sad song, but I must warn you. Don't know how much Aylwin told you . . . he may not even know it all. You were wondering how your uncle has been managing to hold on to the crown."

Radgar nodded. "He's bribing the earls with my inheritance?"

"He can't be. That would take enormous amounts of money, because every earl knows his own fyrd would turn on him if he got caught. Your uncle would have to sell off lands to finance it, and he hasn't, not that I've heard of—not on Fyrsieg, certainly. You may equally ask how Wulfwer avoids challenge. The tanist is good, but there are men around Catterstow who could take him."

"Foul play," Radgar said, a sick expression curling his lip. It was not a question.

Leofric nodded grimly. "Royally born, throne-worthy candidates have had very short life spans in Baelmark lately. Not counting Swetmann, who played by the rules and lost, two Tholings and a Nyrping have died since your father burned—fine strapping young men. Sudden sickness in two cases, a ship that vanished without trace in calm seas in another. Nothing open, you understand, nothing that could start blood feud."

"That's horrible! If taking bribes is a crime, then why isn't that? Why doesn't the country rise against him?"

Wasp suppressed a smile. Did Radgar really expect honor among Baels? Could such monsters obey rules, even among themselves?

"And who's to lead a revolution if not the earls?" the ship lord snapped. "And in Catterstow, who but the tanist?"

Radgar pulled a face. "There too?"

"Same picture. Remember Roðercræft Oscricing?"

"Vaguely. Older than me. About Wulfwer's age."

"A friend of his," the ship lord said grimly. "A *close* friend. Roðercræft's your uncle's marshal, and he either doesn't keep the house thegns under control or he has them under much better control than he should. When I was marshal, I never asked a thegn to do anything I would be ashamed to do myself, because I would have expected him to refuse a dishonorable order. There have been rumors. . . . A couple of young ship lords vanished without trace; two others were crippled in fights that no one witnessed. These were all men who were being encouraged by their friends to challenge the tanist. No proof, of course, but Roðercræft and his thugs cast long shadows.''

Radgar shook his head as if violence in Baelmark was beyond belief. ''I can't begin to imagine what Dad would have thought.''

''That's not all,'' Leofric said. ''Brimbearn Eadricing?''

''Yes! Great fighter, wonderful man. Remember him spending half a day teaching a bunch of us kids how to tie knots.''

''One of the best, a Cattering of the Þærymbe line—not truly royal, but certainly noble enough to be earl or tanist. He could have taken Wulfwer if anyone could. He had just started rallying support when a rabid fox wandered into his house and bit him.'' Sunlight flamed on the eyepatch. ''Guard your ward, Sir Blade. Baelmark needs him.''

Radgar still looked incredulous. ''You are telling me that my father's brother—who is also now my mother's husband—will try to have me murdered, or else my cousin-stepbrother will?''

''Atheling, I would never insult your noble line by suggesting anything so shameful. I merely warned your Blade to beware of treachery.'' With a sad smile, Leofric leaned on the oar, bringing *Faroðhengest* around a headland.

''You are only at risk if you're a threat to them,'' Wasp said. ''Can you renounce all claim to the throne?''

Radgar hesitated. Oars creaked, creaked, creaked. The rowers finished one song and started another.

''Well?'' The ship lord's one-eyed smiles were peculiarly sinister. ''Answer his question, Atheling.''

''I could renounce thegnhood, so I could never be counted throne-worthy.'' He glanced at Wasp to see if he was being believed. ''It's been done often enough, even by some of my bloody-minded ancestors.''

''Will you?''

Radgar could be as inscrutable as the bottom of the sea when he wanted. ''I may. First I must sneak ashore unobserved and arrange a secret meeting with my mother. She will have advice to offer, I'm certain."

In Drachveld he'd said he could never be king and wasn't qualified anyway. Now he was less sure. Thegn Leofric seemed pleased by the change.

• 2 •

Had Radgar not been dazzled by the sight of his homeland he would have been paying better attention. He would have guessed what the sailors were up to. He had barely set foot on the shingle before Aylwin and Oswald grabbed him and hoisted him up on beefy shoulders. His shouts of warning were drowned out by a roar of approval from the others. The entire *werod* set off in parade.

"Æleding!" they shouted, *"Æleding! Aldes sunu!"* In moments they were riding a human wave. Everyone threw down tools and joined in. Louder and wilder grew the acclaim. Soon a thousand, then two thousand people, were clamoring through the streets, bearing Radgar to the seat of his ancestors as if he were already earl and king. Cwicnoll rumbled and the crowd roared right back.

"Radgar! Radgar Æleding cumeþ!" They made it a marching song: *"Rad-gar Æled-ing!"*

Helpless, Radgar could only sit up there and wave to friends. They were all his friends, apparently, the whole population. That was illusion, because ahead stood Cynehof, where a king who had clearly outstayed his welcome crouched in his web—a king with unscrupulous house thegns, with dark unspoken ways of averting rivals, with a tanist who never had to face a challenge. Leofric was behind this demonstration, burn him!

"Æleding! Radgar! Aldes sunu!"

Where was Wasp? He would know that this riot was well intentioned, but could his binding accept that? Radgar's fragile ambitions would die in the shell if his bodyguard began slaughtering his followers.

Across the great yard before the hall swept the crowd, almost to the shallow steps that spanned the full width of the porch. Radgar yelled a warning. Aylwin and Oswald cursed and halted. A drawn sword barred their way. The swordsman's chalky pallor and the madness in his eyes were enough to stop the commotion on the spot.

"Wasp!" Radgar shouted. "It's all right! Set me down, you idiots! Wasp, they mean no harm!" He was dropped on his feet ungently. "Wasp?" The crowd surged around, enclosing them all, clamoring to know what the holdup was.

"Where are they taking you?" Wasp spoke through clenched teeth. His rapier flicked to and fro like a cat's tail, responding to every move made by anyone, causing those within reach to back hard against the press of the mob, leaving a space around him.

"We're going to see the King, of course," Radgar said. He had no choice now; Mother must wait. "Put away your sword. *Now,* Wasp!"

But Wasp continued to flick *Nothing* around. "Going to see the King *where*?" he snarled. "Armed or unarmed?"

Flames! Why had Radgar not thought of *that* problem before a Chivian saw it? In theory he had two choices. If he veered off to the right, he could go through the gate into the palace enclosure. There would be *cnihtas* on guard, but they would admit an atheling and his Blade without argument. Or he could head for Cynehof itself, which would normally be empty at this time of day. Except it obviously wasn't. There were *cnihtas* aplenty in the porch and armored house thegns, including—now that Radgar took the trouble to look—a very large one standing in the doorway with his arms folded. His scarlet cloak and crested helm identified him as the marshal, Roðercræft. King Cynewulf must be holding court inside.

No one entered a mead hall bearing arms except the

cnihtas and thegns of the King's own *werod.* To do so was challenge. Radgar was not armed, but Wasp was and no foreigner should bear arms without royal permission. Roðercræft could arrest him if he wanted—or die trying, maybe.

Storm and fire!

Everyone began talking at once. Leofric: "You'll have to leave him behind—" Aylwin: "Make him put that thing away!" Oswald: "He's crazy!"

"I can't leave him behind," Radgar said. "He can't leave me and he can't give up his sword. Ship Lord, present my respects to the marshal and explain."

"Marshal can't admit him." Leofric sighed. "I'll appeal to the King. You wait here." He strode off angrily.

"All right, Wasp. Put up your sword. I'm not going anywhere without you."

With an obvious effort of will, Wasp slid *Nothing* back in its scabbard. The triumphal procession had collapsed.

· 3 ·

It had been a very near thing—a Blade should not be expected to watch his ward being mobbed by a pack of filthy Baels. Even when Leofric returned with royal permission, Wasp was still shaking. He followed Radgar up the steps, past the glowering house thegns in their mail shirts and steel helmets, past *cnihtas* no older than himself. Many thegns had gone on ahead, yielding up their swords at the door. Others followed. Led by Marshal Roðercræft, the procession headed into Cynehof.

Even on a hot afternoon, fires smoldered on the central hearths; but the great space was cool and dark after the glare outside, pungent with odors of ancient meat and drink, smoke and men. With no windows except the two open gable ends, vast wooden walls soared up to a web of blackened beams. Their upper reaches bore sooty, greasy shapes like fungi, probably ancient battle honors. Enthroned on the low platform at the end of the hall sat the King, with a dozen house thegns at his back and a golden crown on his head. There was no sign of the Queen, but she must have heard the news by now. Wasp assumed that a mother would prefer to hold such a reunion in private, although he remembered little about his own mother. He did know something about kings' behavior—mostly Ambrose's, of course, but the lectures had mentioned others. Cynewulf was holding court, which was not something done very often, because crowns were actually highly uncomfortable things to wear. The gathering could not be a welcome for Radgar. There would not have been time to organize it even if a messenger had galloped a horse up from the beach.

Wasp trod at Radgar's left heel all the way to the dais. Not surprisingly, he sensed the same black glow of danger on Cynewulf that he had seen on Ambrose. Perhaps all kings would look like this to him now because all kings were potentially dangerous. The house thegns scowled at the armed foreigner, ostentatiously clutching their sword hilts. Did they really think they could stop him if he intended to harm their King? No private Blade would be allowed this close to King Ambrose.

Radgar bowed and then waited with eyes lowered to be recognized. The hall fell silent. Wasp did not bow, because Blades were treated as invisible at formal ceremonies. Admittedly Baelmark might not know that Chivian custom. He could see no one there fitting the description of Wulfwer, and if anyone should toll his Blade alarm bell loud and clear, it ought to be the nefarious cousin.

Cynewulf was older than Ambrose, a fat little man, instantly repellent. His bright henna fringe of beard looked dyed and somehow accentuated the sagging flesh around his mouth and the scrolling red veins on a bulbous nose, while the splendid, bright-hued velvets and silks and furs of his clothing made their occupant seem coarse and dissipated. His fat fingers and even his thumbs were loaded with gold and gems. When at last he spoke, his voice rasped like a blunt saw.

"Radgar Æleding, our beloved nephew and stepson! You are welcome back after so long."

Radgar bowed again. "And glad indeed to be here, most gracious uncle."

"We mourned you for dead. Where have you been these many years?"

"In Chivial, lord."

His Majesty's pout conveyed Royal Displeasure. "Willingly?"

"No, lord," Radgar said calmly. "When I escaped from the fire, I was abducted by a member of the Chivian delegation. He deluded me with lies and betrayed my trust. I was snatched away to Chivial and locked up in Candlefen Park, prisoner of my mother's family."

So intently was Wasp analyzing the house thegns' chain mail and planning how he would go about killing its wearers that he took a few moments to register this outrageous falsehood. He hoped his start of surprise was not noticed.

"Kidnapped?" Cynewulf said. "A member of our house? This is intolerable! This may be cause for war. King Ambrose shall hear of our displeasure."

The shifty eyes and wet lips were those of a velvet-clad rat trying to bluster at a very large and hungry dog. Radgar had told the *Faroðhengest* sailors about Ironhall, so he could not expect to get away with this Candlefen nonsense for very long, yet he sailed blithely on over a sea of lies.

"It was King Ambrose who learned of my predicament and ordered me set free. He apologized profusely, and I expect his ambassador will soon deliver a full apology to your kingly self. As a token of respect, Uncle, he donated me this Blade. It is an honor much esteemed in Chivial, and one I could hardly refuse. As my lord is aware, Blades have only limited freedom of action, being compelled to stay in close attendance upon their wards. His presence here is unavoidable and not intended to offend."

Having been acknowledged, Wasp made a token bow, one that barely reached his waist. The King smirked.

"A Blade? Hardly more than a dagger, by the look of him. Such a gift should require our royal approval. But if the lad is your special friend, he is acceptable to us." He heaved himself to his feet and addressed the hall. "This is a happy day for us and our dear queen, for our shire, and for all of Baelmark!" He held out his arms to his stepson.

As Radgar sprang up on the dais to accept the embrace, the onlookers dutifully broke into cheers. Wasp kept his eyes on the guards, who had now decided to find him amusing. He did not know Baelish ways well enough to know what was amusing or not amusing. *Special friend* . . . that remark could have been an innocent, even gracious, dismissal of Radgar's breach of etiquette. Or it might be a sneer at a young man who arrived with a boy companion.

Smiling maidens brought drinking horns so Radgar and his uncle-stepfather could quaff ceremonial mead. Red hair looked *much* better on women than it did on men. If Wasp was ever going to accept Baels as people, he would begin with the girls.

"Tonight let the fyrd feast!" Cynewulf croaked. "Then we shall hear more of our dear son's ordeal. It may be that we shall take steps to punish those responsible. Radgar, your mother most ardently awaits the son she has so long believed lost to her."

"And eagerly I go to her, lord. But a duty first. . . . By descent from my warrior ancestors, I claim the right to bear arms and beg your noble leave to be counted among the fyrd of Catterstow."

Cynewulf's beard twisted in a foxy smile. A silent alarm screamed in Wasp's head, setting his teeth on edge.

"We certainly cannot deny your lineage, Son, for it is our own. By all means, tonight you will take the oath. We shall find you a worthy heriot and will happily accept you as *cniht* in our hall. Admission to the fyrd, of course, is not wholly in our power to grant. But we can help you find a worthy ship lord to take you *færing,* so that you may prove your valor. Roðercræft?"

The man with the golden boar crest on his helmet thumped his chest in salute and barked, "Lord?"

"Tell me again of this plan for a *færing* that you have been bleating in our ears for so long."

"I dared to ask my lord's leave to raise a *werod.* So I might accompany my brother Goldstan. He goes on the *færing* that my lord graciously approved."

"Ah, yes. Remind us again of his objective?"

Roðercræft hesitated a moment before saying, "Chivial, lord. For slaves and booty. My lord expressed the opinion that one cannot expect a treaty to endure so many years—my lord—without a minor accident now and again. And that we owed it to our Chivian friends to keep them on their toes. My lord."

"So we did, so we did!" Cynewulf smacked his lips. "And if we were to deprive ourselves, however briefly, of your invaluable services as our marshal, dear Roðercræft, would you be willing to admit our nephew to your *werod* so that he might display his mettle in the manly skills of raiding?"

The house thegn turned his helmet toward Radgar. The face inside it had been assembled from badly dried bricks. "No *werod* would ever turn down a man related to your noble self or your great warrior son, lord." It was curious that the marshal aroused no sense of danger in Wasp, but perhaps he registered as no more than a tool.

Leering, Cynewulf waved him back to his place. "Then we must give the matter our most urgent attention. How does that prospect attract you, Radgar? A chance to demonstrate that you are your father's son, yes?"

"I am at your lordship's command, always," Radgar said with astonishing self-control. Could he not smell the trap? The stench of it filled the hall.

"Ravaging the coasts of Chivial would not disturb you unduly?" Wheezing, Cynewulf settled himself back on the throne.

"There is no coast I would sooner ravage, lord. *I bear no loyalty to Chivial!*"

Cynewulf smiled tolerantly. "We are delighted to hear it. *Cniht,* conduct the atheling to our gracious queen."

· 4 ·

Ward and Blade headed for the door. The audience of thegns was drifting out, arguing and muttering.

"Well, friend," Radgar said in Chivian, "now do you understand why I tarried so long on Starkmoor?"

"We none of us choose our family." Who would expect the King of the Baels to be a benevolent monarch?

"One week!" Radgar's voice was soft but his green eyes shone with fury. "Just one week! Can you keep me alive for a week?"

"I was planning longer than that."

"I should never have brought you here, but if you can stand it for a week, then we can leave and find somewhere sane to live. Oh, that rogue! That carrion! Did you hear him?" This was the first private conversation the two of them had shared since the morning they met Aylwin.

"He's going to make you a squire?"

"A *cniht* is lower than a squire, not much more than a page. That doesn't matter!" It did matter—his laugh was bitter. "I'll shave the freckles off them in sword practice!"

"The oath?"

"No, no! The oath is nothing. He has to swear to be worthy of my service. He never was and never will be. I mean, didn't you see his reaction?"

"You lied to him."

"And he knew I was lying! He was expecting a different story."

"You're sure?"

"Yes, I'm sure."

"You know him better than I do."

They had reached the hearths and Aylwin, who was seething, teeth grinding, hooves pawing the turf. He fell into step alongside Radgar. "Goldstan! Goldstan? He's going to give you to that Goldstan *niðing?* You're a *Faroðhengest* man! You're one of us, one of Leofric's *werod*!"

"He's another friend of Wulfwer?"

"Yea!" The sailor waved a fist like a mace. "Trustworthy as a stone boat."

"So Radgar goes off *færing* with Roðercræft and Goldstan," Wasp said, "and of course I accompany my ward. Baelmark never hears more of us?"

Aylwin ignored him.

Radgar said, "Did you discover why he's holding court?"

"He's expecting the earls. The witenagemot is meeting."

Aylwin had spoken with no great interest, but Radgar whistled in astonishment. "Spirits of chance are playing tricks!"

"Good or bad?" Wasp demanded. Blades were naturally suspicious of coincidences.

"I don't know. If you think the thegns are tough, my waspish friend, wait until you meet the earls!"

"Tougher?"

"They handle bears with bare hands."

Beyond the doors, in dazzling sunlight at the base of the steps, Leofric waited with a group of dignitaries. The square had filled up as word of Radgar's return spread through the town.

"Some witan eager to pay their respects, Atheling," Leofric said. "Of course you remember *Ealdor*—"

"No, no! I am only a *cniht* who had a famous father. Present *me* to *them*."

The ship lord shrugged, but obviously approved. "*Ealdor*, you remember Atheling Radgar?"

The first man to be presented was not the oldest. He must originally have been tall, but his back had curved so much that he had great difficulty looking anywhere but straight down. He twisted his head around to smile sideways at Radgar. "Welcome, oh, welcome, son of Æled!"

Radgar dropped to his knees and held up both hands. "Ceolmund Ceollafing! How could I forget my father's chancellor and noble predecessor? I am your servant, *ealdor.*"

"Nay, lad, I hope I can soon be yours!"

"Dangerous talk!" Radgar made no effort to rise or release the older man's hands. "But if you promise never to cuff my ears again as you used to do, then I shall promise never to cuff yours—in spite of oaths I swore several hundred times."

"Oh, boy, this is a happy day, for that is your father's smile to the life! You cannot begin to guess how we miss your father! Or how welcome you are, back from the dead." The former earl tugged at Radgar to rise. He lowered his voice to a husky whisper. "But take care, take care, Atheling!"

A couple of house thegns had drifted close, watching and listening. Few in the group had noticed them. Wasp did not care if the upper crust of Catterstovian society chose to reveal dangerous loyalties, but too much loose talk might increase the risk to Radgar. As his ward was about to be presented to the second wita, he spoke up loudly. "The Queen is waiting, Atheling."

Leofric took in the situation at a glance. "He is right. A loving mother must take precedence. Will you meet with us when she gives you dismissal?"

"If I may take my leave now, *ealdras,* I shall greet every one of you with proper respect then," Radgar told the group—and then made a fast round of them right there, clasping each hand briefly and speaking the man's name. After so many years, it was an impressive display of memory.

He turned quickly to the *cniht* the King had sent to escort him—a lanky youth with brown eyes and the start of a brownish beard. He would have attracted no notice in

Chivial and looked quite human to Wasp, so he probably regarded himself as seriously deformed.

"Rædwald, isn't it?" Radgar said, winning a huge grin. "Last time I booted your butt, you were only half that size. Lead the way, please." With the witan's good wishes ringing in his ears, he strode off at a steaming pace around the side of the great hall.

Wasp hurried after. "You still thinking of leaving? They're all determined to make you king."

"Yes, I'm leaving!"

"You're just saying that because you think you're putting me in danger! Well, that's what a Blade's for—to be first up—and I won't let you run away from your duty and destiny on my account. That may be exactly what Ambrose had in mind when—"

Radgar laughed and thumped his shoulder. "No, no! That isn't it. I would never throw your life away, friend, but neither will I ever insult you by refusing to take any risks at all. That would waste the sacrifice you made when you chose to become a Blade. Being king isn't possible—the old men just haven't thought it through yet. It's even worse than I thought. First I'd have to become a thegn, and Cynewulf would make sure I died in training. If I did survive, I'd need a ship of my own and a *werod* to man it. That takes massive amounts of money, and he controls all my inheritance. Supposing I lived through the *færing* and managed to establish a suitably gory reputation, I'd still have to challenge Wulfwer. You heard what happens to men who even think about doing that."

Young Rædwald, having explained the visitors to the guards on the gate, was leading them through the palace complex, a maze of covered walkways, lawns, shrubbery, trees, and free-standing buildings—kitchens, storerooms, and isolated sleeping quarters. The teeming boys and women carrying linens or provisions stepped aside to let swordsmen pass, bowing low if their burdens permitted, but Wasp was seeing so many opportunities for ambush that he could barely follow Radgar's argument.

"The lands alone will kill me."

"What lands?" The last thing they needed was more motive to worry about.

"You didn't hear my dear uncle offering to hand over my inheritance, did you? Not likely! Even if he can't hold the throne much longer, that doesn't mean he's going to die. All he need do is refuse the challenge and retire to private life to enjoy himself. Kings get rich in Baelmark, and the war made Dad very rich. So you just keep me alive for a day or two, my trusty Blade, while I find out who killed him. Then I'll tie you up so you can't interfere when I peel him down to the bones. After that we'll sail away."

"Fob your grandma!" Wasp said. *Tie him up!* "You want to be king and you'll die trying. You going to refuse Leofric? All those men who carried you shoulder high, who stood at your backs just now in the hall? You going to leave them to Cynewulf? I don't think your father would have done that."

"My father did nothing rashly. 'When you hunt the wolf remember the she-wolf'—that was his motto. If I tried to follow this trail, my lad, it wouldn't just be the she-wolf circling back on me. It would be a whole pack. I'm only a boy who knows nothing about the business of ruling. The thegns are ashamed of their earl and hope to use me to depose him. Leofric, Ceolmund, and their friends were men of power under my father, and Cynewulf has shut them out. They think they can get back in. None of them want *me,* Wasp. They all just expect to *use* me and I refuse to be used!"

"Then I suggest—"

Without warning a monster shape loomed up ahead and Wasp hurled Radgar aside and whipped *Nothing* from her scabbard. . . .

False alarm. The apparition was only a team of four big men laboring under the weight of a dressed ox carcase. Filthy and unkempt, wearing only a single grubby rag apiece, they staggered on by without even glancing aside. The blankness of their faces made Wasp's flesh crawl. If the raiders at Haybridge had found the badger hole, he would now be a mindless wretch like them. That might be his fate even yet. Would it be possible to enthrall a Blade? The two enchantments were mutually incompatible, so one would negate the other; but he knew of no way to determine which would prevail without actually trying it.

Angry at himself, he sheathed his sword and turned to check on his ward, who fortunately had landed on grass and was still lying there, watching him with much amusement.

"You couldn't throw me around like that before you were bound, you know? What a mean, tough Blade you are! What's wrong?"

"Thralls."

Radgar scrambled to his feet and shrugged. "They're dead, Wasp. No one can reverse the conjuration, any more than death can be reversed. The body goes on. It ages and eventually dies, but the spirit has fled." As a Bael he saw nothing wrong with thralldom. Had Ironhall done him no good at all?

Rædwald led them to a much-ornamented cottage, the largest and most decorated Wasp had yet seen. When the guide tapped and then opened the door, Wasp shouldered his ward aside and strode in first to make sure all was safe. The women sitting on the couches sprang up with cries of alarm.

The three young ladies-in-waiting went scurrying out, none of them sparing a glance for Wasp. He nodded his thanks to the *cniht,* then closed the door and turned to inspect the room. His ward was enveloped in a mother's fond embrace. At first he had put his arms around her to return the hug, but he soon let them fall, enduring her affections with a puzzled, uneasy expression while she wept, laughed, and kissed.

The big perfumed salon was grander than anything Wasp had ever seen in his life. An intricately carved and gilded spiral stair led up to an upper level, which he assumed would be the sleeping area. The ground floor was a single big chamber furnished to bursting with soft chairs and couches upholstered in brilliant silks, thick, bright rugs bearing tables of marble, onyx, and alabaster; statuary, rich drapes, shelves of precious ornaments; flowers in crystal vases. The shiny paneling of its walls bore many paintings set in golden frames. His mind was sent reeling by the impact of so much wealth, a room full of pearl and rainbow. He remembered the magical treasure houses in the stories his mother had told him when she tucked him in . . . also dragons' hoards. Whoever had designed the room had displayed excellent taste; but this was pirates' loot, paid for with the blood and tears of innocents.

Radgar had never said what his mother looked like. She was tall, but Wasp could discern almost nothing else about her. Inside her voluminous clouds of cobalt silk, she might be fat or skinny, stooped or straight. Her hair and neck were hidden by a white head cloth and pale green wimple. Her heart-shaped face was so heavily painted that it seemed curiously devoid of character. He wondered why a woman would conceal herself so. Her attendants had not been packaged like curd in a cheese bag.

At last Queen Charlotte stepped back a pace, dabbing her eyes with a piece of lace. "So tall, so manly! Taller than your father."

"Greetings, Aunt." Radgar still seemed puzzled.

She either did not hear the slur or else ignored it. "I can see the Candlefen chin, but all the rest is your father. Wonderful, wonderful . . . But why, darling? Why did you hide away all these years? So cruel! Why not tell me you were alive? Even if you were a prisoner, could you not have sent word, just a word to let me— *Who's he?* What is he doing here?"

"Sir Wasp, my best friend and my Blade."

"Send him away. This is a private meeting. By the eight, if I cannot have a few minutes' confidential—"

"Can you leave us, Wasp?"

"No, sir." Who could tell who might be lurking upstairs?

"Sorry, Mother. Don't worry. He's a Blade and utterly trustworthy."

"Ridiculous!" said the Queen. "A Blade? That boy?"

"He's already killed one man in my service."

"Oh, really, Radgar! Stories!" The lady pulled her son

over to a multicolored embroidered couch. He was still only thirteen to her. She sat so she did not have to see the boy by the door, and Radgar joined her, not quite reluctant but certainly not enthusiastic. "Now tell me exactly what happened!" she said. "Where you went. Why you went—"

"Shall I start at the point where I woke up and found my door bolted?"

Again she ignored the implications. "Start by telling me why I have been left for five whole years believing my only son was dead, with not so much as one word to tell me he was alive."

"In Chivial, in Ironhall. But why not ask your husband, my lady? He knew."

"Oh, what nonsense!"

"No. Cynewulf knew I was alive and where I was."

Careful! Wasp thought. *You don't know that, you only suspect.*

The Queen raised her chin. "I refuse to believe it! Stop slandering your uncle . . . I mean your, er . . ."

"A little more than uncle, Mother!" Radgar pulled away and stood up. "I was deceived and abducted. Had I known you were alive, I would certainly have let you know where I was. When I found out, I came as fast as I could. Now, why don't you tell me why you jumped into bed with that man right after Father died? 'With unseemly haste' was what I was told. Does that mean you began right after Father died or before?"

"Silence!" Queen Charlotte sprang up almost as nimbly as he had. "You will not speak to me like that! I married your uncle because I love him, and who are you to question my right? *Men!*" Her voice grew louder, shriller. "You are as bad as your father was. All my life I had been treated like a brood mare of a rare bloodline—auctioned off to the highest bidder, *stolen,* forced to produce offspring whether I wanted to or not. You think I asked to have you implanted in my womb? No, I was given the choice of submitting or being forced, no other. Your father was a killer and a rapist, and you accuse me of not being faithful to his memory? Flames and death! Why *should* I be faithful to his memory?''

Radgar's cheeks burned red as his hair, but he held her furious gaze. ''You forget how long I slept downstairs, lady. Often I heard you asking him to . . . telling him you loved him. I heard you. I heard you cry out with rapture in his arms. Call him a rapist and I call you liar.''

''And that is worse, I suppose? Oh! Oh!'' Incoherent, she began striding back and forth across the room, weaving between the cluttered furniture with the skill of long practice. ''Were all my efforts to educate you wasted? You approve of abduction?''

''Not much, but it is a Baelish tradition. You were luckier than most women carried off by raiders, luckier than almost all women, because you became a queen. You were happy—I heard you say so many times.''

''I made the best of my captivity. What was I supposed to do—starve myself to death? Jump off a cliff?'' She came to him and yelled in his face, ''Your uncle is the first man I ever met who spoke to me as if I mattered. He—''

Radgar shouted her down. ''That is not true! I heard Father offer you your freedom many times. He would send you home with a shipload of treasure, he said, if that was what you wanted. He adored you!''

''Send me home without my child! You were the Cattering heir, so you had to stay.''

''Except that. When did he ever refuse you anything else? Show me all my bastard half brothers and half sisters, because I never met any of them.'' He pushed her when she swung a hand to strike him. Overbalancing, she toppled down on the couch and he leaned over her, bellowing. ''A Baelish king faithful to his wife? It's unheard of! And you agreed to the marriage! If you had no choice it was because your own family had left you none, and at least the pirate offered you a virile male body to live with instead of that rotted husk of a duke.''

''You think that matters so much to a woman?''

''Obviously not, if you prefer the walrus you sleep with now.''

Screaming, she tried to rise and he pushed her down.

"Mother, you despised Cynewulf. You made jokes about him, even to me. You hated him."

"That is not true." She tried to be emphatic and sounded oddly unsure.

Radgar straightened. "No? Very well. Whose bed did you sleep in on the night Father was murdered?"

"Murdered?"

"Murdered. Tell me what you remember of that night. Fat Boy offered to leave the feast and take you home. What happened after I went upstairs?"

She seemed convincingly incredulous. "I went to bed, of course."

"Whose bed?"

"Mine, of course! Your father's bed! I put myself to bed. I had sent the girls off earlier, you may remember. They had laid out everything. . . . Next thing I knew was your father shaking me awake. He had smelled smoke the moment he came up the stairs. He sent me down and ran up to rescue you, but the fire blazed up so quickly—"

"No, Mother! That may be the story you told the world, but it won't do for me. I *saw* him, Mother! I saw him lying on the bed with his throat cut. He was murdered."

She shrank down on the couch, white-faced and horror-struck, staring up at him. No actress could fake the pallor that showed under her paint.

"But . . ."

"But what?"

"But that's impossible!"

"Not impossible. Fire was my bane, remember? Healfwer made me proof against fire. I saw Father with his throat cut."

"No!"

"Yes! If you were in his bed when he came back from the feast, then it must have been you who did it. So it must have been you who went up and bolted my door. You set the house on fire, then wakened—"

"No!"

"Then whose bed were you in, Mother?"

She shook her head, seeming more confused than indignant.

"*Whose,* Mother?" Radgar bellowed.

She bellowed back, "*Nobody's!* You remember how the house thegns let us in and then I kissed you and sent you upstairs. We were right at your uncle's door and he had some rare brandy he wanted me to try. Your father didn't know brandy from small beer. And . . . I fell asleep in the chair. I've never admitted that. But it was your uncle who wakened me. By then the stairs were a furnace."

Radgar folded his arms and looked down at her with undisguised contempt. "In a chair? Does adultery only count in bed? You went upstairs with me first, so you must have gone back down."

"No. I sent you up without me." She glared up at him indignantly.

"Strange! I remember you going up one flight with me and saying good night outside your own door."

"Well, I do not! You were a very tired boy. Your memory is playing tricks."

"Or yours is. Go on with the poem."

"I am telling the truth," she said very firmly, but not looking at him. "I admit I haven't told this before. It might be misunderstood, but it was only an innocent chat—a quiet drink, talk of peace coming . . . That's all I remember until the house was full of flames and smoke and Cynewulf was helping me out through the window. Radgar, I swear that's the truth!"

"So it wasn't you who bolted my door and then lay in wait for Father to come home?"

"Of course not!" the Queen said hoarsely. "And if you think either Cynewulf or I could have cut Æled's throat you are a fool. There weren't a dozen men in the fyrd who could outfight him." Her rage and fear and incredulity had faded into a sort of bewildered resignation that Wasp found nastier than almost anything else in the sordid story.

"Perhaps he was drunk."

"Æled? He wasn't." She smothered a sob. "I'd watched him all evening and he hardly drank anything. I never, ever, knew him too drunk to defend himself."

Radgar gazed miserably at her for a while. "I don't know what to think. Wasp, have you any suggestions?"

"Was King Æled drunk enough to go to bed without noticing you weren't there, Your Grace?"

"No." She did not look up. "I mean, he must have done. It was dark. . . ."

"Mother," Radgar said, "your story has more holes than a mackerel net."

"Did Cynewulf drink any of the brandy, my lady?"

"I don't remember."

That was the only credible answer, after so long. "Your brother, Your Grace—Lord Candlefen. Do you know how many Blades accompanied him?"

She shook her head. "I have no idea."

"Cynewulf's room was at ground level? Front or back?"

"Back!" Radgar said sharply. "Of course!"

His eyes said it all. Forget rabid foxes, ships vanishing, virile warriors perishing of sudden fever, fires consuming whole buildings in minutes. . . . Conjury sometimes, no doubt, but no need for an invisibility cloak in this case.

"I don't believe your second husband killed your first husband, my lady," Wasp said. "Physically he wasn't capable. But I think he knows who did."

"He opened the shutters to let him in," Radgar agreed. He went down on one knee and clasped her hands in his. "Well, Mother? Are you a fool or a murderess? *Answer me!*"

She choked and then gasped out, "Neither! I have told you the truth and you have no right to come back from the dead and torment me. How dare you reproach me for marrying the man I love? You were dead. My husband was dead. My family had rejected me, that slop-bucket brother of mine. Those first terrible days, Cynewulf was kind and sympathetic and supportive, and eventually he confessed that he'd always loved me from the first day he set eyes on me. And I had to confess that I had always really loved him—not admitting it, ever, even to myself. I may even have hidden my feeling behind little jokes. . . ."

Radgar leaped to his feet with a howl. "*Stop!* You are

raving! You did love my father! You did detest Cynewulf. I don't know what he's done to you, but you must have been there when he let the killer in, and I can't *stand* it!" He ran to the door and was gone, leaving it open behind him.

Hurdling stools and tables, Wasp followed.

· 5 ·

Three cabins along the path, Radgar was leaning against a tree, face in hands. He said, "Go away!" in a thick voice.

Wasp ignored the order and stood guard in silence for a while. When that didn't work, he grabbed his tall friend with both hands and hauled him loose. "You are allowed to weep on your Blade's shoulder," he said. "It's part of the service."

Radgar let himself be turned around. He seized Wasp in a hug that almost crushed him—he had always been stronger than he looked. "It is possible, isn't it?" he mumbled into his Blade's ear. If he was not actually weeping, he was close, and that was very strange. That had never happened before, although Wasp had wept in Radgar's arms often enough—long ago, as the Brat, but especially last winter, after the fire in West House.

"Of course. You mustn't blame her for anything that happened. No one can resist a conjurement. Probably two of them in this case." Blades had to know about conjury—so Radgar knew the answers as well as he did—but theory was about other people and the real thing hurt. "The first one would bring her back down to his room. Probably some trifle he palmed on her earlier. Did he help her on with her cloak? Give her a ring or a necklace? Doesn't matter—it would be easy. She comes to him. Then the love potion in the brandy. Seal it with a kiss, or . . . or . . . something.'' Something not to be mentioned. ''From then on . . .'' From then on she would be his, but Wasp couldn't bring himself to say so.

''I will cut off his skin and make him eat it.''

''Good idea. Ahem! We have company.''

Radgar sighed, braced himself, and turned to meet the newcomer.

The man scurrying along the path toward them appeared to be making a very hurried search for something lost, but it was only the grotesquely bent Ceolmund. When he came within reach, he clutched Radgar's arm and addressed his belt buckle.

''Just want a word in private with you, Atheling, a warning.''

''As many words as you wish, *ealdor.*'' Radgar bent to listen, putting their heads close together and turning a chat into a conspiracy.

''Leofric wants to see you as soon as you're free,'' said the former chancellor. ''But you wash down his words with a mouthful of doubt, won't you? Remember your father always said that Thegn Leofric would rather fight than think and there was nothing wrong with his fighting.''

Radgar laughed. ''I'd forgotten that.''

''Leofric's too impetuous!'' said Ceolmund. ''Don't let him rush you into anything. Listen to me, son. You've heard about the witenagemot, of course?''

''Just that the King has summoned it and the timing seems like a very odd—''

''No, the King hasn't! The *earls* called it! First time in a hundred years . . . !''

The toothless old man was so excited that his speech came out in a spray, and Wasp had trouble understanding it all. ''Few days ago . . . Earl Ælfgeat of Suðmest . . . raided Suðecg . . . waded across at low tide . . . Suðecg's fyrd absent, *færing* in Skyrria . . . massacre . . . Earl Æðelnoð dead.'' Seemingly one duty of Baelish kings was to keep internal bloodshed within acceptable limits, and this time the rules had been badly broken. The other earls had called the moot to discuss it. "Which means to discuss his part in it, of course—Cynewulf's!"

"And what was his part in it?" Radgar asked grimly.

"Oh, he provoked it. There will never be evidence, of course, but no one doubts it."

"So now he's facing a revolution?"

Ceolmund shook his head as if scanning the ground underfoot. "It won't come to that. They're going to tell him very firmly they won't stand for being murdered, and then all go home again. That's what I want to warn you about. There are one or two of them with ambitions, but there isn't anyone who can rally anywhere near enough support for a challenge. Æðelnoð was the last throne-worthy candidate in sight."

"Surely not! I remember him and he was pushing forty even then. Jovial chap. Smart, but no great fighter. I seem to recall Dad saying he was a good strategist and a lousy tactician. A Nyrping, wasn't he? But quite a minor branch."

"He was the best we had left," the former chancellor insisted.

"Flames!" Radgar muttered, shocked.

"So beware of loose talk tonight, my lad. Some of the earls will promise you anything, but none of them can deliver. Of course your uncle will hear everything that's said. It's much too soon to look for support."

"I shall be guided by you, wita."

The old man showed his gums in a smile. "Whenever possible stress that you are a personal friend of King Ambrose, as well as a relative of his. The earls will like that; they don't want war. The young *fyrdraca* thegns do, of course, but they always do. The earls are happy with the peace. Now run along and I'll follow."

"I am fortunate to have trusted and tested witan like you to guide me," Radgar said.

A few minutes later, as he and his ward were nearing the gate, Wasp was astonished to notice him grinning like an idiot. Considering all that had happened already that day and might happen before it ended, this seemed a singularly inappropriate reaction.

"Something funny?"

"Just thinking about Ceolmund calling Leofric impetuous. My father used to say that Ceolmund slept with a boat in his bedroom in case of tidal waves."

Brawny Aylwin and four of his shipmates stood outside the gate, all still wearing their homecoming finery, complete with flashing gold and jewels.

"Came to take you to Dad's house," he informed Radgar. "He wants you to meet people, eat something. This way." He took Radgar's arm; and the rest fell in behind, repeatedly jostling the Blade just on principle. "Me and the others here have been talking to the rest of the lads, as many as we could find."

"And what conclusion did you reach?" Radgar asked blandly.

"We decided we're going to vote you in right away. You're going to be a *Faroðhengest* thegn, one of Leofric's *werod.* None of this Goldstan and Roðercræft *scytel*! You're one of us!"

"I am honored beyond words. But I am not yet even a *cniht.*"

His friend snorted. "Well, the moment you get your heriot tonight, we'll all go out to the square and vote you in."

"I am fortunate to have trusted and tested shipmates like you," Radgar said.

Leofric's house in Waroðburh was not especially grand by local standards, although it would have brought admiring gasps in Chivial. His *home,* as Aylwin explained, was on Frignes, an island Æled had given him, and he only stayed in the city when he had business. As now. There were at least thirty people crammed into the main room, quaffing ale or mead from horns while they waited to meet the atheling. Obviously they were important members of the local nobility, yet half a dozen were women, which Wasp found surprising.

Not once was Radgar at a loss for a name and a personal anecdote. These usually concerned some appalling mischief of his boyhood. Either he was deliberately trying to deter his admirers by making himself seem irresponsible, or he had been such a hellion in his youth that there were no other stories. It made no difference. They were all determined to welcome him back as a long-lost son. He told the correct, Ironhall, version of his story, dropping the Candlefen fiction he had given his uncle. Asked whether he had stayed away willingly or been a prisoner in Chivial, he grew vague. As Wasp knew, there was no simple answer to that question.

More *ealdras* drifted in later, including Ceolmund, but when all the greetings had been exchanged, it was Leofric, as host, who presumed to climb up on a stool and offer Radgar public counsel. The ship lord was reveling in his self-appointed role of kingmaker, eyepatch flashing fire.

"This witenagemot is a wonderful opportunity!" he proclaimed. "The earls are tired of the criminal who rules Baelmark by terror. They are confused by the lack of an obvious replacement. They will welcome the chance to rally behind the Æleding himself, Atheling Radgar, the lost heir miraculously returned to us."

Pause for applause.

"Remember the Treaty of Twigeport, which ended the war. Few of you here will know this, but Atheling Radgar played a vital role in the negotiation of the treaty, although he was only a child at the time. Without him, it might never have been signed. It was a good treaty, as written—a much better one than Baelmark would have obtained without his efforts. Had his father survived, the terms would undoubtedly have been honored. Alas, they have not been honored under his uncle! Tribute has not been paid, forbidden duties are levied, ports are closed to our shipping. Hardly a clause has not been violated! This, too, must trouble the earls. Their income is down, because trade is depressed by Chivian duplicity and yet they are not allowed to loot Chivial as they formerly were."

Pause for more applause.

"The King of Chivial is a rogue, who goes back on his word! Atheling, you must distance yourself as far as you can from Ambrose. Stress how you languished in Chivian captivity these last six years. Promise to restore Baelmark to the greatness it knew under your father. Promise to enforce the terms of the treaty, by war if necessary. The earls have come to the witenagemot hoping to find a new king. That day has not yet come for you, because you must first win the tanistry and then the earldom of Catterstow. But you are young, and a few more weeks will not hurt. The witenagemot is a wonderful opportunity for you to start rallying support, lad!"

This was exactly the opposite of the advice Ceolmund had offered earlier.

As Leofric stepped down from the stool, Radgar stepped forward and hugged him. "I am indeed fortunate to have trusted and tested witan like you to guide me, Ship Lord."

· 6 ·

In ones and twos the earls were arriving for the morrow's moot, marching their *werodu* up the hill to Cynehof. The visitors surrendered their weapons at the door, but even unarmed they conveyed menace.

Each earl paid his respects to the King sitting on his throne in bloated splendor; each was offered a horn of mead by the Queen herself. This charming family gathering on the dais included neither Radgar nor Wulfwer. The tanist's absence was commented on, but Aylwin reported that even Wulfwer's *werod* did not know where he was. King Cynewulf completely ignored his newfound stepson and if his wife protested this slight, he ignored her opinions also. The atheling was relegated to the milling crowd on the floor, where he was almost impossible to defend properly. At times the pack around him was so tight that Wasp could not have drawn *Nothing* had he tried, but Aylwin and his burly cronies were staying close, and in that sweaty scrimmage their fists would be more effective than a rapier.

Radgar was a new wolf in the sheepfold of Baelish politics. Every earl wanted to meet him and assess him, and so did every thegn in the Catterstow fyrd. He knew almost all of them by name. They asked questions—the same questions over and over—and with admirable skill, he cut out a path of his own between Leofric and Ceolmund's conflicting advice.

One of the first to interrogate him was one they called Big Edgar—the man who had slain Earl Swetmann, now Earl of Hunigsuge. He was by far the largest man Wasp had ever seen. He had to stoop to speak to almost anyone, even in that assembly.

"In Chivial," Radgar said. "In Ironhall. That's a school for *cnihtas*."

"You were captive or guest?" growled the big man.

"I was hiding."

Edgar's tone became menacing. He was known to be a close crony of Cynewulf's. "From your uncle?"

"From whoever murdered my father."

A blood feud made a perfect excuse for his long absence. A boy could always be allowed time to grow up before he had to seek vengeance. He did not have to accuse the Chivians of keeping him prisoner and he could not be accused of selling out to them, because they had not willingly given him his board. But Radgar had not previously mentioned the murder in public, and Wasp wondered why he was doing so now—what had changed?

"Murder?" the big man said. "Can you prove that?"

"I have good evidence, yes."

Then Edgar asked what all the earls would ask eventually, the question that had unexpectedly overshadowed even the matter the witenagemot had been called to consider: the death of Earl Æðelnoð. "What are you going to do now?"

"Track down my father's killer and kill him, of course."

"It was almost six years ago. How are you going to prove anything after all this time?"

Radgar smiled up confidently at the giant's scowl. "There is evidence, *ealdor.* I will have the true story before this night is out." More he would not explain, not even to Wasp's whispered entreaties.

So it went, as the day aged into evening and then dark. Crammed to its walls, the great hall buzzed like a giant hive while frantic servants struggled to set up tables for the feast. Cwicnoll rumbled menacingly in the distance. The earls were furious about the Suðmest affair; several of them mentioned the broken treaty and one or two even muttered about the other mysterious deaths. They wanted a change of monarch in Baelmark, but Wasp thought none of them was impressed by the new candidate. He looked weedy alongside brawny rowers. He had not been tested in battle. When asked about contentious matters, he had to admit complete ignorance of everything that had happened in the last five years, even the endless boundary disputes between shires that were the perennial rash on the Baelish body politic. His royal blood could not be denied, but that alone did not make him throne-worthy.

His Blade was going insane. He could sense danger ebbing and flowing through the hall like smoke, but like smoke it eluded capture and inspection. In the crowd he was unable to distinguish the sources. The most obvious threats were Cynewulf and his mysteriously absent tanist, of course, backed up by the sinister Marshal Roðercræft and the house thugs; but other thegns in the fyrd must have ambitions to rule Catterstow and some earls must consider themselves throne-worthy. If the unknown who had killed King Æled was not one of the above, then he was another with a strong motive to strike soon and often.

Admittedly murder in the middle of a state banquet was unlikely, at least by open violence, and Wasp was the only armed man in the hall other than the house thegns. Assassination by conjurement would take time to arrange. Poison was another possibility, but Radgar was not drinking anything. When the feasting began, Wasp would have to watch that his meat and drink came from the general supply—to try to act as taster at the King's table would be gross insult.

Surely no Blade in the history of the Order had ever faced a worse challenge so soon after his binding.

Yea, life was tough.

It was only going to get tougher.

Several times Cwicnoll roared and made the ground shake. Once he savaged the hall as a terrier treats a rat, rattling it so fiercely that scores of men fell over, the fires blazed up on the showers of fat dropped on them, ceiling beams creaked and groaned, weapons on the walls rattled. The occupants ignored his tantrums—not just the warriors, but women too. For a while the reek of sulfur made all eyes weep and all throats cough, but that was a good excuse to drink more.

One promised event conspicuously failed to occur. King Cynewulf must have forgotten his morning promise to present his nephew-stepson with a heriot and swear him in as *cniht*. Radgar made no move to remind him.

The sky beyond the two triangular windows turned to indigo; sizzling hearths shone brighter in the gloom, gilding the limbs of the sweating, near-naked thralls turning the spits. At last the King called for candles, and slaves began setting out food. Leofric and Ceolmund dragged Radgar off to sit among the Catterstow *ealdras*. Wasp did not presume to join them on the benches. He stood at his ward's back and gnawed juicy beef ribs, dribbling grease on him.

Radgar was amazingly cheerful, as if battling wits with men who might want to kill him was no more stressful than Ironhall fencing practice. He still refused to explain his mysterious hints about evidence. "What can the witan do tomorrow?" he demanded with his mouth full. "There isn't a single royal earl at the moment."

Leofric shrugged. "Æðelnoð was the last adult Nyrping. His boys won't be contenders for ten or fifteen years. The Tholings are down to daughters who need a generation to produce sons. Scalthings are even rarer than Catterings. The tanist of Weðe is a Scalthing, but not ambitious. Can you blame him?"

"That leaves Wulfwer?"

"Your cousin shows no signs of opposing his father. He knows he isn't earl material, let alone throne-worthy. If the witenagemot really wants to jettison Cynewulf this time, it will have to promote a new family to royalty."

The Baels exchanged glances that suggested they had been trying not to think about this topic.

"Can it do that?" Wasp asked.

Radgar answered without looking around. "The earls can rally behind anyone they like."

"It's been tried?"

"Often. It's even succeeded, but it always leads to civil war."

Fires and candles dwindled and died. The King and Queen had long since retired and so had most of the earls—tomorrow might be memorable. Only the youngest and most raucous of the thegns remained, drinking as if it were a duty, singing foggy sea chanties, quite incapable of noticing anything untoward. One by one they rose and staggered out into the moonlight or else slid to the floor to join the slumbering *cnihtas* already there.

Radgar was still awake and apparently waiting for someone or something. Even Leofric and Aylwin were conscious and close to sober. They kept trying to persuade Radgar to go home with them and spend what was left of the night in their house, and he kept refusing without explaining. He had moved a bench to what seemed to be a special place and there he remained, wearily slumped back against the wall. The two thegns flanked him; Wasp just stood and listened as the others talked tactics, explored possibilities, weighed theories. However much Radgar still insisted that the throne was beyond his grasp, he had not lost interest. Wasp thought he wanted it. Perhaps he wanted it mostly for his father's sake, but he wanted it.

"Cynewulf knew where I'd been . . . and that I was coming home. . . . Can't prove it, but I'm sure. . . . Perhaps I was seen in Thergy? You think that could be why he prompted Ælfgeat to go after Æðelnoð? Perhaps his friend Ambrose sent word. Is Healfwer still alive, Leofric? . . . never realized what a superlative conjurer he is. . . . So Cynewulf learns I'm alive and on my way home . . . decides to clean up the odds and ends like Æðelnoð. . . . Must admit it's cleared the slate. . . ."

"So you are the only threat left?" Wasp was bone weary. He could not sleep, but he needed a few hours' rest. He wondered how Radgar could keep his eyes open. And why he did.

"It's made things interesting—this moot." His pauses were growing longer. "Really like to know where Cousin Wulfwer has got to. . . ."

The hall trembled faintly; the volcano rumbled. A stench of ash and sulfur drifted through the hall. None of the sleepers stirred. Radgar yawned and stretched.

"Think it's time! Aylwin, can you lift Wasp?"

The Bael spared the Blade a brief and contemptuous glance. "How far do you want him thrown?"

"Not far. Remember the five swords that used to hang right over where we're sitting?"

His companions all peered up into the darkness.

"Vaguely."

"My father pointed them out to me. They were the swords of the five Blades who died at Candlefen."

"Those were sent back," Leofric said. "Treaty of Twigeport, Clause Nineteen."

"Eighteen. I was there in Ironhall when they were Returned. There's another sword up there in their place. I noticed it the moment I came in here this morning—yesterday morning. . . . It's new since my time. What's the story on that one?"

Puzzled silence was the only answer.

Radgar rose and the others sprang up at once, as if

he were already royalty. "Then let's have a look at it, shall we?"

However insane that suggestion should seem in the middle of the night, nobody argued. Aylwin climbed on the bench; Wasp removed his boots and clambered onto Aylwin's shoulders. Then his face was level with an exceedingly greasy buckler that might have hung there for centuries. It was much too slippery to provide any sort of handhold and it might not be firmly fastened anyway. Staring up with only indirect moonlight to aid him, he could make out more shields, a few axes, several antique two-handed broadswords—and one sword more or less by itself that seemed much more modern. He drew *Nothing* and stretched, but reached only the tip.

"Too high."

"Lift him," Radgar said. "And then stand on tiptoe."

Aylwin's reply was quiet and lurid, but he gripped Wasp's ankles and hoisted him up at arm's length with hardly a grunt. He might not have come by his muscles honestly, but they were real muscles. Working more by feel than sight, Wasp managed to slip *Nothing*'s point through one of the mystery sword's finger rings and jiggle it off its peg. It slid down his rapier with a rush that almost stopped his heart, fortunately not killing him in the process. He waited in silence.

"You got it?" Radgar said at last.

"Yes, but I want to see how long this lunk can hold me up here."

That time Aylwin's comment was *really* lurid.

The four of them gathered around a hearth where a few sickly flames still cast some light. Wiped clean of grease and smoke, the sword was revealed as a silver-hilted thrusting sword, slender and straight but not quite a rapier because it had a single edge for about one third of its length. It was no amateur's weapon. The pommel was a cat's-eye and its name was *Fancy*.

Radgar raised it in salute to the darkness. After a moment he sighed. "I claim this. It slew my father."

"Yorick is dead," Wasp said. "No one hangs a Blade's sword on a wall while he's alive."

"But who did that and why? And when? How and why did he come to die here, back in Baelmark?" Radgar strode toward the door. The others jumped up to follow.

"That you will never know," Leofric growled, catching up. "Is this the evidence you were bragging about?"

"Part of it. You told me Healfwer was still alive. You and Aylwin should go to bed, *ealdor.* We have a big day ahead and I'll need both of you bright-eyed and sharp-toothed. Right now Wasp and I have a job to do, for which we need a couple of good horses."

"You can't ride to Weargahlæw in the dark."

"Have to. Necromancy won't work in daylight."

· 7 ·

As they clattered down the steps in the silver moonlight, Wasp said, "This is madness. You don't believe in necromancy!"

"No? I asked Healfwer once if he could summon the dead. He said he could if he had something distinctive, something that had been very close to that person for a large part of his life and had not been close to anyone else since he died. Like offering a scent to a tracking dog."

Obviously a Blade's sword fitted the requirements perfectly, and that one had been hanging on a wall, untouched.

When they drew near the royal stable, Wasp said, "Are you just going to help yourself?"

Aylwin said, "Why shouldn't he? Most of them belong to him anyway."

"The King won't admit that. If he tries to arrest Radgar for horse stealing, I'll have to start killing house thegns."

"Sir Wasp is wise beyond his years," said Leofric. "I have a couple of good mares boarded here. You can take those."

Sir Wasp was seeing assassins crouching in every velvet shadow. Even if those were just his imagination, a ride up a volcano by night ought to seem like safe recreation after this palace of deceits. His Blade instinct did not work for volcanoes.

Leofric threw open a door and shouted at the darkness inside. Almost immediately a pair of thralls hurried out, rubbing their eyes and shivering in the chill. Barefoot and naked, they ran off to the stalls. The thegn said, "You wait here," and followed them.

"Wretches!" Wasp muttered. "Couldn't we have done it ourselves?"

Radgar glanced at him inscrutably but said nothing.

"What?" Aylwin asked. "Why? That's what thralls are for."

"It's unkind. They must need their rest. I bet they spend every waking moment working."

"Of course they do." The young thegn seemed genuinely puzzled by the Chivian's ignorance. "When they're not working they lie down and sleep until someone kicks them and gives them more orders. Unkind? You can't be kind or unkind to thralls!"

Wasp clenched his teeth in case his frayed temper snapped.

"He's right, Wasp," Radgar said quietly. "Thralls are never really awake."

"If thralldom is so pleasant, why don't you get yourself enthralled?"

"People do. It's a form of suicide. And it can be a sort of murder. That's one of the dangers I hope you'll guard me from."

The nightmare conversation ended when Leofric returned with the thralls leading two horses.

* * *

The moon, just past the full, ruled a clear, starless sky. There was very little wind, that fine spring night, but a ride up a volcano by moonlight was not relaxing. It was crazy. Cwicnoll rumbled almost continuously, and red lights flickered in the monstrous cloud over his summit. His name was masculine gender in Baelish and Cwicnoll was definitely *he.* The horses grew ever more skittish as the journey proceeded. Wasp would never be a stylish rider, but he handled horses well.

"What are the lights?" he asked once, as a particularly bright flower of flame lit the sky.

"Pure fire elementals, probably. I think they're getting wilder. You can hear the earth spirits trying to escape, too. We may be going to see a major eruption."

"How dangerous is that?"

"No danger to Waroðburh. The wind very rarely blows ash this way, and lava runs off to the southwest. Cwicnoll rumbled for years when my father was young and then just stopped, about the time I was born. Old wives say Cwicnoll signals a change of earl, but he did nothing for my father's death. The last real eruption was forty years ago. He's all noise."

The mountain roared protests at this insult.

"Of course he may open a new crater. That might put the town in danger. Or spawn a firedrake. There's always that possibility. He did that in my grandfather's day. It destroyed the Gevilian army."

"And your grandfather too?" asked Wasp, who had been eavesdropping on talk in the hall.

Radgar did not answer.

As they rode higher, their view expanded to include scores of islands and islets lying off Fyrsieg like fragments of charcoal inlaid in a sea of lead, their outer edges trimmed with a lace of white surf. Radgar promised an even better view at the lookout called Bælstede, but the upper slopes were mantled in snowy ash, making the rocky terrain treacherous for the horses. When they reached the viewpoint a chilly wind was stirring up clouds that stung eyes and throats. In the gorge leading to Weargahlæw, the trees were loaded and dying, while deep drifts almost blocked the road. Every few minutes the ground shuddered and ominous rattles warned of stones rolling down the hillsides. Now the danger was undeniable.

Wasp bit his lip to stop himself squealing out protests until he could stand the strain no longer. "I can't talk you out of this, can I?"

Radgar sighed. "No, you can't. Oh, Wasp, I wish I didn't have to drag you along. I know it's dangerous. Even if it kills me, I must know who slew my father. *Fancy* is the key to that. You know this!"

"Yes, I know. I understand. Well, let's go on, then." Brave remark by Will of Haybridge! A real Blade would find a way to keep his ward from doing this.

The mouth of the tunnel presented the worst threat yet. As the men dismounted, Cwicnoll roared menace and rattled the world. Rocks skittered down from the cliffs; the horses neighed in terror and struggled. The stench of sulfur was nauseating. Red-flickering cloud adorned the summit overhead, staining the ash-caked scene with blood.

"We'll have to leave them here," Radgar said. "Tether them firmly. Better hobble them too." As he was lighting the lanterns, another tremor produced clattering sounds inside the cave itself.

"Glad we missed that one," Wasp remarked and was pleased at how calm his voice sounded. With any luck they would find the roof had collapsed and blocked the tunnel completely.

No. What they did find was a trail of footprints where ash had drifted into the mouth of the cavern. Many people had passed that way.

Radgar said, "Going out. They've abandoned Weargahlæw. I don't see any signs of Healfwer's peg leg, do you? They probably had to carry him."

Wasp could see at least one print going in, but he was not going to mention it. "If there's nobody left, then we needn't go any farther."

"They may not have all gone. I have to know, but let's be quick about it."

Yet speed was impossible. What once had been a decent

path was littered with rocks, jagged and sharp as glass. By the faint gleam of the lanterns they clambered and scrambled their way along the tunnel, holding their breath every time the ground shook, which was often.

Between cursing wrenched ankles and bruised shins, Wasp said, "This is crazy! You can find conjurers in Waroðburh, surely?"

"Only quacks and bunglers. They enthrall prisoners and cure head colds, but that's about all they can do." Radgar's voice echoed eerily in the gloom. The light of his lantern wavered over the dark rock, roiling the shadows into dancing monsters.

Growl! Rumble! said Cwicnoll.

Rattle, click-click-click, clatter, said the pebbles falling from the roof.

As soon as they emerged from the tunnel and Wasp could stop worrying that the roof might fall on his ward, he was able to start agonizing over the chances of suffocating, for the air was a stinking fog that blocked the light of the lanterns like wool blankets. It was also ominously warm.

"This is crazy! Let's get out before the tunnel collapses and traps us."

"I can't." The fuzzy glow that was Radgar's lantern continued to move away through the murk. "I must know. There's no danger here that you can guard me against, so you go back and wait with the horses. Should be a path about— Ah! Here."

Wasp followed him without a word down a breakneck slope of rubble buried in slippery ash, over an ash-coated meadow, where every step raised more choking clouds, and eventually, after some searching, into a forest of trees bigger than he had ever imagined. The branches had caught most of the ash, but there was enough on the ground to show faint tracks where people had passed. The fog was just as dense, just as painful to the eyes and throat. The mountain rumbled and trembled. Now and again there were nearer sounds of rock falls. He wrapped a corner of his cloak over his mouth and nose, but it did not help very much. He was sweating in the stuffy warmth and the heat of the ash hurt his feet.

Footprints became rarer, the path divided repeatedly, and yet Radgar barely hesitated.

"How can you possibly know which way?" Wasp demanded between coughs.

"I probably know Weargahlæw better than anyone except— Oops!"

The track ended at a stream of boiling water. It was undercutting the roots of living trees, so it could not have been there very long.

"That probably isn't as hot as it looks," Radgar said cheerfully. He scrambled up on a rock and jumped to another, then a tree, the glow of his lantern fading into the fog. Wasp followed.

When they were together again, his ward went on as if nothing had happened. "My last summer here, I was too young to be a *cniht*. I volunteered to feed the *weargas*. Nobody argued! I couldn't lift the sacks onto the packhorse, but I could unload them. I stole a sword and hid it up here, so I could gird it on and ride Cwealm around where no one could see me and tattle. I got to know several of the hermits—some screamed at me to leave them alone, others were pathetically glad of the company. I'd gather firewood and leave it at Healfwer's door, and eventually, grudgingly, he began to accept me."

"You really think he'll still be there?"

"Oh, yes. Certain. He will never go back to the world. He's convinced that he's dead and Weargahlæw is his grave." After a particularly violent coughing spell, Radgar added, "Of course he may be right by now."

Cwicnoll roared and shook, dislodging clouds of ash from the trees. Between tremors, the forest was unnaturally quiet. Nothing lived there anymore. There would be no dawn chorus and possibly no dawn under the choking black fog.

"Is that a light? Or are my eyes playing tricks?"

"How should I know?" Wasp said grumpily. "Mine are full of mud. Yes, it is." They had been struggling through undergrowth that had once fringed a lake and was now in the lake. The water was unpleasantly hot in his boots.

"Thank the spirits, he's awake! He'll probably have his leg on." Radgar handed Wasp his lantern so he could cup his hands to his mouth, although the glow from the window could not be very far away. "Healfwer!" he shouted. "Healfwer, you have visitors. Two visitors, Healfwer."

Silence, broken only by the muffled whistle of steam issuing from a vent they had passed some minutes earlier.

"Healfwer, you are dead and so am I. I am Radgar Æleding, who died in Twigeport. I have come back seeking your *ræd,* Healfwer. I bring the sword that slew Æled. Your enchantments did not fail in the fire. I saw him murdered, Healfwer. I must speak with the dead."

Nothing.

Radgar took his lantern back. "Come on."

He moved off into the murk, with his Blade on his heels. The lake had reached the cottage before them—there must be a foot of water inside. Radgar had said that the mad hermit lived on the ground like an animal, yet the candles burning in there had been lit not many hours ago. There was no especial threat about the place, but Wasp laid a hand on Radgar's shoulder.

"That's close enough."

"Healfwer is no danger! I could knock him over with a flick of a finger."

"But who else is with him? I'm still waiting to meet your dear cousin."

Radgar grunted. "Healfwer! Two dead men to see you."

The door creaked and began to open, slowly in the water. The conjurer appeared, a shadowed figure against the light, but just as Radgar had described him, leaning on a staff, a bag hiding his head. His robe was soaked.

"Remember me?" Radgar said. "I died in Twigeport."

"Dead men do not grow taller." The old man's speech was muffled and distorted, as might be expected from half a mouth.

"This one did. And here is Wasp, whom I slew with that sword he wears. Show him, Blade."

In this madhouse anything was sane. Wasp handed his lantern over, laid his cloak on a bush, and then pulled off his smock, which left him wearing not very much. In the steamy fog, he wished he'd thought to do so sooner.

"Come closer," Radgar said, wading over to the door. "See, Healfwer? The scar over his heart? Turn around. And there's where the blade came out. That same sword he is wearing—I put it right through him. So he's dead, too. We're all dead here. Three dead to speak with one dead."

Nothing showed within the eye holes. "You did not die by fire!"

Uncertain who was being addressed, Wasp said, "No. I died when Radgar put a sword through my heart. It hurt! I could not scream, but it hurt."

"Fire the fate that felled me, though," said the horrible croak. "Water's shallows shaped my weird."

"Fire did not kill Æled either," Radgar said. "Æled Fyrlafing was murdered, and with this sword. It was hung as a prize in a hall, so its owner must be dead. Summon him for us, Healfwer. Summon another dead man, so that dead may speak with dead. Shall I carry you to the octogram, *eald fæder*? Bring his pole, Wasp." He scooped the conjurer into his arms and scrambled up the adjoining bank, the old man's long wooden leg sticking out grotesquely.

Wasp followed, laden with the staff, two lanterns, and his own discarded clothes. Fortunately they did not have far to go. The octogram was hidden under the ubiquitous ash, with only a trampled circular path around it visible. Radgar set the conjurer upright where he could lean against a tree, and used his own cloak to dust off the ground and uncover the marking stones.

Healfwer babbled the whole time, muttering angrily to himself. ". . . never news announce to me . . . Wanting wealth and wonders wrought . . . spawn of thegn and thrall despising . . . if ocean's depths had deeper hugged; then surging sea had shelter held." He coughed wretchedly.

Radgar inspected the water crock. "Still full. Set one of the lanterns there, Wasp. Now, wita, where do we put the sword?"

"Bæl the bane to burn the king!"

"No. I told you—Æled did not burn. What was his bane, *ealdor*?"

The conjurer did not reply. Radgar tried again.

"When you chanted the *hlytm* for Æled, what weird did you see? Was it love?"

Healfwer shouted, "Yea!"

"Ah, now we're communicating. So where do I put this sword? In the middle?"

"Of course, *niðing*," the conjurer snapped. "And whatever you do stay out of the octogram. When day is doubled, duty labors."

Wasp watched skeptically. He had never put much stock in Radgar's tales of one-man conjurations, and firsthand experience of the enchanter failed to reassure him. The old man's wits had flown south with the swallows a long time ago.

The ground trembled, the mountain roared. Somewhere, and not very far away, a long thunder of falling rocks became a crashing-down of trees. As soon as he could trust his feet again, Radgar planted *Fancy* in the center of the octogram, needing three tries before he found a spot free of roots, and even then not pushing the blade in very far. He retreated to the edge of the little clearing and said, "Ready, wita!"

The conjurer lurched forward to the edge of the octogram, went around it a short distance and stopped. Silence fell, except for vague gurgling sounds of steam and spouting water. They seemed to be coming from several directions now, so perhaps the whole crater was going to fill up like a soup pot. The first Blade ever to let his ward get boiled alive . . . What were they waiting for? The old man clearly didn't even know what was expected of him, although he had positioned himself opposite the jug and lantern, where death point would—

"Hwæt!" he cried, and began screeching out an incantation, invoking the spirits of death. Few of the words were

audible and fewer made any sense, but he never paused or hesitated. After a verse or two he reeled partway around the octogram and chanted some more.

It took a long time. Even when the ground swayed, the ancient cripple kept his balance. He carried on without pause, not allowing the bellowing of the volcano itself or screams from the steam vents to distract him from whatever he was croaking. It was a remarkable display of endurance. Either the two lanterns were dwindling or the fog was growing thicker. The one on the octogram was only a faint golden blur. Even the one at Wasp's feet seemed to be fading away. He could barely see Radgar at his side, although he could hear him coughing. The mist seemed especially thick inside the center, around the sword.

The conjurer's chant rasped away into choking coughs somewhere on the far side of the clearing. Forest and volcano fell ominously silent.

Came a faint, gossamer whisper in the night: "What goes? Who calls?"

The hair on the back of Wasp's neck stirred. That was not Radgar's voice nor Healfwer's, and it had come from the center of the clearing. If he let his imagination run away with him, it could pick out shapes in the mist, like a man kneeling, hugging the blade. . . .

The voice sighed again. "Command me. . . . Who calls me? Who commands? What goes?"

Wasp jumped as Radgar spoke from the darkness at his side, his voice almost as gruff as Healfwer's. "I command you! I, Radgar Æleding, command you."

The apparition—if it was not entirely Wasp's imagination—was upright now, on its feet, peering. "Youngling? So tall now? Is that you, Youngling?"

"I am he. Speak your name!"

"Ah! I have no name now, none. You knew me as Geste, Youngling."

Radgar moved forward a couple of steps. He was just visible, hardly more solid than—than that wisp of mist that could be mistaken for a naked man. Wasp went to stand beside him, ready to haul him back if he tried to enter the octogram.

"Say by what name King Ambrose knew you."

"Yorick," sighed the ghost. "Sir Yorick of the Loyal and Ancient Order."

"Then speak! Who slew my father, Æled Fyrlafing?"

"Why, that was I, Youngling. Know you not that by now?"

"How did you get in?"

"By trade, Youngling, by trade!" The whisper rippled with amusement or mockery. "Fair trade. Cynewulf let me in and I gave him the throne he wanted. I'd already given him the woman he lusted after—aye, she was there, asleep on the bed with half her clothes undone. Twas fair, a most fair trade!"

Radgar spoke through a coughing fit. "Go—on! Say—happened next."

"Why, he led me upstairs to wait and then went back down to the woman." The apparition kept fading and re-forming, illusion wandering around the octogram as if seeking a way out. Still the faint mocking whisper: "When Æled came, I gave him time to draw. Still fair! I told him the names of the five he had slain: Sir Richey, Sir Denvers, Sir Havoc, Sir Panther, Sir Rhys. Good men, good men all! I told him it was his turn now, but I let him try a little sword work with me, so he knew it was hopeless and he must die. I explained that his wife was part of his brother's price so he would die unhappy. When he began to weep I let *Fancy* cut his throat."

"It was easy for you, wasn't it? Easy for a Blade!"

"Easy as stamping on a bug, Youngling. I didn't hurt him, though. I could have hurt him a lot."

"And what happened after that?"

Wasp had an impression of Yorick now. The faint image painted on the mist was that of a wiry, dark-hued man, stark naked, with long rat tails of hair below his shoulders and a wild bush of beard. All imagination, of course. There was nothing there but fog.

"Why, nothing happened, Youngling, nothing! I went downstairs again. I'd done what I wanted and I expect your uncle had, too. I left the way I came, by the window. I waited around to watch what happened when he torched the house.''

''You bolted my door first!'' Radgar screamed.

''Not me, Youngling, not me! I had no orders for you, no grudge either. Didn't know you were there. Never made war on children. I'd kind of taken a fancy to you by then, anyway. Could've killed you easy enough at sea later. You know that, Youngling!'' The ghost sounded quite offended.

Wasp realized he had unconsciously edged forward until his toes were almost on the octogram. The apparition was staring straight at him now. Its face and eyes were those of a corpse, completely dead. Yet in other ways it seemed like a living man. It was shivering, and its breath puffed visibly in the dawn chill. A corpse could not breathe, and a ghost should not be covered in gooseflesh. Even its wrongness was horribly familiar in a way Wasp could not place. He had seen those eyes before.

''A Blade!'' it said softly. ''Will you leave a brother to suffer so?''

Wasp's hackles rose again.

''Why did you board the boat?'' Radgar demanded.

Much to Wasp's relief, the ghost turned away and began wandering restlessly around the octogram. It left no footprints on the ash. ''Why, to save you, Youngling! I told you I'd taken a fancy to you. Didn't like that hulking cousin of yours. Didn't want him to get you.''

''To save me *why*?''

The ghost sighed. ''To sell, Youngling, to sell! I'd avenged my men, but I was thirty-six years old and nobody had made me rich yet.''

''You tried to sell me to King Ambrose?''

''I wanted to be sure my work would be adequately rewarded. Fat Man shows a nasty frugal streak at times.''

''So that's how he knew I was alive! What went wrong? Wouldn't he buy?''

''Hard man, he is. He set the Dark Chamber on me, and I only just got out of Chivial with his inquisitors snapping at my ass.'' The apparition had drawn close again. "If he'd caught me, he'd have found out where I'd hidden you, and that would have been the end of the game."

"What was he going to do with me if he got me?"

Yorick shrugged. "Up to him. I was offering one healthy atheling with no strings attached."

"He wouldn't deal, so you came back here and tried my uncle?"

"Clever lad you are, Youngling, clever lad."

"And what happened then? How much would he pay for me?"

The ghost looked up and sniffed the air. "Dawn coming? How long can you hold this conjuration?"

"Answer my question!"

"Nothing happened then. Everything stopped happening."

Radgar was shouting now, his voice cracking with emotion. "Cynewulf outsmarted you too! You didn't have much success extorting money from kings, did you, Yorick? He caught you and made you tell him where I was, but he wasn't like Ambrose—he couldn't get at me in Ironhall. So he just waited, knowing I would appear eventually. You he killed. He hung your sword on his wall!"

"What? My *Fancy*!" The ghost threw its head back and howled, long and shrill, and Cwicnoll rumbled in answer. Wailing and lamenting, Yorick flickered over to the sword and tugged on it with both hands, a figure of mist straining in vain to pull steel out of the ground. It did not move. "Shame! Shame! Take *Fancy* home! Take her back to the Hall! Don't leave her here. Tell them Yorick herds pigs if you must, but leave not my poor *Fancy* here alone."

Then Wasp understood what was so horribly familiar about that shaggily bearded apparition. "Radgar! He's not dead! He's a thrall!"

The thing in the octogram dropped to its knees beside the sword, caressing it, kissing it, whispering.

"Is that possible?" Radgar yelled.

The conjurer, wherever he was, did not answer. But why would it not be possible?

"Thrall?" moaned the ghost, embracing the sword, weeping. "Find it, Youngling! Find it and kill it."

Herding pigs? Somewhere on this island of Fyrsieg a *Blade* was toiling naked in the King's fields, herding pigs? Wasp ground his teeth. How Cynewulf must enjoy that!

"Answer my questions," Radgar shouted. "Why did you reveal the ambassador's instructions?"

Yorick continued to stroke and nuzzle the sword hilt, yet he answered clearly enough. "Hard it is to kill a king, Youngling—if you want to live to brag of it. I needed to meet Æled alone. Made friends with you so you would arrange that. You did, but he was too smart . . . brought company along. Didn't matter. I closed the deal with your uncle, and after that the treaty was nothing. Fat pension to Cynewulf and forget what the paper said. Ambrose happy, Cynewulf happy. Me happy. All I wanted was revenge, and I got it without your help."

"Pension? Throne? What else did Cynewulf get? You said you'd already given him the . . . given him *my mother*! How?"

"A draft, Youngling. Slip it to a woman and she goes to sleep. Then you enjoy her. She's yours to enjoy ever after."

Radgar moaned.

Wasp said, "So Ambrose put you up to all this? Ambrose?"

Yorick sighed like wind in treetops. "Too late, brother! It's dawn. New day . . ." The whisper faded. "Fare well, Youngling. . . ."

No light penetrated the fog and trees. There was nothing in the octogram except the sword, and never had been. Even Healfwer had gone. A steam vent whistled and splashed nearby.

Wasp shivered as if he had a fever. "He's dead, isn't he? A thrall can't be restored?"

"No. He's dead. Villain that he was."

Wasp went over and pulled the sword out of the ground. It came easily for him, although his hand was shaking. "I'll take this and one day I'll send it back to Starkmoor. I owe him that much."

"Not yet," said Radgar. "I will need a good blade before this day is out."

Hard it is to kill a king.

VIII

· 1 ·

Radgar was barely conscious during most of the trek out of Weargahlæw. He had wanted to find Healfwer and convince the crazy old man that the crater must soon be his grave, which the maniac knew perfectly well and longed for. Wasp forbade it and forced him to abandon the wita to his chosen fate.

It was dawn, the ghost had said, and yet there was no way to know that in the fog-filled crater. Steam, hot water, foul gases were bursting forth everywhere. Paths vanished into pools of bubbling mud, lakes had flooded huge areas of the forest, and Radgar's memory of the route was useless. More than once he passed out completely from the fumes and would have lain there and died had Wasp not half dragged, half carried him onward. That was his binding at work, of course; but superhuman endurance must demand a price eventually. In the absence of daylight and landmarks, the only guide to direction was the relentless rumbling of Cwicnoll. They must head away from the summit to find the tunnel. The summit was no longer their greatest peril. The ancient crater of Weargahlæw was coming to life under their feet, steaming and shaking, reeking of sulfur.

Why did it hurt so much? He had long since guessed who had killed Dad, and should have been glad to have his suspicions confirmed. Almost six years had passed since the death of Æled; it was a nightmare from a world long gone. The bereaved boy who had suffered so abominably was gone, changed by his ordeal and the years in Ironhall into another person altogether, a capable young man who could survive in the world, if he must, entirely on his skill with a sword. He was no longer that child, so why did he hurt so much?

The cave passage was even harder than before—more obstructed by rocks. Wasp found a way through and brought them both out safely, although rubble was falling all the time. Half crazy already, the horses were thrown into frenzy by the sight of these two filthy and bloody relics, yet Wasp managed to soothe them enough to be ridden. There was a diffuse sort of daylight at Bælstede, but the wind had risen and was lifting ash in choking clouds. At times the falls seemed fresher, hot and deadly. Radgar just followed his Blade's orders, paying little attention to where he was going as they started the ride home.

Was it not justice that Æled had been slain to avenge men he had caused to die? His killer, Yorick, had already paid. Must his accomplice, Cynewulf, also die, the wheels of slaughter rolling on forever? Was it not justice that the woman Æled had stolen and then come to love had been stolen from him in turn and so provoked his death? She could not be blamed for what had happened then or since. She had done no wrong, so why could her son not forgive her? Why could he not judge her as a person instead of an ideal?

Villain! If ever a man deserved to die it was Cynewulf. *Hard it is to kill a king and live to brag of it.* There, certainly, Yorick's spirit had spoken truth. Had it told the truth about the murder, though? Not the whole truth and more than the truth. To bring a king to justice was never easy. It needed better evidence than the reported gabbling of a conjured thrall.

When they reached the forest, where the trees gave some shelter from the choking ash, Wasp pulled his horse back level with his ward's. He looked tired enough to die of exhaustion. His eyes were open sores under white eyebrows, his clothes caked with blood and ash; even the fuzz on his lip had grown to a milky mustache. Poor Wasp! Few Blades had ever been in a worse predicament than he was in now, less than a month after his binding.

A boy had been sent to do ten men's work. He spat out mud before he spoke.

"You better now?"

"Just tired." The very word made him yawn. "You Blades are lucky you don't get tired."

"We do get tired. We just can't sleep when we rest. What are you planning, Atheling?"

What indeed? He had learned the truth about the murder, but it had brought him no closer to justice or vengeance. If he swore blood feud against Cynewulf, or just went for him with a sword, the house thegns would kill him, and Wasp too. No question about that. "Advise me."

"You won't listen."

"Try me."

"Become king. Isn't that what you want?" Wasp's hoarse croak made the question almost a statement.

"Yes." Radgar was too weary to lie anymore. "But it isn't possible. It's an illusion, Wasp." From *cniht*'s oath to coronation oath had taken Dad six years, and he had been the youngest king of Baelmark in over a century.

"Then run away. Hide—back in Chivial or Thergy or anywhere."

Run? Radgar rode on for a while, trying to think the unthinkable. "I can't. Aylwin, Leofric, the others who have helped me . . . Cynewulf will kill them."

"Certainly. Take refuge with a friendly earl, then."

"That means civil war!"

Wasp stared at him with scarlet-rimmed eyes. "Yes. That's why I said to become king. Any other way we die."

Hard it is to kill a king. Easy for a king to kill. Send the brat off *færing* with Goldstan and Roðercræft and start writing the funeral invitations.

A few moments later Wasp added, "You knew this would happen if you came back. You can't run and you can't hide. You have to go on."

But there was no way on.

When they reached farmland, the weather had turned, wind veering to the northwest. A steady haze of ash swirled over the landscape, prickling eyes, gritting in teeth.

Cattle bellowed unhappily on the pastures. Thralls digging ditches and planting beans were dusted like ghosts with it.

On this wider trail Wasp fell back again. "Any good ideas yet?" He looked half dead already. Blades who lost their ward usually went insane and oftentimes berserk. What happened to a Blade who saw no way out? How much of this punishment could Wasp take?

"Friend, do you trust what the ghost said?"

His Blade scowled. "Some, not all. I think it was trying to defend Ambrose."

Soon after that a party of a dozen horsemen trotted out of the city in their direction. Wasp rode forward to intercept, but their leader was Leofric and suicidal heroics were not required. He reined in to watch Radgar's approach, glowering disapproval.

"You are still alive, then?" He wheeled his horse in on Radgar's right as Aylwin and the others took up position in the rear. If the atheling's return to the city could not be kept secret, it must be made a formal indication of support, obviously.

Radgar remembered how to smile. "Only just alive."

"What did you learn?"

"That no one can guard a front door effectively when a traitor inside is opening shutters in back."

Relief lit up the thegn's craggy features and was instantly suppressed. "Healfwer was still there? I heard Weargahlæw had been abandoned."

"He's all alone and determined to die there. He did summon Geste's spirit and it confirmed what we had surmised, but I don't know if I totally believe it. Geste killed my father and claims Cynewulf was in on the plot—but it may have been lying!"

"Don't worry about that," Leofric growled. "If he didn't do that murder he's done lots of others. From the look of you, you need a quick rinse in the palace hot springs, a change of clothes, a bowl of chowder, and as much sleep as you can grab before noon. You must be present at the moot."

"I'm not a thegn. Roðercræft will keep me out."

The blue eye glinted. "Let him try."

Radgar smiled his thanks. "Two seconds in hot water and I'll be asleep. Carry me into the hall and wake me up when the proceeds get interesting."

"They may get very interesting." Leofric was almost smacking his lips. "There's at least three candidates trying to raise support for a challenge. The odds are that none will succeed. That's when we push you forward!"

"I'm not even a *cniht* yet."

"Oh, we'll find some way around that."

As Dad had said, there was nothing wrong with Leofric's fighting.

"Get your lazy carcass out of that bed," Aylwin said loudly, and for about the third time. "Or do I have to tip this over you?"

Radgar forced one sticky eye open. The blankets prickled his skin, the air stank of sulfur. . . . The moot would assemble at noon. . . . Oh, spirits! He opened both eyes.

"Drink it yourself, you overmuscled lout!" With a killing effort he managed to sit up and accept the tankard of spruce beer he was being offered. Gulping down the tangy stuff he registered a fancy tunic laid out on the bed and some glittering things on the stool. Thegn Leofric was going to put forward his protégé in style.

"And hurry! There's trouble." The best that could be said for Aylwin's face was that it was honest. Leofric's son was no wita. Hard work, good humor, endurance, yes; loyalty in abundance, starvation rations of wits. Physical strength, of course. Even before he could afford to have himself enchanted into a leviathan he'd been a hulking lad, but the best conjurers in the world could not enchant extra brains into him, and he wouldn't know what to do with them anyway. Like his father, he had loyalty, loyalty to the death. You asked his opinion only out of politeness.

"What sort of trouble?" Radgar threw off the blankets and shivered as the cool air touched his bed-warmed flesh. The whole room shivered, making the pretty things dance on the stool and the bed ropes squeak. Cwicnoll was still restless.

"Wæps Thegn."

"What about him?"

"He's gone."

"Gone where? Blades never leave their wards." Radgar pulled on breeches and socks. He could hear rain beating on the roof.

"Think he's gone to kill Wulfwer."

"*What?* Tell me!" Moving much faster, Radgar hauled on wool leggings and stood up, tossing the long garters to Aylwin. They were gilt stuff, very royal, and the pretties waiting on the stool were a shoulder brooch as big as one of Aylwin's great fists and a belt buckle almost as large, both of them flashing with gold and deep-red garnets.

Aylwin knelt to wrap the garters around his friend's legs. "He was sitting right outside the door, Radgar. Guarding you."

"Yes." Smock next. This story was going to take some time to extract.

"Dad told me to come and tell him that Wulfwer's back. He went strange, Radgar. Wasp did. I mean his face turned cheese color and he shouted at me that I had to stay and watch you. Made me swear. Then he ran, Radgar."

Radgar wrapped the shiny tooled belt around himself and fastened the ornate buckle. He could imagine nothing that would make a Blade behave like that.

Nothing!

"Did he say anything before he ran? No explanation?"

"Well, he shouted something, Radgar, but I didn't catch it. It was in Chivian. He was sort of excited, see?"

More like clean out of his mind. "You caught no words at all?"

"No, Radgar." There was the cause of Aylwin's distress. His father had probably ripped a thousand strips off him.

"Not your fault you don't speak Chivian."

Aylwin stood up, looking much the way he had looked when he was one third the size and caught raiding the honey jar. "He did say your name and Wulfwer's, and I think Healfwer's."

"And you have no idea where he went?" Radgar stopped with one foot poised over a boot and thought about this. Eventually he put the boot on and stamped it; then the other one, and he still could think of *nothing* that would prompt a Blade to desert his ward like that. Especially in this palace, with a hundred knives sharpened for his neck.

"No."

"When did this happen?"

" 'Bout an hour ago. I'd sworn to stay outside your door, see? So I couldn't go tell anyone till Dad came to wake you. Dad's gone looking for him."

How many people could a Blade kill in an hour? Radgar slung the soft wool cloak around himself, fastening it with the great shoulder brooch. All done. He took up a comb and peered in the mirror. He did not like the gaunt, stressed face staring back out at him. Wasp had broken, but he must not. *The worst thing I did in my short life was bind that boy as my Blade.*

"What exactly did you tell him about Wulfwer?"

"Just that he's back. He was around this morning, so Dad asked questions. Seems the King had sent him off to Weargahlæw to see how it was and pull out the hermits if conditions were too bad. That's all. He rode in before dawn."

Radgar and Wasp must have passed him on the way. Nothing remarkable in that—there were many trails up into the hills. The crater was a royal demesne, so sending the tanist himself in such an emergency was not surprising either. What could Wasp possibly have seen in that information that had provoked him to such madness?

"It is not your fault," Radgar assured the woebegone Aylwin. "I could never say this earlier, but Wasp really isn't old enough to be a Blade. I should have warned him that I was going to refuse binding, but I didn't and he jumped right in the swamp beside me without thinking. He's a great kid, but he's still just a kid."

Aylwin scrunched up his nose in thought. "So why did you bind him? Was that a good idea?"

"No, a very bad one." Radgar looped the baldric over his shoulder and adjusted the hang of Yorick's sword at his thigh. "I had no choice. The alternative was probably chains in a dungeon. Wasp was ecstatic and I hadn't the heart to refuse." By the time he had realized his mistake there had been a dead man on the ground. "Wasp was my best friend in Chivial, the first friend I made there, my Aylwin substitute." The kid brother he had never had. "Now he's snapped like a wet bowstring. My fault, not yours." If Wasp had killed Wulfwer, why wasn't Radgar himself already in chains awaiting trial?

Leofric threw open the door. He shot his son a glare of disgust as he entered. "He's gone," he told Radgar.

"Gone where?"

"Inland. He went to the stable and demanded a horse. The thralls started saddling up Cwealm for him, but then a ceorl asked to see his warrant and he drew his sword."

Oh spirits! "He drew on one of the King's *hengestmenn*?"

"Worse," the ship lord growled. "The man sent a thrall to fetch a house thegn, and the house thegn drew on Wasp."

"No! Didn't Wasp warn him?" This was beyond belief! Probably the Bael hadn't listened, or didn't know what a Blade was. Just a bragging boy . . . "What did Wasp do?"

"He put that needle of his through the man's wrist, made him drop his sword. It wasn't really a fight."

"I'm sure it wasn't."

"He rode off inland. Don't know where. That's all."

"He didn't harm Wulfwer?"

"Didn't go near him, apparently." Leofric sighed. "The King's declared him to be in *unfrið* and Roðercræft's sent a posse out after him. This won't do your cause any good, Atheling."

· 3 ·

Murder his name and murder his nature. At the stable, Wasp had demanded Cwealm because he had been Radgar's own horse and should not provoke any trumped-up charges of thievery. Good idea, but it had not worked—the idiot hand had talked back anyway. Cwealm wanted to argue, too. He disliked having a stranger on his back, and the brief sword fight in the stable yard had upset him. He set out to be difficult and was doubtless surprised to find himself working off his rage by heading up the hill at a full gallop. As a rider Wasp was not in the same class as, say, Dominic or Wolfbiter, but he had grown up around horses and this Baelish mule was going to do what he wanted, like it or not.

"Don't be mad!" Wasp told him. "I'm mad enough for both of us. Don't you know that?"

Cwealm flicked his ears and continued to pound hooves.

Cwicnoll was hidden above a roof of pewter cloud, but the eruption was growing louder, more violent. The rumbling was almost constant, and teeming rain had become a deluge of white mud. Black horse Cwealm was a white horse already. The lines of bent thralls planting vegetables in the fields were lines of smoky ghosts in a snowy world.

Cwicnoll was the threat now.

No Blade in the history of the Order had ever deserted his ward like this, and the pain of it made him want to scream. Perhaps gallant young Sir Wasp truly had gone crazy. He could believe it himself. But even if he were certain of it, he still would not be able to resist the compulsion driving him up the mountain. Back at Ironhall he had been contemptuous of Sir Spender's distress when he was separated from his ward. Now he marveled that the man had not been screaming his throat out. He had even doubted Sir Janvier's proclaimed instinct for danger!

Food and a few hours' rest in a chair outside Radgar's door had helped restore him. It had certainly cleared his thinking, which had been badly muddled by the fumes in Weargahlæw, as well as by sheer exhaustion. Long before that musclebound Bael came rolling along the corridor babbling about Wulfwer, Wasp knew exactly where the tanist had gone. He had worked it out by mulling over the ghost's testimony.

Pension, Yorick had said. Ambrose held Cynewulf on a golden chain. Paying the King of Baelmark a personal pension must be cheaper, probably very much cheaper, than fighting a war or honoring all the onerous terms of the treaty. Cynewulf used the money to bribe the earls . . . some of the earls . . . enough of the earls . . . to keep him in power. And when Radgar had turned up in Ironhall, Ambrose had seen him as a threat to a very convenient arrangement. Had Radgar gone on to Bondhill, all unsuspecting, he would have found the doors locked behind him. No one but Ambrose himself and a few of his Guard would have known that the missing atheling was missing no more.

Radgar had escaped.

Radgar had escaped because his Blade had an instinct for danger! *Cling to that knowledge!* It had worked once, so this journey back to Weargahlæw might not be madness. . . .

Balked, Ambrose had sent his accomplice a warning that trouble was on the way home. Cynewulf had sent his son to consult the family conjurer, crazy Healfwer, who was to the King of Baelmark what Grand Wizard of the College was to Ambrose.

Healfwer was the source of all the evil conjurements.

Radgar would have guessed that without saying so. Wasp had been distracted by the brandy, the potion that Cynewulf had used to enslave Queen Charlotte. That one had come from Chivial, part of the traitor's payoff. Either Baelmark conjurers did not know how to make love potions or Healfwer granted such favors only to the reigning king, which had been Æled then, of course. Which of the two sons had been his favorite? He probably did not properly understand how his evil conjurements were being used. This time Wulfwer would have explained that there was another uppity challenger coming on the scene, but he would not have revealed that the new threat was Æled's son. So the old lunatic would have chanted up another booby trap for him.

If Healfwer was still capable of any normal human emotion, he must have been horribly shocked when his next visitors appeared. In his confused, crazy, fashion he had tried to tell them about his earlier client, complaining about double duty, mumbling about wanting wonders wrought. There had been footprints in the ash around the octogram! Ward and Blade would have picked up those hints if the fumes in the crater had not stupefied them.

By the time Aylwin arrived at Radgar's door, Wasp had worked it all out; he had known where the missing tanist had gone and knew he must have brought back something deadly from Outlaws' Cave. That was the message he had told Aylwin to pass on to Radgar: Accept nothing from Cynewulf or Wulfwer—drink no fancy brandy, pet no cuddly fox cubs.

But by that time, Wasp had lost interest in the tanist. His instincts were howling that the real danger was somewhere else and much more urgent. He had no evidence or logic to support that belief, but it had been growing on him steadily until he was ready to scream. He knew that all common sense argued against it. Alas, just as Ambrose and Cynewulf in turn had registered as dangers, so now the threat was Cwicnoll. That was why, for perhaps the first time in more than three hundred years, a Blade had deserted his ward and gone riding off chasing . . . chasing what? Wild goose or wild *fire*?

Wind and a deluge of mud . . . he was already almost into the clouds. The volcano was invisible, just a constant angry thunder.

His ward was in danger. Somewhere up there he must do battle against someone.

Or some *thing*?

• 4 •

Leofric wanted to put on a show. He wanted Radgar to march up to the door of Cynehof with a *werod* or two at his back. He wanted to plant supporters inside to cheer his entry.

Ceolmund disagreed vehemently, spraying spit at the floor. "Stay out, stay out! Attend the moot, certainly. Be seen taking an interest but do nothing more. They'll argue and quarrel and achieve nothing, and you mustn't be associated with failure."

In this case Radgar had agreed with the old wita, but mostly to avoid exposing his friends to any more danger than he had to. The sinister Marshal Roðercræft would be noting names, and if the Radgar movement collapsed—as seemed inevitable—then retribution would certainly follow.

Not in living memory had the witenagemot been called into session to censure a reigning monarch. The dim hall was already full when Radgar and his supporters gave up their swords to the *cnihtas* and went in. They stood back against the right-hand wall to watch. The earls were there with their thegns—mingling, whispering, and plotting—and Big Edgar was a landmark all by himself. Rows of stools had been set up on the floor for the witan; the empty throne sat on the front of the platform. Radgar noted the seating arrangements with disapproval, for the earls would be facing the moot reeve like children before a teacher. They would not even be at the front, for the first two rows were already occupied by the witan of the king's council.

"Who presides?" he asked Leofric. "Wulfwer?"

The ship lord snorted in derision. There had been no overt demonstration of support, but Radgar had his own party now, led by a score or so of witan collected for him by Ceolmund, older men and women who wielded power in Baelmark—rich merchants and landowners, some of them specially summoned from outlying areas and other islands. They appraised him with shrewd green eyes, cautiously restricting their conversation to reminiscences of how they had served his father in the war or, rarely, his grandfather in the days of the shameful triumph over the Gevilian invasion. Around this cozy gathering stood a living palisade of *Faroðhengest* muscle. The energetic youngsters among them were grinning as they discussed the possibility of some action later. It was not unknown for meetings of the witenagemot to break into riot.

Radgar was about to comment on the number of house thegns present when war horns announced the approach of the King. Spectators moved back, clearing a center aisle. Earls broke off their intriguing and filtered forward to take their seats. One stool was left empty in mute tribute to the slain Æðelnoð of Suðecg, whose tanist was still *færing* in distant Skyrria and thus could not know of his accession.

Another wail outside the doors brought an approximation of respectful silence. Those who had seats rose to their feet as the fat villain himself strolled in wearing his crown and a scarlet, fur-trimmed robe. Roðercræft led a dozen mailed house thegns before him and a dozen more brought up the rear. They made a leisurely progress straight down the center, past the hearths, and at last to the dais. Cynewulf settled on his throne and the guards lined up on either side of him, extending almost the full width of the hall.

"That's disgusting! My father never brought a bodyguard to a moot."

Leofric said quietly, "Perhaps he should have done."

"And he never retained that many house thegns!"

"Yes, he did," Leofric said, even more quietly, "but he never let me parade them around in public like that."

Oh? Greenhorn had much to learn! "Where's Wulfwer?"

Nineteen earls had settled on their stools, but the king's tanist was always an honorary member of the witenagemot. In this case, his absence was especially noteworthy. Even a surly and none-too-bright thrall-born like Wulfwer ought to know that he should be there, supporting his father.

"Well, *ealdras*?" Cynewulf did not bother to raise his voice. "You called this moot." He took a small scroll from inside his cloak and pretended to consult it. "Sixteen signatures, the minimum required under the law of Radgar the Great. Earl Ælfgeat is here with our safe-conduct to answer any questions you may wish to put to him. Who wants to start throwing the dung?" He tossed the scroll away and leaned back contemptuously on his throne, bored already.

"Now!" Leofric whispered. "If they're going to!"

This was the moment for challenge, which would take precedence over all other business. The hall held its breath, but the moment one earl began to rise, two others jumped up also and the chance was gone. It was a fair guess that these were the three with royal ambitions, but clearly none of them had been able to muster the necessary votes, so they were all just hoping to gain notoriety by proposing the motion of censure. Before Cynewulf could even point a finger to recognize one, a war horn wailed again. That was definitely not a scheduled part of a witenagemot debate. Heads snapped around.

Crowds stood taller in Baelmark than in Ironhall, and for a moment all Radgar could see coming in the door was a double line of shiny helmets. The spectators roiled back, once again clearing an aisle along the length of the hall, and then the intruders drew close enough for Radgar to make out Wulfwer in the lead. He had not changed a bit in five years, except to increase in bulk and sheer ugliness. *Hulking* would be flattery, *lummox* only reasonable. Like a two-legged ox, the tanist rolled forward bearing a naked sword. He halted when he reached the hearths and scowled brutishly at his father on the throne. The hall erupted in furious roars of protest.

"This is madness!" Leofric whispered in Radgar's ear. The only challenge that could be delivered in the middle of a witenagemot was an earl's challenge to the King; not a tanist's challenge to his earl. Even Wulfwer must know that.

"It's a trick," Radgar answered. "It has to be." But what trick?

The protest roared on until Cynewulf rose to his feet and held up a hand for silence. He was frowning, but that meant nothing. He could have set this up with his son, planning to deflect any formal protest from the earls.

Now Wulfwer was free to recite the formula. *"Niðing!"* he roared. *"Ga recene to me, wer to guðe! Gea, unscamfæst earming ðu, ic þæt gehate þæt ic heonan nylle fleon—"** The rest of the ancient call to combat was lost in renewed howls from the onlookers.

Cynewulf stood with raised hand, seemingly waiting for silence, but his little eyes were scanning the crowd. He located Radgar and no doubt noted who was with him. At last he was able to shout over the noise.

"Drunken lout! Thrall-born oaf! Why did I ever think I could make anything of you? You can't even issue a proper challenge and you try to do it in the middle of a witenagemot. Well, the fyrd will make judgment between us, but it must wait until after the nation's business is completed. Let the thegn moot assemble on the day after the adjourn—"

"No!" roared a voice from the floor, and the cry was taken up by a thousand throats in a great roar of anger

---

*Worthless one! Come quickly to me, man to battle. Yes, shameless wretch you, I this swear: that I from here refuse to flee—

and disapproval. Even the visitors were shouting, although they should not meddle in local business.

Cynewulf did seem surprised then. He peered narrowly into the gloom as if seeking out ringleaders, but he kept his self-control and when he stretched out both arms for silence the crowd hushed to hear him. "If the honored earls are willing to let our shire moot take precedence, then we shall gladly honor their wishes. The witenagemot stands adjourned until the morrow. Thegns, the fyrd will assemble tonight at sunset"—he was shouting at the top of his lungs—"to decide the issue between us and our tanist in the ways of the Baels."

Leofric had been whispering to Ceolmund and some of the other witan. Now he thumped a hand on his son's massive shoulder. "The Haligdom!" he said. "Go and seize the Haligdom!"

· 5 ·

Upward, ever upward, Wasp drove his horse, going he knew not where to fight he knew not what. Only his Blade instinct guided him through stinking fog and the steady drizzle of mud. The ash fall was so heavy now, and so hot, that if the rain part of it ever slackened he would probably fry. Poor Cwealm, superbly surefooted though he was, found the going treacherous and painful.

Wasp kept expecting a firedrake to come flaming and roaring out of the mist at him. Fight a firedrake with a rapier? Why his Blade instinct would drive him to come in search of such a monster he could not imagine. His mission seemed suicidal. *He* was not fireproof! In spite of the wet, he kept hallucinating a smell of burning—the stench of the massacre at Haybridge or the smell of West House just before Radgar came stumbling through the flames to wrap a blanket around him and carry him out. Twice in his life he had escaped death by fire, and he seemed destined to meet it again.

When the ground began to drop away ahead of him and the wind redoubled its fury, he realized that he had reached the bleak shoulder called Bælstede. Coughing and almost blind from the muddy deluge, he turned Cwealm in the direction of the cave entrance. It seemed that his destination was to be Weargahlæw again. He felt a faint stir of hope—he might not have to fight a firedrake after all, only mad old Healfwer.

Poor Cwealm had been run to exhaustion. He coughed and slithered and sometimes bellowed out his misery; but he kept responding, knowing that otherwise he would get beaten with a rapier.

"Not long now, big fellow," Wasp told him. "Won't be so bad in the gully. I never treated a nag like this in my life before, friend, and I promise I never will again. It's all for Radgar. You remember Radgar . . . ?" Babble, babble! The stallion was not the only one near the end of his endurance.

The defile was not better at all. Cwealm had to plod hock-deep up a steaming river of hot mud laced with rocks and branches. He eventually balked, was beaten, went on a few more steps, and then stumbled. Wasp, deservedly, was pitched into the muck, which was even hotter than he had expected. Once he had cleaned off his face well enough to see, he needed only one glance at his mount to know that this was the end. Cwealm was immobilized, and a damaged leg here had to be a death sentence.

Wasp gave him a hug and wept for him. "I am sorry, friend, I really am sorry!" He could read his own name on the death warrant too, so he wept for himself and his folly, but he also mourned a great heart. "If the impossible happens and I ever see Radgar again," he promised, "I will tell him of your courage."

Then he did what had to be done and did it well, for he had helped his father butcher animals and knew where to strike. He wiped *Nothing* on his mud-covered cloak and set off along the gully alone.

Unlike a horse, he could stay out of the mud river by working his way through the brush and spindly trees that lined the steeply sloping walls; they gave him handholds when he slipped on the ooze underfoot. At least the tunnel would provide shelter from the constant drizzle.

When he came to the end of the little gorge, he thought he was to be denied even that. Rock and mud had cascaded down, building a mound that almost covered the cave mouth. Closer inspection revealed that there was a gap left at the top; and when he had scrambled up to see it, he could feel a wind blowing past his head. A powerful draft was blowing into the mountain, so the upper end must still be open and the way was clear.

Clear at the moment. The ground trembled. The mountain's menacing rumbling never stopped.

Finding the tinderbox by feel alone was a painfully long business, but he located it eventually, and also a lantern with candle left in it. Some of the crushed-fungus tinder was damp, and only after a great deal of striking and swearing did he find a piece dry enough to catch. Then he had light and he was out of the rain, but his clothes were so weighted by mud that they felt like the plate mail he had been forced to wear in Ironhall broadsword training. Perhaps because there was no physical means for him to return to Radgar now, the agony of being separated from his ward had dwindled. In its place had come the numbing pain of total exhaustion.

So what? He was wretchedly uncomfortable. He could not sleep. He set off into the tunnel.

Perhaps twelve hours had passed since he and Radgar had come through here on their way out. Much rock had fallen since then. There was no path anymore. There was hardly a tunnel anymore. In its place he found an unending climb over precariously balanced heaps of jagged boulders, going in constant danger of starting a slide that would crush his feet or bury him totally. At times he was wriggling high above the original roof, hunting for gaps between the heaped debris and the new—no doubt temporary—roof. Sometimes he knew he had found a passage because when he thrust his head and shoulders into the gap he could hear the wind whistling past his ears. That was a reminder that the wind could get through narrower places than he could. The exit, if he ever reached it, might not be Wasp-sized.

Exhaustion, earth tremors, the reek of sulfur, now hunger, and certainly thirst . . . a Blade's lot was not a happy one. The end came without warning. Rocks shifted under him. Then a rising din as more and more of the roof collapsed, both in front of him and behind . . . something came down on his left hand, which held the lantern. He was plunged into darkness, his scream of agony drowned out by noise that seemed to beat the brains from his head. He was pelted by stones, choked by dust. The tunnel collapsed.

When the noise stopped, the draft had stopped, too. He was sealed in, buried alive in the heart of the mountain.

· 6 ·

No challenge had been contested in Catterstow for so long that very few men could remember the last time. Ceolmund had yielded to Æled without forcing a vote, but in his younger days he had shed blood to win the earldom and keep it. He knew the unwritten rules. He knew that the earl would hold court in Cynehof, rallying supporters, plying thegns with ale and mead, bribing ship lords with gold. The tanist challenger must set up a recruiting center of his own and see what he could do with promises. Since the Haligdom, the great elementary, was the second largest building in Waroðburh, the Wulfwer party should take it over as its headquarters. This was especially true on a day like this, when the rain was coming down in tubfuls. But no one had told Wulfwer this and by the time someone did, it was too late. Aylwin and his beefiest buddies had seized the building, and his father was leading the rest of the fledgling Æleding party there in parade. Wulfwer's challenge had opened opportunities.

"Here!" said Aylwin, thrusting a war helmet at Radgar. "Choose a sword."

"Huh?"

The huge circular hall was smaller than he remembered, but still impressive. Often as a child he had huddled in the doorway beside the jeering town brats to watch shiploads of Chivian prisoners being enthralled into useful servants. With the unthinking cruelty of the young, he had mocked their screams for mercy. No one had told him he was doing anything wrong. Chivian crowds had laughed when Baelish prisoners were butchered in public. It had been wartime, and things were different then.

Things were different now. Leofric's *werod* was forming itself into a circle, excluding other thegns. Someone handed Aylwin a shield, and another offered Radgar a helmet and a collection of wooden practice swords.

Leofric explained at his elbow. "They're going to vote you in, Atheling. But they need to know that you can fight."

"I haven't sworn the *cniht*'s oath," Radgar said angrily. This sort of contest was stupid. It would prove little about a man's courage in real battle, yet it was dangerous enough to maim him if something went wrong. The helmet he was holding had a face plate, which meant he would be peering out through two small eye holes, unable to see what he was doing. Ironhall dueling equipment was better, safer, and so varied that he was expert in a dozen styles of fighting. Aylwin would know only broadsword and shield, possibly battle-ax.

"Well you can't back out now," the ship lord said

smugly, walking away and leaving Radgar in the circle of grinning faces.

True! He threw the helmet away and refused the shield. He drew *Fancy,* a cat's-eye sword infinitely better than anything he was being offered. "Come and kill me," he said.

"Flames!" said a muffled voice from inside Aylwin's helmet. "That's a real sword!"

"It's a real sword and I'm going to show you real sword craft. I'll use the blunt side. Now come and kill me."

The spectators fell silent. Aylwin shrugged, flexed his arms, and charged. Reluctant to strike an unarmored friend with even the wooden sword, he tried to knock him with his shield instead. Radgar had expected that. He jumped aside, grabbed the edge of the shield with his free hand, and kicked the back of his friend's knee as he went past. Aylwin hit the tiles in a clatter and his sword skittered away across the floor.

Radgar stepped up on his back. "Next?"

Terrible words came out of the helmet. . . .

"You're dead. I want someone else."

The onlookers jeered uproariously at their shipmate's humiliation, but such tricks did not impress them much. Then Radgar Æleding disposed of two more contenders with equal ease and they began to show interest. There was no elaborate point system—first hit was counted mortal. The next men tried to match his speed and agility and came at him on his own terms, without shield or helmet, just a blade. They did not pull their strokes, either. Men who weighed twice what he did swung two-handed broadswords that would have shattered bones. He did not try to block those; he let *Fancy* nudge the stroke up or down or aside, using their momentum to throw his opponents off balance. They all seemed incredibly slow to him, but he dared not be as gentle with everyone as he had been with Aylwin. He rapped a couple of men across the neck with the back of his sword; he disarmed another by striking his elbow with the flat of the blade. With the sixth man, he accidentally drew blood. The wound was not serious, but honor was satisfied.

"That's all!" He sheathed his sword, pleasantly aware that he was barely winded. By then the ale barrels were being rolled in.

"Can he fight?" Aylwin yelled, and the *werod* roared approval.

They voted Radgar Æleding one of them, and a thegn in the Catterstow fyrd.

If they thought he was good, they should have seen Wasp.

All over Waroðburh the afternoon was spent in argument, wherever two or more thegns were within earshot of each other. War horns blared, summoning warriors to the free ale—in Cynehof, at the tanist's headquarters in the boat sheds, or from Ship Lord Leofric at the elementary. Most men would need to try all three, of course. The rain grew worse, turning everything gray with mud. Messengers departed in fast boats to fetch absent members of the fyrd from half Baelmark. Ancient pirates in their dotage were dragged from their beds, bathed and combed and made presentable. *Werodu* assembled and voted fresh-faced *cnihtas* into full thegnhood.

Radgar stayed sober and listened. Everyone had opinions, from the gawkiest beginner to thegns who had been old in his childhood. He steadfastly refused to express his own opinions. Leofric and Ceolmund were in charge, running the Æleding Party, practically planning his first moves as earl, and it was all nonsense. The fyrd could not vote for him under the rules, and would not vote for him if it could. He was almost certain that Wulfwer's challenge was a fraud dreamed up by Cynewulf. He did not understand the plot, though, and he was offered an infinite choice of theories.

"It is a conspiracy," one elder insisted. "The King and that lunkish son of his cooked this up to distract attention from the witenagemot." He repeated this opinion every few minutes all afternoon.

"The tanist is a Cattering. He thinks his father is about to be deposed and hopes to snatch the throne for himself."

"The witenagemot will not stand for that Wulfwer oaf as king!"

"Who would challenge him? He could slay any two of them at once."

"Radgar Æleding, of course. He is trained like a Chivian Blade."

"No, Cynewulf put his son up to this. He wants to show the earls that he still has the support of his fyrd. The fight will be a fraud. . . ."

"Who cares about the witenagemot? We need an earl who can pee straight!"

"The King wants to drop Wulfwer overboard and he won't go."

"Æleding is too young. Even the fyrd will not accept him and the witenagemot—"

"He is only a year younger than his father was."

"But Æled first went *færing* with us at fourteen. I remember how—"

"True, he was a seasoned ship lord. I remember how—"

Murder and mayhem, tales to make a man's hair stand on end! Radgar had never realized how bloody his father's youth had been. He felt very inadequate and knew he must seem so to these men. He missed Wasp. Already he felt like an unshelled turtle without his sharp young Blade watching over him. He even missed the kid's acid-tongued comments on Baelish customs.

The theories were repeated, rehashed, and embroidered. They grew wilder and wilder as the day went on, but a significant number of them presumed that Cynewulf and his son were somehow conspiring together and that Radgar was in grave danger of dying suddenly, as had so many other throne-worthy men of late. No one could clarify the details of how this would be achieved, unfortunately, but it showed how little respect Cynewulf commanded in his own shire.

When dismal afternoon began to darken into evening, the *werod* clamored to hear from the atheling himself. Reluctantly he approached the upturned wooden bucket that served as a podium. Before he reached it, Ceolmund caught hold of his cloak and pulled his head down.

"You are related to both contenders. You are not strictly a thegn. You don't have to attend."

He was wrong. Radgar had been away for years. If he shunned this contest, the fyrd would lose all interest in him. "No, I must go."

"Then support Wulfwer. If he wins the siding, your uncle will retire. Your cousin will become earl and appoint you tanist, his closest relative."

"No!" Leofric clutched Radgar's other arm. "You must support your uncle. You are his obvious successor. Wulfwer is thrall-born and useless. He has guessed you will replace him and is making a desperate last stand. Cynewulf will have Big Edgar or someone make fillets of him and then you can become tanist."

Radgar smiled thanks at each man in turn and gently pulled free. He climbed up on the bucket. So much conflicting advice swirled inside his head that he did not know what he was going to say.

He looked around at the expectant faces—well over a hundred of them. Of course his new *Faroðhengest* brothers would support him to the last drop of blood—theirs or anyone else's—but there were many other *werodu* represented. He could not ask any man to support Cynewulf, that slimy villain. Nor Wulfwer, who had also tried to kill him.

He must shout, because the great dome had been designed to swallow sound, not echo it. "*Ealdras*, thegns . . . friends . . . I thank you dearly. If I hesitate and stumble, it is because I am truly at a loss for words, more touched by your support than I can say. I know many of you came here to honor the memory of my father, and for that I am truly grateful. I can offer you no more wisdom than you have heard already and I will not presume to steer you in your decision. I am royally born, yes. I will fight any man who says otherwise, but I do not consider myself throne-worthy. Not yet. Someday I hope to win your respect, but I cannot claim it now."

A cloud shadow of dismay darkened the elementary.

Modesty? What sort of a man doubted his own manhood? Glances were exchanged, comments whispered. . . . They had not expected that. From portly landowning elders to horny-handed, rollicking sailor boys, they all wanted him to be his father returned to them. If it didn't work and he died, well it had been a good idea. . . .

Too late he saw that his refusal betrayed those who had already risked everything by backing him—Leofric, Ceolmund, Aylwin, his new shipmates. He had blundered. His Ironhall training had let him down, for he had responded as a dutiful courtier or royal bodyguard might, not as a braggart Baelish atheling. Like Wasp, he had not been ready for this world.

But even as he floundered for some way to repair his blunder, a young man pushed forward through the spectators. His mail shirt and helmet marked him as a house thegn and he must be proud of his status, for he would have been a *cniht* until very recently. He stopped some distance from Radgar and called to him in a voice as thin and arrogant as his orange mustache.

"Atheling, your king summons you."

A premonitory shiver ran up Radgar's backbone. He would sooner drop in on a moray eel in its crevice than answer that invitation. But the spirits of chance had offered him a way out of his error.

"Cynewulf cannot summon me, for he stands under challenge. I have other business to attend to. Go tell my uncle that I will wait upon him tomorrow and will settle then all matters outstanding between us."

The youth stared at him in horrified disbelief, but a deafening whoop of relieved laughter from the crowd drowned out anything he might have tried to say. The laughter swelled to applause and applause exploded into cheers. That was more the sort of talk they wanted to hear.

Spirits! Did they expect him to seize the throne by force? He certainly had less than a tenth of the fyrd here, and already he could see men on the outskirts melting away from a group that had suddenly become dangerous company. Anything less than half must fail. He shouted for silence.

"Friends! Brothers! Baels! I believe my father was murdered and his brother had a hand in that crime, but I lack the proof I need to swear blood feud. I am certain that his son, my cousin, tried to murder me that same night. Neither is fit for the office he holds. They are of my blood but I cannot in good conscience side with either. At the thegn moot I shall stand apart."

A plague on both their houses! That was not a solution anyone had proposed in all the hours of arguing. It was not in the rule book, but Dad had spurned rule books, too. Radgar had only just thought of it himself and saw at once that it was horrible folly, because it must make enemies of both factions. But it was a way out of his dilemma. A roar of approval greeted it. In his strange, soft-spoken way, the young atheling was proclaiming revolution, so perhaps there was a streak of his old dad in him after all. They would follow him—for now.

· 7 ·

The only reason Wasp could not just lie down and die was that there was nowhere comfortable to try it. His world was a bed of nails, a universe of razor edges. He had fashioned his baldric into a tourniquet to stop the bleeding from his crushed hand, and the rest of his injuries seemed to be only bruises, from sole to scalp. Desperately thirsty, he could hear a slow drip of water not very far away. For some reason that sound drove him to rage rather than hope or despair—surely no master torturer had ever subjected his victims to anything worse than this! The lack of a draft was not necessarily fatal, he told himself. It proved that the tunnel was blocked in one direction, not necessarily both. A Blade couldn't give up. He could burst his heart and drop dead, but he could never give up.

Having no idea of direction, he must just head for the drip. He used *Nothing* as a probe to establish where the rocks were and were not, and he began to move. Once or twice he found himself in a large open space where he could find no walls, no roof; at other times he had to wriggle through narrow burrows full of broken glass—that was how they felt, anyway. The drip seemed to be slowing down, and he was tormented by the thought that it might stop altogether. He even began to wonder if it was retreating as he advanced, a phantasm created by some evil spirit to torment him. He seemed to crawl through the nightmare for days, and he never did find the drip. Before he reached it, he saw a glimmer of daylight on the roof ahead.

The Weargahlæw end of the tunnel had been almost blocked by a landslide. A puddle of water had collected there and he was able to slake his thirst. There was even a heap of natural porridge where the meal sack had burst; he forced himself to swallow some of the muck just to make his belly stop feeling so empty. His broken hand throbbed with a savage beat, pain echoing all the way through him. Without that he might have curled up and slept away the rest of his life, but there was no way he would ever find comfort again.

He clambered over the debris that had fallen from the cliffs and peered out at Weargahlæw. He could see very little. Storm and eruption between them had turned day to night, but he judged that if the sun had not set it must be about to, because the ruddy glow within the crater itself was brighter than the clouds overhead. He could hear crackling and smell smoke in the stench of sulfur. For the forest to be burning was hardly surprising. A strong wind gusted the muddy rain around—air, water, earth, and fire—all four manifest elements were present in abundance, and that thought reminded him of Healfwer.

Obviously he could never find the conjurer in this mad murk—and it would do no good to do so at this stage anyway—but he had nothing better to try and could think of no better reason for coming here. He scrambled painfully down to the crater floor and limped wearily into the trees.

Radgar must know that Healfwer had been Fyrlaf, but only once had he called the old cripple *eald fæder*—grandfather—in Wasp's hearing. He would brag about great-grandfather Cuðblæse and father Æled, but Fyrlaf was rarely mentioned, as if the shame of what the former king had done to the Gevilians still lingered. Cuðblæse had died fighting a drake. Æled had lured his to the sea and quenched it. Healfwer-Fyrlaf had driven his monster against the invaders, and only after it had destroyed the Gevilians had he plunged it into the healing sea. How? And what had happened after that? He had mumbled something about the water not being deep enough. If he had fallen on his left side and the drake went over him . . .

Mad and hopelessly crippled, he had been exiled to Weargahlæw and publicly written off as dead. Why so much shame? Was it possible that he had not merely directed the firedrake but had actually *summoned* it, much as he had summoned Yorick's ghost? Firedrakes were supposed to be something that just happened, like thunderstorms; but a skilled conjurer might be able to create one, especially during a volcanic eruption, when fire elementals swarmed. That would be a terrible crime, invaders or not. And last night the madman had heard how one of his sons had murdered the other. How much crazier could a man become?

Something had summoned Wasp, drawing him here. He paused at the edge of a steaming lake whose far shore was hidden in the trees. He would have to wade that and hope he did not get boiled on the way. . . . Something in Weargahlæw was a mortal threat to Radgar.

IX

· 1 ·

From the Haligdom to Cynehof in a downpour was far enough to soak a man to the marrow of his bones. Cowering under his cloak, Radgar paused on the edge of the square to glance back at his followers: Leofric; Ceolmund; and better than two hundred thegns, ranging from striplings like Wasp—and where was poor Wasp?—to elders so ancient they could barely totter along on the arms of brawny grandsons. He had lost his Blade and gained a retinue. Satisfied that it had not melted away yet, he uncovered his head, squared his shoulders, and led the way toward the gaping porch.

A few score sword-girt men lingered at the base of the steps, some of them huddled under thrall-held umbrellas. These must be the cautious ones, waiting until they could back a clear winner. Around the edges of the plaza, a forest of hats, hoods, and umbrellas covered ceorls and *lætu* and also many women and children, no doubt families of thegns. None of them had any say in a change of earl—and the result of the vote would make no difference to their drab lives anyway—but they probably enjoyed watching the atheling lead in his army. Could they tell that he was an illusion and it was really led by the ghost of King Æled? His followers were not following him, they were pushing. He had never dreamed that he might win acceptance solely on his father's reputation.

He strode up the three steps, and for the second time that day surrendered Yorick's sword to the house thegns. Many feet tramped up behind him.

The big hall was dim and clammy on this dismal evening and at first glance seemed almost empty, because the occupants were packed in along the walls. Although the scents of generations of feasting still hung in the air, tonight the hearths in the center were cold. Beside them stood three elderly witan in heralds' tabards, adjudicators acceptable to both candidates. Two men who had preceded Radgar into the hall went to them, bowed in unison, and then parted, going to stand on opposite sides of the hall—most likely brothers, prudently dividing the family vote.

Honored guests had been arrayed on benches on the dais at the far end: earls, wives, mothers, grandmothers, a few children close to adolescence. At the extreme left of the platform Cynewulf slouched on his throne, crowned and sumptuously robed in crimson, but scowling. Queen Charlotte sat very erect on an ornate chair of narwhal ivory at his side. Behind them stood grim Roðercræft, watching as his armed minions kept order in the assembly.

Wulfwer stood on the extreme right, ignoring the low milking stool that his father had generously provided for him. With massive arms folded, he was glowering brutishly at the unfolding drama. He had done much better than Leofric and Ceolmund had predicted he would. More than a quarter—perhaps almost a third—of the thegns had assembled on his side of the hall.

Every eye fastened on Radgar as he approached the witan, for it must seem that he could decide the fate of the kingdom. If he took his retinue to Wulfwer, he might tip the balance in the tanist's favor, or at least make it very close to even. This was another illusion. His supporters were following him only because he had promised to take no side. Before reaching the waiting elders he stopped and folded his arms like big cousin Wulfwer. He did not attempt the scowl, but smiled instead at the three old men. His followers bunched up at his back, and the hall stilled into a puzzled silence.

It did not last long. The rafters creaked first, then the walls. The floor lurched under his feet and kept on lurching, so he staggered wildly. Everywhere men tripped and stumbled, the woodwork screamed in every joint, and all noises seemed to merge in a single monstrous roar as the world danced. It was the worst quake he had ever experienced. Dust poured down from the roof and swirled up from the hearths. After an excruciatingly long time, the motion faded and then stopped.

He hurried forward to assist the three witan, who had landed on their backs. Dust settled and fallen men climbed sheepishly to their feet, but neither Cynehof nor its occupants seemed to have taken any serious harm. The siding would continue, because no red-blooded, redheaded Bael would ever accord a mere earth tremor any more respect than he would spare for a rough sea. They made their buildings to survive and so would they.

As he returned to his place, one of the witan came shuffling after him. "*Ealdras!* You must go to one side or the other." He lacked about a dozen teeth for true clarity of speech.

"We take our lead from Atheling Radgar," Leofric said.

"*Æleding!*" roared the men at his back.

The old man looked to the upstart, frowning angrily under bushy white brows. "You must choose sides."

"I will take no side, and my companions are of like mind."

"That is not allowed."

"I cannot choose between those two offal buckets."

"So leave, if you shun your duty!" Outrage made him shrill.

"I will not leave."

"*Ealdor* Ceolmund! *Ealdor* Leofric! You know that this is improper."

"Unorthodox," Leofric admitted.

The wita's slurred complaints grew shrill. "You are breaking the customs and abusing our ancient rights. You must decide between the two men. If you do not like the result you can challenge again. Dividing the fyrd into more than two factions risks standoff and open warfare."

That was probably true, but Radgar could not change his tactics now. He glanced around to make sure his band was still with him and was amazed to see that he had gained at least another fifty men. The fence-sitters were entering now, and most of them were joining his party. Perhaps he had misjudged their motives.

"We shall not take sides, *ealdor,*" he said. "Go and count those who did."

As the old man hurried back to discuss the bad news with his associates, Leofric adjusted the thong that held his eye patch. Two men left Cynewulf's supporters and strolled over to join his dissidents. This devious strategy had been suggested and arranged by Ceolmund, whose thinking was as twisted as his backbone, and it worked beautifully. Three innocents decided to follow the shills' example and then four from Wulfwer's side did the same. More came, and suddenly there were hints of revolution in the air. The witan began bleating; the King roared in fury.

A war horn's wail signaled the end of the siding; the great double doors were slammed. The judges announced that changes were not allowed and every man who had moved must return to his original team.

They would have done better to threaten Cwicnoll. No one obeyed, and more men defiantly left the sides and strode over to join Radgar's center party. He turned to share glances with Leofric and Aylwin, struggling to keep his face from displaying his excitement. This was working far better than they had predicted! He could not guess how long his supporters would back him, or how far, but he now had about as many as Wulfwer. Suppose he finished up with more than either father or son? Or even more than both together! If Cynewulf had provoked this challenge to impress the witenagemot with his support, then he had harpooned himself.

A warning frown from Leofric spun him around again and cracked his jubilation like glass. Queen Charlotte had left her ivory chair and was advancing along the hall to chide her unruly son. Every eye in the hall was on her and every eye would watch their meeting. It was another of Cynewulf's sly tricks, and Radgar's hatred burned up hotter. Never since his first days in Ironhall had he ever truly lost his temper. He had believed the dragon burned out of him and gone forever, but now he knew it could rise again. Alas, this was not a childish fistfight where anger was both sword and shield; in a battle of wits anger was snare and impediment. He wrapped his mud-soaked cloak around himself and waited.

Queen Charlotte moved with grace in trailing robes of rich burgundy. Jewels glinted on her hands, at her neck and ears; a silver coronet shone in her high-braided hair. She did not look old, although she was of an age that saw most women ravaged by childbearing into toothless, white-haired crones. She held out her hands. When he did not take them she clasped them nervously before her. Peering up anxiously at his face, she spoke only to him, although at least a hundred men would hear.

"You have greatly angered your king, Radgar!"

"My king was murdered and that man helped."

"Silence! I will not listen to such sedition. Why did you not come when you were summoned?"

"Because I feared for my life." He noted that her voice was slurred, her breath reeked of wine. Being married to Cynewulf would drive anyone to drink, but perhaps his own behavior had not helped much lately.

"That is madness!" she bleated. "The King seeks only your advancement. He approves of you and always did. Wulfwer has ever been a great disappointment to him and now has had the folly to challenge. You can see he has lost, the fyrd siding against him. Your uncle—stepfather, I mean—Cynewulf wants you to be his tanist now."

"Oh, Mother! *Dear* Mother! You always believe whatever you want to believe, don't you? You refuse to see the shadows or think what may lurk in them. No wonder life always disappoints you!" He wanted to shake her. He needed to hug her. He fought down both impulses. "You are a fool to believe one word that man says."

She frowned as if the world had become difficult to understand. She whispered, "I can't help loving him, Radgar."

His heart twisted. "No. And I can't help loving you, Mother."

"Oh, Radgar!" Again she reached for his hands and again he kept his arms bundled in his sodden cloak.

"But him I hate." Rage burned in his throat like lava.

"Pity him, Radgar! Pity him! Now he must choose a champion to fight his own son. Help him! He says you are the finest swordsman in Baelmark?" She could not believe she had really produced such a monster.

"Probably." If Wasp was not present— Where was poor Wasp now?

"All he asks is that you will hurt Wulfwer as little as possible. In return, he will appoint you his tanist and in a year or two—no more than three years, he promises—he will step aside and let you be King of Baelmark. Oh, Radgar, this is a wonderful—"

She stopped in dismay. The bitter laughter had exploded out of him before he could stop it.

"Cynewulf wants me to fight Wulfwer for him? Fight him and let him off with a slit nose? Oh, no! Go tell your pillow partner, Mother, that if I ever see that brute spawn of his at the far end of my sword, I will spill his bowels all over the floor. And if I ever become tanist I will do the same to him within the first hour. It would be both duty and pleasure. Take that message back to your fat friend."

She recoiled, ashen-faced. "Radgar! You forget who he is!"

"No, Mother. I will never forget. He kills by treachery and evil conjurations. The man who slew Dad has testified that Cynewulf let him into the house that night. He raped you with a conjured potion and tried to slay me. He is dung, Mother, sewage. Go back to your dung and spit on him for me."

He was shaking, almost sick with the effort of containing his rage. Leofric's hand gripped his shoulder in warning. Queen Charlotte backed off in horror, then raised her skirts and fled back to the dais. All the hundreds present watched the King's face darken as he heard her whispered report.

More thegns drifted away from the sides of the hall to join Radgar. Then a ship lord—a man he did not know at all, even by sight—deserted Cynewulf's side and came to him with his entire *werod* following.

"Declare!" Cynewulf bellowed at the three dithering

witan in the center. Roðercræft shouted to the house thegns, who quickly spread out along the line of royal supporters to block any further desertions.

The judges conferred hurriedly. Now the center obviously held more votes than the tanist's side and possibly as many as Cynewulf's. Two more *werodu* or so would make Radgar the choice of more than half the fyrd, but he was not a candidate. The witan hurried over to the King and bowed to him as the signal that he had won. His supporters broke into cheers, which were drowned out by booing from the other factions.

"May all your victories taste as sour!" Leofric muttered.

Ceolmund cackled. "I wonder what the earls think of this?"

The war horn howled again to hail the decision. Cwicnoll shook the hall peevishly. The groups on the floor merged and began flowing closer to the dais, but house thegns held them back to leave an open space—there was a fight to come. Most of the ladies rose, curtseyed to the throne, and trooped to the far end of the hall, where one flap of the door was opened briefly to let them depart. They did not succeed in dragging their young sons with them, and not one man went. Nor did the Queen.

Wulfwer stripped off cloak, baldric, tunic. Bare to the waist, he stepped down from the dais and tried a few practice swings with his two-handed sword. His coarse face puckered in a gruesome smile, a killer scenting blood. "Pick your man, Father! Who will die for you?"

At the far side of the hall, Cynewulf ignored the jeer. He offered his arm to Charlotte and led her along the platform to the center, then turned to address the fyrd.

"Thegns, we thank you." He could teach a pike to smile. "We shall endeavor to continue to be worthy of your trust. And our dear lady thanks you also. Now, alas, it is our sad duty to empower a champion to redress the insult done to our honor." He was good. Anyone who did not know his slimy habits would find him a convincing speaker. Potbellied little monster.

"Go on, Father!" Wulfwer yelled. "Find a man to die for you. I'm waiting."

"Alas," Cynewulf said. "That the culprit is our own flesh and blood hurts us deeply and we can only hope that he will not pay too dearly for his folly. Nevertheless, this is the price of ambition, and those who venture for great prizes must be prepared to pay great price for failure. Kings and earls would know no peace if the penalty were slight." He brandished his smile again. "We shall be true to the tradition that says a king's champion is showered with enough riches to inspire the scops for a hundred years."

"Or his widow is given a wiser husband!" Wulfwer's *werod* whooped at his wit.

"Quite so," Cynewulf agreed. "But first we have a happier duty to perform." He snapped his fingers and a gangling *cniht* paraded forward proudly. He bore a red silk cushion, across which lay a shining sword. He dropped to one knee at the front edge of the dais, displaying it to the *werod.*

"Honored guests," the King declared, "earls, *ealdras,* thegns. It gives us abundant pleasure to welcome back to his own country after so long an absence, our dear nephew and stepson, Radgar Æleding. . . ." He waited for the cheering and booing to fade. And waited. And waited, tiny eyes flickering from side to side as he assessed who was making the most noise. Eventually he began to speak again, and the noise diminished until he could be heard. " . . . and of our own father, Fyrlaf. The guard is silver and bears the Seven Tears, a fabled set of blue pearls handed down from forgotten ages. These precious gems have graced many crowns and scepters and the flesh of great queens. The scops can sing their history for hours. Radgar, my son, come forward and accept from us this precious heriot."

Radgar's feet froze to the floor. What new treachery was this? Now the King had survived the challenge, to refuse his command would be an *unfrið.* Where had he seen that sword before?

Leofric whispered in his ear: "Don't go! It's another trap!"

At the same moment Ceolmund muttered to his elbow: "You must go or be counted craven."

Nobody had ever said politics would be easy.

• 2 •

Healfwer had very nearly run out of time. Steaming water lapped close to the octogram, fire was licking at the forest canopy over his head, and the air was so full of smoke and fumes that it seemed impossible to breathe. Yet still he was screeching out a conjuration and reeling around on his staff, a bizarre figure silhouetted against the curtain of flame.

"Stop!" Wasp croaked. "Stop it! What are you doing?" The enchanter either did not hear or else paid no attention.

Wasp was floundering through hot water that at times was almost chest deep. His progress was slowed by drowned undergrowth and floating debris, including the remains of the log cabin that had once stood here. Steady seepage of blood from his crushed hand had drained his strength. He could make no speed as he struggled toward the madman on the bank, yet his instinct screamed that Healfwer must not be allowed to complete that conjuration.

The ground moved and a major quake thundered through the crater. The poisonous lake surged. Crazy old Healfwer on the bank fell headlong. The backdrop of fire roared even louder, dropping branches, hurling burning trunks to the ground. Wasp staggered and paddled with his good hand in a desperate effort to remain upright as flaming debris hissed in the water all around.

Gradually the tortured mountain fell still again, and the clamor of falling rock faded into the constant roar of the fire. With wild contortions the old sorcerer struggled upright again and took up where he had left off. He had stripped naked, and the fires' light displayed all his horrible mutilation—old man on one side and on the other a moving corpse, a human cinder with no arm and barely enough stump of leg to hold the straps of the wooden extension.

"Stop! Stop!" Through streaming eyes, Wasp could see that there was something humped on the ground in the center of the octogram.

For the first time Healfwer heard. He looked around, puzzled, and saw Wasp wading toward him. At once he began chanting faster than ever, pirouetting around the octogram on his staff from point to point.

But the water at last became shallow. Wasp could lurch into a run, scramble up the final slope, slithering and blundering. He waved his sword.

"Stop or die!"

Healfwer did stop, leaning limply on his staff, his chest heaving, although it almost seemed that only the human side moved. He barked with a spasm of coughing. His one eye streamed tears, but the grimace that twisted the living half face registered triumph. "Done!"

The smoky air above the octogram glowed with a pearly light and the ash-covered eight-pointed star itself shone even brighter, as if written in fire. The thing in the center was an eagle. It was alive, fierce eye glaring at Wasp, but its legs had been tied to a log. How had a cripple managed to catch an eagle? A bull was how Æled's firedrake had been described, but the one that destroyed Cuðblæse had been likened to a great bird.

"You were conjuring a firedrake!" How could any man be evil enough to do such a thing?

The conjurer let out a screech of laughter. "Cynewulf's crimes compel revenge. But he will not escape me now. Stand aside."

"If you loose a drake here, how can you control it? You mustn't! It may kill Radgar as well as everyone else."

"My foes to fiery fates I send. Radgar is fireproofed! Let all others perish but the noble Æleding as I slew the Gevilians."

"No! Stop it!" Wasp had no doubts that Radgar would see it as his family duty to do battle with the monster if it appeared.

"Too late, slave! The elements are summoned."

The light in the octogram shone through the smoke, brighter than a noonday sun. The eagle stretched its wings and screeched. Burning twigs fell like rain, and Wasp's lungs were bursting. He was going to pass out from heat, loss of blood, lack of air. . . .

"If you won't stop it, I will!" He stepped into the octogram and stabbed *Nothing* through the eagle's heart.

· 3 ·

Radgar had lost his temper. He had not been conscious of doing so, but he was very glad of it now it had happened. He had forgotten how good it felt to throw off the shackles, to be free to do anything he wanted without counting the cost. *Hard it is to kill a king* . . . No, very easy, if you did not care whether or not you lived to brag of it. He smiled at the sight of all the house thegns watching him like cats. He was going to kill their lord right in front of their eyes and they would be helpless to stop him when he made his move.

He stalked forward. Anger rarely made him reckless, only ruthless. He stopped before the human vomit on the dais, the kneeling *cniht,* his mother. . . . He had seen that jeweled hilt somewhere. . . . He made a barely perceptible bow.

"Uncle?"

"We must be speedy," the King proclaimed to the *werod.* "There is no need to drag out this painful business. Son, it is not seemly for a man of your breeding to go unarmed, but before you can be admitted to the fyrd we must witness that you are of noble birth and accept your oath. Thereafter we shall ask you to redeem our honor in the matter of the challenge that has—"

A howl of outrage from the fyrd and even the guests behind him informed King Cynewulf what they thought of a man being delegated to fight his own cousin. Men like Swetmann might slay kinfolk for ambition, but it was not approved behavior. For a king to order such a murder was unconscionable.

"Did not my mother pass on my message, *niðing*?" Radgar yelled. "I told her that Wulfwer tried to kill me when I was a child and if I ever saw him at the end of my sword, I would cut out his tripes. Is that what you want me to do?"

Cynewulf spluttered, unable to make himself heard in the resulting pandemonium. Apparently that *was* what the human fungus wanted, though. Was there no depth to which this human dreg could not sink? Of course not! He had proved that five years ago.

The uproar drained away reluctantly. Radgar said, "I need no heriot, Uncle. I found a sword on the wall. Up there. A king-slaying sword!"

It was a satisfaction to watch the monster glance guiltily at the exact place on the planks and a joy to see him pale. Radgar laughed aloud. He knew he should be content with this small triumph, but now his temper was in the saddle, spurring him on to folly. Now he would tell the world what had happened on that terrible night in Twigeport. Then he would have to swear blood feud. As soon as he began doing that, the house thegns would cut him down, so just enough words to let everyone know what he was doing, then snatch up the heriot sword, and bury it in that royal belly—

"King-slaying sword, *niðing*! I have seen it slay lesser men too. Your tanist can tell us how Hengest and Frecful died, can't you, dear Wulfwer? What matters more is that earlier that same evening—"

"Radgar!" Queen Charlotte shouted. "It is time to take the oath, Son. Behold, everyone, the Queen honors Atheling Radgar!" She reached out in a rustle of fabric and took the sword of Seven Tears from the cushion, needing both hands to lift it.

"Charlotte, no! Do not!"

Ignoring her husband's cry, she raised the blade in formal salute. "Atheling, may all your great ancestors . . ."

"Mother!" Radgar shouted. "You stay out of this! Give me that sword—"

· 4 ·

The moment he struck the eagle, Wasp knew that he had blundered. Instead of blocking the conjuration, he had loosed spirits of death and completed it. The bird had not been there for the reason he supposed. He spun around in time to see Healfwer's half face twist with terror in the instant before he burned away to ash. The battle for Weargahlæw was decided; spirits of fire triumphed over the spirits of earth. The ancient crater roared back into life, consuming forest and every living thing within it in one great blast of flame—everything except Wasp, because he was within the octogram. Then he too was swept away.

Like a crimson-orange rose unfolding, the fiery fountain sprayed into the night sky. For an exquisite, timeless instant the flower hung there, air and fire rejoicing in liberty. Far below, the ice-clad peaks of Baelmark stood as islands in a sea of cloud under the cold stars. Then earth's ancient tyranny reasserted itself. Down the plume plunged, raining incandescent death upon the slopes of Cwicnoll. A myriad elementals battled for supremacy: Fire and water to make lava, fire and earth in burning ash, fire and air, air and rock for thunder, death and chance . . . Roiled together in confusion, the disparate spirits shrieked conflicting aims, while in among their millions one small voice of sentience screamed unheard.

· 5 ·

With the passing of daylight and the King's failure to call for candles, the hall had grown very dim. That changed even as Radgar reached for the sword his mother was so unsteadily holding aloft. A ruddy glow streamed in through the gable window as if the sun were rising again on a clear morning. Radgar hesitated, and then he saw the King. He had turned away, hands over his face in despair. What . . . ?

The Queen swayed. The sword waved uncertainly.

"Mother!" Radgar jumped to aid her and narrowly missed disaster as she swung the blade down.

"It's very heavy. . . ."

She released her grasp. The weapon clanged on the flagstones. He caught her as she toppled and lowered her to the dais.

"Mother, Mother!"

She smiled up at him vaguely. "Dizzy spell. I get them at times. . . ."

Clutching her in his arms, he looked up at the King and read terrible things in those hateful, bloated features, lit by that bloody light. "No, it is not just a dizzy spell!" He had turned his back on Wulfwer, which was folly. "What ails her, Uncle? What foul trickery is this?"

"I don't know what you mean . . ." Cynewulf looked to his son.

The tanist ran forward. "Cut out my tripes, will you? If we must fight, then let us start *now*!" He swung his sword at the kneeling Radgar.

The stroke should have rolled his head on the floor. That it did not was due partly to cries of alarm from the spectators, partly his Ironhall-honed reflexes, and partly because a wild surge of earthquake made Wulfwer stagger and sent his would-be victim tumbling out of the path of the murderous slash. Thunder roared through the hall. Radgar reeled to his feet, ripped away his cloak, and snatched up his grandfather's sword.

Now he would kill Wulfwer. There was no doubt in his mind about that, no alternative. He could see nothing except that detestable face as the tanist leaped in to try again. Radgar deflected the slash: *Clang!* He did not riposte, just smiled. Wulfwer tried again, a thrust this time, parried again. *Clang!*

Clang! Clang! Clang! Clang! Clang!

"Keep trying, Cousin!" Radgar jeered. He was in no danger, although dueling in an earthquake was not part of the Ironhall curriculum. *Clang!* The tanist was far less nimble than he was, so the heaving ground impeded him more. The pressure—*clang!*—he could put in his blade was incredible, but subtlety was not in him. *Clang! Clatter!* Now Radgar danced back before the frantic onslaught, enjoying his opponent's steadily rising panic, but aware that he had total control of the duel. "Hurry! You need to kill me, remember? Right ear!" He cut. Nice sword.

Wulfwer's scream sounded more like fury than pain. He carried on with the battle, streaming blood.

Clang! Spectators tried to clear out of their path, staggering as the ground shuddered. Several times Radgar had to—*clang!*—jump over rolling bodies. He wondered what the fyrd thought of this, the first demonstration of real fencing ever seen in Baelmark. He could tell what dear Wulfwer thought. He knew he was doomed.

"Left ear!" More blood.

"Stand and fight!" the giant howled, eyes wide with fear.

"Come and get me!"—*Clang!*—"You couldn't kill me when I was only"—*clang!*—"thirteen! You tried to"—*clang!*—*clang!*—"drown me. It's harder to fight *men,* isn't it—*Cousin*?"

Tiring of the game, Radgar slashed the tanist's wrist, almost severing his hand. Wulfwer's sword rang on the stones, leaving him staring in disbelief at a fountain of blood. The fight was over.

Simultaneously, the world steadied. Although that strange red light still lit the hall with a gory glow and the mountain continued to roar hungrily, the floor no longer heaved. Those who had fallen scrambled to their feet, or were helped up by others, while Radgar and his cousin faced off in the center, panting, and no one spoke. Then—

"Mercy!" Wulfwer clasped his wrist and squeezed, trying to shut off the flood of lifeblood.

"Speak!" Radgar roared. "Confess! Tell the truth if you hope to live. Why did you challenge your father?"

"Mercy!"

"No mercy!" Radgar swung a woodcutter's chop at the giant's knee, cutting him down like an oak. A thousand voices cried out in horror at this breach of honor. Ignoring them, he straddled the fallen thegn and delicately put sword point on cheekbone.

"One wrong word and you lose this eye. Speak, brute! What was the plan tonight?" He did not recognize his own voice. "You were going to kill me, weren't you? How?"

"The sword!"

"Louder! Let them all hear. Confess or I cut you to pieces."

Wulfwer howled, still clutching his wounded arm in an effort to stem the bleeding. "The sword was cursed. Whoever was first to lift it would be dazed. It wouldn't have killed you! Just giddy."

If Radgar had been first to raise it, he would now be dead. That went without saying.

"I am your bane, Wulfwer. Did Healfwer never tell you that? Were you going to kill me the night my father died?"

"No!"

Jab! Radgar spared the eye but opened the flesh back to what was left of the ear.

Wulfwer screamed. "Yes! Yes! I was going to drown you. Help me! I need healing!"

"Who killed King Æled?"

"Don't know— Father told me to stay in the hall. Said I was to be seen there so no one could suspect me."

"So he told you Æled was going to die before it happened?"

Wulfwer's lips curled back in terror, but then he mumbled, "Sort of . . ."

That was enough.

"Murderer!" Radgar cut his cousin's throat as his father's had been cut. The hall resounded with a great animal sound of mingled cheers and protests: approval, disgust, outrage, and delight. He did not care. Leaving Wulfwer gurgling and thrashing in his death throes, he hurried back to see to his mother, not knowing if it was his legs or the floor that trembled so.

He wondered why there were so many people fussing around her—until he saw the blood. Wulfwer's wild slash, which had so nearly decapitated him, had struck the Queen instead, cutting her chest open, severing ribs. A couple of house thegns were struggling to bandage her, but blood foamed out with every breath. She was unconscious. From what he recalled of Ironhall's classes on wounds, she had only seconds left to live.

"Get her to a healer!" he yelled. He dropped the sword and knelt to lift her.

Four house thegns grabbed him from behind and hauled him upright to face the King.

Cynewulf struck him across the face. "Murderer! You slew an unarmed man—we saw it ourself!"

"Get your wife to a healer, monster!" Radgar squirmed

vainly in the house thegns' grip. He tasted blood, for the rings had cut him.

"That was *unfrið*! You slew our son before our eyes, unarmed and wounded. Roðercræft, take this criminal outside and cut his head off." The King was trying to play an outraged father, but his glee kept oozing around his mask.

He had right on his side. The duel had been completed. There had not even been formal declaration of blood feud. No thegn in the room would see his son slain in cold blood and not then take reprisal. A monarch, especially, must defend his rights and honor. The spectators were roaring, half supporting Radgar and half Cynewulf. Meanwhile Roðercræft's armored toughs controlled the hall.

"Yea, lord!" the marshal said. "A pleasure! Take him, men."

The house thegns turned Radgar around and hauled him along the hall toward the door. Another dozen closed in around as escort. They were all bigger than he was and his sword lay abandoned on the floor. He had played right into the King's hands. He was as good as dead. Bitter the taste of defeat!

Roaring defiance, Leofric and his men charged past the posse and formed up ahead, cutting them off from the exit.

"Release him!" bellowed the one-eyed man, and the men of *Faroðhengest* roared their agreement. It was a convincing roar, but it was bluff. They had no weapons.

Roðercræft was right behind Radgar. He yanked the prisoner's head back and laid an ice-cold dagger across his throat. "We can do it here as easy as outside in the square. Stand aside."

"He deserves fair trial!"

"On the count of three he dies," the marshal barked. "One . . ."

Radgar could barely see his would-be rescuers, for he was forced to stare at the rafters, still so strangely lit by the bloody glow. His case was hopeless, but his plight was his own fault and certainly no reason for his friends to die in a hopeless cause.

"Stand aside, *ealdor*!" Radgar shouted.

Nothing happened.

"Two . . ."

Radgar tried again. "My father would not want the men of Catterstow slaughtering one another for my sake. You cannot rescue me. Stand aside."

Leofric ground his teeth. "He is to be held for trial!"

"Certainly."

It was a lie, and everyone knew it, but Leofric stepped back. "Let them past!"

"Thank you!" Roðercræft said brightly. "So kind! Clear the way." He kept the dagger where it was until the *Faroðhengest* men had moved back to the sides. "Forward!"

So died the last of the House of Catter . . .

Just before the prisoner and his escort reached the doors, the doors blew off their hinges in an explosion of flame. The firedrake standing outside peered in under the lintel.

· 6 ·

Healfwer? Had the old maniac summoned this awful thing, or had the mountain spawned it?

Radgar picked himself up from where the house thegns had dropped him and backed away while he considered the problem. Everyone else had fled screaming to the far end of the hall. His ordeal in Twigeport had left him with a terror of fire, but he had overcome it in Ironhall on the night he had rescued Wasp and the others. Fire no longer scared him very much at all—but a drake was no ordinary fire. Already the heat on his face was painful.

"Healfwer?" he roared.

"Arrrh!" answered the firedrake, almost as if trying to

speak. "Arrrh, arrrh!" It flowed into the hall, tearing away part of the wall.

Radgar turned and ran after the others. There really ought to be a back door to this place. Why him? It would have to be him, of course. He was fireproof and Æled's son; and he must try to do something, because no one else could; and the monster might even be his fault, if his crazy grandfather had conjured it up after hearing the ghost's story. The entire Catterstow fyrd was trapped here in Cynehof along with every earl in the kingdom except one. If the firedrake killed them all, Baelmark would collapse in anarchy.

His mother's body lay deserted on the edge of the dais with the sword of Seven Tears nearby. Even before he reached them, he began to strip, for he knew how clothes prolonged the pain as they burned away. His fingers shook so badly that he had trouble unfastening his belt buckle, but there was no shame in being afraid now, not when the entire fyrd had collapsed in screaming terror. He would not have thought so many men could all fit on the dais, but they could—and on the rear half of it, too. Those at the back must be crushed and suffocating, but they were in less immediate danger from the firedrake's wrath.

He was stamping his feet back into his boots when the firedrake rumbled angrily and surged closer.

"Arrrh!" it said in jets of fire. "Arrrh, arrrh, arrrh, arrrh!"

It was black clinker and burning rock and heat so intense that it was difficult to look at, even along the length of Cynehof. A red haze glowed around it. At times it rose up into a man's shape, although two or three times a man's height, and at others it was merely a fountain of rock and lava, surging and flowing and crumbling, never the same for more than a few seconds. As it progressed it left behind it a smoking, bubbling ridge of broken ground like a solidified wake, so it seemed to be erupting out of the floor, but in its manlike moments it waded forward on massive legs, churning up the flagstones. Even when it was at its most human it had no face, and every move or change of shape caused its outer crust to crack and break off, exposing the glowing fires within.

Once inside the hall it reared up to the likeness of a giant, and the rafters over its head began to smoke. "Arrrh!" it said again, a roar of complaint. The ground trembled.

A dozen men made a dash for the door. The firedrake caught them as they went by, although no one could say for certain whether it swatted them with a giant stone hand or just collapsed in their direction, engulfing them in an avalanche. They had time to scream once and roll over a few times before they became cinders half buried in glowing rubble. Flames ran up the wall beside them. As the firedrake reassembled itself from a new upsurge of lava, the greasy rafters above it ignited. The whole building would go in minutes.

Stripped to his boots, Radgar snatched up his grandfather's sword again. Cuðblæse had died; Fyrlaf been horribly maimed, but Æled had survived. Now it was his turn. Dad had battled his drake outdoors, not trapped inside a tinderbox like this with no room to run. The air was already pain to breathe, and his skin was pumping out sweat so he could hardly see or clutch the sword. He had never realized a firedrake would be so enormous.

He turned to look at the terrified mob behind him and located Cynewulf the Good, still in his crown and robes. Like everyone else he was whimpering and trying to burrow his way into the mob, but his bulk and flab could not displace the tight-locked muscle of the other men.

"Come, Uncle!" Radgar seized a handful of ermine-trimmed velvet. "If I must die, then you certainly die first." With the strength of youth he hauled the King away from the crowd, ran him across the dais, and hurled him off. Screaming, the fat man sprawled down on the floor.

"Arrrh, arrrh!" The firedrake lurched slowly forward. It was almost to the hearths now, plowing up the floor like a man wading through slush. All the front end of the hall was ablaze. "Arrrh?"

As the King scrambled to his feet, Radgar jumped down

after him and prodded with his sword. "Move! Die on this blade or move!"

Wailing and struggling—and bleeding, for Radgar had no time for mercy—Cynewulf backed toward the firedrake. "What are you doing?" he screamed. The heat became unbelievable, but worse for Radgar at the moment than for him. His fur collar and crown protected his neck and head and the rest of him was well shielded.

"I want the truth! Whose idea was it to kill my father?"

"I know nothing about—*arrrh*!" Cynewulf's scream sounded very much like the firedrake's roar, octaves higher. With one slash, his grandfather's sword had opened Cynewulf's garments from collarbone to waist, and opened the flesh under it also. Blood spurted even redder than the robes. "It was Ambrose! That Blade he sent promised me the throne. His orders were to get a peace treaty and kill Æled."

"Ambrose *ordered* him to kill my father?"

"Yes! Yes! He had never forgiven him for the Candlefen *færing*."

"And the Queen? Speak!" Radgar drove his victim onward, ever closer to the raging furnace of the firedrake.

Cynewulf fell back from the sword, clothes smoking, hair and beard frizzling in the heat. "Charlotte was my prize, my price! I had wanted her for years. Mercy, mercy!"

"You showed no mercy, *niðing*! Tell of the rest of your crimes. How did you manage to hang on to the throne? Speak! I will make you speak!"

The King tumbled to his knees, writhing as the heat worked through his robes. "I confess! I confess everything. I used a conjurement on your mother. I take Chivian gold—four hundred thousand crowns a year Ambrose sends me to turn a blind eye and keep the peace."

The firedrake continued to move closer, coming slowly, cascading lava from its joints. It glowed brightly in the dense smoke that now filled the hall, looming over the two men like a sun in cloud. Radgar could hardly breathe for coughing, but he forced out one more question.

"And Æðelnoð?"

''He was plotting treason!'' Cynewulf screamed. ''When Ambrose sent word that you were on your way home, I knew he would conspire with you against me.''

It was enough, more than enough. If any witnesses at all survived from this disaster, Cynewulf would be condemned forever in the annals of his country.

''Up!'' Radgar dropped his sword and used both hands to drag the wailing monarch to the firedrake. Lava spewed up from the floor. The fat man's garments burst into flames. So did Radgar's boots. Screaming, he hurled himself aside, rolling away in agony. Cynewulf was trapped and engulfed, although in the smoke it almost seemed as if the firedrake lifted him up in both hands and peered at him curiously while he burned away.

· 7 ·

Radgar hauled himself back from the edge of madness. He could indulge in faints and hysterics later. First he must deal with this fiendish thing before it killed everyone in the hall. He snatched up his sword again and also—with some vague instinct that it was important and should not be lost—the golden crown of Baelmark.

Dad had told him, ''I just made it notice me and then ran like an otter for the water.'' But Dad had met his firedrake in the open air. This one was blocking the only way out.

Somehow he must attract the firedrake's attention and lead it back the way it had come. If he merely angered it, it might charge straight at the fyrd. If he did not do something soon, everyone would broil or suffocate. Shuddering, he ran at the monster.

Strike it and get past it and keep running—simple but almost certainly impossible. It had collapsed into a heap again and seemed to be trying to rebuild its manlike form once more. Why did it choose that shape? Screaming in fury and agony both, he scrambled up the rising slope. Aiming at where its heart would be if it were human, he drove the sword into a crevice, hoping to vault over that hint of a shoulder, come down on the far side, and keep on running. That did not happen. He had expected his blade to meet resistance, but the molten inside of the abomination was runny as water, so the sword went in up to the hilt. A huge slab of the outer crust broke off, releasing torrents of fire and lava. The fiery avalanche swept Radgar down the firedrake's left side and rolled him across the floor until he hit the wall. There he lay, at the monster's mercy.

The firedrake did not turn on him as he had expected. It roared as if it, too, was in pain. It went straight out a side wall, which exploded into fiery ash. Radgar was ripped and bleeding, bruised in a thousand places, but out there was rain and cold ground, so he scrambled up from the rubble and lurched after it. His quarry was fleeing and, houndlike, he must pursue, his insane hatred burning hotter than the drake itself.

Some crazy citizens had gathered to watch the destruction of Cynehof. They fled as the monster churned toward them, moving almost as fast as a man could run—as fast, anyway, as a seriously injured man running on raw feet.

Like a dust devil crossing a field on a summer day, the firedrake waded through Waroðburh as if seeking to escape the puny figure behind it. Whatever Dad had said about being chased by his firedrake, this one fled, a complete reversal. Clothed in steam and flame, it mainly followed the winding streets, but at times it cut corners, and then buildings vanished in spouts of flame, raining burning debris and starting a thousand fires. Only the torrential rain and the wide spaces between houses saved the entire city from destruction. In retrospect, Radgar remembered very little of that mad pursuit. Some deep, hunter instinct continued to function and he ran through pain and exhaustion, driven insane by hate. This was what anger was for! Once or twice his quarry wavered, as if about to turn and fight, but each time it resumed its former downhill path before he reached it.

At the harbor the drake seemed to sense its bane, the sea, for it veered off course and moved along the beach, exploding boats and longships. Radgar tried to cut it off, screaming at it. He had lost too much blood; he was almost too weak to brandish what remained of his sword. Just as he decided that he would have to close with the monster again, it turned away and waded through a rocky outcrop to the water's edge. Without hesitation, it plunged off. A single mountain-sized scream, and the drake was gone, the harbor had a new pier. Radgar was deluged in boiling spray, which was a welcome relief after what had gone before.

The only way out of his torment was to faint, so he did.

• 8 •

He lay on a very hard surface, wrapped in a cloak or blanket. He could guess that he was in an elementary, because conjurers were chanting, sending waves of spirituality washing over him and through him, healing, soothing—and just as flaming well! He felt as if he'd been grated like carrots and threshed like grain. Still, by rights he should have been burned to ash a dozen times over, so he should not complain. The voices seemed distant and had a curiously muffled tone that told him he was back in the Haligdom.

He kept his eyes shut, feeling the spirits working their miracle and enjoying it, for the fading away of pain was intense pleasure. Even when the conjurers completed their incantation and fell silent, he had no great inclination to return to the world. Cynewulf was dead and Wulfwer, too, so it would be a better world. So was Charlotte Ældeswif, poor soul, and Wasp also, if he had gone back to Weargahlæw. Neither had deserved the troubles life had given them. The witenagemot would elect a new king, no doubt, and the runner-up would immediately challenge.

So? Radgar had a good claim now, after defeating the firedrake. But a great weariness had settled over him. No! Let them kill one another off to their hearts' content, to the last tanist. He had survived his first taste of political life, if only barely, and one sip was enough. The estates that rightfully belonged to him would make him very rich, so all he need do was stay off the booming sea and never go a-*færing* on the western wind. Then no one would try to involve him in politics. He could grow fat and live to a ripe old age on the fame he had earned that night. He could acquire a concubine, just to find out what all the fuss was about, and perhaps in time a wife. He had conquered a firedrake! That was good, very good. *Radgar Dracanbana!* His father would have approved. He was a worthy Cattering, fit to stand with his ancestors.

Yet he still had unfinished business. Cynewulf was dead and Yorick as good as, but the real culprit behind his father's murder was still very much at large.

"He's frowning," said Leofric's voice. "Is that a good sign?"

He tried not to react, but then his mouth smiled so he opened his eyes and looked at a complete ring of faces peering down at him—red beards, white beards, no beards, male and female. Few of them were recognizable against the light of the lanterns hung high on the eight pillars. Someone was being extraordinarily extravagant with lamp oil! He moved a few muscles experimentally and everything seemed to be present and functioning. His feet hurt. He tried to speak and nothing happened, but then strong arms raised him and a beaker was put to his mouth. He drained it six times before uttering a sound, and the first words he spoke were a demand for more. They sat him up so Aylwin and another man could slide a tunic on him, dressing him like a child.

The great dome seemed almost empty, although it held the eight conjurers and a score or so of his shipmates from *Faroðhengest.* It was good to be alive, to see those smiles. Why, though, had he not been treated in one of the smaller elementaries—and why all by himself? There would be many injured people in Waroðburh after so many fires. The rain was still falling, for he could hear its deep drumming on the roof, but there was another noise that he could not identify, a vague rumble like surf on a rocky coast.

"Well?" Leofric demanded. "Nothing's missing. All we can see wrong on the outside are some bruises and gashes, and they should clear up very shortly. How do you feel on the inside?"

"Weary. A bit sore, still."

"Spirits, man! Is that all? After what you did?" His single eye glistened. It was not like him to show such emotion. "These learned people have done wonders for you and want to be the first to thank you for what you did. Do you feel up to that?"

"I must first thank them for what they have done for me."

They helped him stand. Reluctantly he accepted the stool they brought, for he was absurdly shaky and his feet hurt, which was a novel humiliation for a man who had not known a day's ill health since childhood. Aylwin knelt to dress him in leggings and garters without as much as a by-your-leave. The exuberance of the conjurers' thanks was yet another embarrassment. Three men and five women . . . he had never had people fawn over him before, except some of the sillier juniors at Ironhall the day he bested Wolfbiter at fencing. He had only done his duty, he insisted, and without their healing skills he would not be here now.

Then—over his vehement protests—Leofric knelt to kiss his hands, followed by Aylwin, Ceolmund, and his *Faroðhengest* brethren. They hailed him as hero and *dracan-bana*, talking much nonsense. They all had an ominous sparkle of excitement about them. They did not seem to realize that

Radgar Æleding had decided to retire from political life, and he was beginning to suspect that telling them so would make very little difference to whatever it was they were plotting. No one threw away this much lamp oil just to heal one battered boy. The door was being opened and closed, as if people were going in and out, and every time it opened the sound of heavy surf surged briefly.

"Have I passed the test?" he demanded sourly. "Am I making sense? No slobbering, gibbering, or detectable hallucinations?"

The ship lord raised his golden eyebrows. "All right *so far.* I think we can turn up the heat a little."

"Please! Can't you find a more tactful turn of phrase?"

Leofric chuckled approvingly. "This is yours." It was a lump of metal. It had once been a sword but half the blade had melted away and the pearls were gone from the hilt.

"My grandfather's," Radgar said. "Hang it in Cynehof if you want. When it's rebuilt. Yes, I'd like you to do that." Fyrlaf was another who must have died tonight in the eruption.

Leofric laughed. "See to it yourself. I think this is yours, too."

It was a badly misshapen tangle of metal, but before being half melted it had been the crown of Baelmark.

"Where by the eight did you find that?" Was this why they were all grinning like idiots?

"On your head, of course. You wore it when you chased the firedrake out of town."

"Spirits! I did? Did I?" He could not remember.

Aylwin guffawed. "That and nothing else. There are seventy-seven beautiful maidens lined up outside, all *very* eager to meet you."

First in when doors were opened was the Catterstow fyrd. The leaders began chanting *Rad-gar! Rad-gar!* in time with their feet—and the beat was picked up by all the rest, a great snake of warriors, hundred after hundred. When the front ranks reached the circle of Leofric's *werod* standing guard around the hero, they divided and encircled it. The followers pressed in around. *Rad-gar! Rad-gar!*

Radgar stood on a stool in the center and watched the cordon grow to fill the Haligdom—a multitude, all facing him, cheering him: *Rad-gar! Rad-gar!* It was an extraordinary sensation, far stranger than he would have guessed. He had never been worshiped before. His throat hurt. He could not speak. Few were armed, for the firedrake must have melted all the swords stacked in the porch. Behind them came wives and children, even ceorls.

And finally came the earls and their *werodu,* anxious to see what the locals were up to. They clustered near the door, glowering suspiciously. Big Edgar of Hunigsuge was there, and Ælfgeat of Suðmest, whose sneak attack on Suðecg had caused the witenagemot to assemble. With both the King and his tanist dead, there was no king in Baelmark. At least three of the earls had ambitions. All nineteen of them might be dreaming of glory now. So who was in charge? Probably Ordheah of Hyrnstan; he was senior.

The chant of *Rad-gar!* was being drowned out by a rising chorus of *Hlaford Fyrlandum!* That made the earls scowl even more, for the song was a royal honor. But Radgar remembered the last time he had heard it, the night his father died. So he stood and wept while everyone else rejoiced.

At last he raised his arms for silence; and the tumult subsided to a low rumble, merging with the volcano's grumbling. Before he could find his voice, Aylwin bellowed at the top of his big lungs, "Catterstow!"

"Catterstow!" roared the fyrd in response, and there was frenzy again: *"Catterstow! Catterstow! Catterstow!"*

Earl Radgar of Catterstow! Could this be real?—the sea of faces, the acclaim? Why could his mother not be here to see it? Or Dad? Or even Wasp. Realizing he was going to start weeping again if they didn't stop, he raised his arms again.

"I am deeply honored! You want me as your earl?"

Stupid question—it set them going all over again.

Leofric gripped his arm. "Claim the throne, too, lad. You're the only royally-born one among them. It's yours."

Ceolmund grabbed his other wrist and tugged for attention. His voice squeaked down near Radgar's knee. "No, no! Wait until they call a proper moot! You must not seem too eager."

It so happened that both of them had managed to find bruises to squeeze. Radgar shook free of them.

"What are you going to say?" Leofric demanded.

He looked down to meet the stare of one eye and an emerald. "I haven't decided yet, thegn."

Leofric managed a smile. "Forgive me, Æleding. Very much Æleding!"

"I will try to be. Thegns! *Ealdras!*"

His shouts brought an attentive, excited hush. Before he could open his mouth, Aylwin, that well-meaning sailor idiot, set the half-melted crown on Radgar's head and bellowed, *"Halettaþ hlafordne Fyrlandum!"**

More tumult—wild cheering from the Catterstow fyrd, booing from the earls' *werodu.* The crown was heavy and painfully knobbly, but Radgar left it where it was. Yet again he gestured for silence, and the din sank to a low surf sound.

He could see that the earls were not convinced. Fighting firedrakes did not necessarily qualify him for kingship.

"Before I can even think of being your king . . . before I even think of giving you my oath as earl, there is another oath I must swear. Hear this one and then decide if you want me. Listen!" He might not get the words exactly right, but he could certainly come close enough. He roared out the ancient and most terrible of curses:

"Woe to Ambrose Ranulfing, King of Chivial! For the evil he has done me, I swear I will not rest from strife until his blood has soaked the land, balefire has eaten his flesh, and the winds have scattered his name. May I be counted *niðing* if I show fear or mercy to him or his."

Shock! The silence was absolute. Even the rain seemed to have been frightened away. In real life blood feuds were

*Hail the Lord of the Fire Lands!

either a grave breach of the king's *frið* or mere romantic nonsense in scops' ballads.

"Ambrose ordered the murder of my father. He broke the terms of the treaty he had signed. He perverted our ancient rights with wholesale bribery. If you take me as your king, then you get a war as well. The killing will come again—the looting, raping, burning. There will be booty and pillage aplenty, but you, *ealdras,*" he yelled, pointing at the earls, "will have to win your riches honestly, by deed of arms. You heard what Cynewulf confessed. There are traitors among you, cowards who took the foreigner's gold."

Big Edgar had the strongest lungs in the Haligdom. *"Are you calling me coward, Æleding?"*

"Wear the skirt if it fits, *ealdor.* Coward or bribe taker. Or prove me wrong—come with me when I sail against Chivial, for I swear that I will harry it as it has never been harried, until it screams for mercy and Eurania is appalled. My sword will glut on blood until I have taken Ambrose's head, but no more will his carrion gold fatten cowards' bellies in secret. I do not know the traitors' names yet, but I expect my uncle kept a record somewhere. So, are you with me, Earls? And if you are not then yes, I call you cowards! And traitors. And *niðingas*!"

Had the firedrake not destroyed the swords stacked in the porch at Cynehof so that almost no one was now armed, those words might have started a massacre. Or perhaps not, because the earls' *werodu* were looking deeply troubled by this talk of bribery. The first earl to speak up was not Edgar but another of Cynewulf's accomplices, Ælfgeat. Shouting, "Death to Chivial! I side with King Radgar!" he plowed into the crowd. His *werod* cheered.

It was Big Edgar who made it through first, though, hurling men aside until he could grab Radgar's hand and swear to be his man, faithful and true, and death to Chivial. So Radgar swore to be his lord and worthy of trust. When he had done that ten times, he was King in Baelmark, lord of the Fire Lands.

*   *   *

The last of the nineteen was the most junior, only a month in office and little older than Radgar himself. When he released the man's hands, Radgar was so shaky from sheer weakness that he descended from his stool by falling into Aylwin's arms. Held upright, he made appointments, good until further notice—Chancellor Ceolmund, Marshal Leofric, and Tanist Aylwin. That involved more oaths.

"Now," he said, "start running the kingdom, because your sovereign lord is going to bed now and will sleep for a week."

Twisted Ceolmund uttered a brief but ominous laugh. "As my lord commands. *Ealdras,* in the absence of our sovereign lord, the tanist will convene the war moot here at noon. King Radgar expects all of you to attend on pain of death."

The earls chuckled, but even in his weariness Radgar sensed the undertow of danger in this raillery. Besides, the thought of Aylwin trying to run a moot was bloodcurdling.

"It can't wait?"

"You have just declared war, lord," his government told him blithely. "Is it your royal command that hostilities commence immediately and without notice? If so, you will be accused of treacherously breaking a treaty and the Chivians will undoubtedly take reprisals against every Bael they can catch. We must have two hundred ships in foreign waters at the moment. Your lordship might even consider issuing a royal decree right now . . ." And so on.

He did not quite say that some of the earls were planning to head straight home and send out the foxes while the chickens were still snoozing on their roosts. But he meant that. He implied that only Radgar could rein them in.

Ironhall had not taught much of this.

· 9 ·

Rain still fell on Waroðburh, but an honest man reigned in Baelmark. Catterstow had an earl it was not ashamed of, the guilty had died, and Cwicnoll was starting to sound sleepy. Things were looking up.

On the other hand, when the new monarch hobbled out of the Haligdom, he encountered the beginnings of a civil war. Loyal subjects were trying to organize a torchlight procession to carry him home to his palace, and both earls and fyrd claimed the right to bear him on their shoulders. Only Radgar himself could settle that argument, so he demanded a horse instead, earls to follow in single file and order of seniority on the right, ship lords likewise on the left and everybody else *shut up*! Life was going to be full of tricky decisions like that from now on. Men ran to obey.

The air reeked of ashes. Even over the muttering rumble of the crowd, he could hear faint chanting as casualties were treated in the smaller elementarics. Huge areas of Waroðburh must lie in ruins, although he could see no fires still burning. His the task of rebuilding his capital. He also had a war to launch, a government to organize, family estates to run, a mother to mourn. As he drooped there in the drizzle, waiting for the horse to appear, he wondered why in the world he had been such a fool. For Dad? For a mother who would have been so proud to have a king for a son? His father would have reserved judgment, he thought, saying he had not won the crown honestly but this would not matter if he wore it wisely.

Where, by the eight, was the accursed horse? He could

have walked to the palace sooner. He was swaying on his feet, yet men kept chattering at him—bowing, fawning, even kneeling in the mud to kiss his hand, reminiscing about their adventures *færing* with his father, daring to comment how much *my lord* looked like *my lord's honored father.* He must be the first man in history to win a kingdom on the shape of his ears, but many of those bloodthirsty old monsters were weeping with joy, and every one of them must be answered courteously and hailed by name if possible.

Then a disturbance, a man trying to break through the mob: "Radgar! Radgar! Radgar!" That was Aylwin's bullhorn voice. Perhaps he had brought the seventy-seven beautiful maidens?

No. He heaved a few more earls aside and appeared, flushed in the flickering light of the torches, panting but maidenless. "Radgar—I mean my lord—he's asking for you! He's hurt but they think he'll live. Wants to see you. He's hurt quite bad, Radgar. This way—"

"Belay! Now, from the beginning. Who's asking for me?"

Aylwin had paused only to suck in one more enormous breath, and now he blew it all out in another torrent of words. "They found him floating facedown in the harbor but the healers were sure he was a thrall because he was a foreigner and he had nothing on and besides they were sure he was dying and they only just got around to treating the thralls and then he told them what he thought of them and they realized he wasn't a thrall at all and— What? Oh, that Chivian *hæftniedling* of yours. Yes, sir, er, lord, I do mean Wæps Thegn."

10

It was one of those spring mornings when the whole world erupts with life—lambs bouncing, birds screeching insults at one another from every bush, and butterflies flying complex colored patterns in the hedgerows. After a two-week tantrum, Cwicnoll had repented of his ill humor and gone back to sleep for another generation or so, trailing hardly a wisp of smoke from his fancy new cone. The woodlands of Hatburna had never seemed lovelier. King Radgar slid down from Isgicel's back and looped his reins around a sapling. Then he continued along the path on foot. It was possible that the patient was still asleep. . . .

He wasn't. Outside the royal cabin lay Wasp, stretched on a couch, staring at the boughs overhead and covered from toes to chin by a fleecy rug. He had not heard Radgar's approach over the noise of the waterfall. He looked up and scowled. Visitors not welcome.

Kings could ignore such hints. Radgar dropped to his knees on the grass. "Came to ask if you want to go riding!" Royal grin.

"No."

Royal frown. "Bathing, then?"

"I can't swim. I doubt if I could even get on a horse. Go *away*!"

"What *do* you want?"

"To be alone."

That was all he ever wanted.

Radgar sighed. "Anything except that. I need some fencing practice. I'm getting rusty."

Wasp looked straight at him for the first time. His pallor

was not so extreme as it had been. His physical injuries had pretty much healed, according to the doctors—other than the loss of his arm, of course, but even enchantment could not replace a missing limb. Mental . . . That was more tricky, the healers agreed, and then they would mumble. They thought he would recover in time. They hoped he would.

"A one-armed fencer?" the patient sneered. "My balance is hopeless. Just walking I stagger and trip over my feet. You have ten thousand pirates—go and practice on them."

Radgar tried the grin again. "I don't dare. They might learn Ironhall technique from me and then challenge. Come on, Wasp! So you lost an arm? You'll learn a new balance soon enough. It wasn't your fencing arm. It wasn't the hand you write with. And you saved a king. Anything I can give you is yours. Just name it, friend. Land? Tell me you like Hatburna and I'll give it to you. Ships? Money? Slaves? Women?"

"Women?" Wasp snapped, displaying some welcome emotion. He heaved himself more upright with his right arm—his only arm. "Explain to me why this patch of woodland is swarming with pretty girls all of a sudden. Redheads, brunettes, blondes . . . all simpering and puckering red lips at me. 'Fresh towels, Wæps Thegn.' 'Your wash water, Wæps Thegn.' 'Some iced wine, Wæps Thegn?' You are a *pimp*, Radgar Æleding! You think you can distract me by throwing girls at me?"

There was enough truth there to warm Radgar's cheeks, but not enough to make him feel truly guilty. "I didn't mean to be a pimp! I hadn't learned then what happens when a king expresses a wish. I just said I hoped my dear friend Wasp would feel happier soon. Everyone in earshot assumed that meant I would shower treasure on anyone who could make you smile. Next time I rode over here, I found the place swarming with daughters, sisters, cousins. . . . Take whatever comes your way, I'd say."

Wasp struggled off the couch and stood up. His left sleeve dangled pathetically empty. "I told you. I just want to be left alone, with nobody in sight or sound. If I'd wanted to swarm I'd have called myself Bee, not Wasp. You want to please me? Go away!'' He turned as if to leave.

Radgar sat back on the dewy grass and leaned his arms on his knees. ''I was going to ask you to be my *drhytguma.*''

Wasp went rigid. ''Your *what*?''

''Bridesman . . . like best man.''

That won a reaction almost like the old Wasp, the missing Wasp. He swung around, eyes wide. ''*You!* Married? That's pretty fast work, isn't it?''

Radgar shrugged. ''Politics. When the first *færing* goes against Chivial, I'll have to lead it. Have to prove I'm my father's son. The witan all agree I ought to sire an heir before then. In fact they more or less told me they won't let me go until I do.''

Obviously intrigued, Wasp said, ''Does she have a name? Where did you find her?''

''Her name's Culfre, eldest daughter of the late Earl Æðelnoð, so she's a Nyrping. It's a good match—she has two younger brothers who will be the first royally born contenders I'll have to worry about, but they're less likely to challenge if their sister is queen. May not work, but that's the theory. I'm told she's very sweet-natured and a real looker.''

They would tell him that if she had three eyes and a beard. The prospect was almost as scary as having to fight another firedrake. Two days to go . . .

Wasp said, ''Hmm.'' Then he pulled a face, a very cynical expression. ''How does the Lady Culfre feel about being a political pawn and broodmare? One foal right away, please! Have you thought to ask her?''

This time Radgar felt his face turn brick red. A king must learn to be more impassive. ''Yes, I have. Ceolmund and I picked her out as the most suitable candidate and I wrote her a private, personal letter, explaining the situation and asking if she would be interested. I stressed that it was entirely her decision and if she did not like the terms, then nothing more need ever be said.''

''And?''

"Her fourteen-year-old brother wrote back that his sister would be honored to marry the King, and he consented to the match, subject to suitable terms . . . and so on."

For a moment Wasp looked ready to grin. "So her mother reads her mail? Women don't get much say in such matters in Chivial, either. Your mother could have told you that. No, I won't be your best man. Put me in a crowd now and I'd go screaming mad. Ask Aylwin. He's the best man around."

"Not so, Wasp," Radgar said quietly. "You're the finest man I know." Besides, anything a king did had political repercussions. Aylwin and his father were uppity enough already.

Wasp bit his lip, his eyes glistened. "Half man!" He turned his back. "Go away, please," he whispered. "Oh, please!"

"In a moment. There's something else I must ask you. I'm sorry, I've tried to ignore it and . . . Well, I must know. When I stabbed the firedrake, just that one time in the hall, a great chunk of it fell off."

Wasp waited, not looking around, not speaking.

Radgar took a deep breath and asked it. "Is that why your arm—?"

"No. I told you. You hurt us, yes. I very nearly lost control of them when you did that. If they'd broken loose, we'd have . . . they'd have wrecked the hall and . . . It would have been a massacre. Our—I mean *my* arm came after, when the spell was broken. The water wasn't quite deep enough, that's all. My arm was left exposed. I got off lighter than Fyrlaf. Now, please, please, can I be alone? Come back in a year. Maybe then I'll know who I am."

Radgar sighed and stood up. Whatever the horrors of the firedrake enchantment, it had burned away Wasp's binding. He was a free man, no longer a Blade.

"Of course. Just one more thing. I tracked down the ship lord who sacked Haybridge and slaughtered your family."

He waited, staring at Wasp's back, but Wasp just stood there.

"He knew about the treaty. He was on his first *færing*

with his own ship, so I suppose he— He knew, he disobeyed the royal command, Wasp. You want him put on trial, I'll do it. His *werod* were just following orders, but he'll be found guilty and enthralled. If you want, I'll give him to you then and you can do anything you—''

''Do whatever you want,'' Wasp said hoarsely. ''Go away.''

''I'll cut his head off, then. Oh, Wasp! I can't give you back your arm, but I can give you flaming near anything else in the world you can dream of. I want you as my advisor, my trusted companion—as my fencing partner, so I can keep up my skills and no blustering Bael earl will ever dare challenge me. My friend, I owe you my life, although no Blade ever saved his ward by anything remotely like the means you used. It cost you. I'm sorry. I'm grateful. Anything you ever want, just ask.''

''Right!'' Wasp roared. He spun around, stumbled, flailed his arm, and recovered his balance. *''Stop the war!''*

''What?'' Anything except that, Radgar thought.

''Stop the war. Is that so hard to understand?'' Wasp's face had gone from pale to scarlet. His eyes were fever bright. ''You're going to start the horrors all over again—*færing,* you call it? I call it rape, theft, murder, slaving, bestiality. I saw it happen at Haybridge and it marred my life. It cost me everyone I held dear.'' Shouting, he advanced, and Radgar stepped back, almost tripping over a tree root. ''You think that's why I agreed to be your Blade, you barbarian Bael—so you could start the war all over again?''

Radgar just stared at him.

After a moment Wasp crumpled. He looked away, mumbling, ''Sorry, Your Majesty. Mustn't speak like that to a king.''

Radgar went forward and hugged him. Wasp tried to break loose, but the King was stronger and had two good arms.

''I had to do it, my waspish friend. Stop squirming! It was the only way I could get the throne. *Will* you hold still!''

"No! Let me go. Please! Please!"

"No I won't. Listen! I'm three-quarters Chivian by blood and I'd been living in Chivial for years. Half the earls thought I was a Chivian spy and the other half were worried about losing their bribe money."

Wasp had stopped struggling, but he was shivering. "You didn't just call for war! You swore your precious blood feud against Ambrose himself. You expect Chivial to hand over its king in chains? The war you're starting won't ever end. It can't. If you want to show your gratitude, King Radgar, then give me that—call off your war! Start right there!" He stopped, choking and gasping.

"I can't. Maybe I made a mistake, but there is no way I can undo it now. We all make mistakes, Wasp. Sometimes the consequences are terrible. Remember Dad's motto about the she-wolf? We all of us forget the she-wolf sometimes. Look at Gerard of Waygarth, drawing his sword against an army of Baels—and think of everything that followed. My father thought he could steal the throne by stealing a wife. Well he did, but he got a lot more than he expected. Crown Prince Ambrose talked his father into starting a war and it turned on him. My father trusted my uncle and died of it. Yorick thought he could sell a prince like a cask of stolen wine. And you? You insisted on being bound as my Blade. I warned you then that I was a Bael. You wouldn't listen. Did you think I was just a rabbit in disguise? You destroyed the firedrake and saved my life. I'm very grateful for what you did, but I'm still a Bael. This war is your she-wolf."

"You're saying it's my fault?"

"No, because that would mean that you owe me now, and that isn't true. Do you regret saving me?"

Wasp seemed to think for a moment, then he sighed. He leaned his head against Radgar's shoulder and awkwardly returned the hug, one-armed. "No, you big monster, I don't regret it one bit. I owed you that, remember? I'd do it again, even if I knew you'd go and start another war." He sniffled. "I'll be honored to be best man at your wedding."

Radgar laughed and squeezed him even harder. "And best friend evermore?"

"And still best friend, always."

"And you don't mind me throwing girls at you?"

"I'll try to get used to it," Wasp said.

AFTERMATH

&

So war came again. Chivians called it the Second Baelish War, but to the Baels it was always Radgar's War; and the thegns soon swore that he was an even better fighter than his father before him. Ironhall had not taught him siegecraft, logistics, or strategy, but he had witan aplenty to help him with those. What he had learned in his lonely exile on Starkmoor was how his opponents thought, and no military skill is better rewarded. Perhaps King Ambrose guessed as much, because the story of their meeting and how the lost atheling had found refuge in his cousin's realm was totally suppressed, the darkest and deepest of all state secrets.

Years passed. Chivial bled. Chivial burned. Its commerce wilted. Lord high admirals came and went, earls marshal rose and fell, yet Radgar Æleding was always where they were not. Lacking the manpower to conquer the country, he could still strike far inland, looting, slaving, and sacking. Even the Baels grew bored of war and sick of slaughter, yet it seemed that no one knew how to end the pain.

· 1 ·

Spry, trim, and clean-shaven, mijnheer Vanderzwaard seemed younger than his twenty-eight winters, yet he was one of the most respected and envied burghers in Drachveld. He owned a mansion in town, an extensive estate on the Willow Canal just outside the city, and shares in many profitable enterprises. His aristocratic young wife had already given him a son and a daughter and was still renowned for her beauty. Her wit, charm, and skills as a hostess made the Vanderzwaards bright lights in the younger set of society and frequent guests at the palace. Their marriage was reputed to be one of fairy-tale happiness.

One fine morning in the late summer of 368, mijnheer Vanderzwaard had his men row him into town in his launch and then walked along Cowrie Street, heart of the financial district. Nimbly dodging hawkers, delivery boys, drays and wagons, carriages and carts, he came at last to his place of business. Its discreet entrance was identified only by two unobtrusive brass plates. The first said:

CONSUL-GENERAL OF BAELMARK

and the other, even smaller:

HOUSE OF VANDERZWAARD
MARITIME ACTUARIES

Through this unassuming portal flowed gold in tidal-wave quantities. Hardly a ship that flew the flag of Chivial or had business in Chivian waters did not avail itself of the services of Vanderzwaard, either here or with its branches in Fitain, Isilond, and Gevily. The House of Vanderzwaard specialized in warranty against a single peril, one that other brokers of maritime insurance were happy to shun entirely—Baelish piracy. Mijnheer Vanderzwaard's methods were unorthodox. He never asked for particulars of the vessel or its cargo. He merely sold pieces of parchment that would, when shown to a Baelish ship lord, cause the man to sigh, salute, and sail away. The Baelish blockade of Chivial was now so tight that almost no cargo entered or left that country without safe-conduct from the House of Vanderzwaard. Would-be blockade runners ended in Baelish hands, with their cargo and craft confiscated and their crews bound for the slave markets. The value of a Vanderzwaard passport was measured in bushels of gold.

Whistling cheerfully he came, garbed in the height of fashion, which this year involved ruffs like cartwheels, flowerpot hats with brims even wider, voluminous and elaborate doublets and knickerbockers. His entire outfit today was white with gold beading; long dark tresses hung loose down his back. His fashionably gloved left hand clutched the scabbard of his rapier stiffly, but he swung his right arm nimbly enough and that hand was bare. An elegant gentleman was mijnheer Vanderzwaard, but he was a swordsman first.

Arriving at the consulate, he trotted up the steps, turned the handle, and strode forward into a dim anteroom smelling of ink, candles, polish, and leather. It held about two dozen comfortable chairs, some well-stocked bookshelves, and an oaken writing desk. Here Hans, his industrious and ingenious bookkeeper, spent long days standing at his desk, tallying incredible numbers in a great ledger and shuffling callers in and out of the mijnheer's chamber. He also embezzled money for the benefit of his parents and sisters at an incredible rate, apparently unaware that his employer knew very well what was going on and had so far been content to watch in amused silence. There was lots more where that came from.

It was only as the heavy door thumped shut at his back that mijnheer Vanderzwaard sensed anything wrong and by then it was too late, because two of the intruders were already behind him with swords drawn. A third was holding a dagger at Hans's throat. *Blades!* With a mental scream of fury at being suckered so easily, Vanderzwaard whipped out his rapier and leaped, landing with his back to the bookcases.

He had always known that the Order neither forgot nor forgave, and the murder of Sir Janvier must remain as unfinished business in its annals. Evidently that account was about to be closed. He could have had very little hope against even one Blade nowadays, and three were a certain death squad.

"How do you work?" he snarled. "All together or one at a time?"

"I so sorry, *mijnheer Wesp*," said one by the door. "Did we startle you?"

Flames and death, it was Bullwhip! He had put on weight and his face looked more like a pudding than ever. The other was Victor, still as blond—pale and skinny as a victim of the coughing sickness. They would both be full knights by now, released from their binding—available to take on a little unfinished business, no doubt. Hungry and desperate, quite possibly. In their Ironhall days he had been able to thrash either of them with one hand behind his back, but now his left arm wasn't behind his back, it was eleven years gone and although grueling practice had taught him how to fight again with a prosthesis in its place for balance, he could never hope to achieve his old Ironhall standard.

Then Wasp looked at the third man and sheathed his rapier, ignoring Victor and Bullwhip. The third man was Durendal, who was in a class by himself and always had been—right from his beansprout year, according to the legends. Wasp had seen him fence only once and then he had made even Wolfbiter look like a crippled turtle. He was tall for a Blade, although not as tall as Radgar—dark-haired, bony, aquiline features with heavy eyebrows, dark eyes of startling brilliance.

Flames! Wasp did not want to leave his wife a widow, his children orphans. Things had been going so well. . . . He made a courtly bow.

"Sir Durendal! I am honored. I did not know a man of your eminence stooped to executions."

"That is not why we came, Sir Wasp." Durendal's voice was deep and melodious. "I am sorry if our precautions lead you to believe otherwise." He removed his dagger—an ornate and valuable-looking sword breaker half an arm long—from the vicinity of Hans's gullet and slid it back in its sheath on his right thigh. Then he stepped well clear of Hans. "Would you be so kind as to explain to your scribe that we intend him no harm? He ought to be sent home to change, but I prefer to keep him here until we have cleared up any misunderstandings."

Wasp hoped his own face was not displaying anything like the expression of sick terror that he could see on Hans's. "They mean you no harm," he said in Thergian. "I know them." Then he caught a whiff of what had upset Durendal. "Don't sit on the furniture, will you?"

"I apologize for our unorthodox entry, Sir Wasp." Durendal negotiated as he fenced—graceful and deadly. "Desperate situations require desperate remedies." He offered a hand. "We have met before, but I confess I do not recall you, brother."

Of course not. He would have noticed the tall redhead standing beside him that night, but Wasp had never been memorable like Radgar. "When you came to Ironhall to bind Wolfbiter. I remember you, Sir Durendal." He had first seen Durendal a few years earlier, when he returned to Ironhall for a second binding, but they had not met then.

The visitor withdrew his ignored hand with no sign of annoyance. "If you would be so kind as to spare me a few minutes I hope we can do business together. Even if we do not, I swear that we mean you no harm."

"Then I swear not to throw you all out on your ears," Wasp said curtly. "Pray follow me."

Being the finest swordsman of his time, Durendal had succeeded Montpurse as Commander of the Royal Guard, although he must have been dubbed knight by now—Wasp did not keep up with the affairs of the Order to which he had so briefly belonged. The man had a reputation for honor, but the effort it took Wasp to turn his back on the intruders told him that he did not trust the protestations of friendship. Their respective nations had been at each other's throats for eleven years now, and nobody remained untouched by the steady piling up of hatred. Whatever the Blades' purpose in coming, it was not to reminisce about old times on Starkmoor.

He led the way into his office, which was large and bright, offering an unexpected view of the Grand Canal. The furnishings displayed the sort of pleasing simplicity that comes only at incredible cost—a half dozen chairs grouped around a solid oak table, an escritoire, a cabinet for refreshments, a few candelabra, some oil paintings. The intruders had been sniffing in there already, for on the table lay a folded and sealed parchment he had not seen before. He walked around to the far side as Durendal closed the door. The henchmen having remained outside to guard Hans, the two of them faced off across the table.

The visitor gestured to the letter.

"Tell me," Wasp said angrily.

Those brilliant dark eyes were missing nothing, studying him as intently as if swords had been drawn already. "A royal pardon for all events related to the death of Sir Janvier, companion in the Order. It applies to both you and your ward, although I doubt he will be interested."

"What makes you think I am?" In theory, Wasp could overcome this visitor with a surprise attack, lock the door, and escape out the window. With only one arm it would be tricky, but it might be done. Against any man except Durendal he might even try it.

"It is not meant as a bribe, Sir Wasp."

"It looks like it."

"Then appearances are deceptive. I insisted on that pardon as an expression of good faith, nothing more. I am satisfied that you acted that night in the best interests of your ward as you saw them. I also insisted that your name be entered in the rolls of the Order—you were never expelled, because you had never been recorded. As of now you are a companion in good standing. Obviously your binding is no longer operative." He tried a smile. "I am most curious to know by what means—"

"I fail to see where this is leading," Wasp said angrily. He had noticed that repeated word *insisted,* and knew he was intended to notice it. "My allegiance lies with Baelmark. I am no longer bound to King Radgar, true, but I serve him loyally and always will. I could add that King Ambrose himself ordered me to do so, but I have no intention of testing that argument in a Chivian treason trial. Kindly state your business, Sir Durendal."

"To end the war."

Flames! Wasp took a deep breath. "I have no authority to negotiate."

"I do. I want you and me to settle it here and now, across this table, as brothers in the Order who should trust each other to speak without deceit. You have the ear of King Radgar and I am Lord Chancellor of Chivial."

Oof! Wasp should have known that and had not. Montpurse was gone, of course, after many years as Ambrose's first minister. The replacement appointed last Firstmoon or thereabouts had been a Lord Someone, a name that had meant nothing to him. Now his ignorance had put him one point down in the match—a match in which he had nothing to win and his life to lose. If Durendal couldn't wring out a treaty, he might yet settle for settling old scores instead.

"I beg your lordship's pardon. May I ask if the government of Thergy is aware of your presence here in Drachveld?" Wasp saw no reaction in those obsidian eyes—he had never met a man so unreadable—but he suspected that he had just evened the score. Durendal must be under enormous pressure to conclude the meeting speedily and return to his ship.

"It is not. This is a very brief and very private visit. May we sit down?"

"I prefer to stand. State your terms, my lord. Why should Baelmark end the war?"

"Because it is ridiculous, uncivilized. Baelmark is not big enough to invade and conquer Chivial, but you have command of the seas and can prevent us building and training a fleet to use against you. The result is bloody stalemate. It causes suffering and waste and tragedy. Must it drag on forever to so little purpose?''

That was all very true. Even in Baelmark everyone was sick of the war, but Chivial was hurting much worse, as Durendal's presence here proved. Radgar had learned his craft well.

Wasp shrugged. ''Chivial is doing the bleeding, not us. Did you know we now use gold bricks for ballast? They conserve cargo space.''

If the Chancellor saw the humor in that remark, he contained his amusement admirably. ''Your 'Maritime Actuary' scheme is highly ingenious. I could hardly believe it when it was explained to me. Who invented that?''

''One of His Majesty's witan,'' Wasp said modestly. The very best part was that piracy had become almost bloodless and yet the noose around Chivial had never been tighter. ''I do believe King Radgar earns more from duties on Chivian foreign trade than King Ambrose does.''

''I am certain of it,'' Durendal said coldly. ''What are his terms? What might he be persuaded to accept, do you think, brother?''

That presumed brotherhood was really beginning to rankle. Wasp took a turn to the window and back. ''This would be the fourth set of negotiations.''

''And you were one of the Baelish commissioners each time.'' Durendal had done his homework.

''I swore I would never get involved again.''

''I have wide authority to settle the matter. You are conversant with the problems. My sources insist that you are the King's friend and most trusted advisor.''

Why the sudden rush? Was the new guard dog just trying to show his royal master he could bark louder than his predecessor, or was there a new scent on the wind?

''Every time,'' Wasp said, ''the talks broke down over the same point—King Ambrose must make public acknowledgment that he ordered the murder of King Æled and must apologize for it as a barbarous act unbecoming a civilized monarch.''

Durendal displayed an excellent set of teeth. ''I have

discussed this at length with His Majesty, and so did Lord Montpurse when he was chancellor—"

"Ah, yes!" Now Wasp recalled that Montpurse's head had dropped in a bucket just after the new chancellor took office. "What exactly was the case against Montpurse—*brother*?"

He had found a chink in the armor. Something terrible burned up in the midnight eyes and a warning pallor outlined the strong cheekbones. Wasp had drawn blood—and might be about to die of it. Durendal took hold of a chair back with both hands, knuckles blanching as if he were trying to break it.

"That is a very long story, Sir Wasp," he said hoarsely. "Let us deal with the war first."

"As your lordship wishes. We can reminisce about old friends later."

"The fact is that even the greatest of men may have a weak point. I honestly believe that King Ambrose is a great man, but he has failings, too. Thirty years ago, as Crown Prince, he was grievously humiliated in his cousin's house at Candlefen Park. He has admitted to me that he talked his father into starting the First Baelish War over that affair. That war dragged on for years and was finally settled the day King Æled died."

"Was murdered."

"Was allegedly murdered. The evidence has been disputed and the accused, Sir Yorick, is long dead. It was Ambrose who sent him to Baelmark, and Ambrose is the only man living who knows exactly what instructions he gave his former bodyguard. His version—and he is thoroughly convinced of this in his own mind, I am certain—is that he expressly forbade Yorick to take revenge for the Blades who fell at Candlefen." The Lord Chancellor studied his audience in search of a reaction and then shrugged. "Whether that is what an independent witness would have heard, I have no idea, but kings' instructions can be very deniable, Sir Wasp. Their memories are often very supple, too. We all tend to remember things as we want to remember them; this is a universal human weakness and in my experience the great are as prone to it as the humble. For better or worse, this is what my master now believes—he is convinced that he not only did not order the murder, he expressly forbade it.''

Wasp also leaned straight-armed on a chair back, staring across at his visitor. ''In that case he chose a bad emissary. He should have foreseen the danger.''

Durendal raised his heavy black brows. ''He might be willing to admit that much. I cannot promise but—''

''It would not suffice. Your king's memories may be supple, my king's are totally rigid. His father was murdered. The deathbed testimony of three men confirmed the sequence of events. The war goes on until Ambrose issues a confession and apology—not a mealymouthed diplomatic weaseling, but an explicit admission of guilt and appeal for mercy. Radgar swore blood feud. To accept anything less than Ambrose's head would be an enormous concession for him to make.''

For a long minute they stared at each other defiantly, like duelists planning their next moves. This moment had been foreseen, of course. Without some new stroke in mind, Durendal would never risk a clandestine dash into a foreign country. The Thergian government would blow all the tiles off its roof if it discovered him here, chief minister of a foreign power threatening the consul of another with drawn swords. How long before the day's crop of merchants arrived to buy safe-conducts? How long could Bullwhip and Victor hold them at bay when they did? Durendal did not have long to try out his new gambit. Here it came.

''I understand,'' the Chancellor said, staring very hard at Wasp, ''that Queen Culfre recently died.''

Implications swarmed like bees. Words flashed out in thrust, parry, riposte—

''Could you deliver that?''

''He suggested it himself.''

''Would she agree?''

''She will do her duty.''

''Indemnities also.''

''Of course.''

''That is still not an apology!''

Durendal smiled. He glanced down at the chairs and then cocked an eyebrow at his reluctant host. The man had incredible style.

Wasp said, "Please do be seated, my lord," and pulled out a chair for himself. Needing time to think he spoke of Culfre, a safe topic requiring no thought. "Her life was very tragic. She almost died losing a baby a few months after their marriage and her health never recovered. More children were out of the question. But she never complained, was never bitter, even as she suffered. Her death was a release. Radgar has not slept alone these ten years, but he has always been discreet. He showed her great kindness and respect, and he never flaunted his mistresses. He refused to put her away, as kings are wont to do with wives who cannot bear heirs." As King Ambrose had done with his first wife.

"The Princess will be reassured to hear this testimonial."

Not so fast! "I repeat, a princess is still not a confession and apology."

"But as good as." Durendal leaned back and stretched his legs. "You understand, Sir Wasp, that everyone in Chivial has been taught since birth that Baels are ogres, lower than beasts. They live in caves and eat children. King Æled is officially described as a pirate chief. I believed much of this nonsense myself until a few months ago, when the war became my business and I started asking questions. Few Chivians ever return from Baelmark, but there have been embassies, both ours and other countries', so I was able to find people who had been there. I was astounded to learn that the average Bael lives in much better conditions than the average Chivian, that the nobility has more . . . Well, you already know all this. Chivial does not know it. The rest of Eurania is not much better informed. Ambrose is aware of the truth, of course, and has been for years. Were my royal master to sign a treaty with yours and seal it by giving his own daughter in marriage, this would be a recognition of equality. Perhaps it is not the explicit apology Radgar seeks, but it would be a very great concession. He and his house would be elevated to truly royal status in the eyes of the world, and Baelmark would no longer be dismissed as a brigands' nest."

Wasp smiled for the first time. "You are eloquent, brother, but Radgar has never been much impressed by fine words." Was it possible? Spirits, could they stop the madness and suffering at last? It had all begun with a wedding. Perhaps another could end it. "As I recall, King Ambrose has one son and one daughter?"

"Crown Prince Ambrose is a very loud and still-damp-at-times heir apparent. Princess Malinda is almost seventeen now—not a legendary beauty, but attractive enough to speed any man's heartbeat. She is, um . . ." Durendal cleared his throat. "Were I not being a diplomat at the moment, I should describe her as a strapping wench. No weakling, certainly. His Majesty has just announced his betrothal to Princess Dierda of Gevily."

"And expects to produce several more children? Is he capable?"

The Lord Chancellor of Chivial shrugged. "His current mistress says he is. Fifty-one is not really old."

"Still fat?"

"Fatter."

If Malinda was seventeen the match was not unreasonable. Radgar had recently turned thirty. Negotiations would have to be set in motion quickly, for he needed another wife to secure the succession. Which explained Durendal's flying visit. There were always Baelish ships in port willing to whisk Wæps Thegn back to the Fire Lands. . . . He was about due for another trip there anyway. Could Radgar be persuaded that the hand of Ambrose's daughter was the only apology anyone would ever wring out of the man, and that the rest of Eurania would see it as confession and surrender?

"Will it work?" Durendal asked quietly.

"I have no idea," Wasp confessed. "I have known Radgar since we were children, yet he can still astonish me. He owes much of his success to being completely unpredictable—as Chivial well knows. I have seen him be gentle, ruthless, generous, and implacable inside an hour.

The only thing predictable about Radgar is that he always gets what he wants.''

``That is a habit of kings,'' Durendal said with feeling.

``Quite! But the prize is noble and worth pursuing at any odds. I will convey your proposal to him.''

Wasp rose and went to the escritoire. Needing several trips, he returned with paper, ink, and a handful of quills. From the cabinet he brought two glasses and a decanter of schnapps, but what he was really after was a few minutes to regain control of himself, because he kept imagining the astonishment on Radgar's face when he heard the news. To burst out laughing at this stage in the negotiations would not be good diplomacy.

He sat down again and proposed a toast to fruitful negotiations.

Durendal concurred. His eyes opened very wide as the schnapps kicked him on the palate. He coughed.

``What other terms are you offering, my lord?'' Wasp put pen to paper. His guest did the same, so they could produce identical memos. ``Heads of Agreement, This Seventh Day of Sixthmoon, 368. King Radgar to marry Princess Malinda. All conditions of the Treaty of Twigeport to be reaffirmed and reinstated. And in addition . . .''

· 2 ·

Inevitably, rumors of the proposed match were soon tiptoeing through the courts and capitals of Eurania. King Ambrose had already set tongues wagging by contracting marriage with a princess a month younger than his own daughter. It was no surprise that he should plan to rid himself of the daughter, because wise monarchs avoid exposure to ridicule, yet no one really believed that he would be so cruel as to send her off to dwell among savages on barren ocean rocks. By fall the story was confirmed. Commissioners from Chivial and Baelmark, meeting secretly in Drachveld, had signed a treaty to end the long war, and the betrothal was part of it.

Then the scandal thickened. Ambrose, it was said, had sent his Lord Chancellor to inform Princess Malinda of the arrangement. That being the first she had heard of it, the aforesaid Princess struck the aforesaid Chancellor so hard that her rings cut his face open. There was known to be no love lost between those two. She had then—if one believed the more outrageous versions—stormed into a formal state reception and shouted abuse at her royal father in front of the entire court and diplomatic corps. The enraged King had ordered his renowned Blades to remove the Princess, but the Blades had ignored the command. Malinda had gone on to accuse her father of abusing all three of his previous wives and of selling her to a gang of slavers to escape from a war he was incapable of fighting. At that, the King had either knocked her to the floor or stormed out of the hall—or both. Courtiers all over the continent sniggered loudly and waited eagerly for more.

There was more, although little of it was ever confirmed. The Princess swore she would not speak the marriage vows; the King threatened to lock her up in the Bastion; only when jailers came for her with manacles did she lose her nerve and submit. She wrote to her royal fiancé, swearing that she was overjoyed at the match and entering into it voluntarily—but at the formal betrothal ceremony she seemed close to tears. The families of all the Princess's ladies-in-waiting raced up to court and snatched away their respective womenfolk—daughters, sisters, aunts, or dowager mothers—before they could be loaded into pirate longships. The King's own marriage had been postponed until spring. Long Night was not a happy festival in the Chivian court that year.

Some things were certain. Although news of the treaty had been greeted with jubilation throughout the land, the prospect of the second in line to the throne being married to a foreign pirate was wildly unpopular. The King called Parliament into session so he could bask in its praises. He prorogued it very quickly when it began debating the succession. His ability—or inability—to father more sons was none of its business.

Winter could not last forever. On a morose, drizzly day in Thirdmoon, 369, Princess Malinda married King Radgar of Baelmark in the palace of Wetshore, a league or so downstream from Grandon. Everything had gone quite well until then.

Arrangements for the wedding had been organized by the Princess herself and the Thergian ambassador on behalf of the Baels. The ambassador was reliably quoted as saying that King Ambrose, who normally meddled in everything, was so engrossed in organizing sumptuous month-long celebrations of his own forthcoming marriage that he had not noticed what his daughter was doing. He became memorably enraged when he discovered she had omitted everything that normally defined a royal occasion—balls, banquets, parades, masques, fireworks, and extravagant pomp. Royal weddings were invariably held in Greymere Palace in the capital. She had chosen instead a ramshackle edifice, impossibly inadequate, and scheduled for demolition. The guest list omitted, and thus insulted, three-quarters of the nobility and diplomatic corps who were entitled to invitations. By the time the King learned all this, it was too late to make other arrangements. His daughter would be married like a fishwife's daughter, he bellowed—small beer, sausages on sticks, and straight into bed.

The gossips sniggered that this must be the whole idea. The young lady was letting the silence speak for her, showing what she thought of the match. No one believed her protestations that she had moved the event out of Grandon only because the populace would riot in protest, and she did not want anyone hurt or killed for her sake. Worse, although the Baels had offered to provide a caravel to transport the bride to her new home, she had requested that they send a dragon ship instead. That was, she explained, a tradition in the family. At that point Sir Bandit, Commander of the Royal Guard, stepped between the King and his daughter. . . .

Only two attendants would accompany the Princess into exile, Lady Ruby and Lady Dove. They were about her own age, but she hardly knew them. They had accepted the honor that nobody wanted—so it was said—because Ruby had no backbone and Dove no brains. Their respective families had pressured them into it because the King had bribed or coerced them, and if he had settled for only two, he must have had to pay dearly—large estates had changed hands.

The Thergian ambassador certainly passed all this scandal along to his royal masters, who in turn informed their Baelish friends.

It was too late to make changes. The wedding proceeded as planned.

The groom was not present in person, of course. Monarchs never visited other realms except in the ways of war, and in this case King Radgar was so feared and detested in Chivial that he would have been torn to shreds had he set foot in it.

A former minister and longtime advisor, Thegn Leofric, had been called out of retirement to be his proxy. Although he was too polite to mention the fact while he was there, this was not his first visit to Chivial. He and the King's father, Æled, had shed blood there side by side on their first *færing*, almost forty years ago. Later he had lost his eye in a bloody sea battle off Brimiarde, and of course there had been the Candlefen caper. He had even seen Wetshore a couple of times from afar. The Chivians' greatest dread had always been that Baels would sack their capital, so Radgar and his father before him had feinted at the mouth of the Gran often enough to make Ambrose keep his forces concentrated there, leaving the rest of the coast more vulnerable. The palace itself had never been molested, because the shores of the estuary were flanked by tidal mud flats—deadly terrain on which to beach dragon ships. With peace now restored, the royal architects presented plans for a grandiose ornamental pier to commemorate the happy occasion. The Princess specified a simple, temporary, wooden jetty.

Here, on a very wet morning, Leofric disembarked from *Wæternædre.* Her escorts, *Wæl* and *Wracu,* stood offshore—and all alone, because the sight of three dragon ships had been enough to empty the mouth of the Gran of other shipping. He was greeted by Sir Dreadnought, Deputy Commander of the Royal Guard, backed by a flurry of multicolored heralds. The thegn confirmed that his *werod* would remain aboard, as had been agreed. The war was still too recent for either side to trust the other. He was then conducted off to the palace and a tense audience with His Majesty.

Wæternædre loaded six chests of the bride's luggage and withdrew to drop anchor beside her sister ships.

The wedding took place the following morning.

· 3 ·

Like all state occasions, even that meager ceremony ran late. Nevertheless, tides would not wait for royalty, and at the agreed hour of noon, *Wracu* was rowed in. As she approached the jetty, her *werod* could hear bugles being blown up on the meadow, which was probably a signal to speed up the final farewells.

A spiteful wind stirred the dismal drizzle. River and clouds were leaden; leafless trees on the bank equally colorless. Doubtess the courtiers were all bedecked in dazzling splendor, but the Baels down on the water could see nothing of the ceremony, only the bank itself—which was admittedly a brilliant grass-green—and the steps leading up from the jetty, which were fresh plank color. From farther out they had glimpsed the tops of gaudy canopies and striped awnings.

A dozen or so Blades in the blue livery of the Royal Guard appeared and lined up along the top of the bank. If they were intended as a warning to the visitors, they failed to intimidate anyone. There would be a lot more where they came from, though, and probably a regiment of cavalry just out of sight.

The rowers sat in patient silence, huddled under leather cloaks and never taking their eyes off their leader. They were all veterans of many *færings* during the long war, and every man of them must be remembering similar occasions when the signal they awaited had been a call to battle. This was supposed to be a peaceful and festive outing, but they would not relax their vigilance. Marriage or mayhem, their smiles conveyed the same eagerness for action.

The ship lord waited a few minutes for the wedding party to appear, or at least a herald to bring an apology and explanation. When neither happened, he waved an arm and the *werod* threw off coverings and sprang into action. In seconds they were up on the jetty. The Blades on the bank displayed excitement. There was shouting, running back and forth, and more bugle blowing. Another dozen Blades arrived as reinforcements.

Commander Bandit himself in his silver baldric came to see what was happening. Nothing was happening. There was no reason to worry. The other two dragon ships were still at anchor far out, almost at the limit of visibility in the misty rain. Seventy-two bare-chested pirates had lined up along the jetty, thirty-six on one side with drawn swords and thirty-six on the other with axes, a narrow aisle between them. No doubt the Chivians saw naked savages, brutal predators, but by Baelish standards they were an honor guard in formal dress. What if it had been agreed that no Bael would come ashore? What if their formal dress was skimpy to the brink of indecency? From boots to steel helmet every man flashed and glittered with a fortune in battle honors—golden necklaces, rings on arms and fingers, elaborately jeweled and enameled belts, buckles, and baldrics. Rain made their bronzed skin shine also, but none of them looked in the least cold. Most of them were grinning widely at the effect they were producing.

The only Bael who might be classed as decently dressed by Chivian standards, and the only one lacking flashy gold and jewels, was the ship lord himself, who had remained on board. Nobody was looking at him. He was watching the Blades, though. There were Blades up there who had known a certain Candidate Raider twelve years ago—Bandit himself, for one, although he had been a very new soprano when Raider disappeared. They might never have equated the lost *Raider* with the monster *Radgar* but they ought to recognize faces. Oak, Huntley, Burdon, Denvers . . . It was Foulweather who suddenly screamed in astonishment and pointed at the ship lord.

Radgar waved back.

Of course it was only a few minutes before Ambrose was informed and arrived at the top of the steps, swaddled within a living hedge of Blades.

Radgar waved again.

The King of Chivial did not look pleased. Nay, His Grace seemed close to having an apoplectic fit. Down there—his longtime foe, the murderous pirate king, the monster to whom he had been forced to sacrifice his only daughter . . . *and there was nothing he could do!* He did not return Radgar's wave. Obviously he slammed the door on any prolongation of the wedding ceremony, though. In moments the bride appeared on Leofric's arm and began her descent of the steps.

Radgar watched her approach with a strange inner turmoil. All his life he had been able to make up his mind quickly. At times, as when he lost his temper, he made it up much too quickly. Conversely, when there was no urgent need for a decision, he could always set problems aside. But this matter of his second marriage presented complications he had still not resolved. It was more than half a year since Wasp had brought the proposal to Waroðburh, grinning like a moray eel. The witan had debated it at interminable length. Baelmark was sick of war—children wanting their fathers, wives missing their husbands, husbands worrying that their wives might be entertaining the thralls. But the King had sworn blood feud! How could he back down from that most terrible of oaths? Radgar had spent many days pacing the moors or riding the hills, wrestling with all the implications. And even now, as his bride descended the steps, he was still not certain what he should do.

And what he *would* do might be quite different anyway.

She was wearing a very simple, ankle-length blue gown with an open skirt displaying a kirtle of cloth of gold. Anything more elaborate would have been absurd for an ocean voyage in an open boat, and the lappets of her gable hood would keep the worst of the weather off her face. She was tall—he had been warned about that as if it were a flaw—but very little else about her person could be discerned. Her hair was dark brown, he had been informed, and so long that she could sit on it, but at the moment he would not have been able to tell if she were as bald as a turtle. He noticed a total absence of jewelry and wondered if she were again making the silence speak for her. High cheekbones. Sensuous lips! Maybe even *voluptuous* lips?

She looked even younger than he had expected, more vulnerable.

It was highly unlikely that Princess Malinda had ever seen a hairy chest before, other than on a shepherd or plowman in the far distance. It was equally unlikely that she had ever been so close to naked swords, but she showed no hesitation as she reviewed the unexpected honor guard. Leofric fell back and let her proceed alone, and she came marching along the jetty, glancing at each face in turn—right, left, right, left. . . . As soon as she passed them, the thegns relaxed their stony stares—older men nodding approval, youngsters grinning lecherously. They liked the look of their strapping new queen.

She reached the end of the guard, the end of the jetty, the stern of the ship. She was pale but well in control of herself, not revealing the turmoil she must be feeling at this crucial transition in her life. The boardwalk was roughly level with the rail; Radgar had thought to outfit the warship with a stepladder. He offered a steadying hand and she climbed down, muttered thanks without really noticing him.

The two ladies-in-waiting had been found and were now descending the bank, escorted by a Blade. The crest of the bank was packed with neck-craning courtiers—barons, viscounts, earls, marquises, dukes, government officials, military officers, consuls and ambassadors, and their grand ladies, all bleating like goats at their first sight of a dragon ship and real pirates.

Leofric was showing his age now. Old wounds were acting up. Instead of jumping aboard, he hobbled down the steps, although the men would never let him hear the last of that. He pulled the royal signet ring off his finger and returned it to its owner, accompanying it with a roll of parchment—the marriage contract, of course—and also a meaningful nod. That might be the briefest report any wita ever delivered, but Radgar understood it. The ship lord approved of the Princess and believed that she was there of her own free will.

Did anyone other than Ambrose possess free will in the court of Chivial?

Before the Blade and two women reached the jetty, Leofric took hold of the steering oar and shouted, "Board!"

Fast getaways were a Baelish specialty, frequently a matter of life and death, and always one of the first drills a *werod* practiced. In two precisely timed waves, seventy-two Baels boarded in a double crash of boots on the gratings. *Wracu* lurched violently. Malinda staggered.

Steadying her elbow, Radgar said softly, "My lady, I am Radgar Æleding."

"Good chance to you," she replied absently. "Thegn Leofric, you need not wait for those two women. Go without them. Depart at once, please."

She knew how to give orders. Leofric said, "*Gea, hlæfdige!*" without even a glance to Radgar for approval. "Cast off!" Two cables were flipped and two oars pushed.

Wracu slid away from the jetty and began to turn as the wind caught her. Seventy-two ports were flipped open and seventy-two oars run out.

Then the words registered. Malinda spun around. *"What did you say?"*

She had been sent a drawing of him. He had picked out the least flattering of half a dozen, not wanting to raise false expectations. He hoped she was not disappointed—he prided himself that he wore his years better than she could have expected. His figure was still that of a youngster, and no silver glinted in his trim copper beard. Princess Dierda of Gevily had not fared so well in the stakes matrimonial.

He smiled and repeated his previous statement.

"Your Grace!" She tried to kneel and his hands flashed out to catch her arms.

"You don't kneel to me!" he said sharply, but the contact was a mistake, informative for both of them. She felt his strength. He learned that her arms were as thick as a man's and not flab, either. As her stare turned to a blush, he released his grip. He felt the first stirring of lust and suppressed it, determined not to let his *beallucas* make this decision for him.

They wanted to, though! He had known a girl with lips like those and she had been a hurricane in bed. . . .

"My pardon if I startled you. Did not your father tell you I was here?"

She shook her head, eyes searching his face, perhaps wondering where the fangs and horns were. She had the golden eyes of the House of Ranulf.

"Did he even tell you that we knew each other of old?"

"Why . . . No, Your Grace." She looked around. *Wracu* continued to drift slowly away from the jetty. The ladies-in-waiting and their Blade escort had stopped, uncertain whether or not to continue. Up on the bank, her father was peering over the heads of his cordon of Guards, and the fury on his fat face was clearly visible.

"He assured me, Your Majesty, that he had good reason to believe that you were gracious in your person and of gentle manner."

"How kind of him!" Radgar said angrily. "Such was not his opinion when we met twelve years ago. It seems he came very close to lying to you about our acquaintance. Would you agree that he was trying to deceive you?"

Leofric waited patiently for orders. The sailors smirked as they watched their monarch's wooing. Malinda, understandably, was at a loss for words.

Radgar raised his eyebrows. "An honest answer, my lady! Did your father deliberately hide from you the fact that he and I know each other personally?"

Reluctant to call one or other king a liar, she said, "Perhaps he forgot a brief—"

"I am sure he did not. What other tricks did he use on you? What threats did he make to force you into this marriage?"

"Your Majesty, I wrote to you! I testified before the—"

"Yes, you did, because I would not sign the treaty until I was given assurances that you were not being forced into a union you found distasteful. I must still hear it from your own lips."

"Your Grace . . ." The multitude onshore had fallen silent, staring at the longship. *Wracu* had turned almost right around and was drifting upstream in an eddy. Her oars remained spread like wings, her crew sat patiently.

"Why did you not wait for your two ladies to board?"

Malinda was understandably bewildered. "My lord husband, why don't we sail?"

"Later. Because you knew they did not want to come? Because they had been forced into accompanying you? So what about yourself? You are happy at the prospect of spending the rest of your life in Baelmark bearing my children?"

"I am honored to wed so fine a king!"

"Oh, rubbish!" He despised himself for bullying the child, but the marriage had not been his idea. He was sworn to avenge his father's murder. "You may be terrified or disgusted or shivering with excitement. You cannot possibly feel *honored.* I'm a slaver and a killer of thousands. But my mother was forced into her marriage and I will not take you as my wife unless I am convinced that you are truly happy at the prospect. I think you were bludgeoned into it. Speak! Persuade me otherwise."

She gasped. "Unfair, my lord! I have told you already and you refuse to believe me. You call me liar?"

"I call your father worse than that. Did you not accuse him of slaving?"

Color flamed in her cheeks and she dropped her gaze. "I may have used intemperate words in the shock of—I mean—The news was sprung on me. . . . I promise most faithfully, Your Grace, that I will never presume to speak that way to you."

That was the worst thing she could possibly say. In his lonely deliberations, Radgar had realized that what he wanted more than anything else was someone to talk back to him. Nobody dared contradict a king, or call him a fool, or tell him he was making a mistake. They all waffled and mumbled. Even Wasp and Aylwin these days—make a man rich and he has too much to lose. Culfre had been a dove, all sweetness and feathers. Argument was what a king needed, argument from someone whose interests were the same as his own, who had no hidden purposes or allies. Yes, a lusty mate to wrestle in bed would be welcome, but he could buy those anytime.

Before he could find words, Malinda spoke again, trying to sound defiant. "I am of the blood, so I will marry whom I am told to marry. I have always known this was my purpose, and I presume to say, my lord, on first sight you seem much less offensive than other suitors whose names have been bandied around me in the past. The Czar-evitch is a congenital idiot. Prince Favon is said to be fatter than my father. The Count of—"

"I am flattered," Radgar said dryly, "but I did not mean Radgar Æleding as a two-legged male animal. All men are much the same in the dark. Most women close their eyes in the action, anyway. Kings also marry sight unseen, lady, and it is not your appearance that makes me reluc-tant—far from it! No, I mean any king of Baelmark. My name in Chivial is held in low esteem."

Her chin came up. "You will force me to beg? A royal marriage is often a bridge between former combatants.

What of the treaty? If you refuse me, must not the war continue?''

Now the tide was carrying the longship slowly downstream and farther out over the rain-speckled water. The crowds on the bank continued to buzz with puzzled comment. Everyone must have guessed by now that the man holding up proceedings could only be the Monster himself.

Radgar shook his head sadly. ''I could have ended it any time in the last ten years, my lady. I did not want to retract my juvenile boasting and that is a foolish reason, mere pride. As it happens, there are legends of heroes who swore blood feuds but then became entangled in coils of love and so were forced to recant their oaths—I am sure you can fill in the details for yourself. Thus marriage to you would provide a face-saving excuse for me. Strange that it was your father and not I who thought to roll you up in the treaty scroll.''

She opened her mouth and then closed it quickly.

''Aha! You thought the match was my idea?''

''That was what I was told, but I thought it was Lord Roland's.''

''Durendal?'' Radgar said scathingly. ''No. He has too much honor to sell a lady, but he fetches when his master throws. It was your father's idea. He was desperate to end the war, and evidently he lied to you yet again. Well, I will end it without you, I promise.''

''Oh!'' She stared hard at him, as if anyone could read a killer's thoughts in his face. ''You swear that?'' She could not have imagined this discussion in a lifetime of nightmares.

''I swear that. You are free to go.''

''You shame me!''

''I honor you, mistress. My father carried off my mother by force, but I refuse to abuse a woman so.''

Fire flickered in those golden eyes. ''Indeed? What of the thousands you carry off into slavery?''

''Except that. That is war, and I hate it. I do truly intend to end it now, Princess, and you need not be sold into slavery. I give you back your freedom.''

''You shame me!'' she repeated uncertainly.

"I shame your father. Having shown the world how low he will sink, I am content. Go in peace. You need not breed pirate babies for a living."

Abandoning the unequal struggle, she bowed her head and whispered, "I will obey Your Majesty's command."

Radgar raised her hand to his lips. "My loss, Princess. This was not a pleasant nor an easy task. Take us in, helmsman."

"Yea, lord!" Leofric said angrily.

· 4 ·

The old pirate had not lost his touch. In that calm he could have moved *Wracu* by himself with just the steering oar, but he nodded to the aft pair of rowers, Aylwin and Oswald. Expertly the three of them swung her around and backed her until her stern nudged the end of the jetty with a barely detectable bump. Radgar moved the steps into position and held Malinda's hand to steady her as she disembarked. For a moment she looked down at him with a plaintive expression that made him want to cut his own throat.

"Who knows, my lady, once peace has been established between our two nations, what the future may hold? I shall still need a wife, and you a husband. I may yet press my suit on honorable terms. I bid you good chance."

She blinked at him in confusion and then turned to begin her lonely walk back to her own people. Her two ladies in waiting had already gone. Some Chivians who had ventured down to the jetty now fled back up to safety, joining the crowd struggling for a view. *Wracu* began to drift away again.

"Steady as you can," Radgar said.

"You never had the least intention of taking that girl!" Leofric snapped—not loudly, but audible to at least some of the crew.

Radgar spared him a brief glance. "Not so."

"She wanted to come."

Then she should have said so more convincingly.

Receiving no answer, Leofric said, "She despises her father!"

"So she should."

"You'll never find a better wife than she would have made."

"It was a very close call."

The old warrior could not know that the finest string of rubies in the entire world presently nestled in Radgar's pocket, safely out of sight but available had he needed a wedding present. He did not produce it. He just forestalled further argument by repeating, "Steady as you can, helmsman."

Glaring but obedient, Leofric concentrated on nudging the ship's bow around to meet the ripples, making her as stable as possible. Up on the bank the wedding guests were still babbling in amazement. There must be some clever people among them, though, people who would realize that no bride meant no wedding, no wedding no treaty, no treaty no peace. In a few seconds someone would start taking precautions. In the meantime Ambrose himself was standing there at the top of the steps, glowering over the heads of the Guard, who were all intent on the Baels—show a Blade a sword and he could see nothing else. Sending the *werod* ashore earlier had been a typical Radgar ruse to distract his opponents' attention from some other front, force, or—in this case—weapon. He had won a dozen battles with feints no more subtle than that.

The Princess reached the landward end of the jetty and the Blades on the slope moved aside, emptying the stair for her. They cleared a path right to the King's toes. A blind limpet could not miss at that range. Radgar stooped and lifted away the leather sheet covering the crossbow. He took up the bow, already spanned, and laid the bolt in the groove. He had practiced at least an hour a day for the last half year—unheard-of dedication for him. In one swift motion he stood erect, aimed, and squeezed the trigger. *Thwack!* said the bowstring.

"Get him?" asked Leofric, who had been watching the river for stray ripples, but the question was drowned out by the *werod*'s scream of triumph and howls of horror from the crowd onshore.

"Right between the eyes. Isn't that what I promised? Make a wake, helmsman." There might be bowmen up there on the bank, and one dead king was enough.

Leofric responded with a yell and a thump of his mallet on the rail. Seventy-two oars bit the river, sending *Wracu* bounding forward. She was capable of astonishing speed in calm water, and the scene ashore dwindled fast behind her.

Radgar drooped on the rail, limp with unexpected reaction. It was over! Finished at last, Dad avenged.

Avenged in plenty! A major riot was developing. Screams drifted over the water. The biggest drawback of the Blade system was that the poor dupes went berserk when their wards died, especially if the death was caused by violence. Bystanders and horsemen were fleeing in all directions, even plunging into the river, although some of those might be demented Blades trying to attack the longship. Ambrose would have company on his last journey.

Farewell, Fat Man! Imagine that pompous fool thinking his daughter would buy his way out of a blood feud! Now the King of Chivial was a sickly three-year-old boy. Chivians would scream treachery, but in a month or two they would be ready to settle. They had no option, thanks to Wasp's blockade.

Wasp was going to be devastated. Radgar did not want to face Wasp.

"You haven't done your reputation much good," Leofric said sourly. He had the crew singing their stroke now and could spare some thought to nagging his monarch.

"What reputation?" Radgar leaned his elbows on the rail and stared at the flat shore receding, the palace that had come into view, the rain. . . . "Chivians have been demonizing me for years. How can they complain if I start running true to form?" Realizing he was still holding the bow, he hurled it overboard and watched it vanish in the murky water even before the ship carried him away from the spot. "Ambrose did not bargain in good faith. He forced his daughter into submitting and then claimed she was marrying voluntarily. That's what we tell the ambassadors."

"*Scytel!*" Leofric said. "You just made a serious mistake!"

"Shut up, old man!"

Dad was avenged, that was all that mattered.

Now he could get on with his life.

Would take some getting used to.

Pity about the girl. She'd have made a fine queen.

• Epilogue •

Year 369, A Year of Sorrows:

In Thirdmoon the spirits took the spirit of Ambrose, King of Chivial, the fourth of that name, betrayed by Baelish treachery in the twentieth year of his reign, and his body was returned to the elements. His successor, the fifth of the name of Ambrose, being an infant in his fourth year, was smitten by fever and his body was returned to the elements, the crown of Ranulf then passing to his sister, the Lady Malinda, a virgin unwed. . . .

Annals of the Priory of Wearbridge